Night Glitter

Also by Jill Shure

Jeri Devlin Rose Series:

NIGHT JAZZ

NIGHT CAPS
(Cocktails inspired by *Night Jazz* and *Night Glitter*)

Betsy Ross Series:

A CLAUSE FOR MURDER
(Coming Spring 2010)

Night Glitter

Jill Shure

Syntax Books

Carlsbad, California 92011

Night Glitter

All Rights Reserved © 2009 by Jill Shure

Published by Syntax Books

For information go to website: Jillshure.com
Or email: jillshure@Yahoo.com
or
The Bookmasters Group
30 Amberwood Parkway
P.O. Box 388
Ashland, OH 44805
1-800-247-6553
www.bookmasters.com

This a work of fiction. Any references to real people, events, businesses, organizations, and locales are intended to give the fiction a sense of reality and authenticity.

ISBN: 978-0-9824105-1-6

Printed in the United States of America

Acknowledgments

To Bert, the person who supported me in every sense of the word.

I also sought help from the people listed below. They gave me their best cheerfully and honestly, and I appreciated their generosity. Thank you Bert Shure, Lyn Larsen, Caroline Tolley, Mary Waleski, and Joe Marich.

The San Fernando Valley, 1933

"Harder, Big Blackie. Faster, boy. Hurry, before the posse gets here!" Big Harriet shrieked for the third time since dinner. The banging of her headboard against our shared wall picked up speed. The gasps, sighs, and "hot damns" in a male voice grew louder.

The cotton in my ears barely muffled these theatrics let alone the radio music, suspenseful dialogue, and advertisements which provided a backdrop for the performances in the next room.

… yes, ladies, with new improved Lux soap …

"Thatta boy, sugar! Come to Mama," Big Harriet bellowed.

… what's more, Lux won't fade colors like so many other detergents …

No doubt Harriet was much more involved with *Chandu the Magician, Helen Trent*, or *Fu Manchu* than the guy in the saddle. She could've been hemming a dress or painting her toenails while her clients rode into the arms of ecstacy. After all, a job was a job in 1933 and you did what you had to do to survive. I'd heard it a dozen times from the gals here at The Rainbow Brothel. Not that I'd been desperate enough to sell myself … so far.

Now there was a loud gasp followed by Harriet's dramatic

sigh. Meaning it was over.

I felt so spent, *I* could've used a cigarette.

Too bad I could still hear my cousin Jimmy on the other side of me. He'd been hammering away on his old typewriter for six hours straight, rushing to meet a story deadline for *True Detective* at two cents a word.

Seated at my frilly dressing table, surrounded by torn yellowed lace and faded pink satin, I tried to focus on the figures I'd scribbled on a paper bag. Because a bill had arrived today from my husband Lex's sanitarium with a warning to pay up or else. A bill which could've been the national debt, considering I was down to my last ninety bucks and hanging onto this rundown cubbyhole by my thumbnails.

According to my calculations, after I paid my cousin Lorena ten dollars for rent and five for eating privileges, I'd have seventy–five dollars left. Money now squirreled away in the lining of an old coat crammed in the back of my closet. And that was *before* I paid a dime toward Lex's bill. Of course I could pawn my clothes, those reminders of better days. But a pawnbroker would give me next to nothing for my things. So once again, I decided to wait and see.

Without warning a door slammed, shaking the whole house.

"Sonofabitch!" a voice screeched, as footsteps thundered past my room.

Heart pounding, I tied my robe sash tightly and hurried to see what the ruckus was about. Peering into the hallway, I spied Big Harriet. *Naked.*

"Open up, you fucking faggot! Open up 'fore I break down this door and kick your teeth out!" Harriet shrieked, as she pounded on Jimmy's door with her fist.

Wild–haired with lumpy flesh and a pockmarked face, it was hard to imagine any man wanting Big Harriet, let alone paying for her. Including the scarecrow of a farmer who emerged behind her now, *Big Blackie* himself. Unshaven, with wispy hair and missing front teeth, the pale farmer staggered out of Harriet's room scratching his soiled long johns as if he raised field mice in there.

Apparently, he didn't mind the five–inch scar across Harriet's left rear cheek where her drunken husband had shot her one night during a fight. Or the map of stretch marks which spread across her body like irregular seams from the five kids she'd borne then dumped in foster care. Or the fact that she didn't seem to have a single muscle under that sea of quivering flesh. To me a grizzly bear was sexier than Big Harriet.

Without warning, Jimmy's door flew open. Rage distorted his handsome features as he glared down at Harriet. "What the hell do you want?"

"You better cut that fuckin' racket out. I got customers. Payin' customers. So you shut that thing off, before I cut your thing off!"

"Don't threaten me, you revolting cow. Get your pathetic body out of here and keep your big mouth where it belongs." Jimmy slammed his door in her face.

Snorting, Harriet turned and caught me watching. Placing her hands on her flaccid hips, she narrowed her eyes. "Whadaya think you're starin' at Jeri Rose? Think you're too good for all this? Well get used to it, lollipop. You ain't no princess now. You is livin' in the same crap house we all is." With that, she grabbed her shocked john's arm, dragged him down the corridor, and slammed her door behind them. A heavy silence filled the house. Then I heard Jimmy drag something cumbersome across the floor and brace it against his door.

Back in my room, I tried to calm down. A moment later, the typing began again. Then I heard Big Harriet say, "You up for seconds, handsome?" This was followed by more moaning and the sound of Harriet's bed creaking like it had an engine inside it.

Once again, I cursed the thin walls covered in flowered paper and stains from roof leaks and other mysterious sources in shades of dried blood and snot. I took in the nails stuck in the walls which held up my hats and coat. And the hole under the window, where I'd stuffed newspaper to keep drafts out. And my narrow closet where mouse droppings appeared every morning.

Not that the other girls complained. But many of them came from farms where a bowl of grits or turnip greens was a blessing. Where a Saturday night beating by a drunken father was a weekly event. And delivering a baby pig was as common as my reaching for a diet soda and flipping on the TV back in the future. Back before I'd awakened in 1929 and made the mistake of sticking around long enough to live through these hard years of the Great Depression.

Mostly, I wished the old house had a fire escape in case one of the girls fell asleep with a cigarette clutched between her fingers after a busy night of drinking and entertaining johns. Because the whole place would cook up like last year's Christmas tree. And me with it.

Dropping onto my bed, I stared over at that sanitarium bill and thought back, back before all of this.

ONE

New York, October 1932

The October rain had left its wet misery on everything. Rivers of oily run–off overwhelmed gutters. Pools of water dictated where pedestrians walked. Trolleys and omnibuses up and down Fifth Avenue created waves perfect for surfing. On Riverside Drive the air hung heavy from the constant downpours. After a morning spent shopping at Saks and Bergdorf's and a fast lunch at a drugstore, I'd slipped into a matinee of *The Grand Hotel*, starring Greta Garbo, John Barrymore, and Joan Crawford. I emerged to face something akin to the Great Flood. Even in 1932, the worst year of the Depression, with a dollar bill fluttering in my fingers, the taxis had sped by. Until I was forced to take a subway then walk the rest of the way home.

At last, soaked to my girdle, I reached our grand Riverside Drive home, Lex's house before he married me. Out front, a haggard soul who'd been hovering under the neighbor's front stoop, stepped forward, startling me.

"Can ya help a fellow in need?" The man asked, extending a shaking hand, his ancient hat crushed low over his weathered face.

Avoiding his touch, I handed the vagrant a coin.

In a flash, Bobby Peacock, our new bodyguard, appeared with a gun in his hand. "Beat it, buster. Beat it before I get tough with ya," he barked. The ragged man backed away. Then he turned and hurriedly limped down the street, glancing back nervously in case Bobby intended to follow.

Bobby held the door open for me. "You okay, Mrs. Rose?"

"Fine. Just a little wet."

"Raining cats and dogs," Bobby said, sending me a slow grin, flashing teeth so white that most girls probably melted to the floor when confronted by his dazzling smile, large dark eyes, and curly black hair.

"Yes, it is," I agreed, pressing the elevator button to go up to the second floor.

Bobby resumed his position by the vestibule door. A comic book waited on a nearby window sill. Cigarette butts rested by his feet. Gazing out a window, he took out his revolver, twirled the barrel, then practiced aiming it through the glass.

A minute later, I exited the tiny elevator to our foyer. My new Delman shoes made a squishing noise as I crossed the walnut floor to drop my packages by the gold love seat. My hat, a Lilly Dache exclusive, came apart in my hands.

It was almost five. Tired and hungry, I kicked off my shoes, tiptoed to the kitchen, and stuck my head in. "Hello, Mrs. Graumann."

Mrs. Graumann grabbed her heart. "*Mein Gott*, you scared me," she gasped, then resumed beating out a grease fire in the sink with a dish towel. On the counter a leg of lamb, covered in onions, carrots, salt, and pepper, waited to be shoved in the oven.

"Mrs. Graumman, doesn't this recipe call for garlic?"

"No, madam. I follow the book, like always," she said, her

round face dripping with sweat.

"Yes, but I thought we'd settled this."

Mrs. Grumman sighed. "If you wish." Shaking her head, mumbling in her native Austrian tongue, she went back to a huge straw basket and pulled out a garlic bulb.

In the living room, our housekeeper Keely sat on the sofa. A *don't bother me* expression covered her face as she darned one of Lex's socks and listened to a radio show.

"Saks will be delivering my packages by six," I called out.

Keely grunted.

I could hardly complain. Fresh flowers filled the house. The hardwood floors shone, the carpets appeared freshly swept, and the furniture smelled of bees wax and lemon oil. In our bedroom, I dropped onto the edge of our bed, glad I had time before dinner. A good hour before Lex came home from work.

He'd recently reopened Rose Construction in spite of obstacles that would bury most men. Like the Great Depression. And a two–year court battle followed by a short prison sentence based on allegations of embezzlement, racketeering, and construction fraud in the 1920s. As well as a murder charge for supposedly gunning down Carmine Ascencio, a brutal gangster who'd plagued New York in the 1920s. Ascencio was the type of vermin nobody missed, except for his wife and nephews, Nicky and Tito Desanto, vengeful young thugs with a thirst for blood. The very reason Bobby Peacock stood guard downstairs.

For now, the murder charges against Lex had been dropped. But the specter of illegal activities hung over us like a bad smell.

In our bedroom, I stepped out of my sodden things and rejoiced in a hot shower. Then I slipped naked between the sheets and drifted off. I woke to find Lex frowning down at me.

I sat up, startled. "Honey, what's wrong?"

"Why aren't you getting ready? It's after seven and we're meeting the Maitlands at eight."

"We are?"

"I told you this morning. We're going to El Morocco."

"I must've forgotten. Besides, Mrs. Graumman made a delicious leg of lamb and –"

"So let her eat it. Just hurry up and get dressed."

Which was how the argument started.

"… what have you got against the Maitlands?" Lex demanded, ripping off his shirt and tie.

"Because Margaret Maitland acts like she saw me selling ten cent dances down on Broadway?" I said, sliding into the seat by my dressing table. I grudgingly began to paint my face. Thanks to the humidity, I hadn't bothered with a robe. Not that Lex noticed. Here I sat, naked except for lace panties and a dab of My Sin between my breasts, and all he wanted from me was an argument. Whereas the sight of him without his shirt filled me with all sorts of ideas.

At thirty–three, he still had a rock hard abdomen and the tightly muscled arms and shoulders of a prize fighter, having been one in his youth. His eyes were still a fiery blue, when not marred by too much gin. And his brilliant smile and thick dark hair still made my heart quicken. Too bad he'd stopped coming near me weeks ago.

"If you hadn't made such a big deal about wearing black lingerie," he said, tossing his cufflinks on his dresser.

"I told Margaret Maitland I found it attractive. Big deal. Just because she probably wears a horse blanket to bed. '*Only common girls wear black lingerie,*' I mimicked. "What makes her such a fashion expert? Years of milking cows in Nebraska?"

"One darn dinner out and you throw a fit," Lex said.

"One dinner? We go out every night."

Lex suddenly looked tired. "Fine, we'll stay home tomorrow night. It just so happens I owe Roger Maitland plenty. He helped me out big time this year against those jackals who meant to lock me away for life just for being Jimmy Walker's friend."

Mayor Jimmy Walker was in trouble now, too. In fact, he'd resigned from his position as Mayor of New York. But I couldn't help remembering him during better days. Nights when he and his dazzling showbiz friends joined us for dinner at the Casino in Central Park, the best nightclub in the city back in 1929.

"Roger Maitland didn't do you any favors," I said. "His help wasn't exactly free. And you already paid your dues. Remember? Three months upstate in a cell. You've told me a dozen times, the case is over."

"You're in a swell mood," he said, marching into the dressing room, a moment before the whine of the pipes and the rush of water indicated he'd ducked into the shower.

Confused, I put my head down on the dressing table. I was in a bad mood. For some reason I felt edgy and nervous. Like I expected bad news any minute. Maybe it was because Lex and I'd been so in love once. Because the bumps in our road had been smoothed over by a driving passion for each other. Until recently, when he'd begun to avoid me. When he claimed to be too tired, too busy, or on the verge of a bad cold.

Keely knocked and entered. She had several fur coats draped over her arm. "What'll it be tonight? The mink, the ermine, or the sable?" she asked in her heavy Bronx accent.

I glanced at the costly furs, wishing they made me happy. "Neither, I guess. They're too hot. Just bring me my fox scarf."

Why had Lex lost interest in me? Up until last summer our sex life had been the racy ingredients for books currently sold in brown paper wrappers. At the hotel in Atlantic City, we'd swum, eaten, danced, and spent hours pleasing each other on every piece of furniture in our suite. Right up until Lex caught a cold.

Since then, he'd avoided me like I'd grown a heavy mustache and stopped bathing. But I hadn't. At twenty–seven, my breasts were still high and firm, if fuller than the fashion pundits liked. No wrinkles marred my face. And my figure had remained slender and toned thanks to daily walks up and down Riverside Drive, a throwback to my life in the future when I'd been a fanatic about dieting and exercise.

"Better get a move on or you'll be late," Keely warned.

Lex's telephone rang in his dressing room. The shower screeched off.

"Oh, it's you," Lex said, chuckling. "Of course I am. But I thought we agreed you wouldn't call me here."

Keely and I exchanged looks.

"I'm not making excuses," Lex said, using his knee to shut his dressing room door. Fortunately, the lock didn't click. And the door slipped open to expose Lex in his private sanctuary. So that I could easily watch him. And if he didn't mumble, I could hear him, too.

"Okay, I promise. Sure, but I have to go now," he said.

My hands shook as I penciled in my brows, smudged a light veil of shadow over my lids, applied rouge, then painted my lips. Finished, I turned to Keely, who helped me into my brassiere, girdle, and stockings.

"… you're making this very difficult," Lex said, fastening pearl buttons to his dress shirt. "Swell, Thursday for lunch." He hung up.

My heart sank. So there really was another woman. Now everything made sense.

Without a word, Keely held out my new black Milgrim

evening dress. I stared at her and the dress wondering if I could continue this charade. I felt like hurling a vase at Lex and screaming. Instead, I used my dressing table for balance as I carefully stepped into the gown to avoid snagging my stockings or mussing my hair. Keely hooked up my dress. Then I slipped on my diamond earrings, a wedding gift from Lex. But what did diamonds matter if I'd lost his love?

Side–by–side, Keely and I stared into the armoire mirror. Keely grunted her approval.

Keely had arrived a few months after our wedding in 1930. A short, ample bosomed widow of forty–three, with monstrous blue eyes and a nose like a pickle, she'd immediately informed me about her bad feet, ailing back, and female troubles. I'd taken to her instantly. In truth, Keely was inexhaustible and fiercely loyal. In many ways, she was the mother I lost as a teenager to an air crash that had killed both my parents back in the future.

Through the open door, I watched Lex dab on aftershave then light a cigarette. In seconds, he convulsed into one of his coughing fits, a remnant from his cold last summer. At last, between coughs, he finished tying his tie. A moment later, he ambled in looking pleased with himself. Keely headed into the bathroom to straighten up. And I fussed with my hair, fighting the tremor in my hands.

"So, who was that on the telephone?" I asked, struggling to sound light hearted.

Whistling, Lex pulled on his dress jacket and studied himself in the mirror above the bureau. "Just a business acquaintance. He had a hot tip about a construction job he might throw my way. Better hurry or we'll be late." Satisfied, he strolled out into the living room.

I ached to scrape the glow right off his face. But I didn't. Because I always felt sick after we fought. Because I couldn't imagine life without Lex. Still, it was hard to believe I'd once been a career woman with a job in advertising and a MBA from UCLA, instead of a suspicious housewife digging for clues of her husband's infidelities.

I pulled on my long kid gloves and stood. Which was when Keely rushed out of Lex's dressing room, a crumpled handkerchief in her hand.

"Wait a second, ma'am. I got somethin' to show ya," she said.

"*Jeri,* for heaven's sake, what're you doing?" Lex yelled.

I glanced at the handkerchief. There weren't any telltale lipstick prints. Just Lex's monogram LNR, for Lester Nathan Rose and a few tiny brown stains. "I don't understand —"

"Jeri, if we don't leave now, we'll be late." Lex thundered.

"I better hurry. We'll talk in the morning," I told Keely. Tossing my fur scarf around my shoulders, I rushed out, my new shoes pinching like the devil. But if I wore an old pair, Mrs. Maitland would notice. And knowing her, she'd be rude enough to mention it, too.

At hour later, seated at a table for six at El Morocco, I sipped a highball and tried to nod at appropriate times as Margaret Maitland chattered on about the ills of drinking and numerous other subjects her women's club was vitriolic about. Prohibition still hovered over the land, making the sale of liquor illegal in 1932, but few people – other than the likes of Margaret Maitland – still believed the law made sense.

"My, my, Lex is a wonderful dancer," Margaret Maitland suddenly said, gazing with adoration at Lex as he led Margaret's younger sister Doris around the floor in a foxtrot. "So handsome. You don't dance, do you?" she said, malice in her small brown eyes.

"I do but —"

"You and Lex are really such opposites. How did you two ever meet?"she asked, eyeing my dress as if I'd found it in a box of

Cracker Jacks, though it was the very latest in chic.

"At the Plaza Hotel. I was on my way to a party and —"

"Oh, yes, you already told me. Doesn't Doris dance divinely? But then she's so accomplished at everything she does."

Doris Fox was blonde, blue–eyed, and twenty–five. Lex had left me to dance with her three songs ago.

"… and Doris paid over five hundred dollars at Bonwits' for that dress. It's by Scaparelli."

"It's lovely."

Doris's gown had no back and almost no front. Not that Doris needed much coverage with her flat chest. Yet she was stunning with honey–toned flesh, slim hips, and lovely shoulders, the very image of the current ideal in beauty. Every man in the place had given her a second glance. And if Lex ever sat down again, one of her young admirers might even get the chance to dance with her.

Now, as Mrs. Maitland babbled on, I wondered what Keely had meant by showing me Lex's handkerchief. I definitely hadn't seen any lipstick prints.

"… and our father insisted that Doris get that diamond and platinum necklace. I mean the way Daddy spoils her," Mrs. Maitland said clucking disdainfully, though she'd gotten her point across: Her family had money – still. "Did I tell you that Doris also plays golf? And my, my, what a knack for decorating. Her house is exquisite. Every time she throws a luncheon or bridge party – oh, but you missed the last one didn't you? Sick again, were you?"

"I must've been if I missed her party."

"She's divorced, you know. But somehow, divorce suits a girl like Doris."

Mrs. Maitland would make cold blooded murder sound appealing if Doris did it.

"Doris won't last long out there. Any man would be proud to

have a gal like Doris on his arm. *Poor thing* married a fool who lost his shirt during The Crash. Then he had a breakdown. I mean the poor man stopped shaving and spent weeks hunched over a gin bottle, raving about Franklin Roosevelt – *that Bolshevik.* I don't know how Doris took it for so long before she filed for a divorce."

Lex wasn't really looking at Doris. He was looking at me.

"… then he had that car accident," Mrs. Maitland prattled on. "Not that anyone believes it was an accident. Going over a bridge in broad daylight – my word. But Doris got everything. And when you get right down to it, a ten thousand dollar life insurance policy and that beautiful house gave her a nice start. Not that our daddy would ever let her struggle. He just adores her. But then everyone adores Doris. Now, which finishing school did you attend? Or were you the one who was sent home in disgrace? Poor me, I get so confused."

"Wellesley, "I lied, naming the familiar women's college to avoid more questions. Since Margaret Maitland had probably never heard of UCLA.

"Oh, a smart one. Well don't be too smart. Men don't like smart girls. Just girls with common sense. A girl with too many brains has a way of shutting a man down."

"Is that so?" I wondered if this dim–witted wisdom could have merit. Maybe my brains were the problem in my marriage.

"My mother always knew best. She was the one who gave me that bit of advice. Isn't that so, Roger dear."

Roger Maitland responded with a cold stare and a loud belch before focusing on the dancers again. An awkward silence filled the moment. Margaret Maitland glanced at her husband looking dejected. Sighing, she rose to her feet. "I think I'll visit the powder room. Coming?"

"No thanks," I answered, relieved when Mrs. Maitland's broad ass faded down the aisle of tables. The woman was everything

I didn't want to be: An aging matron who'd lost her husband's interest and filled her days with bridge parties, shopping, women's clubs, and gossip.

Without warning, a waiter stepped into my line of vision and set down two fresh drinks.

I eyed the cocktails. "We didn't order these."

"No, those gentlemen sent them over," the waiter said, indicating a table across the dance floor. "A Merry Widow set up for you, madam. And a Roman Punch for your husband."

My heart pounded. Across the crowded club, the restaurant captain had just seated five men, all in dark double–breasted suits. The two ugly mugs in the center belonged to Nicky and Tito Desanto. Nicky DeSanto had the wiry hawk–nosed look of a weasel. Tito looked like a giant who'd sucked his thumb too long or suffered from adenoid problems. Both men hated Lex, believing he killed their Uncle Carmine, their loving uncle who'd probably bounced them on his knee as toddlers then taught them how to point a Tommy gun and squeeze the trigger.

In truth, Lex's bodyguard Harris had shot Ascencio. Harris had told me this himself the night it happened back in the summer of 1930.

Since then, Lex had refused to discuss the shooting, meaning I probably didn't have all the facts. But as Lex always said, "The less you know, the less you can tell anyone. And the safer you'll be."

The orchestra finally took a break, and Lex and Doris returned to the table.

"What's this?" Lex asked, picking up his drink and taking a small sip.

"We have company," I said.

Before Lex could follow my gaze, a shadow fell across our table. Everyone, from Mr. and Mrs. Maitland to Doris fell silent. Eyes wide with alarm, we stared up at our visitors.

Nicky and Tito Desanto positioned themselves behind Lex and me. Harris, Bobby Peacock and two other men then encircled the interlopers. And each of them had a hand jammed inside his jacket.

Chewing on a toothpick, Nicky flashed a cocky grin at Lex. "Nice night, ain't it. Me and my boys just wanted to send you our regards. But I see you ain't had time to enjoy your drinks. If you ain't got any gin, we could set you up."

Tito chuckled, revealing huge gaps in his teeth.

Nicky abruptly placed his hand on my neck. I froze. Lex bolted from his seat, blood in his eyes.

"One thing about you, Lex," Nicky said, running a lone finger down my exposed back, "you got swell taste in dolls." Grinning, Nicky's hand suddenly moved to the top of my breast, above my bodice.

"Get your fucking mitts off her," Lex growled, his face red, his breathing heavy.

Mrs. Maitland's eyes widened. Clutching her silk handkerchief, she exchanged horrified glances with Doris and Roger. No doubt this would be our last dinner with the Maitlands.

Hands up, smiling, Nicky Desanto backed away. "Be seein' ya, Lex."

A sigh of relief went around the table as the hoods strutted away.

"The idea," Margaret Maitland said. "To think they let rubbish like that into a place like this."

Still standing, Lex took my elbow and pulled me to my feet. "Please forgive us. I have an early meeting tomorrow," he explained to the Maitlands.

It took us forever to move through the mobbed room. Gentlemen in dress suits and women in low cut gowns, witnesses to the scene, devoured us with their eyes.

"What if they're waiting for us outside?" I asked Lex as he guided me toward the door.

"Just keep moving."

For two years since Ascencio's death, the Desanto brothers had tried to provoke Lex into a confrontation. Our telephone rang after midnight, jarring us from our dreams. Neighbors complained of suspicious cars prowling past their Riverside Drive houses at all hours. And no matter where we dined and danced from the Stork Club to El Morocco, the Desanto brothers often found us and ruined the evening.

"But they could've shot us at any time. They seem more interested in scaring us," I told Lex, as we settled back in Lex's grand old Dusenberg.

Lex frowned. "Shoot us with dozens of witnesses around? That's not their style. They prefer dark alleys, parking garages, and abandoned warehouses."

I was suddenly grateful that Harris and Bobby Peacock sat up front, as we sailed over city streets and a damp breeze cut through the windows.

"I didn't know you had an early meeting tomorrow," I said.

Lex chuckled. Leaning forward, he made sure the curtains between the front of the coach car and the back were closed tight. "I don't. For once the Desanto brothers did us a favor. I couldn't wait to get out of there. One more golf story or narrow–minded remark about Jews, niggers, and WOPs, and I would've told them all where to go. Besides, you're no Lillian Gish.[1] You looked so miserable, I didn't have the heart to make you stay."

"What about Doris? She seemed *very* broad minded."

Lex chuckled. His gaze roamed over the neckline of my dress then back up to my face. "Just another dull debutante next to you, my dear. Besides, I wasn't up for another fight about black lingerie."

I laughed. "You ass."

Then we were in each other's arms, making up for weeks of silence. As Lex's lips crushed mine, my loneliness receded for the first time in over a month. There, in the back seat he was mine again. A hungry passionate lover who yanked at my bra and tore at my stockings. Until I lay beneath him with nothing more than his muscled flesh to send warmth through my thighs, chest, and belly. As his warm lips roamed over my breasts, neck, and throat, I shut out all the annoying thoughts that had plagued me for weeks. Until I rejoiced in my husband's burning loins.

"Jeri," he murmured, as he plunged inside me, indifferent to the sounds of the wheels on the road, the distant horns, and the voices in the street. "I love you," he cried out, as he road a wave of passion and finally fell away, a satisfied smile on his lips.

At home the next morning, I woke happy for the first time in weeks. Sunlight crisscrossed the walls of our room in spite of the heavy drapes. And even thought the spot beside me was empty, I assumed Lex was having breakfast. Or he'd already gone to the office. I sat up slowly, savoring my mood. Then I glanced at the clock and saw the time. Eight–thirty. I hadn't slept this late in months. If I meant to get a walk in before my hair appointment, I'd have to hurry. But a second later, Keely entered looking as if she'd just lost her favorite cat.

"Keely, be a dear and get me some coffee and juice," I said, about to jump out of bed before realizing I was naked under the covers. "And grab my robe for me. It's freezing in here."

With a sigh, Keely trundled over to the armoire and withdrew my robe.

"What happened? Was Mrs. Grumman rude again?" I asked, slipping into the itchy wool robe, wondering why wool flannel robes were so fashionable.

Keely shook her head, looking dejected.

"Then what is it? You look positively miserable." I hoped it was nothing too tragic. Something that would spoil my rare good mood.

"Best pay attention, madam," Keely said dramatically, dropping down on the edge of my bed. "You know I love you like you was my own daughter."

"Of course. But can't we talk while I dress?"

Keely followed me into the bathroom. And while I donned my current workout wear, a cotton blouse, a loose wool skirt, an old cardigan, and the heaviest sneakers sold, Keely rambled on about her sick uncle, the Irish potato famine, the British army, the Irish priests, and every other reason she and her brothers had for coming to America twenty years ago.

I listened, hoping we could finish this before nine, so I could dash out and keep on schedule.

"… then six weeks ago, I was helping the laundry gal. And I seen more of these." From her uniform pocket, Keely withdrew the handkerchief from last night. "Of course I seen spots on pillow slips and the likes before. Didn't think much of them at the time. But now, with the Master actin' so strange – and that cough of his, I'd have to be blind not to see the truth. Had me an uncle that passed away from the consumption."

I gaped at her. "What're you talking about?"

Keely rambled on about her uncle and her fear of dying, as the word *consumption* echoed in my head. It was an old word for one of the mostly deadly and terrifying diseases of the times, tuberculosis.

"… the poor man went mad. Didn't want no hospital," Keely babbled. "Had no money for one anyway – them days, before state hospitals. They call it the white plague, ma'am."

"Keely, you have no idea what you're talking about," I snapped, annoyed by her absurd conclusion. TB was a disease isolated to poor immigrants living in crowded tenements, prison inmates, and residents of third world countries. Of course I'd heard about the sanitariums. I'd even met a wealthy young man who'd somehow caught the deadly disease while traveling. But Lex didn't fit into any of those categories.

Or did he?

I thought back to his earlier lung ailments which had started during World War I, when Lex had been sprayed with mustard gas. And his bout with pneumonia right after we met, when I'd been forced to smuggle my limited supply of antibiotics from the future into his hospital room to save him. And his recent imprisonment at Sing Sing.

"It can't be," I said. "He's just taken up boxing again to keep in shape. Maybe he just had a bloody nose or —"

"I seen this before, ma'am. A deep cough that won't go away. Stained pillows. I best be packin' my things. I got a family that needs me, and this…" she held up the linen handkerchief "… can spread. I'll make up the spare room for you. You'd best be movin' outta his bed. Then I'll be gettin' along myself."

I glared down at Keely, angry, panicky. "Keely, this is ridiculous. You have no proof about this. You can't walk out on us over a few silly spots on a handkerchief. I'm sure there's a better explanation. And if – God–forbid – Lex really has TB, you can't leave me when I need you most."

Keely patted my hand. "See a good doctor, dearie. Then help him."

"This is insane. I don't believe you're doing this."

"Love you like you was my own kin," Keely exclaimed, grabbing me in a bear hug before letting go to wipe her nose and eyes with her own handkerchief. "May the Lord look after you Jeri Rose and the master."

Without warning, Lex marched in, dapper as Prince Charming in a business suit. "Dinner at home tonight. See you around six."

Stunned, Keely and I watched him strut out. He didn't look sick. This morning his back was straight and his blue eyes were clear and lively. Yet the stained handkerchiefs and his cough were evidence of something. The cough had lingered after his chest cold had gone. And sometimes he perspired. He often looked pale and tired. And once or twice he'd been so exhausted that he'd spent an entire weekend in bed sleeping. Yet he refused to visit the doctor or even allow a house call.

Still, Keely could be mistaken. She was no physician. Last summer, she'd insisted I was pregnant due to an upset stomach. And she'd been wrong then. She'd probably jumped to the wrong conclusion now, too.

"Call your doctor," Keely said. Head down, she quietly exited our room, shutting the door behind her.

I stared after her, feeling anxious and aggravated. Lex couldn't be sick. Not after last night. Not after we'd been so happy. I picked up Lex's old dough boy picture off his night stand, a photograph taken when Lex was in Paris in 1918 right after the war. Even in a sepia toned picture of Lex squinting in the sun with a strange mustache, he was handsome. He just couldn't have TB.

Nevertheless, I dug out my phone book from my night stand and found our family physician's number. I stared at the number. I didn't have to call anyone. I could simply do nothing. I could order a veal roast for dinner or have Mrs. Grumman reheat the lamb. I could buy a new dress or have a facial or a mud–bath. I could push this whole miserable idea out of my head. Then I recalled how Lex's shirt collars didn't fit him anymore. How the cough had hung on.

Taking a deep breath, I reached for the telephone and said a silent prayer.

TWO

Seated behind a small desk overflowing with files, the new lung specialist, Dr. Bloom, studied Lex's records. Lex and I sat in hard chairs and waited for the doctor's verdict. Fidgeting, Lex crossed and uncrossed his legs. At last he reached inside his coat pocket and withdrew his gold cigarette case and lighter. Kicking his chair, I glared at him. Ignoring me, he snapped his lighter open and lit his cigarette.

Dr. Bloom glanced up. "Mr. Rose, I don't allow smoking. And if you choose to become my patient, you'll give up it up for good. At any rate, they won't let you smoke at any of the sanitariums. So I suggest you reform now."

Lex sheepishly crushed his cigarette in an ashtray the doctor offered.

Dr. Bloom instantly emptied the ashtray in a trash can. "From today on, Mr. Rose, your health will be my concern. I wish to give my patients the best chance of recovery. But I'm sorry to say, you do have tuberculosis. Your health report indicates a history of lung ailments, and I'm afraid you were vulnerable to the disease." He handed us several booklets. "These will help you make decisions and answer many of your questions. Now, Mr. Rose, I'd like a private word with your wife."

Pale faced and glassy–eyed, Lex stood. He spoke softly, politely. "Of course. Take your time. I need to call someone anyway." Head down, he quietly left.

My shoulders ached from the tension. My mouth was dry and there was a feeling that this had to be a bad dream.

"Mrs. Rose, I'm sure you have questions. Questions you might not wish to ask with your husband present," the doctor said.

"I don't understand how he caught the disease."

"Someone coughed on a train. Or a cleaning lady or laundress from a crowded tenement, where the disease flourished, may have visited your home a number of times. Or Mr. Rose visited somewhere exotic and caught it there. Usually the disease is the result of repeated exposure, over a period of time. But not always. Being weak from previous illnesses, he had poor resistance. But he definitely has consumption. An advanced case, I'm afraid."

I thought of Lex's months in prison with all those men. A prison was the perfect breeding ground for every kind of disease. And yet I had no proof that he'd caught TB there. A few drops of sputum sprayed in the air by a cough or sneeze could spread the disease on a subway, a bus, or in a crowded department store, according to what I'd read.

I studied the skeleton Dr. Bloom had mounted on a wall behind him and tried to comprehend the practice of having somebody else's bones on display, knowing that the collection of bones had been a human being once with the capacity to love and hate. Perhaps the skeleton had been a patient who'd succumbed to consumption.

"In the meantime, Mrs. Rose, please don't dwell on the negatives of this disease. Try to remain positive about your husband's future. There's no need to upset him even more," Dr. Bloom said. "For the next few days, until we find him a sanitarium, I suggest you encourage him to follow the prescribed routine. No smoking, quality foods, lots of rich milk, and constant rest. We've had remarkable turnarounds with some of the more advanced treatments."

I'd read about these treatments. Collapsing a lung was usually at the center of them. Usually they filled the lung cavity with gas. Sometimes they put heavy weights on the patient's chest. These methods were meant to rest the lung, quiet it down until a capsule formed to encase the lesion and put the patient into remission. The capsule seemed to be made of fairy dust and delicate spider webbing which formed over many months, as long as nothing disturbed the process, like any normal activity such as standing, combing hair, or even playing cards. But did these efforts work?

Now I waited for the doctor to allay my fears with a positive remark about what Lex and I could hope for. Back in the future, patients had a right to hear everything, good or bad. They had a say in their treatment and were encouraged to question their physicians. There was the Internet for information, too. But in 1932, the medical community believed that patients shouldn't be upset by the truth. Patients were expected to passively follow their doctor's advice, no matter how far fetched.

"Why are the sanitariums up in the mountains?" I asked.

"It's believed the disease doesn't do well at such heights. Just read the literature about Doctor Trudeau. And since constant close contact with a sick patient is dangerous, I suggest you move to a different room and keep your distance," the doctor added.

Thanks to Keely, I'd already moved into the guest room.

No doubt other questions would crop up. For now, I felt like shutting my eyes and sleeping for a month.

Dr. Bloom led me to his door. "I understand how upsetting this is, but we want to keep you healthy."

I mulled this over. " Doctor, please forgive me for getting

personal, but how do *you* treat your patients without getting sick yourself?"

"I've already had consumption. It's gone for the time being. Many doctors in the mountains will have the disease, too. But if the ill keep their mouths covered during a sneeze or coughing spell, the disease won't spread."

I stared at Doctor Bloom, surprised by how normal and healthy he seemed.

"Decide quickly on a course of action for your husband, Mrs. Rose. Time might make the difference. I suggest Saranac Lake. It's not far from the city, and it's quite picturesque, even if your husband isn't a candidate for one of the bigger places like the Trudeau Clinic."

"Why's that?"

"The bigger places don't have time to cure every case. But there are dozens of other places, smaller houses which follow the same regimens and in some cases are friendlier, more intimate. Call me in a day or so and let me know which place you've chosen. I'll be happy to send them Mr. Rose's records and assist in any way possible."

"Of course we'd like a place where there's music. Lex is very fond of music."

"There might be a radio or a piano, depending on where he goes. For now, Mr. Rose needs quality food, rest, and quiet."

Rest and quiet? It might as well be enemas and icy showers. Lex liked cocktails before dinner, beautiful women in low cut gowns, and jazz. Dr. Bloom sounded as though Lex was about to be embalmed.

"One last thing. And please be honest. Is my husband's case hopeless?" I asked.

The doctor's gentle gaze focused on my face. "Where there's life there's hope, Mrs. Rose. Yes, he's ill. A bad case. But I've seen these things turn around. Nobody's hopeless. If he wants to get well … if it's meant to be …"

On my way out, Dr. Bloom didn't offer me his hand. I wondered if my being in a small room with the doctor had put me at risk.

Clutching a pile of brochures about diet, exercise, and rest regimens, I headed down the hall to find Lex. The brochures sounded so upbeat, as if all you needed was a good attitude and fresh milk and you'd be back home, healthy and happy in no time. But I'd gone to the public library yesterday and read about the disease. One in four died in spite of the current cures. Bigger clinics kept the serious cases out to keep their statistics steady. Many patients, who left sanitariums believing they were well, returned within five years. Or they died at home.

In the hospital corridor, the smell of alcohol, ether, and hospital food filled me with dread. When I reached the admissions area, Lex was just stepping out of a telephone booth. Without a word we exited outside to our car. Harris gently helped me in.

Lex slid beside me and instantly lit up a cigarette. "I'm absolutely starving," he said. "What about a good delicatessen?"

I studied him. My hands shook. His didn't. My stomach was in knots yet he was hungry.

"Let's just grab something fast at the Automat," I said, thinking of all the arrangements we needed to make.

But as the car swung into traffic, inertia washed over me. My whole system seemed to go into shock. Because if Lex had an advanced case and was doomed, as I suspected, what was the rush? The doctors could say what they liked, but if one in four died anyway…

***

Lex stared out the car window. He'd suspected he had

something serious ever since that awful cold got him down last summer. Still, hearing it from the doctor felt like a death sentence.

Beside him, Jeri gazed out her window, sniffled, and wiped away her tears. Her pale, frightened face broke his heart. Yet it was time to cut the ties and let her go. *Make* her go, even if he had to be cruel. She deserved someone healthy, not a guy on the run from mobsters with a bad lung. A husband who could make her sick. Maybe he'd even insist on a divorce. He just needed time to work up to it. He studied her. So lovely with the wind blowing through her hair from the open window. He ached to touch her. But if he did, he might wind up crying himself.

***

At the Automat, Lex and I found a table. Harris sat two tables away and read the paper. Lex smoked and stared pensively across the room at several sorry characters struck down by the times. Men and women who were glad for a clean place to sit, a hot cup of coffee, and a donut. Along with them, there were women shoppers, businessmen, and mothers with children.

I sipped coffee, too upset to eat.

"The doctor was very optimistic," I abruptly said, fighting for the right tone, the right thing to say. "Many people do get better."

Lex studied me, a sardonic lift to his brow. "That's very enlightening."

"If you go to a place upstate, I could move nearby. Some families rent homes up there. Then I could visit you regularly. Whenever I was allowed."

"I told you not to marry me," he abruptly whispered, looking stricken, as he put down the cigarette he'd been smoking and began to cough. Looking embarrassed, he quickly covered his mouth with a handkerchief.

Someone on a train coughed, the doctor had said.

It seemed surreal to be discussing something so life–shattering here at the automat where you dropped a nickel in a slot, lifted a glass window, and pulled out a piece of pie or a ham sandwich.

I stood. "Let's go home."

With a handkerchief still over his mouth, Lex followed me out. His beautiful blue eyes told me he'd read my mind, seen my terror of catching his disease. I'd intended to be brave. Instead, I'd been relieved when my own x–rays had been clean. Poor Lex. How awful to have a contagious disease for which there was no cure.

At home Lex listened to the radio and read while I telephoned private cure cottages from a list the doctor had given me. I managed to sound upbeat as I questioned the different sanitarium directors. Many places had no bed space. And deep down, I doubted Lex would be able to follow the endless rules believed essential for getting well. Not that most of the rules printed in the Metropolitan Life's *Optimist Guide* made sense to me.

For instance, patients were required to drink huge amounts of milk and stuff themselves with at least five full meals every day. Crocheting was considered good for you. Playing solitaire was not. To me, rest, a good diet, and fresh air couldn't hurt a person, but I doubted they'd cure anyone as sick as Lex. But I'd come from the future when doctors knew better and the current strain of tuberculosis had been eradicated decades earlier.

Right after I found him a bed at a place called Mrs. Jankel's Cure Cottage, Lex announced his latest news.

"If I'm going to die, I might as well have fun first," he said. "So, I've booked us on a steamship to Cuba. Mrs. Jankel and her cures can damn well wait."

THREE

Havana Cuba, November 1932

I could tell the red head had nothing on beneath her thin purple dress. Sweat stains had formed under her arms, between her breasts and buttocks. Under the lights, her greasy makeup looked bright orange. And perspiration had caused the green shadow on her lids to bleed into the black kohl painted around her almond–shaped eyes.

Still, the street girl dancing with Lex was beautiful.

High breasted and slim, with a round bottom, she had full lips which she kept parted in a seductive smile. Now, she turned her back to Lex, stuck out her buttocks, and gyrated wildly to the band's African rhythms. Facing him again, she undulated seductively in time to the music, then ran both hands over her full breasts, until her nipples hardened beneath the thin material of her dress.

My stomach clenched as she moved toward him. Smiling, she slowly ran her tongue over her rouged lips before wrapping her arms around him and grinding her pelvis against his. I watched this assault, feeling sick, furious. Stuck between Harris and Bobby Peacock, I chomped on a piece of ice from my third rum drink and thought of what I'd say to Lex when he got back to the table. *If* he ever got back to our table.

After too many rum punches, Harris and Bobby Peacock were bleary–eyed and hungry for the young *chicas* that filled every chair and doorway of the Rio Rosa Club. Girls in tight dresses and promising smiles. Girls who promised a visit to paradise – for a price. Not that Harris or Bobby would dare leave me. Not after Lex had given them orders.

"Watch her," Lex had barked over an hour ago on his way to the bar where he'd met the redhead, who now held him by the neck and was sucking on his throat like she meant to draw blood. Although Lex wasn't exactly peeling her off him or complaining.

At least the Desanto brothers weren't stalking us here. And Hollywood movie legend Lupe Cardona, the Guadalajara Spitfire, was at the next table giving her handsome blond escort an earful.

"… and you are *not* thee only man for a woman like *Lupe*," the star said in broken English, in between mopping her face with a powder puff and painting her lips with enough rouge to lacquer a sofa. "So, do not pat yourself on thee back. Many men have fought to thee death for Lupe's love."

"Name one," the blond man said.

"*This* is exactly what I mean. You *no* want to dance. You *no* want to make love. You *no* want to do nothing no more. I still young, I still beautiful. I no want to be buried alive at twenty–one."

He shot her a look.

"I still look twenty–one, no?" she said.

Sighing, the blond man stared into space as if he'd heard it all a thousand times.

"You see, you jus' did it again. You all thee time making faces. All thee time pretending to be tired, or bored or – I do not know. Maybe you no like Lupe no more. Maybe you like to sleep with thee other *chicas* here. Thee *putas*. Someone with thee yellow hair and breasts like casabas instead of little Lupe."

Was it possible she meant me? After all, I had blonde hair and considerable cleavage.

Tonight, the Guadalajara Spitfire wore a shimmering white frock trimmed in ostrich feathers and a matching hat. No doubt the dress was meant to be glamorous. But to me she looked as if she might take flight any second and join the cockatoos out in the entry. The blond man looked familiar, too, only I couldn't place him.

Tonight, I'd donned a daring black silk creation embellished in sequins with an extremely low back. It accentuated my tan and kept me from roasting in the island's cloying heat. Lex had chosen the design from a Mainbocher original he'd seen back in New York. He'd had a side street tailor named Mr. Ramon whip it up for a song right after we landed here three weeks ago.

Tonight, he also wore a Mr. Ramon creation. A double-breasted white suit which camouflaged the eight pounds he'd lost. So that no one would guess he was sick – unless he coughed. Except that his cough seemed to have vanished since we'd arrived in Havana. I suspected it was the sun and sea air. Or the Cuban women.

Now, Lupe agreed to let the Russian fortune teller, Natalia, predict her future. Natalia had been making the rounds, claiming she'd been the Romanoff's mystic before the Communists shot Nicholas and Alexandra and their children. I was dying to ask her why – with all her psychic abilities – she hadn't warned the Czar to take the fastest train, horse–sleigh, or goat cart out of town to save himself and his family. Instead, I sat back, grateful for the distraction. Anything was better than watching Lex and the redhead.

Natalia quickly shoved a chair between Lupe and the blond man, ordered a cognac from a passing waiter, then leaned forward as if she meant to divulge Judge Crater's whereabouts.[2]

"You have heard the name Rasputin?" Natalia said, dark eyes flashing.

Lupe and the blond man nodded.

"Many times I meet Rasputin at palace in St. Petersburg. He vas big like bear. That Monk vant every woman in Russia," she said, shuffling a card deck that looked older than she did, with her vulpine features and spiraling tangle of dark hair which sprang out from under her gypsy scarf like the wires from a busted radio. "Rasputin proposition me many times."

"So you were forced to give in?" Lupe asked.

"No. He vas pig. When I resist, he say terrible things about me. He hate me after that."

Now, Natalia rattled off her psychic talents. Besides reading cards, she could see your destiny in the stars, your palm, and possibly the dregs of a rum punch for one American dollar.

"Read thee cards," Lupe said, her large dark eyes intent on the ravaged deck.

"Two times you must do cards like so," Natalia advised, shuffling the ancient deck hand–over–hand.

Impeded by her gaudy rings, Lupe's little fingers held the cards tentatively as she followed the psychic's directions. When Lupe finished, Natalia counted out ten cards. She deftly placed them in a pattern then stared at the results as if she was engrossed in a full length movie starring Greta Garbo and Ronald Coleman. "You vill be *big* success in work," Natalia finally said, stabbing a card with a boney finger.

A darn good guess, considering Lupe was already a major star and the daughter of Caesar Cardona, a rich studio boss.

"What about love and passion?" Lupe asked, glaring at her blond escort.

Natalia dealt out more cards. "You are woman who need strong man – man with hot blood. Man with much fire in veins. You are woman who burn with explosive desire."

The blond man sighed and stared miserably at the dance floor. Lupe shut her eyes, pressed her diamond studded hand to her tiny breast, then crossed herself.

"Also…" Natalia added, narrowing her dark eyes dramatically, "… I see intruder."

Lupe and the blond man exchanged glances. I pictured a burglar climbing through a window with a knife and a gun.

"A dangerous woman will come between you and your heart's desire. A blonde woman," Natalia added.

Lupe's jaw dropped to her feathered chest. Then she nodded as if she'd suspected as much. With a wave of her tiny hand, she dismissed the fortune teller. "Pay her, then order me another drink," she told the blond man.

Natalia gathered up her long cape and unfashionable dress. Bowing, she scraped her coins off the table, swept up her cards, and disappeared into the mob. As soon as Natalia had gone, Lupe faced the blond man. Her dark eyes were filled with tears. "I never forgive you for this. Even thee Russian puta can see you no love Lupe no more. We are finished."

"Be realistic," the blond man said. Turning to get the attention of a passing waiter, he caught me eavesdropping. After a quick once-over, he winked. Then a slow smile spread across his face.

Embarrassed, I stood, intending to escape to the ladies room. But Harris bolted to his feet, too. "Pardon me, madam. But where are you going?"

"I thought I'd find a sailor and bring him up to my room."

Harris's eyes widened.

"Relax, I need to powder my nose," I said, sounding testier than I meant to. Harris stepped aside. Dodging my way through the crowd, I combed the gyrating bodies for Lex and the redhead, but there were too many people dancing now. In the ladies room, I touched up my lipstick and searched the crowd for the redhead, thinking she might've come in to wipe the sweat off her breasts. But she hadn't.

Minutes later, I braved the packed club again to return to my seat. I'd almost reached our table when I stalled in route. Lupe Cardona had abandoned her chair in favor of Bobby Peacock's lap. With her arms wrapped around Bobby's neck, Lupe smiled spitefully at the blond man at the next table, grabbed a fistful of Bobby's black curls, then pressed her mouth to his.

In a flash, I reversed directions and headed toward the club's front door, a challenging goal thanks to the wall of people. But a moment later, I froze when a stream of sharp staccato sounds from outside cut through the din. The musicians abruptly stopped playing. The dancers paused. Patrons listened and waited. The disturbing noises grew louder, clearer. *Gunfire.*

FOUR

My heart raced. Fear filled the faces around me. Voices rose as patrons speculated about the meaning of the gunfire. Did the shots signal a Cuban coup, a violent change of power? I pictured men running and bodies crumpling in the streets.

A corrupt leader named Machado currently ruled Cuba. But from my history classes back in the future, I knew that a man named Batista would take control soon. Fidel Castro would follow in 1959, after the Cuban Revolution. But I had no idea about Cuba's struggles in November of 1932.

Standing on my toes, I scoured the crowd for Lex. In a flash, Harris appeared beside me. His hand was inside his coat on his gun.

"Relax, I'll see you get out safely," Harris said.

Then a short mustached man in a white dinner jacket pushed his way through the crowd, rushed onto the stage, and grabbed the bulky microphone. "Ladies and gentlemen, señors and señoras. Please be assured there is nothing to fear from thee guns. Tonight thee news is *very* good. It is an honor to tell you, that thee American election has finished with Mr. Franklin Roosevelt defeating President Herbert Hoover."

The audience cheered. Drums boomed. Glasses crashed against the floor. Men spun women in the air, and everywhere people shouted. More gun salutes came from the street. And I finally spotted Lex. The brassy redhead gripped him around the waist as she urged him through the crowd toward the exit. In a heartbeat, Lex and the girl evaporated into the tangle of people. I caught a final glimpse of Lex's head towering above the others before they slipped out the club's door.

I was about to charge after them, when Harris grabbed my arm. "Wait."

"Not on your life." I yanked my arm away and darted into a narrow corridor through the impenetrable maze of chairs, tables, and sweaty patrons. I emerged from the club in time to see a cab rumble down the street past white colonial buildings, vacant lots, and tropical vegetation. My heart sank.

"Taxi?" a young boy about fourteen in a uniform two sizes too big asked.

"Did a couple just come out here? A tall man and a ... never mind," I said, discouraged by his vague expression.

"Taxi?" the boy repeated.

I shook my head. A sigh of misery broke through my self–control. A couple strolling inside the Rio Rosa glanced curiously at me.

Then an American voice rang out. "It can't be that bad."

With that, Lupe's handsome blond escort emerged from the shadows into the light. Up close, exposed by the club's lamplight, he was incredibly attractive. His clear eyes sparkled like blue glass. He had thick blond hair, a perfect jaw line, and straight white teeth.

"I beg your pardon?" I said.

"Care for a walk along the Malecon?" he asked.

I glanced from him to the sleepy sea bathed in moonlight, across the street. "Sorry, I don't know you and —"

"Franky Wyatt. Nice to meet you." He stuck out his hand.

Taking his hand, I was surprised by how cool and dry his palm felt, how familiar his name sounded. But I was no easy pick up, not even for a Lupe Cardona castoff.

"Jeri, that is, I'm Mrs. Rose," I said. "You'll have to excuse me. I'm heading back to my hotel." Turning away, I crossed the boulevard. The traffic had dwindled to a few cabs, a few private cars. But Havana was no ghost town in the early hours of the morning. Couples still emerged from the Rio Rosa, laughing. Music and voices still spilled into the briny scented air from nearby parties and clubs. And everywhere, lovers embraced.

I glanced back to find the blond man trailing me. "Are you following me?"

"You don't own the sidewalk, do you?"

A few feet down on the Malecon, the drive which hugs Havana's harbor, I dropped down on the low wall. After slipping off my heels, I reached under my dress to unhook my stockings from my garter belt. After stuffing my stockings in my purse, I stepped onto the cool walkway and headed toward my hotel. Hanging back a few feet, Franky Wyatt kept pace with me.

"Was that your husband? The one dancing with that street girl?" he called out.

Stopping, I gave him a dirty look. But I couldn't help noticing how boyish–looking he was, how well–built. "What about him?"

"I spotted you the moment we sat down. Lupe caught me and got pretty steamed. She's not wild about other women in the first place. And you, in that dress … it's one reason I'm walking home alone."

"Lupe Cardona was jealous of me?"

"Jealousy is her trademark. Or one of them. Like having a rotten temper and a powerful father."

"I'm flattered. I don't feel very … well, let's just say I don't feel very enticing."

"Too bad. This town's the place to feel enticing." He moved forward and fell in step with me. "It's those palm trees and that ocean breeze. They do more to people than the rum punches and cigars. Pretty soon you forget rational behavior and you sink into the mood."

Maybe he was right. I'd noticed the effect the climate had, too. But getting into a discussion about passion in the wee hours of the morning with a total stranger while walking home in the dark seemed like a bad idea.

"Ever been to California?" he asked.

The question surprised me. California was where my former life had been, back in the future. Where I'd spent my first twenty–five years. "I used to live there before I moved to New York. I'm going back one day."

"The palm trees are different," he observed, gazing up at the swaying trees. "No coconuts. And it's not as humid. I prefer it there. The mountains and open spaces. The chaparral and sage brush."

"I prefer the beach. What about Lupe?"

"Nightclubs."

I laughed. "Is Lupe your girlfriend or fiancé?"

"My wife."

I studied his familiar face, still unable to place him. He was famous but in an obscure way.

"She took off with somebody else," he stated flatly.

Bobby Peacock, I thought. Bobby would be in trouble if Lex found out.

"I'm used to it," Franky admitted without malice.

Me, too, I almost said. But that wasn't true. Because Lex had ceased to flirt with other women after marrying me. Until he got sick.

"Excuse me for being nosey, but why do you stay with her?" I asked.

"We have a daughter. It's complicated."

California didn't have no–fault divorces in the 1930s. His predicament wasn't unusual. Courts uniformly gave children to their mothers no matter how neglectful.

We ambled on, watching the water lap against the pilings. It felt freeing. And I liked this man. His looks, his dry humor. He was so different from Lex. Lex was a New Yorker with all that moniker entailed. Lex was exciting and full of nervous energy. Franky Wyatt was a Californian, quiet and easy–going, like an afternoon at the beach with a good paperback.

"Won't Lupe mind you walking home with me?" I asked.

"She might if she saw us together."

"What would she do?"

"Well, if you were an actress, she'd have you banished from every major studio in Hollywood. She'd make sure you never attended any party worth going to. And she'd tell every newspaper columnist to describe you as frumpy. Except you aren't an actress, and I'm sure we won't run into her."

"Why?"

"Fresh air. Lupe hates the stuff. And she'd never strip off her shoes and go barefoot on the sidewalk. She prefers oriental rugs and other people's backs."

I digested this unflattering profile of the star.

"So that was your husband?" Franky asked, changing the subject.

"Yes."

"And that young girl – a friend of yours?"

"He has his reasons. You wouldn't understand."

"You'd be surprised."

"We have no proof anything wrong happened. Besides ... he's ill."

"Nothing like a trip to a sanitarium for that. I know plenty of people who take the cure every year to dry out. Get away from the booze, the gossip, the studios."

"I meant, we should have gone up into the mountains weeks ago. But Lex insisted we come here first, for a last fling. You see, he knows things are hopeless and ..." I stopped walking and stepped over to the wall and stared into the dark night. I fought my urge to cry, amazed that I'd blurted out my troubles to a stranger.

The blond man halted, too. "Sorry. It's really none of my business. I shouldn't have said those things. Will you accept my apology?" His voice was filled with compassion.

"Yes, thank you," I mumbled.

We continued walking in comfortable silence. I was aware of our footfalls, the gentle sea, and the rustle of the palm trees. We passed ancient buildings and heard the African beat of Cuban music bleating from inside hotels, restaurants, and bars.

A short time later, I recognized our hotel where Lex had taken a four room suite with an extravagant living room, a room for Harris and Bobby Peacock, plus separate bedrooms for Lex and me. With Lex being contagious, it made sense. But the distance between our rooms had added distance to our marriage.

I suddenly wondered if Lex might've brought the street girl back to our suite. A few weeks ago, he wouldn't have dared. But everything had changed now that he understood he had a short future.

Franky and I circled to the front of the hotel and paused by the drive leading to the lobby. In the glare of those unforgiving lights, I gazed into his face. It would be easy to lose myself in his lustrous blue eyes. Eyes which could guide aircraft through storm clouds. He wasn't as tall as Lex. But he was every bit as handsome. I stared down at my bare feet and crossed my arms over my chest to control my sudden, powerful desires. "Well ... thanks for walking me home.

The doorman can find you a cab … "

Then I made the mistake of noticing his lips, his honey–colored skin, his strong chin. A compelling need to touch him overwhelmed me. Then his hand was on my back. And my face was against his. Our lips met in a blinding hunger. I tasted rum and desire as his tongue probed mine. A rush of warmth filled my insides. His hungry mouth, strong arms, and the heat burning through his jacket enveloped me until I clung to him satisfying a craving that sent waves of powerful yearning from my heart to my loins. I ached to fill my senses with the firm flesh on his neck and throat. I longed to run my hand over his bare chest, and fill my lungs with the scent of his skin, a fragrance as pure as a freshly laundered shirt. So different from Lex who smelled like a highball and costly cologne.

As his body molded to mine, the painful night melted away. I felt an urgent need that reached inside my belly and reminded me that I was still young, still alive. It seemed like an hour before we pulled apart, and he gently rubbed his cheek against mine. Then, with his arms still around me, he fixed his gaze on my face. I felt as if I'd escaped inside a dream then abruptly returned to a grim reality. I felt exposed in the hotel's unflattering yellow light with my hair straying from the tropical breezes and my lips stripped of rouge.

"Sorry for your troubles," Franky said, as his fingers traced my chin and his eyes searched mine. "You're very lovely." He stuck his hands in the pockets of his slacks beneath his white dinner jacket and headed back in the direction we'd just come from. I watched him go. I felt as if I'd lost a dream, something unreal. Yet, within that kiss there had been the promise of survival no matter how many times I stumbled through the days and nights ahead. Still, a gnawing guilt chafed against this new knowledge. Because I'd never desired another man since I'd fallen under Lex's spell three years ago.

Seconds later, I reached the entrance where a uniformed guard on a chair slept with his legs splayed out, and a newspaper with headlines about Roosevelt's victory spread across his thighs. Lex stood behind him. A cigarette burned between his fingers and an agitated expression covered his face.

"Have a nice time?" he asked sarcastically, meaning he'd seen Franky and me kiss. "Where are Bobby and Harris?"

"Doing the tango together last I looked." Passing him, I headed through the lobby. The wall clock above the registration desk said it was after three. Meaning it had taken Franky and me close to an hour to walk back from the club. "I didn't expect you home so early."

"I was tired," he muttered.

I studied him. There was a glow on his forehead, meaning he might be feverish. "What happened to your girlfriend?"

"Can't I dance with someone without you turning into a policeman?"

"That was dancing?"

"What happened to your boyfriend? Or did you admit you were married?"

Lex's sarcasm was meant to show his indifference. But underneath, I heard fear.

"Let's finish this in the morning," I said, as we climbed into the gilded elevator cage. I wasn't sure if I wanted to cry or kill him.

When we entered the suite, he turned right for his room. I crossed the living room to my own smaller bedroom. I switched on the light and began to undress, tossing my things on an arm chair. Through my open door, I watched Lex unbutton his shirt, yank off his bow–tie, and kick off his pants. Down to his shorts, he peeled off his bedcovers and flopped face down with a contented grunt before rolling on his side. He'd managed to keep his looks from his thick dark hair, clear blue eyes, and muscled physique in spite of the booze, cigarettes, weight loss, and deadly disease.

In seconds, he began to snore softly without coughing.

I quietly entered his room and turned out his lamp. His breathing sounded steady. No rattle tonight. The sleep of a peaceful child. *Poor Lex.* All the drinking and womanizing couldn't save him from the truth. That within days we'd be at the sanitarium, a convalescent home which offered hope – providing he followed the rules. But we both doubted he had a real chance of recovering no matter how many half–hearted promises the doctors made. Doctors didn't have antibiotics or penicillin yet. And they wouldn't be able to cure tuberculosis for years.

In the bathroom, I studied my face in the mirror above the sink. I didn't look very different from the twenty–five–year–old girl who'd arrived by some miraculous fluke three years ago. That modern young working girl from the late twentieth century who went to bed one night in a New York hotel room and woke up a stranger in 1929. But I'd definitely changed. I'd fallen in love and become dependent on a man. A businessman with mob connections. A man who'd introduced me to love and passion. Deep down, I probably still had the backbone and perseverance to survive without him. The problem was, the Depression made everyone's survival uncertain.

Reaching for the faucet, I began to fill the tub. A cold bath would cool me down and help me sleep. But as I knelt to test the water's temperature, I spied a strand of brassy orange hair and a wad of crumpled toilet paper with garish lip prints on the floor by the wastebasket. As if the redhead from the Rio Rosa club had aimed at the wastebasket and missed.

In the morning Lex woke with a cough and a 101° fever. Stuck with remedies like aspirin, steam baths, and hot tea with honey, I felt powerless and afraid. What if we had to miss the steamship trip back to New York in two days? What if Mrs. Jankel gave away Lex's room at her cure cottage? What if Lex couldn't catch his breath and the doctors here in Havana couldn't help him?

For those long hours – the morning after the blond man and the redhead had drifted in and out of our lives – when Lex's fever spiked and his breathing became an uneven rasp, I prayed for help and guidance. By late afternoon on the second day, Lex was breathing better and his fever had dropped to just above normal. Meaning we were able to file up the steamship's gangplank as planned.

As the ship sailed out of the Havana harbor, Lex and I stood together at the rail and enjoyed the disappearing Cuban coastline. In the late afternoon sun, Lex looked tanned and fit in his new navy blazer and white pants. No one would guess that he was on his way to a sanitarium. Or that one night soon, he wouldn't be able to catch his breath, and he'd cough up a clot and drown in his own blood.

Unless I could get him back to the future.

FIVE

Four days later, we arrived in New York Harbor.

"Home, sir?" Harris asked, opening the Dusenberg's doors for us outside the pier.

Lex shot me an indulgent look. "No, Harris, the Grand Biarritz."

The Grand Biarritz Hotel had been my residence from the day I arrived in 1929 to the spring of 1930. It had also been my portal from the future to the past. But the portal had closed. Now, in the early November afternoon, I'd convinced Lex to give me a last chance to see if we could open that portal and travel to the future where doctors could cure Lex. Lex didn't have much faith in time travel. To him, this was just another postponement, another blessed few days outside the sanitarium. The reason he agreed.

The hotel lobby smelled of cool marble, lemon oil, and fresh flowers, just as it had in 1929. The desk clerk, an officious looking young man, examined Lex's signature in the guest book and handed him a key. "Do you require a bellman for your luggage?"

Lex pointed to our bags. "My man is bringing them in. And send up a bottle of gin," he added, sliding a bill toward the clerk's hand.

"Sorry, sir. I can't take that." The clerk returned Lex's bill, hit a bell for assistance, then leaned forward and spoke softly. "Your bellman can get you anything you need, sir."

Lex seemed amused as we rode up in the familiar elevator, strode down the hallway and stopped at room 552, my old room.

"This is definitely more pleasant than a sanitarium," he quipped, unlocking the door.

Inside, it was like stepping back in time. How many days and nights had I sat at the small round table mulling over my fate? How many times had I tossed a frock or stockings over one of those delicate green arm chairs? Or cried myself to sleep in one of the twin beds? How many times had I wished the old Crosley radio on the night table would be transformed into the Magic Fingers Massage Machine, a time machine. A machine which had transported me into the past and might very well send Lex and me into the future.

For three years, I'd tried to reconstruct the events which had led to the massage machine's appearance. It seemed to be tied to the discovery of a small piece of hotel stationery. An elusive slip of paper which either read: The Roosevelt Grand, the hotel's future name, or the Grand Biarritz, the current name. Once the paper was discovered, the room would grow murky. Then the massage machine would appear on the night stand by the bed in place of the radio.

The massage machine had a slit for a quarter and a tiny lever with three speeds, mild, medium, and strong, determining how intensely the bed vibrated. And possibly, how far back or forward in time the hotel guest traveled.

Unfortunately, that darned scrap of stationery was missing. I'd made a point of storing it in a small file with the rest of my mementos from the future. But the paper scrap seemed to appear arbitrarily. And it wasn't with my things now.

After our luggage arrived, Lex ordered a bottle of gin from the bellman. Lex had several strong belts, then fell asleep on the second twin bed by the window. The same bed he'd occupied after he received a gun shot wound in July of 1930 in a battle with mobster

Carmine Ascencio. The same night my brother Paul and his wife Sylvia vanished from this very room. Too bad, I had no idea where in time they'd gone. Because Paul had been my last living relative. Back in the future, we'd been extremely close. And by the summer of 1930, we'd managed to rekindle our relationship. Then, without warning, we'd unearthed that scrap of hotel stationery. The room changed. And I chose to remain behind with Lex when Paul and Sylvia had disappeared in time.

Now I prayed for a similar miracle to save Lex. I didn't need to return to 1997. Any future date would work as long as there was a cure for the current strain of tuberculosis.

While Lex snored, I dug through the file's mementos on the second bed. But the scrap of hotel stationery wasn't with the photos of Paul and me as kids at Disneyland. I sifted through the contents several times hoping to conjure up that scrap of paper. Without luck.

As Lex's labored breathing deepened, I probed under the beds, in the closet, behind the bureau, and the night table as I had in 1997. But tonight my hunting expedition produced nothing more than a palm–full of dust. With a sinking feeling, I saw how fate had played its hand. Lex was doomed to the sanitarium just as I was doomed to follow my own course in life.

"Your brother Paul and his pain–in–the–neck wife are probably hiding in Chicago or Detroit, glad they got out of town with their necks," Lex always said, when I tried to convince him that Paul and Sylvia might be living in the year 1956 or 2006.

"Lex, I was there. I saw the hotel room change. I heard the air conditioner, and the television— "

"Honey, your brother owed money everywhere. Not only to Ascencio but Macy's and Saks, you name it. They aren't on a spaceship, Jeri. They're in Toledo or Baton Rouge. You just refuse to believe your brother would leave us holding the bag and skip out on his debts."

This was the gist of a conversation we'd been having for two years.

By ten that night, I knew my time travel scheme had failed. I undressed and fell asleep in the second twin bed. We stayed at the Grand Biarritz Hotel for three days hoping to find an outlet to the future. But we never did. On the fourth morning we returned to Riverside Drive. And I packed the items Lex would need up at Mrs. Jankel's Cure Cottage at Saranac Lake.

SIX

We left at six in the morning for Saranac Lake. The sky was
an iron gray with mounds of ominous clouds, and the temperature had
fallen to a grim thirty–five degrees. I'd hardly shut my eyes the night
before. Now, in the back of the old Dusenberg, frigid air stung my
face and ankles, areas not covered by my mink coat, stylish hat,
elegant shoes, or the fur rug which covered our laps. Lex wore his
new camel hair coat. He smelled of hair pomade and cologne. I'd
chosen a new brown wool suit and a matching hat. We looked as if
we were off to an afternoon cocktail party or a fancy luncheon, not a
trip to a sanitarium.

A few miles out of the city the views through the Dusenberg's
windows changed from city to country. We sped through small towns
of Northern New Jersey and Upstate New York as Harris steered the
car around deep pits on the unpaved country roads. We passed
woodlands barren in the late fall, and farms with faded houses and
barns where cows and horses grazed. Many properties lay abandoned,
foreclosure signs nailed to a tree or fencepost. We hardly spoke
during the long drive.

Smoking a cigarette, Lex silently stared out his window. I
tried to contain my fear while imagining what he must be feeling. We
stopped once to stretch our legs and relieve ourselves at a café. At

some point I fell asleep with my head on Lex's shoulder.

Three hours later, we rode up a bumpy dirt road to Mrs. Jankel's Cure Cottage, an enormous Victorian house with the prescribed wraparound porch. The house had a fresh coat of white paint and a deep green trim. Under the sullen winter sky, Lex and I gawked at the enormous house, while Harris removed Lex's luggage off the back of the car. Then the three of us silently crunched across the gravel walkway, past dead flower beds, to a flight of wood steps which led to the porch. On the broad front wraparound porch, we self–consciously clumped past prone patients wrapped in heavy blankets, stretched out on cure chairs. The wood beds reminded me of the Adirondack chairs of the future which could be made to sit up or lie flat. Most of the patients dozed. A few silently watched us. One young male patient smiled and waved.

A hand printed note had been pinned to the door. *Welcome. We're busy right now. Please have a seat inside and wait quietly. And remember to cover your mouth when you cough. Thanks, Mrs. Eva Jankel.*

A bell jingled announcing us. Entering, we found ourselves in a large, dark reception area. Smells of damp wood, alcohol, and institutional cooking filled the house. A reception desk with a line of pigeonholes stood against the back wall. A sign on the desk advised us to, "Have a seat in the parlor." Off to the side, pamphlets about patient care and local shops covered a small round table. There was *The Journal of Outdoor Life* and the *Optimist Guides* which urged a positive attitude in TB patients. I'd already read this utopian tripe back in the city.

The town of Saranac Lake had its own train station, thirteen drugstores, five undertakers, fifty–three private physicians, thirteen private–duty nurses, seven churches, two banks, two apartment hotels, nineteen sanitariums, a hundred–fifty cure cottages, and the well–equipped Saranac Lake General Hospital. But there was still a shortage of space for people with consumption.

Now, the three of us practically tiptoed into the parlor, a large room filled with ornate Victorian furnishings. Every inch of the decor from the floor to the ceiling seemed to be made of dark wood and dark fabrics, casting the space in gloom. The three of us stood frozen in the center of the large space, afraid to sit or touch anything, let alone talk. Then, from somewhere in that great old house, we heard a piano playing.

A man's wistful voice rang out.

"… I'm always chasing rainbows, watching clouds drifting by. My schemes are just like all my dreams, ending in the sky…"

Without warning, with Harris looking on, Lex stretched his arms toward me. Maybe it was the music or the oddity of the moment, but I instantly understood. I tentatively stepped forward and accepted Lex's embrace. Then he led me in a slow, gentle waltz. Today, my legs didn't wobble or acknowledge the gravity of the situation. I blocked out the smell of camphor and the overpowering sadness woven into the faded rug and nubby green draperies. I shut my eyes and followed my husband's lead to those tender notes, feeling his broad hand holding mine and his muscled shoulder beneath his jacket.

In that instant, we transformed Mrs. Jankel's grim parlor into the Casino in Central Park, three years ago, October 24, 1929. I could almost smell the bootleg whiskey and cigars, and hear the boisterous laughter, the clink of glasses, and the music. I recalled our first kiss on the dance floor. For a few moments, we hung there, lost in memories.

Then a woman's rang out. "Mr Giananetti!" The music ceased. "You're supposed to be having your dinner, not playing the piano. Now get on with you, before I'm forced to spoon feed you myself."

Without warning, a woman with wild silver hair rushed out of a side door by the reception desk, chewing food and drying her hands on a clean white apron. "Sorry, but you've come at dinner time," she scolded. "We're very busy. Come back later when we're finished —"

"Mrs. Jankel? I'm Lester Rose. *Lex*, if you please," Lex said.

Mrs. Jankel paused to study Lex, and her demeanor instantly softened. A smile spread across her kind face. She reacted the way most women did when confronted by Lex. "I'm Eva Jankel. Nice to meet you, Lex." She did not reach for his hand. "Now, Lex, the nurse is just finishing up your room. So be a lamb and come with me. We'll get you settled right after dinner. Have you eaten yet? I can see we need to fatten you up." Taking his elbow, she led him toward the door she'd just come through. "We've got a nice roast today with plenty of mashed potatoes, corn, and spinach. And apple pie with cheese. And the richest milk anywhere. Your room is a lovely one with a wonderful view. You can see the lake from your upstairs porch. Don't worry about your things, we'll bring them up for you after dinner."

Lex glanced nervously back at us, like a small boy being led away on his first day of boarding school.

"Come back in an hour," Eva Jankel called over her shoulder to Harris and me.

Hanging onto my purse, I felt faint, as if I were the one being taken away. When the door swung open, I glimpsed the dining area where a group of adults, surrounded by nurses, sat family style at a long table.

A nurse ladled food onto a woman's plate. "Come on, Mrs. Silverman. Eat up. You don't want to go back to bed rest all day, do you?"

Then the door swung shut, leaving Harris and me alone in the reception area where I stared at the closed door feeling as if someone had punched me in the stomach.

"Hungry, ma'am?" Harris suddenly asked. "I could drive you into town and find a café."

"No, I ..." I felt too upset to speak, as if my whole being would crack if I tried to answer. As though I'd start to cry and never stop.

"A walk by the lake then?"

Outside, we followed a dirt road. Me in my dressy high heels and mink coat. Harris in his driver's uniform which consisted of jodhpurs, a trim long dark jacket, and a black cap. We trudged over thick tree roots, fallen trees, and a dense blanket of pine needles. We battled fickle winds filled with the scent of pine and lake water. When we reached the lake, an enormous body of gray water, which rose like a vast ocean in the insistent breeze, we stood in the shadows of a small inlet on a low cliff above the water's edge. Houses surrounded the lake. Some were private homes for the rich. Others were small sanitariums like Mrs. Jankel's cottage. The acclaimed Trudeau Clinic was somewhere nearby. I'd written the Trudeau Clinic several letters. In the end Lex had been rejected. They claimed to be too full.

While my legs, ankles, and nose felt frozen from the late fall chill, Harris seemed indifferent to the cold. He stared across the lake, his pale face a solemn etching.

"Don't give up on him, ma'am. He's a fighter," he said. "If it hadn't been for the mustard gas in the war ... there were none like him. Nor will be again. You had to have known him then, as a lad of seventeen. He was so dedicated, so brave, the best soldier out there. Not many knew his true worth."

Against my will, tears filled my eyes. I'd meant to act brave and look my best when Lex and I said goodby. Maybe my vanity was silly after all we'd faced together these last two years, but having his last impression of me looking puffy–faced and tired with mascara trailing down my cheeks seemed pretty tragic, too.

Turning, Harris and I hiked back to the cottage. Our feet crushed the pine needles and fallen leaves. Harris's stern face brimmed with the first sorrow he'd ever shown in the three years I'd known him.

Back at Mrs. Jankel's, in Lex's tiny room, I tried to absorb the endless rules rattled off by Miss Bronson, the head nurse. A tall, hard–faced woman with a long sharp nose, dark hair pulled back tightly under her white cap, she seemed as brittle as dried spaghetti.

"… patients will remain in bed without exception for the required month or more until the doctor permits otherwise. You bathe nightly in your bed. A full bath is given once a week on a specified day, which you will be told about later."

"How can he bathe in bed?" I asked.

"We manage a thorough sponge bath daily. The bed pans are under the bed. Patients must ring for help. In case of an emergency, tap loudly on the side of the bed with this metal spoon. Never cough into the open. These are paper handkerchiefs. Use them. Deposit your soiled ones in this paper bag. This cup is for sputum. If you have any questions, refer to your book of rules there by your bed."

"Sounds like boot–camp," Harris muttered.

Lex sat on his bed, his gaze locked on the view out his window, as if dreaming of happier days. "I'd prefer a private hospital," he'd insisted from the start, though each state had established public TB sanitariums and a private home would be costly. But he'd already learned that though smaller establishments followed the same strict rules for patient care as the larger sanitariums, they were often more flexible.

No doubt he intended to break every rule that didn't suit him.

We left Lex alone to change into bed clothes and followed Nurse Bronson for a tour of the house. The cottage smelled of disinfectant, urine, food, alcohol, the lake, and sorrow. My fears of catching the disease increased with every step. And my heart pounded frantically at the thought of saying goodby to Lex.

Back in Lex's room, after our tour, I jotted down a list of additional things Lex would need. Lex remarked about the glorious view while eyeing a tall slim nurse and two other female patients as they headed downstairs for a walk. But seconds later, when we were about to say goodby, he grew quiet, awkward. Dressed in a gown without pockets and his robe, he didn't seem to know where to put his hands. And he wouldn't look at me. Instead, he gazed up at the ceiling or down at the floor.

I wanted to tell him how much I loved him, that I'd write every day, that I'd wait forever. But once again, we'd lost our ease with each other. At last, he peered out the window and I waited, feeling waves of sadness and panic that this might be our last few seconds together. Outside, it began to rain. I knew I'd never forget the grimness of the cure cottage. The awkward silence other than the heavy patter of rain. And the smells.

When Lex finally spoke, his gaze was fastened on the view through the doors to the second floor wraparound porch. He stared at the winter trees bereft in the December chill, at a man wrapped in a blanket on a recliner, his wire–rimmed glasses down his nose, his mouth open as he snored.

"Listen, darling…" He began.

I shut my eyes and swallowed. He hadn't called me darling in a long time and his voice was a breathy whisper.

"It was always you. No one else. You may think … it was otherwise. But you have to trust me about this. So when you think of us, think of us the way we used to be. Out on top. Dressed to the nines. On our way to see Jimmy Walker, the Mayor of New York."

"You don't have to explain." I reached to touch his lapel, as my eyes welled up again. "You just need rest and good food—"

"Go west, Jeri. Back to California where you'll be safe, away from the Desanto brothers and all our troubles here. See your family and friends. If I had the lungs, I'd have moved us there myself. The movies are still making dough. Harris can get you set with train tickets and whatever else you need. Then go. And don't look back."

"Sure, maybe I will."

He abruptly took my hand, surprising me. I thought he meant to touch me, to make contact. I felt as if I'd been holding my breath for eternity, and now I could breathe again, now there was hope for us. Then my fingers felt the cash, a big wad of bills. I studied the money then his face. Those brilliant blue eyes of his were filled with tears, too. Then, we were in each other's arms.

"You're still the most beautiful doll in New York," he cried into my ear. "So when that fat movie producer asks you to sit on his lap, remember who you are, who we once were."

A moment later we parted. Lex instantly waved at a passing nurse and sent her that fifty–dollar grin that had always made women swoon. His shoulders were back, his chin was out, as if he were gliding past the ropes at the Stork Club, heading toward his table, after slipping the Captain a sawbuck for a spot down by the orchestra. In that final instant, he'd managed to push back his obvious horror and persuade the world one more time that he was the invincible Lex Rose.

Outside, Harris waited in the rain, stone–faced, pale, his hands hanging by his sides. He studied a nearby mountain as if he intended to climb it later and needed to discern the correct route to the top. I felt hollow, yet relieved, too. Lex and I had done the hardest thing of all. We'd managed to hide our fears and part as friends. Lex would probably never return home. This view of the world would be his last. He would eat well, sleep well, and gaze endlessly at the tall pines.

Then one night he wouldn't be able to catch his breath. He would hemorrhage. And I would get a telegram. And I'd learn to survive without him.

That night, back home in bed on Riverside Drive, I couldn't turn off my mind. What was Lex thinking? Was he staring up at the ceiling, contemplating his own death? Maybe he couldn't catch his breath and he was coughing. Or would they give him a sedative to sleep his first night?

Alone in the dark with the servants snoring soundly upstairs, the grand old house on Riverside Drive echoed with emptiness. Over and over, the image of Lex putting on a hearty grin as he met his nurse and the doctor swam through my head. And the memory of his pale face peering out his upstairs window as Harris led me back to the car for our return trip to New York. I'd never forget the misery in his eyes or his half–hearted wave.

In the morning, the unruffled spot beside me brought home the truth. Lex was at Mrs. Jankel's Cure Cottage. And it was still raining.

"I'll wear my gray Mainbocher," I told Keely, minutes later, as I stepped from my shower and steeled myself to face the day.

With Lex gone and the threat of tuberculosis with him, Keely had agreed to stay on with me. An hour later, dressed in my new grey suit trimmed in Persian lamb, a matching beret, long grey silk gloves and a valuable pearl broach pinned to my lapel, I could've been an elegant committee woman on her way to a luncheon.

Downstairs, Harris held open the Dusenberg's door.

"Manhattan Trust and Savings," I said, sliding in. This morning, everything from Harris's hands to the back of his head, spoke of his sorrow over Lex. "Harris, are you okay?"

"It's not just Mr. Lex, ma'am. It's … Bobby, Bobby Peacock."

"Bobby? What's wrong with him? Don't tell me he's sick, too."

"Police found him this morning, Mrs. Rose. Found him with a slug in his back down by the river. Been dead a couple of days."

Bobby Peacock. To me he'd been a handsome young thug paid to guard Lex. Another employee. A soulless young man with a fast gun. I suddenly pictured him with Lupe Cardona on his lap. "What happened?"

"Dunno yet."

"Did he have a family?"

"Seems he did."

Depression washed over me. There were too many things to live down. And now Bobby Peacock, too.

Twenty minutes later, a bank officer named Deekin Ferber faced me from across a wide desk. A set of papers sat before him and glasses clung to his beak of a nose.

"Good of you to come, Mrs. Rose. However, when I wrote your husband, I had no idea he would send you. But since you've come today …"

Bad news was coming. "Yes, we were away. And then Mr. Rose … he had to leave town again. I'm afraid I never read your letter."

"I see." He glanced at me, saw the tears in my eyes, and looked stricken. "Mrs. Rose, are you unwell? May I get you a glass of water?"

"No, thank you. Please continue."

Mr. Ferber opened the file, cleared his throat, and stared down at the papers before him. "We'll get right to it then. You see, Mr. Rose has been a good customer for many years. He profited during times when a great many others fell short. But recently, Mr. Rose has been spending beyond even what he can afford. Until, well, here is your final statement."

Final statement? It seemed the devil had appeared in the form of a soft–spoken, little bald man in wire rimmed glasses and a dark grey suit. This bank hadn't closed its doors or gone on a holiday like so many others had recently. The marble pillars and shiny wood cubicles still broadcasted stately grandeur and stability. But the bracketed figures before me were my worst news yet. I began to shiver until the numbers grew hazy.

"Mrs. Rose? Please, let me get you water or …" Harris and Mr. Ferber rushed to my side.

"No, I…" Holding onto the chair arm, I managed to stand. "I'm fine, really." It seemed Lex had spent us into a penniless state. Okay, he'd never been frugal. But I'd counted on his business acumen, his common sense. Unless the TB had affected his brain, a possibility. Or he just chose to ignore the facts and go on believing Rose Construction would rise from the ashes and save us. In a daze, I shook Mr. Ferber's hand. Muttering apologies, he and Harris helped me out the revolving door.

"Mr. Rose had another account downtown," Harris said in a discreet voice, as we reached the car. "Perhaps he had something there."

So Harris drove me to the other bank, the United Savings and Trust. But when we arrived, we found a sign taped to the door: *Closed. Come back Monday.*"

The problem was, today was Monday.

Harris shook his head. "Trouble ahead, madam. Looks like another bank failure."

I wanted to scream, to ring Lex's neck. For his insane spending, for getting TB, for leaving me alone to clean up this mess. My head began to spin. I felt nauseous. "Harris, pull over!"

Harris screeched to the curb and rushed to open my door. I

staggered from the car and was sick in the gutter. After, I wiped my mouth on a clean hankie and crawled back inside the car. "Harris, think. There must be a strong box or a vault. Something we've overlooked."

Only yesterday, Lex had handed me fifteen hundred dollars, an extraordinary sum in 1932. But it wouldn't support us now. Not when Lex's private sanitarium would cost thirty–five dollars a week, and we had no money coming in to pay for it.

"There might be something at his office. In the safe," Harris said.

But the safe was bare, too.

Afterward, over coffee and donuts at the Automat, I stared into Harris's face. A face which never showed fear. "We need to sell everything," I said. "You'll have to help me. Especially with the cars."

"What about Lex's mother, Mrs. Stern? Perhaps she'd be willing to help out. She used to be quite well–off. And she still lives here in the city, down in Gramercy Park," Harris said.

"No, we can't ask her." Ida Stern, a vain selfish woman, had barely hidden her hatred of me for the last three years, during the few times we met for birthdays and holidays. Begging her for help was beyond imagining.

The following day, down at Mr. Leavitt's pawn shop, my diamonds, gold, pearls, and furs were as common as autumn leaves on a windy October day. Harris negotiated with the pawnbroker, but it was no use. Nothing was worth anything anymore.

During the following week, I gave the servants notice, sold off our possessions, and packed. For me the sumptuous world of the 1920s had finally ended, albeit over two years after *The Crash* had wiped out everyone else. There was no going back.

SEVEN

The December winds spoke of a cold New York winter as Harris pulled the Dusenberg to the curb by Pennsylvania Station ten days later. I gazed up at the grand old train station, afraid.

"Better go in, Mrs. Rose. Cold out here today," Harris said, taking my hand to help me out. Harris and a train porter quickly removed my luggage off the back of the car. And I searched my purse again, checking on my tickets and money. Back in the future, I'd flown around the world, taken travel for granted. Now, as the wind whipped my face, fear gnawed at my gut. I longed to be back on Riverside Drive in bed. Except my bed had been sold along with the rest of our furnishings and the house itself to a French diplomat who planned to move in tomorrow.

"Harris, would you mind parking the car then meeting me inside by the information booth?"

"Certainly, madam."

Inside the old Penn Station, a mass of humanity crossed floors where thousands of glass bricks had been imbedded. Travelers patiently sat on long benches, their heads bent over newspapers, Bibles, and dime novels. Women knitted. Children played hopscotch. People leaned against the walls and waited. I studied the building's tall spires, the light filtering through the glass, and the huge board which listed the trains with bold names like The Montrealer, The Orange Blossom Special, and The Broadway Limited, my train. Loudspeakers echoed across the grand expanse of the room announcing incoming and outgoing trains. Shops and restaurants, decorated for Christmas, lined the arcade, a metal–faced boulevard of shops. With a pang, I realized I was about to miss Christmas in New York.

After nearly three years in New York, I'd be back in California in a few days. A very different California from the one I'd left. In the late 1990s, Los Angeles had been a sprawling modern world with a population of over nine million people. In 1932, the population was just over two million.

At the newsstand, I bought a *Herald Tribune*. In the news, Joseph Stalin's second wife, Nadezhda Alliluyev had died under mysterious circumstances, possibly by her own hand. Telephone service between the US and Hawaii was now possible. Picasso had just finished *Girl before a Mirror,* and *Buck Rogers* had just begun airing on CBS radio. The top songs of the day included "Brother Can You Spare a Dime?" and "Night and Day" from Cole Porter's Broadway hit *The Gay Divorcee.* The year's new books included, *Tobacco Road* by Erskine Caldwell. *Light in August* by William Faulkner, and *Brave New World* by Aldous Huxley, a science fiction novel about the future when art and relations would be controlled by technology.

At last, I spied Harris cutting across the enormous room. That pale lined face made my heart ache. Ever since I'd known Lex, I'd known Harris. Silent, chalky as Milk of Magnesia, Harris had always been there to help shoulder life's weight. He'd always been around to protect us from Ascencio and now the Desanto brothers.

"Your luggage has been loaded onto the train," Harris said, joining me, glancing at his watch. "You might want to check on it in

Chicago. Just send a porter to the baggage car and slip him something for his trouble."

"Is the train on time?"

"Yes, madam." Feeling in his pocket, he fished out the keys to Lex's Dusenberg. "You'll want these. And the receipt for the garage where it's parked."

I'd been waiting for this moment. "No, Harris. I'd like you to keep the car. You'll take care of it for me."

His eyes widened. "But madam —"

"Lex would want you to have it. Maybe one day, he'll need the car again. And you'll have it. And we'll find you."

"As you wish." Then staring at a large wall clock, he said, "Seems like a long time since Mr. Rose brought you out to the car that night at the Plaza Hotel."

"A long time."

"He was in love then, even if he didn't know it. I saw it on his face. So take care out there, madam. And write. Write to Mr. Rose often. Even if he doesn't write back. Sometimes you have to ignore what he does, look past it."

Tears filled my eyes, and my nose began to run. I rummaged through my purse, relieved to spy a clean handkerchief. "What will you do?"

"Wait for Mr. Rose. I'll stand my post and watch for him as always." Harris was referring to their years together during the Great War.

"Where will you stay?"

"Out on the Island. A place called Montauk where men still fish. My dad fished. And I always thought I'd try it someday."

"You know I would've brought you with me to Los Angeles … if I'd had the money. Have you got any family at all?"

"Just a half–sister. And Mr. Rose."

Then the loudspeaker blasted, echoing across that hollow palace. "The Broadway Limited, track four." We heard a deep rumbling, a warning that my train was on its way. Harris grabbed my things. "Better get you downstairs."

We moved quickly across the station, then down the steps with the rest of the passengers. My heart was pounding, and the cold air ate through my sheer stockings. Below, by the tracks, the air smelled dank and sooty. Harris seemed so strong, so capable, I had to bite my tongue to keep from begging him to come with me. To serve me as he'd served Lex. But I couldn't promise him anything. Not a place to stay, let alone wages. I'd be sharing a room at a women's hotel out in Hollywood, watching every penny.

At last, with a gust of steam, the train chugged through the tunnel. Hissing steam, it jolted to an abrupt stop.

"You've got a nice stateroom," Harris said, instantly moving to a train door. Taking my hand, he helped me up the narrow iron stairs to the metal platform by the train's parlor car. Then he handed me my jewelry box, hat box, and overnight bag.

I gazed down at his lined face. "Thank you. Thank you for so many things."

"You will always be my mistress, madam. And if you ever need help, write me. And – God willing – I will come." He handed me a slip of paper with nothing more than an address: Stoneyhill Road, Montauk, Long Island, New York.

I dropped the paper in my purse, rummaged for yet another clean handkerchief, and dried my eyes. When I looked up, Harris was gone.

I'd meant to shake his hand, to tell him I'd write. I meant to ask him for a telephone number. Leaving my things behind on the platform, I raced back down the train's steep metal steps to the landing. Looking left and right, I combed the crowd for him. I finally spied him rushing up the stairs to the station's waiting room. Desolate, I turned back to the train. I paused to stare at one of those lucky men who'd bypassed the Depression. A luxuriously groomed woman in magnificent furs and an elegant hat clutched his arm.

"Mr. Rockefeller, your private car is ready, sir," a conductor said.

Then I was winding my way down a Pullman car to my private stateroom, a final indulgence. A place where I felt safe. In the tiny room I set down my things on the seat beside me, leaned back, and shut my eyes. The train abruptly shifted. Out my window, a young black man pushed a cart filled with luggage. And a conductor studied his timepiece. With a quiet lurch and a cloud of steam, the train slowly rolled out of Pennsylvania Station. Grunting and sputtering, the train headed down a blackened tunnel until it emerged from the darkness of the station into the pale light where a reluctant sun gave off a sad and hopeless illumination.

I thought back to my arrival in the past and how it happened. In July of 1997, my brother Paul flew to New York on business. And vanished. For months I commuted east looking for him. That October my boss at the advertising agency fired me. She insisted my head wasn't in my marketing job anymore. With little else to do, I flew to New York to search for Paul. At the Roosevelt Grand Hotel, I checked into Paul's former hotel room. I searched every inch for clues of his disappearance but found nothing more than a scrap of hotel stationary with a different hotel name. Then I noticed the Magic Fingers Massage Machine, a machine which promised a relaxing massage. Curious, I dropped a quarter in the slot, turned out the lights, and drifted into a bottomless sleep. I woke the next morning to discover I'd gone back in time almost seventy years. Unfortunately, the Magic Fingers Massage Machine no longer sat by the bed. And I could find no way back to my own time.

Panicked, I threw on clothes and hurried down to the lobby. With the help of the hotel manager, I learned that my brother had stayed in the hotel in 1929, too. A hotel now called The Grand Biarritz. Frightened and alone, I decided to see if Paul had become a stock analyst again. Unfortunately, I'd arrived on October 24, 1929, the first day of the stock market's five day slide to *The Crash of '29,* and the Great Depression. Meaning the area around Wall Street was pandemonium.

Unable to get close to the brokerage houses, I wandered into a nearby restaurant. By coincidence, Paul was lunching there, too. But when I waved at him, he didn't respond. And before I could introduce myself, he paid his bill, rushed outside, and sped away in a cab. Only one thing seemed promising. I'd heard him tell his lunch mate that he planned to attend a party that night at the Plaza Hotel.

That night, dressed in a Vionnet original from Saks, I lost my nerve to crash the party. Which was when I spied Lex. Tall, dark–haired, with incredible blue eyes and a confident swagger, he was the most desirable man I'd ever seen. He noticed me, too. And before I knew it, he'd whisked me inside the party and introduced me to a wide assortment of people. Including my brother Paul. But once again, Paul didn't recognize me.

However, Paul and I soon became close friends. He even warned me to be careful with Lex, a notorious womanizer. Then, one night, Paul confessed to having amnesia, having been knocked down by a taxi outside the Grand Biarritz Hotel. Eventually, I explained that I was his sister, that we were both time travelers from the late twentieth century. My photographs from the future helped convince him that my stories were true.

In 1930, Paul married Sylvia, a vain brat whose family had been crushed by the stock market crash. And I married Lex.

Soon Paul confessed to Lex and me that he was indebted to

loan shark Carmine Ascencio. Knowing how dangerous Ascencio was, Lex agreed to intercede on Paul's behalf.

To be safe, I moved out of our home on Riverside Drive and into my old room at the Grand Biarritz. Paul and his new bride Sylvia followed, taking the adjoining room. Unfortunately, Lex was shot that night during a gunfight with Ascencio and his cohorts. Ascencio was killed.

Using the hotel's back entrance and service elevator, Harris and I brought Lex up to our room. A doctor sewed Lex up and gave him a strong sedative. But in the early hours of the morning, the police arrived in search of Lex. Harris, who'd stood guard in the lobby, phoned to warn me. After convincing Paul and Sylvia to switch rooms, Paul and I moved Lex to a bed in the adjoining room. The police arrived at my old room to find Paul and Sylvia instead of Lex and me.

When the police left, Paul knocked on my door to return photographs from the future that I'd lent him. Somehow the elusive scrap of hotel stationary was mixed in with the photos. This time the name on the stationary said *The Roosevelt Grand*. In a flash, the light in the room dimmed. Once again, The Magic Fingers Massage Machine materialized on the night table. Soon the glow of a television set and the sound of air conditioning convinced me that we were about to experience more time travel. Caught between both rooms and the choice of going forward in time with my brother or staying behind with Lex, my husband, I chose Lex. I jumped through the portal between our rooms and landed back in 1930.

The connecting door slammed shut. And though I knocked and knocked that night, no one answered. In the morning, another hotel guest occupied my old room. Paul had disappeared again. And I remained behind in 1930 with Lex.

EIGHT

Hollywood, 1933

"Maybelle, telephone," Mrs. Whitcombe said, handing a short brunette the phone, before cheerfully resuming mail call. "Peaches, you got two letters. Connie, two postcards. Verna, a letter."

Mrs. Whitcombe owned The Bayridge House and she had yet to call my name in three months. Once again, the pile of letters had been dispersed without a word from Lex.

"Honestly, that husband of yours oughta be scalped," my roommate Carol Ann said, rising off the ancient parlor chair and smoothing down her slim ankle–length skirt. Carol Ann wasn't bad looking with her peroxided mop of curls and well–painted face. But she was pushing thirty and had yet to land a role with more than one line of dialogue in six years.

"Come on. Let's get lunch then go through the trades," she said. "My new *Photoplay's* in, too, with Gable on the cover."

"You go. I don't feel like meatloaf again."

"Well, who does? But it sure beats starving," she said, catching up to several other gals heading toward the dining room.

The Bayridge catered to what I considered *wannabes*. Girls who'd hopped a bus one day and left behind their dreary small town lives to become Hollywood film stars. Not that all the girls fit the bill for the cover of *Modern Screen*. Some were downright chubby. Others were pert seventeen year olds, girls who made me feel like my teeth should be soaking in a jar. There were several knockouts, too, at least by current standards. In this era, you had to overlook bowed legs, over-bites, and flab around the middle. This generation hadn't heard of nose jobs, extreme workouts, or lyposuction. Most of the girls came from hamlets where a dentist was a rarity, let alone an orthodontist. Many of the *wannabes* hadn't made it to the eighth grade. But all of them had tried their hands at permanent waves, mascara, powder, lipstick, and a sultry smudge of eyeshadow.

Seated in the parlor by the faded Christmas tree, a reminder that the holidays had passed uneventfully, I clutched an unfinished letter on my lap and eavesdropped on the conversations swirling around me.

"… so I says to this guy, the assistant to the assistant, you put your hand there one more time, and I'll use my toenail clippers on you. So the guy laughs like it's the funniest thing he ever heard. And that's how I landed the job. I made the jerk laugh," a stumpy blonde bragged to her friend.

It was almost noon. In a few seconds, Mrs. Whitcombe would announce lunch and the girls would stampede into the dining room. I'd lost my appetite. Partly because Lex hadn't written. But mostly because lunch usually consisted of dark brown meat sliced to the thickness of notepaper with a roadmap of gristle, mashed potatoes like glue, gravy like colored paste, and green beans cooked about a year.

Once again, I pulled out my pencil and tried to finish my letter to Lex. Writing Lex made me feel less guilty about being healthy and free.

> *… and the girls here are great. There's always someone to talk to and someone trying out for a big*

part. We all go to Central Casting regularly but since
King Kong finished filming, things have been quiet. I
thought I wasn't getting picked for jobs because of my
wedding ring, so I took it off. But I still didn't get any
work, just a lot more propositions.

I crossed out that last bit. Maybe he wouldn't find it funny.

So as much as I love Hollywood, I'm looking for a real job
with steady pay.

Upstairs in the room I shared with Carol Ann, I finished my letter with a promise to write again soon, providing Lex wrote me back. Then I stuck the envelope in my purse beside my note to the *Los Angeles Times'* Classifieds. This was my third attempt to reach my family, the Coopers. According to what my mother always said, the Coopers had been victims of the Dust Bowl and migrated to the San Fernando Valley in the early thirties. By the time I was ten, all of them had passed away or disappeared. This latest notice repeated what my last two said.

Family member looking for the Ohio/Kansas Coopers. Please
contact Jeri Rose, c/o the Bayridge House. Hollywood.

"I used to feed my dog better back home," Carol Ann announced, bursting into our room after lunch. After tossing her magazine on her bed, she flopped down on her stomach. "You going with me to that audition tomorrow? They're casting for another big musical starring Claudette Colbert."

"Not me. I can't sing or dance, remember?"

"They won't notice with those gams and the way you fill out a chemise."

"Frankly, I don't understand how you keep it up. Spending every day down at Central Casting, always hearing the word *no.* Don't you ever get discouraged?"

Carol Ann groaned. "Don't tell me this is another

heart–to–heart on life in Hollywood. Cause I got better things to do."

"Guess I should level with you. I'm leaving."

Carol Ann sat up. "Leaving? You only been here two months. Why throw in the towel so fast? Especially with your looks."

"I've been here over three months. And I need a real job."

"Don't we all. What're you gonna do, sell encyclopedias?"

"I don't know. Maybe I'll do bookkeeping or teach school."

"Pull my other leg," Carol Ann said, tossing down her new magazine.

"It's the truth."

"You ringin' a school bell? I don't see it. Besides, the pay stinks."

"At least it would be steady. My husband's bills won't go away just because I land an occasional walk on. Beside, my being an actress was his idea, not mine."

"I ain't puttin' you down, honey. Some days … well, I ain't the youngest gal here. But, aw shucks, Jeri, just when I decided you're okay, you're leavin'. I hate breakin' in a new roomie."

I smiled. "I'll miss you, too."

"Gosh, but I don't see you bein' a desk jockey or stuck in a classroom with a bunch of grimy kids. Me, I hated school. Just the thought of it makes me sick. If I left here I know what I'd do. And it wouldn't have nothin' to do with a bunch of snot–nosed brats. I'd go straight down to one of them places that caters to fine gents. Then I'd close my eyes and count the patterns in the wallpaper and collect a whole lotta greenbacks."

"You're joking."

"Hey, it's all acting, ain't it? I've done my time on casting couches here in sunny Hollywood. And I never got more than a few bits for my troubles. So what's the big deal? I know a few spiffy places right around here that wouldn't be half–bad."

"Really?"

"Ever heard of Mrs. Small's? A guy told me she's got a place right off Sunset. Then there's a place out in the valley. The Rainbow. If things got rough, that's where I'd go. I met the lady that runs the joint. I was waitin' tables at a swanky private party at The Ambassador. And she asked me for a highball. So we got to talkin'. You'd never know she ran one of them places. She was just a regular person, only prettier. She looked like she stepped right off the cover of some fancy fashion magazine. Glamorous but lady–like. Of course my old mama would drop dead with heart failure if she knew I worked in a place like that. But I wouldn't exactly write home with the news. And at least I'd be able to send her and Pop a few bucks regularly."

"Seems like anything would be easier than breaking into pictures," I said.

"But you've hardly given the business a chance," Carol Ann said.

"I can't afford to."

"Just come with me tomorrow. Please. We can have lunch after. I know a real nice beanery nearby. Just think of it as a great adventure."

"You should be in sales. Okay but this is my last try."

NINE
Lex

Lex strained to listen. Someone had opened the door to his room. Probably the nurse checking on him. Mrs. Jankel's Cure Cottage had bedded down for the night. As usual, he felt isolated and afraid. He wondered if he'd ever sleep. He got so little activity during the day that he needed sedatives at night. Too bad they left him exhausted and depressed.

Outside an owl hooted. Winter. Would he still be here by spring? Or would he be dead? *Focus on something else ...your other life,* he told himself.

He began to play the game. Where would he be if he weren't here? With Jeri at a nightclub or a grand restaurant he decided. She'd be in a new gown by Lanvin or Scaparelli. The music would be mellow jazz by Paul Whiteman. Or maybe they'd go to the Savoy in Harlem. A half dozen friends would be seated at their table, though he couldn't picture their faces. That was okay. He and Jeri had gotten stuck with a lot of phonies after he'd been indicted for everything from embezzlement to murder. So far, none of them knew where he was now. He could've been dead. No one suspected he was stuck up here in a sanitarium, stuffed like a pig, and bored.

At least Jeri had sent him another letter. He'd read it over and over. He even dictated a response to Nurse Nancy.

"Just give me the address and I'll send it right out," Nancy said brightly that morning after breakfast.

"Later. I might want to add something. Do me a favor and put it on my dresser."

"That's the fifth time you refused to let me mail a letter for you," Nancy said, her big brown eyes full of compassion. "You don't have to be ashamed of being sick. It's not your fault."

"I promise to mail it in a day or so." Or whenever his mother Ida made the trip up here. Ida would take his letters back to the city and mail them from there. That way the Desanto brothers couldn't trace him up here in Saranac Lake.

He hadn't meant to write Jeri at all. That way, when he died, she'd take it on the chin. He'd done everything to push her away. Flirted with other women, even pretended to have affairs. But he wasn't ready to cut the ties completely. Not when her letters meant so much to him.

"Guess what I know?" Nurse Nancy said. "You're famous." From inside her uniform pocket, she withdrew a page from an old *Herald Tribune* and handed it to him.

Rose Still Smelling Sweet, the caption read. He studied the grainy picture of himself in the witness box giving testimony during the Carmine Ascencio murder trial.

A wave of panic washed over him. He was a sitting duck here. No gun, no bodyguard, wearing a nightgown. Even Nurse Nancy wouldn't stare down a thirty–eight for him in case Nicky or Tito found him as easily as Nurse Nancy had dug up this stupid article.

"Gosh, I didn't mean to upset you," she said, seeing his expression. "We're not supposed to upset the patients." She automatically felt his forehead to check for a fever.

"You're not upsetting me," he said, desperate to chat with someone about something besides his fever, his cough, or his bowel habits. "It's grand to have a little intelligent company."

She smiled, relieved. "I guess it isn't really breaking the rules if I talk *and* straighten up." She hung up his robe, lined up his slippers under his bed, and opened his window wide. "You should be outside. It's cold but sunny."

"Sure." He grinned at her and she grinned back. Leaning on Nurse Nancy, he slowly climbed from bed and settled into a wheel chair.

"Gosh, they're awfully strict here, aren't they? Sometimes I'm afraid I'll start to protest when they won't let a big strong guy like you read the newspaper or use the telephone. I don't think that's half as important as sleeping well and getting plenty of nourishing food."

"I knew you were a smart girl," he said.

After she wheeled him outside on the screened porch, she placed him in a recliner. Once he was wrapped up like a mummy in his blanket, she served him water.

"I'll check on you in a little while," she said, disappearing inside. Instead of snoozing or staring at the familiar scenery, he fantasized about her. He wondered if Nurse Nancy had ever *cousined* with a patient, a term for a secret sexual rendevous.

"Keep a positive attitude," the doctors always said. "That's an important part of your cure."

Well, he felt very positive toward Nurse Nancy. Nancy with her small waist, large breasts, and slim ankles. But for some reason, he didn't actually desire her. He could've fooled himself into believing it was because of the TB. But he knew better. He missed Jeri.

He'd been strong, refusing to make love to her back in New York, pretending to be interested in other women. He'd only slipped once, that night after dinner with the Maitlands. Even then, before the lung specialist gave him the bad news, he knew something was seriously wrong with his health. Ever since he first coughed up blood. Plenty of guys in prison had coughed themselves blue at night. He'd seen more of it during the war. And as a kid growing up in the tenements on the Lower East Side. He'd known whole families who coughed. But he'd never met a soul who beat the disease.

At least he'd kept Jeri from getting sick. He could be proud of that. And the fact that he'd left her twenty thousand dollars in his account at The United Savings and Trust, meaning she wouldn't have to worry about money for a while.

***

The next morning, Carol Ann directed me through the Paramount Studio lot to Arnold Walter's office. I grudgingly followed her into a large room where two dozen girls sat on hard benches lining the walls. I felt like a total fraud. What did I have to offer a Hollywood producer except the obvious? And the idea of crawling under a desk or having sex with any of the paunchy, dog–faced producers I'd already met, made me gag.

"How about movin' down?" Carol Ann barked, making two other girls seated on a bench slide over to make room for us.

A bored looking clerk in black pants, a grey vest, and rolled up shirt sleeves, appeared. "Elma Dweeder," he read off his clipboard.

"Oh, that's me." A sweet strawberry blonde stood and patted down her coiffed head. She disappeared down a hall behind the clerk.

"Elma oughta change her name and drop a few pounds off her can," Carol Ann said.

"What should I say when this guy asks if I can dance?" I said.

"Honey, take a hard look at your competition."

I did. For starters, the girls were shorter, plumper. They had curly bobs, thin tweezed brows, and the current long skirt, shimmery blouse, and high heels. "What's your point?"

"They're skags compared to you. So just do what I told you. When you get inside, do a slow turn like we practiced. Betcha anything, you'll be posing on top of a wedding cake in some big production number in a silk chiffon gown, earnin' seventy–five smackers a week in no time."

"Jeri Rose," the clerk called.

My heart flipped. I slowly rose. Carol Ann waved me onward. Clutching my purse, I followed the clerk down a short hall to a tall door. Before the clerk could knock, the door flew open. A blond man charged out. Rushing past us, he accidentally knocked my head shots out of my hand.

"Sorry, Miss," he said, as we both stooped to collect them. Which was when he finally looked at me.

It was *Franky Wyatt*. The handsome young man who'd walked me home in Havana then kissed me. A kiss which had given me quite a few sleepless nights.

His blue eyes widened. "Sorry," he said, rising to his feet and handing me my pictures, letting his fingers graze mine. Then he tipped his hat and disappeared down the hall. And I stepped inside Arnold Walters' office.

The room had two large arched windows, potted palms, and a cloud of cigarette smoke hovering above three suited men seated around a table. The big shot in the center, presumably Walters himself based on the size of his chair, waved his cigar around in a circular fashion. "Honey, let's have a slow turn."

Chin up, chest out, I took my time, feeling as if I might faint.

The three men exchanged glances. Then Walters said, "Pictures?"

I handed him my photos. Walters glanced at them then asked,

"Any speaking parts?"

"Not yet." My voice sounded high, shaky.

His eyes narrowed. "How about that profile again."

I turned to my side.

"Lenny, Bill, give me a minute here."

Both men obediently rose to their feet and exited out a side door leaving me alone with Arnold Walters.

Walters came around from behind his desk. Reaching under my chin, he lifted my face and studied me. "Smile."

I grinned.

He studied my teeth. "Not bad." Facing me, he took my hands and held them out to my sides as he took a slow look at my breasts, my waistline, and my legs, until I felt a deep blush covering my face.

"You dance?" he asked.

"Not much, sir."

Chewing on his cigar, he continued to study me. "Still, you can walk and your voice is okay. Of course you'll need a screen test. How about dinner tomorrow night? I'd like to discuss some ideas I have for you."

"Gee, tomorrow night. I don't know if —"

"Just an informal thing, so we can get better acquaintanted. See if you've got the stuff. I'd spend the time now, but I've got a room full of gals out there." He glanced at his watch. "Just leave your number with the girl out front. She'll give you instructions."

"Instructions?"

"Where to meet me. What to wear."

"Sure, thanks." I returned to the waiting room and Carol Ann.

"What happened? What did he say?" she asked.

"I have to see the receptionist."

Carol Ann's face lit up. "Oh, honey, you got it!"

We waited for the sour–faced, dark–haired woman seated at

the front desk to hang up the phone. "Excuse me, Miss," I said. "Mr. Walters wants to set up a meeting for tomorrow night and —"

"Here's the address," she said, scribbling on a piece of paper.

"Thanks, but what should I wear?"

"I'd wear clothes myself. But you can put on a fig leaf, if that's you choice," she said, reaching for the phone.

"Witch," Carol Ann muttered as we left. "Never mind. You can have her fired when you're a big star," she said, gaily rushing down the stairs. "So what did Walters say? You were in there forever. I thought he might be giving you a screen test. Or chasing you around his desk."

"I think that's his plan for tomorrow night. Honestly, I wasn't even sure I should accept."

"Are you insane? Tomorrow night could set up your whole future. You might get a contract. And with your looks and brains, you'll be on Easy Street in no time. 'Happy Days Are Here Again'," she sang gaily.

"By the way, how did your interview go?"

"They took one look and I was out the revolving door."

"Sorry. By the way, did you notice that blond guy who passed me on his way out?"

"Franky Wyatt?"

"You know him?"

"Not personally, no. But my momma and I saw every picture he ever made back home."

"So he was a star?"

"Sure, back before talkies. Poor guy hasn't done much lately. Probably doesn't sound so hot, so the studio dumped him. But he's still got plenty of *it.*"

"That's tough about his career."

"Don't get too soppy–eyed. He's still got a meal ticket named

Lupe Cardona," she said.

And there he was, waiting at the bottom of the stairs, as Carol and I descended. He was a few feet away, leaning against a Packard convertible, the sun shining on his thick blond hair.

Seeing us, he smiled and sauntered over. "Hi, Jeri. Remember me?"

I felt blood rush to my face as I shook his hand and tried to ignore how my insides flipped from just the contact of his fingers. "Sure, hello. How are you?"

His gaze swept over me. "Delighted to see you."

I introduced him to Carol Ann, then Franky pulled me aside. "I can't believe you're here in Los Angeles. When did you get here?"

"A few months ago —"

"Are you alone or—"

"Alone."

A slow smile lit up his face. "Have dinner with me."

For a moment I was too overwhelmed by his startling blue eyes and tanned face to speak. I reminded myself that Franky Wyatt was married to Lupe Cardona. And I was married to Lex. That dinner with Franky could be dangerous considering the way I'd responded to shaking his hand.

So why did I scribble the Bayridge's telephone number on a matchbook and hand it to him?

***

"Wear the green one, " Carol Ann said that evening after another deadly dinner of pot roast and boiled potatoes .

We were upstairs trying to choose the perfect outfit for my big dinner appointment with Walters. Holding a dress up, I studied the effect in the mirror above the bureau. "The whole thing seems fishy. Why didn't Walters just make an appointment with me during normal business hours?"

Carol Ann studied me and my dress. "Big shots do business over dinner all the time."

"They do business at the office, too."

"Dinner, lunch, what's the difference? Now, if I were you, I'd stick to the green silk. With your face and figure, you need something that flatters your figure but also tells him you're a serious actress."

"I dunno. It's kind of tight, don't you think?"

She sighed. "Let's decide tomorrow after we get our hair and nails done. Come on, let's go down and listen to the radio."

"You go. I'll be right down," I said.

She stood in the doorway. "You're gonna write Lex again, aren't you. Months without a word and you're still at it. He must be some kind of man."

I thought back to my first glimpse of Lex that night at the Plaza Hotel in New York, right after I'd arrived back in time. The way my heart had pounded. The instant attraction I'd felt. "Yes, he is special," I said. But writing Lex also wiped out my guilt for giving Franky Wyatt my telephone number. For being attracted to him.

Lying on my side on my bed, I was half–way through my letter, when I heard what sounded like my window opening and the soft landing of a foot on the floor. Turning over, I stared, unable to believe my eyes. Nicky Desanto had used the fire escape to climb through my window.

TEN

I screamed. In a blur, I flew off my bed and lunged for the door. Nicky was faster. He launched himself across the room and grabbed me from behind. Covering my mouth with one hand, he held me still with the other. His breathing was heavy, and I smelled him. That nauseating odor of hair pomade, body odor, and sour breath from a mouthful of decaying teeth.

"Shut up and listen or you'll be sorry. Where's Lex?"

"I don't know. He left me."

"Liar." His hand moved from my breast down to my belly and then between my legs.

I kicked backward, connecting hard. "Help!" I screamed.

"Bitch!" he snarled, striking me to the floor.

Panting, feeling pain across my shoulder and breast, I stared up at Nicky. At the thin mean mouth. And the scars across his right brow and chin.

Grabbing me by my hair, he knelt down and pulled my face to his. "Listen, you stupid quiff. First I'm gonna fuck you. Then I'm gonna fuck up that gorgeous mug of yours."

"Drop dead," I cried.

He slapped me hard across the face. I fell back against the

dresser. Bottles fell. A fiery pain shot through my cheek. My eyes watered. Gasping, I gazed up at him.

"Where is he? Tell me, or so help me —"

Before I could answer, he rushed at me again, pulling me to my feet and ripping the front of my dress down to my bra. Then he shoved me flat across my bed and dropped on top of me.

"Stop, don't." The words slipped out, as one hand slipped beneath my bra and the other reached under my dress between my legs.

"Bet Lex pops right up after he hears I fucked you, then cut you up."

I heard footsteps. It sounded like a stampeding herd thundering up the stairs. A key turned in the lock. Then the door flew open. Mrs. Whitcombe and a dozen faces peered in.

In a flash, Mrs. Whitcombe aimed a shot gun at us. "Let her go. *Now.* Or so help me your brains are gonna cover that wall. And don't think I won't do it."

Nicky gaped, his mouth open. Breathing hard, glaring at Mrs. Whitcombe, he slowly moved off of me. He straightened his tie then retrieved his hat off the floor, never taking his eyes off the huge gun. He headed right at the crowded doorway, roughly shoving his way through the girls. A cacophony of complaints and curses followed him down the hall to the stairs.

"You better hurry, sonny," Mrs. Whitcombe yelled after him."The police are on their way."

I began to shake. To sob. My cheek hurt. And I felt ashamed and afraid.

Carol Ann gently reached for me, helping me sit up. "It's okay, honey. You're safe. He's gone."

Sinking into her arms, I let loose and sobbed. It seemed as if weeks of misery broke through.

"All right, girls. Everyone downstairs," Mrs. Whitcombe told the crowd peering into the room.

A minute later, Mrs. Whitcombe returned with a glass of water, smelling salts, and several pills. She quickly shut the door behind her. "Jeri, drink this."

Sniffling, I took the water and drank, accepting the aspirin tablets.

"Now what's this about, Jeri? Is it money or —"

"I can't say. Look, I better be going. Please, just tell the police it was all a mistake."

She took my hand and gently patted it. "Can't you tell me?'

I shook my head.

"I hate to see you rush off like this. A beautiful girl like you with manners and intelligence is rare. I could hide you. Help you —"

"You were wonderful just now. But I couldn't put you or the girls in that kind of danger. These are tough guys. Mobsters."

Understanding filled her bright blue eyes. "When it's safe, you slip out through the kitchen. Carol Ann can show you the way." Mrs. Whitcombe gave me a quick hug then hurried downstairs.

Carol Ann sat on the bed and watched me pack. "But where will you go?"

"It doesn't matter. Listen. I need to leave stuff behind. Just shove everything under the bed. I'll be back in a day or two for the rest. And don't tell the other girls anything."

"Tell 'em what? I don't know anything myself. Except that you're paid up for two more weeks. And you got a date with one of the biggest producers in Hollywood tomorrow night."

"Tell Mrs. Whitcombe to put my rent toward what you owe. Just keep things quiet. Okay? I'm counting on you, Carol Ann."

"But you're throwing away your whole future."

I paused from packing. "You're a good friend. But it's too

complicated to explain now. One day I'll come back and we'll have a good laugh over this. In the meantime, you go out with Walters tomorrow night. See if you can make something out of it."

"He ain't gonna want me when he's expectin' you."

"Don't be a fool. Grab your chance. As soon as I find a place to stay, I'll call you." I opened the door and listened. The usual sounds greeted me: girls chattering, laughter, and radio music. "Carol Ann, see if the coast is clear."

With a brief wave, she stepped into the hall and shut the door behind her. After a thorough search of the room to make sure I'd packed the essentials, I sat down on my bed and waited. This room with its faded wallpaper of pink roses and heavy furniture had been my home for almost four months. Not a long time, but enough to get comfortable. I recalled how I'd first found out about The Bayridge in the rotogravure section of the *New York Times*. Some movie star had stayed here at the start of her career. A hotel for actresses in Hollywood had seemed like the perfect place to head for, a safe haven where I could start life over. Now I was off again. Me and millions of others struck down by bank failures, house foreclosures, or a need to escape.

Carol Ann returned a few minutes later, out of breath but excited. "They're outside now. One in the back and one out front. One's leaning against a big black sedan, havin' a smoke. I'll show you the way out as soon as the music starts."

"Music?"

"Yeah, the girls are gonna sing. It's Mrs. Whitcombe's idea for a distraction. Then you and I are gonna head out the secret way."

Time seemed to rush by. My cheek, shoulder and breast throbbed. My breathing was fast and dry as we hurried down the back stairs to the kitchen, then down more stairs to a dark cellar. From there we slipped through a side window and dropped down onto an alleyway. Dragging my suitcase, we hurried across a narrow dirt road past garages, abandoned shacks, and garbage bins. We headed toward Sunset Boulevard. Beside the crunch of our feet, I strained to hear the sound of that black sedan. But apparently, we'd fooled the Desanto brothers. We'd gotten out without being noticed.

Minutes later, we reached the bus stop. An old man and two women waited, too.

Carol Ann stared down the street, not looking at me. "It oughta be by soon. You got a nickel for the fare?"

"Sure."

"Keep that mug of yours down. And don't get off till the end of the line," she advised

"Thanks for everything. I hope you get someone nice to take my place," I said.

"She'll probably be seventeen, my size, with a yen for borrowing my best stockings."

"And good luck with Walters. And save my mail, in case any comes."

She faced me, her eyes red with tears. "Know what I think? I think you're gonna miss the Bayridge."

"Especially you," I said.

Then we saw the bus chugging toward us. We quickly hugged.

"I hope you end up real happy," she said as I climbed on board.

Carol Ann watched my bus pull out before hurrying back down the alley. I crunched down in my seat as the vehicle picked up speed. Tears streamed down my cheeks. I'd never felt so alone or afraid. Where would I sleep tonight? What if it rained? What if the Desantos found me? Maybe it had taken them months to discover I'd moved to Hollywood. But now that they knew …

At least Lex was still safe, or the brothers wouldn't be

stalking me.

After what seemed like hours, we reached Santa Monica. Sea air and a dense fog reminded me how close I was to the beach. Lugging my suitcase, I crossed the street, and entered a small café. A bell rang announcing me. The wall clock above the counter said it was just past eight.

"Coffee," the plump blonde waitress asked as she led me to a front table by the window.

"If it's okay, I'd prefer to sit in back," I said, glad the place was empty.

The waitress led me to the last table by the kitchen and dropped a menu by me. "Blue plate special ain't bad. Pork chops, applesauce, and green beans for sixty cents. Coffee's extra."

"Fine." Not that I'd be able to eat, but at least I'd have a reason to sit here and read the newspaper someone had left behind. I quickly found the classifieds and the column for rooms for rent.

The waitress returned with my food. Tears filled my eyes, as I stared at the plate.

"Not much of an appetite, huh," she said, taking a seat nearby and lighting up a cigarette. "Want one?" She held out the pack.

"No thanks."

She glanced at my cheek, at my fresh bruise. "When I'm like you, I can't eat nothin'. Brought you aspirin. Take 'em. They'll make you feel better." She placed two pills by my water glass. Then, she pulled up a chair from the next table and put up her feet with a loud groan. "Gosh, it's good to get off my dogs for a minute. Live around here?"

"No, I … I'm looking for a place to stay. For a week or two. Maybe even a month."

She studied me. "You're in luck. The owner here's got a room out back he rents. I live around there, too. It ain't bad. Cheap, no bugs. He's out back. Want me to ask him for you?"

"Would you?"

"My pleasure. And drink your coffee. It'll help your head. By the way, I'm Sally."

We shook hands. "Katie," I lied. "One more thing. I don't want anyone knowing I'm here."

She gave me a slow once–over. "You ain't in trouble with the law, are you?"

"No, it's my husband. He used to… to beat me until … I couldn't take it anymore."

Her eyes narrowed. "I had me an old man who used to punch me around like he was practicing to be heavyweight champion of the world. So one day when he was out gettin' cross–eyed, I emptied out our cookie jar, took a bus to Reno, and divorced him. You'll be okay here. The landlord ain't big on questions. Just pay him rent, and he'll mind his own business."

My new accommodations were behind the diner off a courtyard. Sally showed me the tiny kitchen, bedroom, and bathroom. "That's my place across from you on the right," she said. "Honey Thresher's flat's on the left. Her old man took a powder around Christmas. The bum left her and the kids without a nickel. But she's swell. Lends me her vacuum whenever I need it. Well, hope you like it here. I better get back to work. Be seein' ya."

***

Right after dinner, after Nancy slipped him the new *Colliers* Magazine, Lex fell asleep. He woke in the dark and heard coughing from down the hall. Here at Mrs. Jankel's, patients were encouraged to control their coughing. He managed to grab his wristwatch and the flashlight, a strenuous move for a TB patient. It was after two. Soon he heard something banging. A metallic sound. The banging seemed insistent. The coughing grew deeper. He thought he heard a woman cry out. But he couldn't be sure. His own heart seemed to be beating at a frantic pace. *Help her*, his mind screamed. He realized it was a metal cup banging. The same type of metal cup that sat beside his bed, the one for sputum.

"Bang it on the bedstead and help will come," he'd been told again and again.

Now, rubber-soled feet raced by his door. He listened, hearing whispers. Slowly, he managed to climb from bed, breaking the most basic rule. No patient was allowed out of bed without a doctor's permission. But whenever he asked when he could expect to do that, or when he could use the bathroom instead of a bedpan, the doctor would smile patiently and say, "You're a very sick man, Mr. Rose. A very sick man indeed. You would do well to consider our advice and count our rules as your route to getting well. The more you battle and question our procedures, the less chance you have of winning this war."

His feet hit the small rug another patient had left behind. His room was freezing, thanks to the open window, the biggest element of the prescribed treatment: Fresh air and more fresh air, on top of more fresh air. Cold fresh air was deemed best. It quieted the lungs and kept the disease at bay – they said. Cold air, rest, and food. No talking, no laughing, no reading, no writing, no walking. Also no real bathing except on Sundays, when Berta, a nurse that resembled a lady-wrestler, rushed him through a tub bath.

Now, praying the floor didn't creak, he inched his way to the door until he could see down the hall. He felt a cough bubbling up. *Don't cough*, he thought. For once, *don't cough*. He peered out. Two nurses rushed right by him.

Out his window, he saw a car pull up. The engine suddenly cut. Doors slammed, then feet pounded up the front porch steps. Seconds later, Doctor Metzger charged past his room, white lab coat flowing. Lex heard anxious voices, hushed voices, and feet squeaking across the linoleum. Then a nurse said, "Mrs. Weiss."

Couldn't be, Lex thought. He'd just seen Mrs. Weiss at breakfast. She'd been made up to perfection, dressed to the nines with a dazzling array of jewelry, and a smile for everyone. And she was only thirty–three. She'd just told him that the other day when they were out on the porch alone with no nurses around.

Tired, he crawled back in bed and fell asleep hoping it wasn't Mrs. Weiss.

Noises woke him again. It took him several moments to realize where he was. It was just beginning to get light out. He heard voices downstairs, outside. He tiptoed to his window with its view of the street. A hearse waited. His alarm clock said it was just after six. Several men in coats and hats emerged from the house carrying a stretcher with a body covered in a sheet. Nurse Bronson followed the body. He recognized her brown cardigan over her white uniform. In the cold, she hugged herself for warmth. In the half–light of dawn, she also appeared to be crying.

Lex quietly climbed back in bed, grateful to be under the covers. He wondered if he would ever get out of here or see Jeri again. Or dance at the Stork Club or El Morocco.

Reaching over, he took the letter off his night table and read what he'd dictated to Nancy earlier.

Dear Jeri:

> *There's no dancing here, no silk dresses, or starlit nights. Only bed–rest and heavy food which sits on my stomach and threatens to turn my insides into concrete. Everyone insists that I must obey the rules in order to win the fight. They call me rebellious, because I listen to the radio or play solitaire. But I'm not rebellious. Just bored.*

Through my window, I hear cars race by. No doubt the occupants fear contamination by us, the ghosts who inhabit this mausoleum. Silence and the heavy–legged cow who bathes me, empties my bedpan, and brings me my meals have become my life. Mrs. Jankel, Doctor Metzger, and Nurse Berta Bronson have forbidden me to move off my bed until the doctor says it's okay. So twice a day, they carry me outside to a stiff chair for my daily quota of fresh air. First they wrap me in a blanket I'm sure the milkman used on his horse. Then I rest some more, while the staff quietly wipes away evidence of my ever existing in that tomb known as room six. Even reading is frowned on during these early months. Too upsetting, too stimulating, they say.

I miss Cole Porter and George Gershwin. I miss Joan Crawford and Marlene Dietrich. I miss you.

Love Lex.

ELEVEN

Loud voices woke me. In the dim light, I studied my surroundings. I was alone. Then I remembered I'd moved into the flat behind the café in Santa Monica. I slipped on shoes and crossed the cracked linoleum floor into my kitchen to listen. Out my window in the courtyard, exposed by a single light bulb, Sally the waitress and a bald man embraced. His suit jacket was slung over his arm, his suspenders hung down around his hips, and his hat waited in a planter filled with dead geraniums.

"What's your hurry?" Sally purred, gripping the guy's narrow back with one hand and using her other hand to keep a ratty blue robe closed in front.

"It's late," he said. "I gotta be up early."

"You had a good time, didn't ya?"

"Sure but —"

"Well, I got rent to pay."

"Look, it's late and my wife —"

"Let her wait," Sally said, opening her robe, showing him her rounded thigh and full breast.

The man's eyes widened. He instantly reached for her. One hand moved up her white thigh and disappeared under her robe. The other cupped her heavy breast while his mouth roamed hungrily over her throat. "You could drive a man crazy," he moaned.

"Lemme show ya *how* crazy."

"I can't stay, I swear. Here, take it all," he gasped, abruptly yanking free. Thrusting his hand in his pocket, he pulled out a wad of bills and stuffed them in Sally's hand.

Sally glanced at the money and let go of his lapel."When ya comin' by again, lover?"

"Tomorrow or the day after." In a flash, he straightened his tie, pulled up his suspenders, and wriggled into his jacket. After setting his fedora low on his forehead, he crossed under the archway and disappeared. Sally counted her money before heading inside.

The next afternoon, a rare rain pounded the café windows when Carol Ann dropped by to return my stuff. She looked like a refugee from a spy movie with her old blue hat pulled down around her nose and enough furtive glances to give me the jitters.

"This is everything," she said, handing me an old laundry bag filled to the brim. "These came for you, too." Reaching inside her purse, she pulled out two envelopes. "Can ya beat it? Lex finally wrote."

"Thanks, Carol Ann. It's good to see you," I said, glancing at the envelopes. Neither letter was from Lex. Keely had sent the first one. And the second envelope had a Van Nuys postmark and the name Cooper on the return address. Seeing the name Cooper, relief surged through me. "I can't believe it. My mother's family finally wrote."

"Glad to hear it."

"No, I mean, I had trouble finding them. And now …" How could I explain that the letter had come from my ancestors. Family members long dead but alive now.

"That's swell because … I got some bad news, too."

My heart lurched. "What?"

"Someone at the Bayridge blabbed about you to those tough guys. They must've showed up again, flashed your picture around, and offered a reward. Some greedy big mouth told 'em about us sneakin' out the back way and givin' them the slip. She even showed them where the bus stop is. Mrs. Whitcombe threatened to toss her out on her keester. But by then, those thugs already had what they wanted."

My chest felt tight. No doubt the brothers would show the bus driver my picture and the driver would tell them where I got off. Then they'd track me here.

"There is one good thing," Carole Ann said. "Franky Wyatt called you. *Twice.* Spoke to him myself. He was so nice, I gave him the telephone number here. Hope it's okay. He's in a real lather to see you. He even sent flowers. The biggest bouquet you ever saw. I would've brought them today, only I couldn't carry everything on the trolley. So Mrs. Whitcombe put them in the parlor and they look swell."

"Never mind Franky. Look, I won't be here after tomorrow. So forget this telephone number. I'll call you when I land someplace else. Now tell me all about Walters, and then I need to go."

She sighed. "It was just like I expected. He gave me the old runaround. Fed me dinner than insisted on showing me his little house in the hills."

It took me a moment to grasp her meaning. "Oh, Carol Ann, I'm sorry. I hoped he had more on his mind."

"He probably did with you. I can't gripe too much. I ate a fine steak before I found out the house was just a little bungalow where he entertains starlets."

I stared at Carol Ann, mystified. "You went?"

"Might as well see what else he was handing out besides a fancy line and a good meal."

"But Carol Ann, you're an actress not a, a —"

"Who says I'm an actress? Beside it wasn't so awful. I went to a fancy restaurant, had a fine meal, and got fifty bucks cash, too. Plus a week's work as an extra which means another forty simoleans in my pocket. That ain't hay."

I felt ill. Everybody in Hollywood was for sale.

Seeing my expression, she spoke stiffly. "Look, honey, it's the way this town works. How else would anyone survive? Maybe *you* would've gotten a screen test. But I bet Walters would've asked you to see his house first, too. Sorry if that shocks you," she said, acid in her tone.

"Carol Ann, I didn't mean —"

She rose, leaving her donut and coffee untouched. "I better get back. It's a long ride."

"Carol Ann, I'm sorry. I didn't mean anything by what I said."

"Don't sweat it. I ain't made of silk."

"Carol Ann, wait."

She already had her coat on and was half–way out the door.

I ran after her and reached for her hand. "Thanks for stopping by with my things. You've been a good friend. Best of luck."

Her expression softened. "You, too. Be seein' ya."

Depression overwhelmed me. I'd lost Carol Ann, my only real friend in town. All because I refused to see that everyone here had a price. At last I recalled the letters in my purse. I tore open the smaller envelope and pulled out a sheet of cheap notepaper.

... and we was real happy to read your notice. Please drop by after church on Sunday for dinner. I have written down the directions since our farm is off the beaten track. The Van Nuys locals know it as the old Thornton place.

Best wishes, Violet Cooper.

I stared, wishing the name made me happier. Because my mom had spoken of Violet often. In fact, she never stopped talking about her family right up until her death.

According to my mother, the Coopers had migrated from Ohio to Kansas after the Great War. When the land dried out and the top soil blew away in the 1930s, they'd crossed the country searching for a new home and ended up in the San Fernando Valley. My actual birth wasn't until 1972, but I'd manufactured a believable place for myself in the current Cooper family tree, just in case they contacted me.

Now, the Coopers might be my salvation.

The next morning the fog burned off before noon leaving a brilliant blue sky and a hot sun tempered by a cool breeze. A few blocks down from the café, I picked up a fine–milled soap for my aunt and a tinned–ham for the family. Excited about meeting everyone, I meant to hurry home, pack, and set out to find them. But as I crossed the street to head home, I spied Tito Desanto leaning against a post outside the drugstore, the very place where I'd picked up the soap. I was lucky, because his head was buried in the newspaper and Nicky was nowhere in sight, though their sedan was parked at the curb.

Keeping my head down and my pace unhurried, I crossed the street and headed through a quiet neighborhood past tiny houses and tiny lawns. When the street curved, I glanced back. So far, no one was following me. Panicked, I tossed my packages behind someone's car and ran. In minutes, I reached my building. Panting and out of breath, I entered the courtyard from the back alley hoping to avoid my neighbors. Unfortunately, I almost stumbled into Mr. Widner the milkman.

He was busy pounding on Honey Thresher's door. "… so ya

better open up, Mrs. Thresher. Cause I know you're in there. Got me a bill here for six dollars and thirty–eight cents. So if ya don't want me callin' the sheriff, ya better get wise."

Slipping quietly past him, I entered my flat, grabbed my suitcase and threw in the rest of my things. Then I peered out my kitchen window, desperate to leave without anyone seeing me. But just then, Honey Thresher stepped into the courtyard to face Mr. Widner.

At thirty–five, her breasts had settled around her waist. Her hair was thin and faded, and her skin looked like a raw chicken's. Except today she'd put up her hair, applied lipstick, and donned a faded pink silk peignoir which lifted her bosom and gave her a waistline, even if the garment had seen too many washes. "Why don't you come on in so we can talk Mr. Widner?"

"Ain't got the time, Mrs. Thresher. Can't leave no cream or milk neither. Got me a bill here for six dollars and thirty–eight cents, and I gotta turn the money into my boss or it's my job. I been lettin' you off for far too long and I can't —"

"Please – just come in for a minute. Surely you can spare a minute."

"No, I can't —"

"Just so I can explain about the bill. Please – the neighbors – I don't want them knowing my business. You can understand that."

Oh, go inside already, I thought, desperate to escape, sure Nicky and Tito were closing in.

"I got me a wife and family to feed," Mr. Widner said. "And if the boss or my wife found out —"

"It's nothing like that. Just a word – please. Don't make me beg. I have a sick baby. He hasn't been fed since …" she choked back a sob. "… since I don't know when. He isn't even a year old yet. So please, I just have to have milk. I've been sick myself and can't feed him enough. Please, Mr. Widner, you have children."

"But I already told ya —"

"I just want to talk to you, Mr. Widner. We can be friends, can't we?" Mrs. Thresher stepped closer, glanced both ways, before she clamped her hand on his arm and yanked him across her threshold.

Just before Honey Thresher's door shut, Mr Widner said, "Wait a second. There's kids here. I can't do nothin…" His voice broke off mid–sentence.

At last, the courtyard was empty. Grabbing my suitcase, purse, and coat, I tore out the back way. In the old days when I had money, I would've paid Honey Thresher's milk bill or tried to shame Mr. Widner into leaving quietly. But I couldn't afford to pay anyone's milk bill now. Or draw attention to myself, an unemployed woman on the run.

On my way to the trolley, I paused by a dark green mailbox to deposit my latest letter to Lex. In it, I said I was fed up with being ignored; that he could at least dictate a letter to a nurse if he wasn't permitted to write himself. I warned him that this would be my last letter until he wrote back. I left out my news about the Desanto brothers, my unemployment, and my dwindling cash reserves. But in the end, I didn't have the heart to mail the letter. Instead I stuffed it in my pocket for later.

It took me almost two hours to reach Van Nuys. One trolley took me part way then I connected to a bus. On the bus, I finally opened the large manilla envelope. Out fell a stack of mail. Unpaid bills, Christmas cards from friends. Even one from the Maitlands.

Best of all there was a letter from Keely.

TWELVE

January 5, 1933
Dear Madam:

I think about you and Mr. Rose every day. Since you left, I been troubled by a bad hip and haven't worked much, so I'm back here in the Bronx with my brothers.

It grieves me to pass on more bad news but here it is. I was up at your old house on Riverside Drive to pick up any mail that slipped by the mailman, like I been doing regularly since you left. The butler who works there has been real nice about saving the mail for me. And as you can see, lots of mail slips by. So there I was on a rainy Monday when who should be watching me from his car, but that Desanto boy with the big head, the stupid looking one. Well, I was just about to ring the doorbell, when he grabbed me from behind. He lifted me right off my feet and jammed me in his car. I might have gotten away, but it was raining cats and dogs and he was fast. He clamped his big mitt over my mouth and tossed me down like a bag of dirty laundry. There I was on the floor of this big dark car, helpless. I don't mind admitting how scared I was. Especially since he had another tough–looking friend with him, the driver.

He warned me that I better listen and not try anything because he needed information and I was gonna give it up one way or the other. They drove me all the way to New Jersey and pretty soon I could see we were driving past farms. And I was sure I was done for. I mean, no one would know what happened to me if they decided to bury me out there. But still, I had hope. Turned out they wanted information about Mr. Rose and you. I knew he meant business so I tried to cooperate. Maybe that was cowardly of me, and I apologize for that, but under the circumstances, I saw no other way. Truth be told, I had no idea where you sent Mr. Rose. Neither Mr. Rose, Harris, or you ever did let on where you finally took him. So I told him the truth, that I didn't know where Mr. Rose went. But I did tell him how you had called Arizona and Colorado. But I never told them that Mr. Rose had consumption. Cause I figured they might start calling around and find him that way. So I told them that Mr. Rose had a girl on the side and you found out, packed your bags and left.

Well, the big lug seemed to buy that. He even chuckled like he got the punch line of some big joke. And even though he still threatened to slap me around, I flat out told him he might as well kill me, because I couldn't give him anything more about Mr. Rose. But I'm afraid I wasn't so smart about you. See, I figured you were so far away that they would never

follow. I told them you went to California. Either San
Francisco or Los Angeles. How you lived there once
and wanted to go back. I got a good hard smack
across the cheek over that one. And I finally broke
down and told them I didn't know one city from the
next out in California and that you went out there
hoping to break into the moving pictures.

That's when he let me go. Right there in the
middle of this broken down farm in New Jersey. He
shoved me out the door and drove off. Well, I was so
glad he didn't shoot me, I turned in the opposite
direction and started running. I finally found a filling
station where they had a phone. A few hours later my
brother Sean came and got me.

I know I betrayed you, and I am sorry for it.
You and Mr. Rose were always good to me. But I just
couldn't be as brave as I wanted to be. So forgive me,
Mrs. Rose.

With greatest respect,
Keely

I read the letter twice, digesting what it meant. Too bad it had
taken weeks to reach me or I would've been on my guard. I was also
sorry Keely had endured so much on my behalf.

From the town of Van Nuys, I had to hitchhike to the
Coopers' place. A local farmer picked me up in his truck then
dropped me off twenty minutes later by a large barrow with squash,
lettuce, and eggs at two cents a piece. A crude sign had been nailed
to a tree with the name Cooper burned into the wood. Hanging onto
my suitcase and purse, I slowly hiked the last quarter mile up a hill.
The Cooper's house turned out to be a small unpainted farmhouse
with a crooked stove–pipe poking out of a sagging roof. Chickens

pecked at the dusty front yard. The barn appeared to be little more than boards nailed together with tar paper over it. In the distance a farmer in a crushed suede hat and overalls led a cow into the barn. And the place smelled as if a septic tank had backed up. Or the outhouse had overflowed.

I ached to turn around and escape unnoticed down the hill.

But just then, the front door flew open and a slim honey–blonde in a starched white dress stormed out. "I told you before, I'm goin' into town for a permanent wave. Then I'm goin' home, and I won't be back for supper," the blonde shouted over her shoulder.

The door opened again. A skinny old woman in a faded dress and apron appeared. "Home, huh? That's what you call home, Lorena? All them fancy women and men …"

A heart beat later, the two women noticed me. They froze, their faces wary.

The old woman's mouth became a hard line."Lookin' fer somethin? Cause we ain't got no food to spare."

"I'm Jeri Rose, your cousin from Ohio. Cousin Emmy's daughter," I said, placing my suitcase beside me then pulling out the Cooper's letter from my purse.

The old woman glanced at the letter then me. At last a smile broke through her scowl. "Bless me, you're Bernadette's kin from Ohio." Tears filled her faded eyes. Without warning, she hugged me. "I'm your cousin Violet. And this here's your cousin Lorena. And you're Bernadette's niece. My, oh, my. Pretty as a movie star, ain't she Lorena? My my, it's good to see you. But we didn't expect you till Sunday. No matter. You're kin and that's all that counts. We got our own Emmy here. Course she's just a wee thing. Only four this spring."

Emmy? Four–year–old Emmy had been my mother's mother.

My grandmother.

Violet led me toward the small faded structure. Before stepping inside, I glanced back at the pretty blonde called Lorena. Standing beside an old model T truck, she watched us.

"Ohio, huh," Lorena called out. "You sure don't look like anyone from Ohio."

"That's because I lived in New York before I moved here," I said, hoping I could keep track of all my lies. But as far as I knew, everyone but my grandmother Emma was gone by the time I was born.

"Hey, Ma. Maybe I will come back for supper," Lorena said, before climbing into the truck.

"Suit yourself, Lorena. You always do," Violet answered.

The blonde laughed then called out the window. "Hey, Jeri Rose. I'm the bad girl in the family." Then she gunned the truck's engine, which coughed a few times, before the ancient vehicle rumbled down the hill, leaving a cloud of dust in its wake.

Inside the dimly lit farmhouse, I followed Violet down a narrow hall to the tiny front parlor. It was a room right out of the Victorian age with overstuffed furnishings, hideous figurines, and painted oil lamps.

"You rest a spell before dinner. I'll be back with a glass of lemonade in a jiffy," Violet said, hurrying off.

Grateful as I was for family hospitality, I couldn't help feeling like I'd wandered into an episode of *The Beverly Hillbillies.*

Dinner was at 1:30 in a small airless room dominated by a long trestle table and brutally hard chairs. Before we ate, my great, great–grandfather Clement Cooper bent his head and said a prayer, his voice reverberating off the walls. Clement Cooper had no front teeth, skin drier than dust, and lips that never broke into anything remotely like a smile. He was probably fifty but looked eighty. As the family bowed their heads and prayed, I peeked at the weathered, pious faces around me. And found Lorena grinning back. I decided Lorena had been adopted. With her shiny permed hair, red nails, and glamorous face, she was entirely different from the rest of the Coopers.

"Back in Ohio, there was twelve of us," Violet explained as she nibbled at the greasy stew made with carrots, peas, potatoes, and bits of thin tough meat. "I was only nine months younger than Bernadette. We was like two peas in a pod before she run off and married a boy from Cincinnati at seventeen. Then I married Clement a few weeks later and we moved to his family's farm outside of Liberal, Kansas, on the Oklahoma border. I never did see Bernadette again. Used to write her twice a year on her birthday and at Christmas. For twenty years I waited for her letters. But when things got real bad, we lost touch. Hard to forgive myself for not writing her. But the land, the crops, and them dust storms… plus them greedy bankers demanding money … we had our hands full. So when the bank took our place, we had to get out fast. Took what we could carry and started for here. I took it hard when I heard about her —"

"Influenza," I volunteered, recalling the date of Bernadette's death from my mother's old Bible. Notations I'd read over and over as a kid. My mother had wanted my brother Paul and me to know about the Coopers and our family's humble past. She'd purposely kept photographs, letters, and an old family Bible on a low shelf in the family room so we could easily look at them and feel connected.

Violet nodded. "Bernadette passed right after we got here. Of course I have a picture of her, memories …" Tears filled Violet's eyes. "Made an apple pie for dessert," she announced, drying her tears on her ratty apron, rising to her feet, and hurrying into the kitchen.

As soon as Violet closed the kitchen door, Lorena struck a match against the table and lit a cigarette. "Tell us about yourself,

Cousin Jeri."

Clement scowled at Lorena. "Ain't none of our business. And I already told you about smokin' in my house. Ain't lady–like."

"I don't mind telling," I said. "My husband Lex is in a private sanitarium back in upstate New York for consumption. When I couldn't find work in New York, I came here hoping I'd be able to make enough to pay his medical bills."

Clement Cooper nodded. "You did right, young lady. We're family. You stay here with us till you get back on your feet. You can bunk with your cousin Lorena." He glared at Lorena. "Providin' she's stayin' here."

"Your room's over the kitchen," Violet explained when she returned to dole out a small slice of pie for everyone at the table. "We stay down the hall. And Rufus stays in the barn out back. He has a bed all fixed up in the hayloft."

I studied Rufus knowing he would be killed in France during World War II. Now, he was a big–eared eleven–year–old. And he was currently using his spoon to lob a pea at Lorena without his father noticing.

When the last piece of pie had been eaten, the coffee pot emptied, and the meager table scraps scraped into a bucket for the farm animals, Violet stood. And I realized the ordeal of dinner was over. Lorena motioned for me to follow, and she led me up a steep back staircase to a tiny room with a narrow bed, a night stand, and a bureau.

"Wanna go someplace?" she asked, standing before the tall bureau mirror, running a comb through her hair, dabbing on lipstick, and plopping a hat on her head.

"Now?"

"Sure. It's not even six. You'll have a lot more fun with me than with those ghosts."

I laughed. Lorena's observations were scathingly accurate.

"I ain't sayin' they aren't decent people," she said, running her fingers over her stockings. "But they might as well be stuffed and mounted over the fireplace. For them, life is work, work, work, and pray, pray, pray. And where's it gotten 'em? This drafty old dump. Now, what've you got to wear besides that thing you've got on?"

"I have a few dresses in my suitcase. But where're we going?"

"Anywhere but here. So put on somethin' that shows your shape."

We'd just opened my suitcase, when Violet appeared at Lorena's door. "Lorena, not on her first night here. Please."

"It's about time you got used to me, Ma."

"Jeri, you don't have to go with her. You can stay right here and rest. We got a new *Saturday Evening Post*. And a radio," Violet said persuasively.

Lorena stopped digging through my things and held up a blue silk evening dress. "Perfect," she announced. "Now, Ma, she wants to come out with me. So go back to your bread–making or knitting and don't fret."

A few minutes later, as the sun cast its warm rays over the desert, Lorena and I climbed into Lorena's old truck. We were backing down the drive, when Violet Cooper appeared by the front door. Her arms were crossed over her chest and she was scowling as we drove off.

Lorena shifted gears, the truck gained momentum, and we were soon rumbling down the bumpy dirt road. "Boy, it's like holdin' your breath bein' with them."

"They seem … angry with you," I said tactfully.

Lorena drove another few yards then abruptly jerked the wheel making the truck ride up the side of the road, where she let the engine stall. Frowning, she said, "You mean they didn't tell you about me?"

"Tell me what?"

Lorena stuck out her hand. "Cousin Jeri, meet the San Fernando Valley's most notorious madam."

"Madam?" It took me several seconds to make sense of her words. "No wonder," I finally said.

"Let me know if you feel faint. I got some pretty potent stuff in my flask to revive you."

"No thanks, I'll survive."

"Didn't mean to spring it on you like that. Usually, it's the first thing my folks apologize about. First, they tell everyone that they're good God–fearing Christians. Then they make excuses about the dust – a hold over from Kansas. Then they pray. And right after all the *Amens*, they confess that I'm a scarlet woman. A prostitute. Then they go on and on about being forgiving which is why they haven't turned their backs on me. When actually it's the money I give 'em."

Lorena didn't look as if she hung out on street corners plying her trade. She could blend in anywhere. In the city, here in the sticks, or back with the movie star wannabes at the Bayridge. Her honey blonde hair was styled in an attractive pageboy. Her make–up was tasteful yet enhancing. And her white dress, which accented her lean shape, would look appropriate on any conservative matron.

"To be honest I'm fascinated," I said.

"Good. You got a place to live yet?" She asked, maneuvering her truck back onto the dirt road.

"Just that room back at your folk's place. Unless it's inconvenient. I still have a little money left."

"I got a better deal for you. And you won't have to look at their sour pusses every morning over biscuits that taste like they were baked before the Civil War."

I laughed, feeling sixteen again. As if my best friend and I were heading to the mall to shop and have a burger. In reality, we were in the middle of a great desert. A terrain as unsettled as the African bush. A land where snakes, bobcats, coyotes, and mountain lions hunted. Where homesteads stretched beyond the horizon, farmers tended sheep, and orange groves perfumed the night. We sped past abandoned shacks, ranches, farms, studio ghost towns, orange groves, and humble dusty villages where ragged country stores pushed Sal Hepitica and Pillsbury flour. It was hard to tell North Hollywood from Van Nuys or Encino.

Twenty minutes later, we pulled into the driveway of a huge old house. Excitement surged through me as I stared up at the faded white building. So *this* was the notorious Rainbow Brothel.

"I'll make you a deal," Lorena said, as we headed inside. "I got an open room up on the third floor nobody uses. It's yours for twelve bucks a month. Food's another five."

"How come nobody else wants it?"

"A man was murdered in that room."

I froze in my tracks. "Really?"

Lorena started to cackle. "No, it's on the third floor. Too many stairs."

"So no one … works up there."

"A couple of girls with regular customers are up there. And there's Cousin Jimmy. He's in the room next to yours. He's a writer."

"But —"

"It beats my folks' place by a mile. And you'll get clean bedding and plenty of hot water for baths. Or you can rush back to the farm if you wanna hear more about moral decency, the perils of crop rotation, and why every girl with a brain oughta be a stenographer."

Lorena had practically read my mind. After one hour at the Coopers' farm, I'd started figuring out where else I could go. "Exactly how many stairs are there?"

Grinning, Lorena led me into the entry where she hung up her wrap. In those few seconds, I glimpsed two girls lounging in the parlor. One had her nose buried in a movie magazine. The other was knitting. Both wore ill–fitting, sheer dresses and dark red lipstick. Neither was even remotely pretty.

I was out of breath by the time I reached the third floor. At the top of the stairs down a short hall, a bored looking brunette yanked on the tie of a tall skinny boy wearing jeans and a huge cowboy hat. After dragging him into her room, she kicked her door shut.

Then we heard her say, "Well, well, Kentucky, darn if you ain't excited to see me."

Lorena barely glanced in the brunette's direction as she stepped into a room and switched on a light. "This is our upstairs john."

The walls were pink. The sheer window curtains above the old–fashioned tub with feet were white. And everything from the black and white tiles on the floor to the sink and commode sparkled.

For a second, The Rainbow House tour brought back my tour of Mrs. Jankel's Cure Cottage. I suddenly wondered what Lex was doing. Was he snoring his head off? Staring up at the ceiling? Or in bed with a nurse? According to my watch, it was 9:30 up in Saranac Lake. The perfect time for a secret rendevous.

Just then another door opened. A handsome young man in a faded leather jacket hanging onto a package tied in string stepped into the hallway.

Lorena grinned. "Jimmy, meet your cousin Jeri. She's taking the room next to yours."

Jimmy stuck out his hand. "A pleasure. Hope I don't disturb you too much. Sometimes I stay up late typing."

"He's a writer, a darn good one," Lorena said.

Jimmy's face brightened. "Says who?"

"Says me. He's also a whiz with a sewing machine," Lorena added.

"I better get going. Got a job tonight tending bar at the local speak. But first I need to mail this," Jimmy said, waving his package at us before dashing down the stairs.

After Jimmy left, Lorena unlocked another door and said, "This here's your room."

THIRTEEN

From his bed, Lex watched his mother Ida Stern pace his small room. An aging beauty of fifty–six, she fussed with her furs, gold bracelets, and leather gloves. At last she cleared her throat and sniffed the air as if his bed pan needed emptying. "My rent's due," she said, pursing her lips and sticking her chin out. "This is unbearable. I'm reduced to begging you for rent money. I don't suppose your dear devoted wife needs to beg for *her* rent money."

"Always nice to see you Mother," Lex said, finding her theatrics reliable and amusing.

Her nostrils flared. "I hate this place. I hate the nurses, the smells, and the cold. And it's so expensive. I happen to know exactly how much a place like this costs. I have friends who've been … sick." She whispered the word sick, as if God in heaven didn't already know about Lex and might be tempted to make Lex really sick if word got out.

"You still look prosperous," Lex said.

His mother bristled. "If you knew what it took to prepare myself for this, this ordeal. The journey up here on that awful train with all those sick people. My furs in tatters. My clothes mended until …" In a flash, her linen handkerchief appeared and she sobbed into it.

Lex studied her. Her fox coat looked new and expensive.

"Even my perfumes are old and stale," she wailed.

"I'll give you a quarter and you can buy more."

She made a sound of disgust. "Well, *I* never had this disease and neither did your father."

"What about my sisters? Or don't diphtheria and the flu count?"

"You would bring all that up. How can you be so spiteful?"

"Anybody interesting around?" he asked to change the subject.

Still sniffling, Ida dried her eyes, pulled out a jeweled compact and fixed her face, applying lipstick with a brush. Then she powdered her nose and fussed with her hair which had crept out from under her stylish new hat. "Just a small dress manufacturer. A nobody. A little man called Sidney Shineman. He makes such awful things I won't even accept a skirt from him. And he's always saying things like, 'How about a little kiss, sugar?' After he's dragged me to some awful little beanery."

"Not El Morocco?"

"I supposed we've been there once or twice. But the rest of the time he always says, 'Business is off this month, honey bun.' Can you imagine anyone calling *me* honey bun?"

"Not really."

She glanced at her watch. "I really must go. There's a late train I'd rather not miss."

Lex studied her. He was always taken back by her ultimate selfishness. He'd known dozens of women. But he'd never met anyone quite like her.

She studied her nails. "And please don't give me that sad–eyed look. I know I promised to stay in town overnight. But I just can't face some awful little room by myself. And it takes forever to get back to the city, and I'm not as young as I used to be." She pulled on her coat which fit over her suit as if they'd been designed to go together. "I don't suppose you can spare anything. I mean, for my rent."

"Sorry. Things are tight."

"You know, Miriam Rosenblatt says everyone in New York, from mobsters to politicians, believes you made off with a king's ransom."

"Do they? Well, ask Mrs. Rosenblatt where it's hidden because I sure could use it."

Ida pursed her lips with annoyance. "Well, then..." she leaned over and barely brushed her lips across his forehead. "I do love you, Lester. Trying as you can be."

He reached for the little drawer in his night stand and withdrew three letters for Jeri. "Send these for me, Mother. They're already stamped."

"I suppose this is necessary with those hoodlums on the loose."

"Just a precaution. The less information around, the better."

Later, seated alone on the train home, Ida debated with herself about mailing the letters. Even in the taxi on her way home from the station she thought of nothing else. How her selfish daughter–in–law Jeri had abandoned Lex when he was sick by moving clear across the country to be with her own family. Breaking Lester's heart.

By the time she entered her building near Gramarcy Park, it was past midnight and the weather had turned frigid. She rode the old elevator up, furious that she had to run the darn thing herself, now that the building only had a part–time operator. She let herself into her crowded two room flat. Her beautiful things from her old apartment were now crammed together like a crowd at Ebbets field.

She'd been there once with her second husband to watch a baseball game and hated every dull minute of it. She took off her hat, hung up her coat, then reached for her purse. She withdrew the letters meant for Jeri and noted that they were all addressed to some rural post office in Van Nuys, California. Taking out the letters, she ripped open the first and read.

> *Dear Jeri,*
>
> *I'm allowed to walk again and shave myself. Tomorrow they're letting me eat with the other patients. I see them drift past my door each day. Few of us look very chic. Up until yesterday, when I finally saw the barber, I was the spitting image of Charlie Chaplin.*
>
> *I've lost more weight. Six meals a day, with pounds of cream and butter, and I'm thinner. So you'd better have my tux taken in again. I may be the size of a greyhound when I get out of here.*
>
> *I've been thinking about Miami lately. And Havana. Even California. I think of you there in the sunshine. The way your hair shines and your teeth glisten when you laugh. I think of us swimming in the surf. I think of you naked after a bath. Then my nurse lumbers in and says it's time for my sponge bath. She looks like a Ukranian factory worker, like something out of a photo in the rotogravure section of THE TIMES about Stalin's new Russia. Tomorrow, I get to eat with the others. For some reason I'm very nervous.*
>
> *Love Lex*

Ida read the letter again as hatred for Jeri and pity for her own reduced circumstances bubbled up inside her. She thought of her former glory as one of New York's great beauties. Of the men who'd loved her, begged for her attention. Like Carl Laemmle the big movie producer from Universal Pictures in the 1920s who'd said she had the looks to be a Hollywood star.

With a sudden jerk, she ripped up the letter, feeling her heart pound as the pieces fluttered across her old Persian carpet. Then she knelt by the fireplace, depositing the paper scraps into the fire. She did the same with the second letter and the third until the whole pile was gone. The paper made good kindling. At least this dreary dump had a fireplace and she'd learned how to build a nice little fire, as long as the janitor, Willy, cleaned it up for her.

***

"… and movie star Gloria Swanson threw a delightful bridge luncheon the other day wearing an aubergine silk frock, the very latest in chic," a gaunt redhead with frizzy red ringlets called Myra read aloud to the other Rainbow girls. "Miss Swanson's guests dined on a variety of tea sandwiches and coconut cake." Myra put down her *Modern Screen* magazine and sighed. "My granny used to make coconut cake."

"Sounds swell, doesn't it," Thelma, a buxom blonde said in her high–pitched squeaky lisp. "One day I'm gonna have my own house and have tea parties and luncheons all the time. Or maybe we can have one right here. Elvira could fix the sandwiches and —"

"For crying out loud," Big Harriet barked. "Who needs a lousy tea party when we're stuck here with each other seven days a week? Read us somethin' about John Gilbert, Myra. Must be somethin' in there about him."

Thelma's eyes filled with tears. "I just thought a tea party would be nice."

"Nice?" Big Harriet snorted, her pockmarked face a mask of disgust.

The Rainbow girls were arrayed across the sofa, love–seat, piano bench, and chairs. They fanned themselves, drank lemonade, smoked, read, and chatted. A new recording of "Isn't It Romantic," played over and over on the Victrola.

It was just past five and too early for the brothel to start hopping. I sat with the girls in the parlor and listened to their usual bickering as they waited for their johns. The girls fascinated me. Even though it was hard to ignore their cigarette smoke, drugstore perfumes, and unwashed bodies. But it was only for a few more minutes because Lorena and I were going out for the evening. As soon as she finished her preparations for a busy Friday night.

"That's a swell new dress," a lumpy blonde named Diedre said to Big Harriet. "Where'd you get the flower?"

"Picked it from the garden this afternoon. Had to kill a bee to get the darn thing. Squashed him like a grape," Harriet bragged, petting the flower.

"How much for the dress pattern?" Diedre asked.

"Two cents down at the Five and Dime on account of it havin' a rip in it. I patched it up with a little flour an' water. Good as new. Thelma done up the dress for me then made one for herself. 'Except hers is red," Big Harriet said.

"I'm savin' mine for tomorrow night," Thelma added.

"I may wear this again, too," Big Harriet said.

Thelma's jaw dropped. "Not Saturday night. You promised you wouldn't —"

"Don't get your britches up. I *said* I might wear it. And why the blazes do you care? No john of yours is gonna see me anyway. Chances are, I'll be upstairs the whole night. I got a lot of followers or ain't you noticed?"

To me, Big Harriet's dress looked pathetically homemade even though it did give her dumpling shape a waistline. She'd also smeared lipstick across her mouth – badly. Although, according to Lorena, the johns usually arrived so stewed with moonshine, they wouldn't notice if she smeared lipstick across her whole face.

I'd been living at The Rainbow for a month now. My room up on the third floor wasn't luxurious. The bed had a lumpy mattress and noisy springs. And I was living at a whorehouse. But the rent was cheap, I had my own room, and I already adored Lorena. She had more brains and energy than any other women I'd met in the past, excluding my former New York dress shop boss Zaza Pavlova.

"Somebody change that record, will ya," Big Harriet said. "I'm worn out from that *lovey–dovey* drivel. Put on somethin' we can dance to."

Thelma began sifting through the thin pile of records. She quickly chose one, placed it on the turntable, then cranked up the machine. Dance music from the movie *Flying Down to Rio* filled the parlor.

"That's more like it," Harriet said, rising off her chair and shutting her eyes, before she began banging her hips from side–to–side, doing her own demented version of the *Carioca*. The other girls joined in. Most of them weren't pretty and anyone wandering in might find them comical. But to me they were heartbreakingly sweet as they let loose.

"Better settle down, ladies. We got company," Lorena announced, charging in.

The girls stopped dancing. Thelma turned down the music. Harriet turned off the big light on the ceiling and switched on a lamp shaded by a gauzy rose–colored scarf. Covered in soft hues, the parlor's garish decor almost achieved a measure of grandeur. The colored glass beads, red–flocked wallpaper, overstuffed furnishings, and gold framed pictures of fox hunting and corpulent ladies from the Gilded Age suddenly seemed magical. Even elegant.

The bell rang. Lorena hurried to answer. The girls automatically adopted seductive poses. They leaned against the furniture with a knee up or a hip out or they crossed their legs and hiked up their skirts to reveal pudgy knees and black lace garters. Lips were puckered or forced into shy grins.

Then two farm boys shuffled in. Their hair was slicked back and they looked as if they'd shaved with rusty knives. Hanging onto their soft hats, they timidly eyed the women. After several quick glances, they each pointed to a girl. Then the four hiked upstairs.

Minutes later, Lorena and I were bouncing over a dirt road on our way to a road house, a current rustic version of a night club. I briefly fretted about running into the Desanto brothers. But I doubted they'd drive out to a saloon in the middle of the San Fernando Valley. The Rainbow was another story. The Desantos had been regulars at many of New York's finest brothels.

A half hour later, we pulled into a crowded parking lot by a lonely adobe structure. A neon sign on the roof read: The Cactus Trails.

"Guess I oughta tell you. I got a fella waiting," Lorena said, as the truck lurched to a stop in the middle of a mud puddle.

FOURTEEN

Lorena pushed open her squeaky door and jumped out. I balanced on the running board, stretched out my foot, and managed a safe leap over the oozing mud without breaking an ankle or my shoe heel. Outside, crickets sang, and the night air smelled of hay and gasoline. Lorena and I'd just reached the club's door when it abruptly burst open. A haughty woman in a shimmering silk dress and a luxurious fur–wrap stormed out.

A tall young man in a dress suit grabbed her elbow. "Damn it, Betty. It was just a big misunderstanding, I swear."

"Don't insult my intelligence with that innocent wide–eyed stare," the woman snarled. "That cheap–bit–of–fluff had her hands all over you. Now hurry up and get your car before we're spotted together, and the press gets wise to us."

Grabbing my hand, Lorena rushed me past the couple through the door.

"Wait, Lorena. That was Betty Blaine, the actress."

"So?"

"So, she's stepping out on her husband. I just read about them in *Modern Screen*. How perfect their marriage is and —"

"Betty Blaine steps out on that rat–of–a–husband all the time. Did the magazine also mention he's a drunk with a lousy temper?"

"No, but —"

"Well, I met Betty Blaine at a party once. She was in the powder room tryin' to cover up a black eye her old man gave her when he was stewed to the gills."

Inside, the stench of cigarette smoke, body odors, beer, gin, and vomit almost knocked me over. Colored lights hung above the long bar. Deep booths lit by small candles hugged two walls at right angles. Behind the bar, couples clung to each other on a small dance floor by a group of black jazz musicians and a lone white female singer in a tight satin dress. Blues music competed with an overall din. Clutching my hand, Lorena directed me through the tangle of revelers to the bar.

"Don't worry, we aren't staying long. My boyfriend's taking us to a party," she said.

I hoped I didn't end up feeling like a third wheel.

"Hello, Mack," Lorena said to the bartender.

"Howdy there," said a paunchy dark–haired man in a full white apron, his face lighting up at the sight of Lorena. "Gin and ginger?"

"For starters."

"How about your friend?" he asked.

"Same as her," I said.

"Been awhile since you've been by the house," Lorena told Mack, as she scrutinized the crowd, her eyes burning with excitement.

Mack shoved a drink at Lorena then leaned in close. "How's Miss Diedre?"

"Pining for you. She wrote you a love note but I got busy and forgot it."

Mack chuckled, revealing brown crooked teeth and an Adam's apple with rhythm. "Tell her I'll be by soon. Guess I can step out one Monday night in ten."

The current song ended and an extremely handsome man in formal wear climbed up on the tiny stage to take the girl singer's place. He had thick black hair, intense dark eyes, and gleaming white teeth. Every girl in the place looked smitten. Then the lights went low except for a spotlight on him.

"More than you know..." he sang. His voice was gutsy and real. He sang as if he connected with the words and the audience.

"That's Walt," Lorena said wistfully. "Once upon a time, I would've licked his boots."

"What happened?" I asked.

"He was perfect, except for being broke all the time from gambling. And a bad habit of accepting money from every available woman in Los Angeles. Too bad he's got a voice like warm coal and the moves to match."

"Sounds like a bum."

"That's the only way I'll have 'em. In case you haven't heard, my taste in men is rotten. Ever been in love, Cousin?" she asked.

"With my husband."

She suddenly looked stricken. "Darn, I forgot. Me and my big mouth."

"That's okay. "

"Guess you were happy."

The truth was so much more complicated. "Yes, I was happy."

An awkward silence followed. Both of us watched the couples move across the scuffed wood floor. The guys in their cheap suits and the girls in their two dollar dresses.

"I found three of my girls in this joint," Lorena said.

"Who are all these people?"

"The gals call themselves starlets but most of them wait tables, clean houses, or stand behind the counter at the Five and

Dime. Some don't have any work. They wear cheap dresses that fall apart in a month. And all of 'em are waitin' for something better. Like a movie producer to discover 'em. Or a guy with enough scratch to marry 'em. The guys are farmers, bricklayers, ranchers, you name it. They hustle for rent money and cigarettes. But for a few hours here, while the gin holds out, they forget. A little dancing, a few laughs, a quickie in the rumble seat of a car – it's what keeps 'em going."

"What about the girls who work for you?" I asked.

"They want a whole lot more." Lorena abruptly froze and her hand crushed mine. "That's him. Over there by the door – no, don't look. Listen, if I get sloppy or start yammering like some Dumb Dora, pinch me hard, okay? How do I look?" Her eyes combed mine for approval. But before I could answer, she dove into the crowd, leaving me alone at the bar. Through the mob, I saw her new love kiss her cheek. Even from across the room, I could tell he wasn't some pie–eyed farmer with a pocketful of quarters looking for a Saturday night bang. According to Lorena, he was Pasadena Society from his manicured nails to his restricted country club.

"Roger Starling meet my cousin Jeri Rose," Lorena said two minutes later, her eyes glistening with excitement and adoration.

Swaying on his feet, Roger gave me a lengthy once–over. Flashing a dazzling grin, he took my hand and kissed my palm. "Beauty must run in your family," he drawled.

I already knew he was a bum. A drop–dead charming bum with a great smile, a movie star profile, and a snazzy line. But a drunken bum all the same.

"Follow me," Roger said, a minute later outside the club as he slid into a magnificent silver roadster and gunned his engine.

"Some car, huh," Lorena said, we settled into her truck. "It's a Bugatti."

I just hoped Roger and his silver Bugatti didn't end up wrapped around a tree.

"So what do you think?" Lorena asked breathlessly as we pulled onto the road.

"Seems swell. But why didn't we just meet him at the party?"

"You need an engraved invitation to get in. Roger's gonna have to do some fancy footwork to get us through the front door. But it's a real Hollywood party."

I wasn't impressed. I'd been to a few Hollywood parties back in the future. And back at the Bayridge too. Many wannabes had attended these drunken festivities. Each prayed she'd make the right connection which would lead to her big break. Instead, most had ended up with a list of broken promises and a hangover.

In the dark, we trailed the Bugatti's tail lights. We bounced over dirt roads and careened around tight curves for what seemed like forever. Without warning, a huge, brilliantly lit Mexican hacienda rose like a monument on a small hill. A sea of cars sprawled across fields, surrounding the main house. Waves of music and the scent of orange blossoms drifted across the desert night. It was after ten by the time we filed up the tiled walkway to the house behind a parade of guests. Inside, a butler took our things. Before Lorena or I could grab a cocktail off a waiter's tray, Roger pulled her toward the large knot of couples moving slowly across a small dance floor by a raised bandstand, where a full orchestra softly played.

Alone, I found myself a comfortable wall to lean against. In spite of the wood floors, rustic paneled walls, mounted deer heads, and a great stuffed bear standing in a corner, the party guests were colorful and well–dressed, as if the Depression had skipped this pocket of Los Angeles. The male guests wore dinner jackets and fine suits. And the women sparkled. Still, this wasn't New York in the 1920s but Hollywood in the 1930s. Not only had the fashions changed, but if you looked closely, the rubies and diamonds were fake. And the glamorous dresses were copies of Vionnet, Mainbocher, Lanvin, Chanel, and Scaparelli.

"Bet you meet someone tonight, too," Lorena had said on the drive over.

But why try to meet someone when I already had a husband? When I belonged back with my own generation. Back in my Malibu condo dressed in jeans and fuzzy slippers, watching TV, and working on a marketing proposal. Instead, here I stood in a girdle, stockings, and shoes guaranteed to give me bunions. Here I was, wishing there was a way to wipe out the Desanto brothers, short of killing them. And find a cure for tuberculosis.

I'd just accepted a glass of champagne off a waiter's tray, when a tap on my shoulder startled me. Turning, I confronted a face I'd been dreaming about since Havana. Except tonight his blonde hair seemed thicker and his face even more chiseled.

FIFTEEN

Franky Wyatt's gaze covered me like a warm glove. Desire clouded his blue eyes as they roamed over my decolletage to my breasts and down the bodice to my legs.

"My God this is a coincidence. I was just thinking about you," he said, leaning over and brushing his lips across my cheek.

My pulse began to race. And I felt a deep flush as a wave of heat rushed through me. "What're you doing here?" I asked, hating the way I reacted to him. Wishing he were shorter, fatter, with a receding hairline and bad breath. Instead, his good looks still took me by surprise. Plus, he was wearing the same white dinner jacket and black bow tie he'd had on in Havana.

"My ranch is just up the road. Care to dance?" Without waiting for my answer, he grabbed my elbow and steered me toward the dance floor, until his arms encircled me and I felt him against me. Even the gentle touch of his hand on my back provoked me, sending waves of desire through my loins.

"I shouldn't even be speaking to you," he breathed into my ear, a whisper which felt like a tender kiss. "I must've spoken to that darn waitress in Santa Monica a dozen times trying to find you. I even dropped by once, but she said you'd gone."

"You mean, Sally from the café?" I said.

"Sure. She was very helpful. In fact I'm seeing her now. We just got engaged. The wedding should be some time in July."

I laughed. "You're welcome to each other."

"Actually, she's not my type. A little too plump."

"What is your type?"

"You."

I can't do this, I thought. But the trouble was I could. I wanted to be good, to behave myself. But he was so close and the flesh on his neck smelled like soap, and the sensation of his calloused hand clutching mine left me dizzy and intoxicated. Lex was thousands of miles away. And Lupe was nowhere in sight. And other couples around us were kissing openly as they shuffled across the hard Mexican pavers, their bare arms grey in the dim light, their dark heads so close they became one.

"After seeing you the other day, I haven't stopped thinking about you," he said, as his lips brushed across my throat.

I filled my nostrils with him. From the aroma of whiskey on his breath, to the scented talc on his skin mixed with a masculine undertone. Then his silky lashes grazed my cheek, his lips tickled my own, and an unbidden urge bore through me like a searing blast. It felt so good to be in his arms. To feel him against me. By now, we were barely moving. Like clay, our bodies molded together, as his strong hands directed me, his warm lips gently probed mine, while his brick hard groin rubbed up against me. The solid and insistent pleasure turned my insides into melted chocolate, warm, smooth, and flowing, until I craved the flesh beneath his clothes. Craved his trim muscled body which I hadn't actually seen, but imagined to be cut like a diamond. Then his lips crushed mine and his tongue entered my mouth, moving in slow gentle circles, as evocative as a wet finger between my legs. His kisses grew harsher, more insistent until I trembled with a need which suffocated my resistance. Until he could've had me there on the dance floor.

At last the song ended, and the room grew too bright. Franky took a step back, and I found myself damp with desire, aware my face betrayed my carnal imaginings. Clutching my hand, he led me outside to a patio where lanterns hung from the trees. I'd barely taken a deep breath of the cool desert air, when he pulled me to him, and covered my mouth with his. There in the dark California night, his lips quenched my yearnings. His mouth was demanding, intoxicating as he devoured mine. His hand rose over my breast, warm and insistent, crushing the silk. Then his hand slid down my bodice to my bare flesh and his warm fingers probed my nipple, pinching it, making me groan. Until I realized how fast we were moving and saw myself as I was. An easy target. A lonely wife thrilled by a handsome movie star's kisses.

I abruptly pushed him away. "Stop, please, don't."

"Jeri," he moaned. "Please."

"I can't do this."

He sighed, dropped his hands, then stepped away. "Sorry. I can't seem to help myself around you. I suppose I should've sent you flowers or French perfume. Or tried harder to find you."

All true, but that wasn't the problem. The problem was, we were married to other people. And I'd never planned to cheat on Lex. Even now, with hardly anything to be ashamed of, I felt guilty for desiring Franky. Guilty because I still loved Lex. And because I understood Franky too well. His persuasive words and kisses were *meant* to drive me wild, to reduce my resistance to dust. And he probably believed he could seduce me, if he was persistent enough and pulled the right switches. After all, even back in Havana with Lex in the same town, I'd let him kiss me. But I was no small town bimbo fresh off the bus with stars in my eyes. I was a modern, educated woman who understood he might quickly tire of me and rush back to his wife. That I might easily be left with a broken heart. So I meant to go on resisting him as long as I could.

"Are you angry with me?" he asked.

"That isn't the reason —"

He abruptly grabbed me and tried to press his mouth to mine.

"Stop. I told you *no*."

Turning his back to me, he moved away and leaned against a low wall. I quickly found my compact and handkerchief to wipe the sweat off my brow, the unexpected tears in my eyes. Then I repaired my lipstick.

"Jeri, what's wrong?" he asked.

"I'm not ready for this. It's too quick. And it's wrong."

"I'm sorry. I know I've pushed you too hard. But … look, can we take a drive? Go somewhere to discuss this?"

Thank heavens my sanity had returned and I was in control again. "Absolutely not. I came here with friends and I intend to leave with them."

Frowning, he pulled out his cigarette case, extracted a cigarette, and lit up. He inhaled slowly. "Who's this friend? "

He actually sounded jealous. "It's not *a he*. It's another couple," I said.

Relief flooded his expression. He took my hand. "Tell them I'm taking you home. Tell them anything. Let's just go. We can drive anywhere you want. Down to Mexico or up to San Francisco. Or —"

"Forget it. I'm married and so are you."

He gazed intently into my face. "But are you happy?"

He read me so easily. "What does that matter? Look, I'm no waitress. I'm a sophisticated married woman not some farm girl you can dazzle with a drive in a fancy car or a bottle of champagne."

"I never said you were. It's just that … we've lost too much time already. Can't I at least see you again? For dinner or drinks?"

"I don't think —"

"Just for fun. I swear I'll behave."

I studied him. Half of me wanted him to ravage me now, here on the terrace. The saner half of me wanted to get on a train and head east to Saranac Lake to Lex's bedside, even if he didn't want me there. But another part of me, the lonely half, the angry person who hadn't heard from Lex in months made the final decision. "I'll think about it."

"I have to be out of town next week. How about next Friday night? A week from tonight?"

"I guess so but…"

He abruptly grabbed me and planted a kiss on my cheek. "Swell. I won't stop thinking about you the whole night. I won't sleep at all."

My own thoughts exactly. I scribbled down the brothel's number on a matchbook for him.

"Why can't I take you home now?" he asked.

"My friends wouldn't understand." My real concern was how Franky would interpret my living at a brothel. Between now and next week, I'd have to find a way to explain things. Or keep him from discovering the truth.

It was after midnight when he left. I stood outside the front door and watched him stride off, hands in his pockets, his collar hiked up against the brisk night air. In spite of everything I'd said, I regretted seeing him go. Back inside the grand house I began to search for Lorena. The bright house lights had been dimmed. Now, light came from candles and lanterns peppered around the enormous great room. Behind the bandstand, candles outlined the black musicians playing trumpets. I studied the dancers hoping to spy Lorena and Roger but didn't see them. They weren't in the parlor, the kitchen, or the dining room. Eventually, I discovered a long hallway which led to the bedrooms. But I couldn't very well pound on the doors and disturb the guests or residents.

At last I found refuge in a small bedroom turned into a dressing area for the occasion. "Lorena?" I called, receiving once–overs from the two other women nursing their finger waves and powdering their noses. Lorena didn't answer. Desperate to kill time, I found a seat and waited my turn for the bathroom.

"Gosh, that guy Nat's got heavy feet," a thin girl griped. "Been on mine all night."

The dyed redhead beside her slapped her comb down. "Stop bellyaching. You ate a steak dinner, didn't ya? And all the gin you could swill. So lighten up. Cause Benny says we're goin' out for fried chicken next Saturday, and Nat's plannin' on bringing you along. And since I ain't eaten this good in months, do me a favor and clam up."

"But he's got that awful dandruff – makes me sick."

"So don't look at it. It ain't like he asked ya to marry him."

"No, but I'm scared he might. And I might be tempted to tell him okay cause at least the poor sap's got a steady job. And boy am I sick of workin' in that house as a maid. One lousy day off every other week. Workin' my tail off. I sure would like a house and kids of my own. Get off my feet sometimes."

"You got squirrels up there," the redhead said, tapping her head. "Whadaya think you'd do raisin' kids? You'd be on your feet more."

"Heck, my mama slept all the time when she wasn't soakin' her feet or crabbin' at us kids till the day she died. The four of us girls did all the cookin' and cleanin'."

"Yeah, but she had girls, didn't she? With your luck you'd have nothin' but boys."

"Well, things gotta get better. If I could just land another actin' job —"

"Say, listen. You got no one to blame but yourself for that one. Agreein' to see that movie producer on the sly. You knew he had a wife and three kids, that he was just playin' house till the thrill wore off."

"I got a speakin' part in a picture, didn't I? And a few bucks on top of that."

"A lousy walk–on part with one lousy line," the redhead sneered. "If I had to sleep with some fat slob for every bit–part I landed, I'd head back to Wichita and marry the grocery boy."

"Maybe you should," a third gal quipped, as she strolled in wearing a fancy fur wrap.

Hearing these young girls squabble about the movie business reminded me of what Lorena had said back at the Cactus Trails. " … some of these star–stuck gals can even act. Put 'em in a costume, and they can play Hamlet's ghost. Too bad no one wants 'em. Most of 'em took a bus here from Kansas. I get the ones that don't wanna make the bus ride back. The ones interested in making some decent dough."

I searched the sprawling house for Lorena again without success. I doubted she'd abandoned me. But if she had, I'd need a ride home. I wasn't even sure if cabs came out this far in the valley or worked this late. It was well past one. I doubted I even had cab fare on me. And it would be damn awkward asking another guest, a stranger, to drive me out to the brothel.

Back in the main dining room, I spied a haughty debutante I'd seen talking to Roger earlier. Now, she and another well–dressed woman sat on a sofa chatting. Plastering a smile on my face, I said, "Excuse me. I'm Roger Starling's friend. Have you seen him around here lately?"

The girl stubbed out her cigarette and eyed me with hatred. "Not really. Maybe he and your friend the whore drove down to

Tijuana." Scowling, she turned away from me and whispered something to her friend who gave me a withering once–over.

Rebuffed and desperate, I could've kicked myself for refusing Franky's offer. I was tired and fed up with the whole scene. Worse, I realized the crowd had thinned out. The remaining guests were sprawled across the furniture, talking softly. Even the band was packing up to leave. Spying a quiet corner with a telephone, I considered calling my Uncle Clement. Except I'd only met him once, and I didn't have the farm's telephone number. Besides, I pictured him showing up in his old truck with his teeth out, a four–day growth of beard, and that smell I'd noticed that day at lunch, as if he'd been cleaning out the chicken house and hadn't bothered to wash afterward. Uncle Clement was out of the question.

Instead, I trailed several guests outside to one of the fields to find Lorena's truck. By now, the air was downright freezing as I searched the vehicles around me. Many of the cars gently rocked with the rhythms of passion. At last, I spied the old pickup. Too bad no one was inside. Only then did I realize my mistake. I should've been looking for Roger's Bugatti. But after ten minutes of dealing with the mud and cold, I trekked back to the house. If Lorena and Roger had decided to take off in Roger's car, I was stuck here. At least until morning.

Back in the great room, I dropped into a generous arm chair prepared to spend the night when a familiar and unusual male voice said, "Listen, doll–face. We got two big pictures starting next week. I could get you a role in either one of 'em. Now, how about a trip to my place. I've got a sweet little bungalow with the best stocked bar in the city. Plenty of anything you want. Not this home–brewed swill either. Every bit of it is imported."

I recognized Harry Deen's voice. He was one of several minor movie producers I'd tangled with when I lived at the Bayridge and went on interviews for acting jobs. Desperate, I took a deep breath and stood. Grinning, I eased over to the side of the piano where I peered down at Deen's bulldog face. "Aren't you Harry Deen, the big movie producer?"

The blonde with Deen scowled at me. But Deen smiled as if he'd just won the Irish Sweepstakes. "Jeri Rose. If you aren't a sight for sore eyes. How could I forget a gorgeous face like yours?" He was staring at my breasts.

Maybe he recalled my name but he'd obviously forgotten the circumstances of our first meeting. How I'd threatened to call his wife when he insisted I climb under his desk to kick–start my career.

"I could sure use a lift home, Mr. Deen," I purred, gazing into his puffy lizard eyes. It was at least fifteen miles to The Rainbow. And Deen seemed like my best bet to get there, even if I'd be forced to do some fancy footwork to avoid physical contact with him. Deen reached for my hand, gave it a damp squeeze, then leaned close, spewing a whiff of sour breath at me. "You got moxie. Moxie in a beautiful doll like you is like Gershwin to me."

Then someone barked, "Jeez, Jeri, where ya been?"

Lorena. Finally. *Thank you, God.*

"We been lookin' all over for ya," Lorena said gaily, linking arms with me and leading me away from Deen who looked stupefied and unhappy.

"Where have you been? I almost had to sleep with that pig to get a ride home," I growled to Lorena.

"Never mind that. Guess what?" Lorena said, her green eyes ablaze with excitement. "We just got engaged."

Roger, who stood a few feet away, gulped what was left in his champagne glass then stared down at his wingtips. My mouth went dry and my heart sped up as I groped for something positive to say. Before I could utter a word, the haughty young woman who'd snubbed me earlier appeared.

Stifling a yawn with manicured fingers, she sneered at Lorena and me then faced Roger. "I'm ready to leave now, Roger. Please get my wrap then bring the car around."

Roger blinked rapidly and his face grew pink. "Right away, Darlene."

Every inch of the girl proclaimed money, from her elegantly coiffed dark hair and her ermine–sleeved silk–dress, to her necklace which probably cost more than the average 1933 worker earned in a year.

Roger shrugged regretfully at Lorena then trotted after Darlene.

Alone with Lorena I said, "I don't understand. If you're his fiancé, who's she?"

"His old fiancé. Get your things. We're leaving." Minutes later, we were trekking across the field toward Lorena's truck.

" … but if he's in love with you, why did he arrange to meet her here?" I asked.

"He's trying to get rid of her but she won't take the hint. He has to be careful how he handles her. Because of her social standing and what their friends will say."

Minutes later, the old truck was bumping across the field toward the dirt road.

"Does he know anything about you?" I asked.

"He thinks I live off a small family trust. I told him that Mumsy and Daddy were hurt by the Crash and had to sell their Tuxedo Park Estate plus their country home in Greenwich. That we moved out here to a ranch so we could keep our thoroughbreds."

"What're you gonna say when he finds out you lied?"

"I'll hit him with the truth down the road. But why spoil the fun now?"

"Because he's not some farmer. Because when you finally do tell him the truth, he'll probably be mad as hell."

Lorena changed gears and sped down the dark road as insects splattered across the windshield. "Look, a guy like that's never gonna marry an ignorant Oakie like me. So don't get in a lather over somethin' that's never gonna happen. Cause Roger Starling's probably not interested in getting his mug in the funny papers over the owner of a whorehouse."

"But you just told me —"

"It's play acting. Didn't you ever play *pretend*?"

"I don't get it. You're such a realist. You face life squarely every day. So why put yourself through this kind of heartache?"

"For the same reason you're attracted to that married cowboy whose career's in the toilet."

Her breakdown of my situation with Franky Wyatt was painfully accurate. "How do you know about Franky Wyatt?"

"I spied you two together. And when things get slow at the house, I read the movie rags with the rest of my gals. Look, I don't care what you do. It's your business. I'm in no position to be judgmental. Live and let live, is how I see it. And you're probably right about Roger and me. It's just that Roger's a gentleman down to his knuckles. He eats on china with silver forks. He reads good books and takes famous ships to Europe. His family belongs to a club where Jews, Italians, and the Irish aren't allowed. Where a gal like me couldn't get through the front gate. But when I'm in his arms, I feel like I'm gonna be in one of those movies where the women always wear satin and the floors shine like glass. And everyone dresses for dinner and goes to swell nightclubs."

"What if he hears the truth about you from someone else? What if he hurts you?"

"Like I tell my gals. Count the flowers on the ceiling and think of recipes when you're doing it. And when it's over, it never happened."

"Does that really work?"

"In the beginning. Later I tell them to think about Friday, pay day, and how it's just before supper. And supper will be steak and mashed potatoes with green peas and Jello. And how every girl at the table can make as much dough as she wants to."

To me, her answers sounded pathetic. But I'd come from the future. I'd started at the top as a wealthy, educated girl. Even back in 1929, I had more to look forward to than Jello. "What if he breaks your heart?"

"You gotta expect a little pain in life."

"Don't you ever want a family or children?"

Lorena pulled up to The Rainbow and cut off the engine. Most of the house lights were out. "Sure I do," Lorena said softly. "I dream about it just like every whore I ever met. But I don't kid myself, not really. Roger is like Fred Astaire in *Flying Down to Rio*. He's so far above me – it's hopeless. But I'm still flattered by his attention. And for a month or two, I get to be the star of a beautiful world where people are polite, rich, and funny. Okay, it's make–believe. But while it lasts, life is swell,"she said, opening her door and climbing out.

It was almost three when we crossed The Rainbow's threshold.

"Go on up." Lorena said. "I gotta see what's doing."

Elvira appeared in her robe. "You all want somethin' to drink?"

"Not me," I said.

"A nice cold beer," Lorena piped up.

SIXTEEN

"Like it fuller up front, Sweetie?" Rose Tencil asked, puffing up my new perm with a comb the following Friday afternoon. The plump middle–aged woman in a pink uniform with dyed red hair and a cheery smile had spent hours slathering my head with repellant chemicals before hooking me up to a permanent wave machine, a piece of equipment with dozens of wires and knobs. Something Dr. Frankenstein might've used to regenerate dead tissue from corpses.

While my hair processed, I searched the collection of movie magazines piled on my lap for news about Franky. He'd awakened the whole house at seven the morning after the party to repeat that he had to leave town for a week but wanted to invite me to dinner the following Friday evening. *Tonight.*

A half–dozen movie magazines later, I finally unearthed *The New Movie Magazine* from January 1931. In an article called "Fallen Idols"about cowboy stars from the silent era and their current Hollywood status, Franky was mentioned along with Francis X Bushman, Bill Hart, and Tom Mix.

According to the story, cowboy movies had faded from popularity. Franky and Fuerte were retired. And Lupe wasn't even mentioned. Although, a more recent article in *Movie Mirror* inferred that Lupe's career had hit a frigid spell, too. The story suggested that

Lupe's one hope rested on her latest project, a musical produced by her father's friend at Warner Brothers. For now, only Greta Garbo, Marlene Dietrich, Joan Crawford, and Norma Sheerer reigned as Hollywood royalty.

Many of the stars were either hiding in Europe from bad box office receipts, waiting for news on their latest picture, or visiting sanitariums for health problems, which might mean tuberculosis, pneumonia, alcoholism, or nervous breakdowns. Based on the vicious gossip in the magazines, *Movie Mirror*, *Photoplay*, *Modern Screen*, and *The New Movie*, the public still feasted on the dirt thrown at Hollywood stars. Exactly like the future.

"…it seems Bob Montgomery's career is soaring while Buddy Rogers is slipping. Buddy seems to be taking himself pretty seriously these days and losing a bit of his charming naturalness," was a typical quote.

By four o'clock I was back in my room to dress for my big date. Through the wall Jimmy's radio blared as he typed away. It was like living next to gossip icon Walter Winchell, except that Jimmy worked on mystery stories for pulp magazines instead of a gossip column or radio broadcasts.

Down the hall, the bathroom had pools of water on the wood floor and a thick ring around the tub. It took me fifteen minutes of cleaning before I could settle in for a hot soak. At five, I laid my dress out on my bed then gently unveiled my new stockings, the sheerest and most expensive kind Bullock's sold at a dollar sixty–nine a pair. Stockings I'd saved for a special occasion. Next came my best bra, an imported white lace chemise, and matching garter belt, items saved from better days in New York. As last, I pulled on my new dress, stepped into the hallway, and knocked on Jimmy's door.

"Be right there," he called.

Down the hall, Uncle Suds, one of Big Harriet's regulars,

waited outside her door. Uncle Suds, a minor bootlegger, made revolting beer which I'd tasted once then promptly spit out.

Suds whistled at me. "Hey, purdy lady. If you ain't a sight for sore eyes."

"Thanks." Suds was another scrawny old man in dirty overalls. All of Harriet's customers looked like refugees from *The Grapes of Wrath*. Dirty, unshaven, and skinny.

"Got me a new bridge comin' for my teeth," Suds said, sticking his tongue in the space where his two front teeth should've been. "Sold a set of old tires and some chickens and now I got an appointment with a real dentist who says —"

Big Harriet's door flew open startling Suds and me. Wearing an old robe, she stepped into the hall and grabbed Sud's arm. "Never mind them teeth, you old goat. Let's get this ride goin' before your old lady comes lookin' for ya." Scowling at me, she added, "And tell that damn pantywaist to turn off his radio. Got me a headache from that racket." With a hard yank, she pulled Suds inside then slammed her door.

A moment later, Jimmy peered out of his room. "Is the beast gone?"

I laughed. "Yep. She'll be busy for the next five minutes." I twirled around in my dress. "What do you think?"

"You're the most beautiful doll in Los Angeles."

"I love it. I can't thank you enough."

My new dress was a copy of one featured in last November's *Harper's Bazaar* by Bernard Newman. Newman had designed Ginger Roger's gowns for *Flying Down to Rio*. The original full length gown was belted at the waist by a wide matching tie sash. It had a very low back and *a bretelles,* a scarf of half fabric and half kolinsky fur around the neckline. Since I didn't have any kolinsky to spare, since it was the most expensive fur in the world, I'd used an old white fox scarf which Jimmy had cleverly attached to the grey satin gown. He'd also cut the dress, pinned it, then finished it on Lorena's sewing machine. The revealing gown fit as if it had been painted on. It accentuated my curves from my breasts to my knees then gently fell to the floor.

"Not bad," he said, fiddling with the fur scarf.

"Wish I wasn't so nervous," I admitted. "Should I wake you when I get in?"

"Only if you've got something shameful to tell me."

I laughed then planted a sisterly kiss on his cheek.

"Hey, Queen Victoria!" Lorena shouted from downstairs. "Wanna come down here and join the riffraff for a beer?"

"Be right there." The idea of sitting with the whores before my date filled me with dread, in case they gave me a hard time about Franky. But since Lorena had invited me, I felt obligated to join her. Back in my room, I checked my stockings, took a whiff under my arm to be sure the talcum powder and deodorant were still working, then did a final turn in the oval mirror above my dressing table. Finally, I locked my door and headed downstairs.

My second day at the brothel, I'd left my door unlocked and a drunken client mistook my room for Georgette 's across the hall. He'd stripped off his dirty clothes and passed out naked on my bed. It took Georgette, Elvira–the–housekeeper, and me ten minutes to drag the sweaty farmer from my bed and into Georgette's room.

But I still had to wash my bedding to get the brewery stench out. Without an electric washer, I'd had to handwash my sheets in hot water, bleach, and a caustic detergent, hang them on the clothes–line to dry, then iron them. I usually left this grueling chore to Mr. Chin's laundry in town. But with only one set of sheets and money problems, I'd started doing my own laundry by hand. Lorena had promised the girls a new Maytag for Christmas, providing all went well and the law didn't shut us down. I prayed she kept her promise.

"Jeri Rose! Will you get down here already," Lorena bellowed again from the first floor landing. "We need an educated opinion on somethin' important."

Two minutes later, I entered the kitchen, feeling awkward and self–conscious. Lorena gave me a slow once–over from my new perm to my shoes. She whistled softly. "Will ya look at you. Girls, we got our own movie star here. That dress sure beats anything in my closet. Maybe you'll lend it to me sometime."

"Anytime," I said.

Most of the girls were half–dressed in cotton lingerie. All of them puffed away on cigarettes making the air dense with smoke. Open beer bottles covered the large table. Georgette had rags in her hair and a bare foot up on the bench beside an open bottle of Cutex garnet colored nail polish. She paused from painting a glossy layer of red on her big toe and smiled at me. "You sure beat any film star I ever seen."

Myra, clad in a full cotton slip, sniffed indignantly at Georgette. "You ain't supposed to do that at the table, Georgette. It ain't lady–like."

"I ain't harmin' anything," Georgette shot back.

"Myra, mind your own potatoes," Lorena barked without malice.

Then, Lorena handed me an enormous white box. "In the meantime, you might need this tonight."

Overwhelmed, I accepted the box. "What is this? You've already been too good to me —"

"Don't worry, it's a loaner. I'll want it back tomorrow."

I lifted off the top and gaped at magnificent white fox fur Lorena had just purchased. "But you haven't even worn this yourself."

"Try it with your dress."

With Lorena's help, I gently placed the stole around my shoulders and tried to ignore the admiring as well as envious looks from the girls at the kitchen table.

"Thanks. It's exquisite." I planted a sisterly kiss on Lorena's cheek.

"Good. Now slide down, girls, and let her in." Lorena quickly made room for me beside her on the bench. As always, the odors of a hot supper filled the room. Tonight, thanks to my jitters, the smells didn't entice me.

"Did I tell ya, that guy Willie's comin' by tonight just to see me," Thelma bragged in her high–pitched squeaky lisp, scratching her plump arm. "All the way from Long Beach. Joe's comin', too. Both of 'em are nuts about me."

"And fifteen other girls workin' here," Myra added.

"But he's sweet on *me* now," Thelma insisted. "He always asks for me. And he always brings me roses. I love roses in my room. They make it smell so nice and add a real homey touch. I read all about roses in this swell magazine that said — "

"Yeah, they cover up that fishy smell, too," Myra cut in, cackling.

Thelma's face darkened. "You didn't have to say that. What in the world's eatin' you tonight, Myra?"

"Knock it off you two," Lorena snapped before turning to me. "Relax and have a beer. We're just getting warmed up for the evening."

I studied the cold beer in front of Lorena. "Is that Uncle Suds' brew?"

"Nah, it's from another supplier. Try it. It's practically the real McCoy."

I took a small sip of icy beer. "Not bad."

Lorena wore a peach satin robe. Her hair had a collection of large clips meant to create the popular ridges. Lorena never personally entertained johns, but she still dressed up most nights. Now, seated in the kitchen with her girls, sipping beer and smoking, she seemed light hearted. But earlier in the day she'd had an ugly run in with two of her girls.

SEVENTEEN

I'd just finished my bath, when I heard loud yelling coming from the second floor. I rushed down to find Lorena charging out of Diedre Bishop's room, a belt in her hand. From out in the hall, I could hear Diedre weeping. Without a word, Lorena marched across the hall into Irene's room. Before Irene had time to protest, there was a hard slap and the sound of fabric tearing as Lorena ripped the girl's chemise. Then I heard a belt snapping against flesh followed by screams and curses.

"Now, pack up your stuff and get out," Lorena growled.

"No, please. It won't never happen again," Irene sobbed. "I got no place to go. Don't make me leave. I swear I'll behave."

"Then keep your hands off my other girls. Or so help me you'll be out in the street."

Lorena stormed out of the room, face ashen, hands shaking.

"Lorena, what happened?" I asked, sick over the scene, wondering what Irene, a pretty blonde from Mississippi, could've done to make Lorena so angry.

"I found them in bed together."

"Irene and Diedre are lesbians?"

"Just lonely. It's a big problem, girls liking girls. But if I let 'em go on like that, we'd never make a cent around here." Flushed and out of breath, Lorena had marched down to the front parlor and poured herself a strong drink.

Tonight, neither Diedre nor Irene sat at the table.

Thelma sighed loudly and said, "Gosh, you're lucky, Jeri. Franky Wyatt's the best lookin' cowboy I ever seen. Back in Ohio, I went to the moving picture show all the time to see him."

"Well Franky Wyatt's darn lucky, too," Myra said. "Goin' out with a girl as pretty as Jeri. If I had her looks, I'd be rolling in lettuce."

"Maybe we can take a peek out the window when he comes," Thelma lisped.

"That would be fine except I'm meeting him down the road at the filling station. Too many pretty girls might confuse him," I added.

The girls glanced down at the table or into their laps. Shame filled their faces. They understood why I didn't want Franky here. I was embarrassed by them and The Rainbow.

"Can you imagine?" Lorena said, joining in. "The poor cowboy with his hat in his hand, waiting in the parlor with a bunch of half–naked girls in their underwear. The poor fella would jump on his horse and ride into the sunset for good."

The girls broke into giggles over that, slapping their thighs, snorting their beer.

I glanced at the kitchen clock and stood. "Actually, I better get going."

"I'll drive you," Lorena said, rising, too.

"It's less than a half–mile walk," I argued.

"The road's rough. Gimme a minute to change and I'll drive you over. Unless you don't want him seeing me either."

"Don't be silly. I'd love a lift. I just didn't want to

inconvenience you on a busy Friday night."

"Where's he takin' you?" Thelma asked. "I know. The Coconut Grove. It's in the Ambassador Hotel. Every movie star in Hollywood goes there."

"Or the Brown Derby. That's just across the street," Myra added. "Or The Pig 'N Whistle by the Egyptian Theater."

"I'm not exactly sure where he's taking me," I admitted. "He just told me to get dressed up."

Thelma sighed. "That's sure swell. You're so lucky. My heart's poundin' from just thinkin' about you goin' out with such a handsome movie star. Promise you'll remember every little thing so you can tell us all about it tomorrow. Like the songs the band plays. What everybody wears. What movie stars show up. And what they eat and drink."

I grinned. Lately, I never felt very lucky. But tonight, just for a little while, maybe my luck had changed. Then Harriet waddled into the room in a ratty terry–cloth robe which looked as if it had been blue once but was now a muddy grey. "Brown Derby, huh?" she said, giving me a challenging once–over. "Is his wife goin', too?"

"His wife?" Thelma asked, as if she'd just heard I tortured kittens.

"You finished with Uncle Suds already?" Lorena cut in, marching back into the kitchen in a pretty blue dress.

"Well, he ain't what you'd call a long–term lover," Harriet said.

There were snickers around the table.

"I had Uncle Suds and a quick bath, too," Harriet said, roughly pushing her way in between Georgette and Myra to get a space at the table.

"He's separated," I replied, angry enough to claw the sour smile right off Harriet's ugly mug.

"You may be pretty, Jeri Rose, but you ain't the swiftest apple in the orchard," Harriet added. "I doubt he's gonna give that Mexican broad the heave–ho for you."

My throat felt dry. Harriet and her big mouth. "You mean Uncles Suds isn't married?"

"Good for you, Jeri," Myra said, smiling meanly at Big Harriet.

Minutes later, Lorena's old truck bumped along the hard dirt road. I fidgeted, thinking about the party last week, how Franky had touched me. How his mouth seemed to reach down inside me and fired up my whole being.

Last night in bed, I'd tried to remember the last time I kissed Lex. It felt like a million years ago, though it was actually last November at Mrs. Jankel's Cure Cottage. Right before I left, we'd kissed. But the moment had been pregnant with our fears and sadness. We didn't linger together long because Lex was contagious. And there was no privacy. At any moment a nurse might barge in to take his temperature or issue another order. And there was my horror of leaving him alone in that unfamiliar place, a grim hospital ripe with institutional smells. A place where he might die.

"Should I lock the outside door tonight?" Lorena asked, interrupting my thoughts.

"What?"

"I meant, do you think you're coming home?"

"Don't be silly. I'll be home."

"Hey Cousin, it's 1933. Just be careful to use that sponge like I showed you."

"I won't need that tonight."

"Don't tell me you left it home."

I held up my evening bag. "It's right in here, safe and sound. But if I do sleep with him … don't you think it's too fast?"

"You mean, you'll lose points in the game?" Lorena frowned. "I'm not the one to ask. I don't play games. Life's too short. But then I haven't had much experience with men where money didn't change hands. Or I didn't get my heart broken. Just be careful in case things progress. And don't worry about Big Harriet. I'll set her straight. Even if I have to use my belt to do it."

Five minutes later, Lorena pulled into Dodd's filling station which was practically deserted in the early evening. The sun still hung over the hills to the west. The smell of gasoline and grease overwhelmed the desert scents of eucalyptus, juniper, and sage. Around us, the land was untamed, a mix of wild chaparral, rock formations, tumbleweeds, and scrubby grazing land for horses, cattle, and sheep. It was hard to believe this wilderness, this desert, would become the sprawling San Fernando Valley of the future.

Mr. Dodd and his son were inside the garage talking. Another man, a small Mexican, worked on a car inside a second shack nearby. A forlorn looking restaurant, called Dodd's Country Café and grocery, sat beside the garage. Behind the restaurant, stood Dodd's private house, another tiny shack with a smokestack.

Opening my door, I climbed out. According to my watch, it was almost six. "You don't have to wait. He'll be here any second," I said, trying to calm the raging wasps in my stomach as I stole a last look in my compact.

"Ever heard of a guy standing a gal up? I better wait with you," Lorena said, studying her face in the rearview mirror to make sure her hat covered her head, since she hadn't pulled out her hairstyling implements yet.

"He won't stand me up. And it's Friday night. You have a million things to do."

"I probably should get going. The girls could be scratching each other's eyes out by now. Call me if —"

"There he is," I breathed, seeing the Packard speed down the dirt road, a spray of dust in its wake. I felt my breath catch.

EIGHTEEN

"Where'd you learn to dance?" I asked, impressed by Franky's competent footwork as he held me close and deftly moved me across the Coconut Grove's mobbed dance floor.

"I never did learn, that's the problem."

"Someone must've taught you," I said, laughing.

"Actually, the studio had a school. In '28, when talkies took off, the big shots decided to turn me into a little gentleman. They sent me to class for walking, talking, chewing gum, picking my teeth in public, and dancing. I aced my teeth–picking class but dancing, well, you're a witness to the results."

"I'd say you aced all your classes."

He laughed then his gaze grew intent as he peered into my eyes. His blue eyes were lucid and gentle. A current shot through me. My heart jumped irregularly. Franky Wyatt's career might be in a slump but he still had eyes that could guide aircraft through a typhoon, and a masculine physique that couldn't be camouflaged by a white dinner jacket.

Here in The Coconut Grove, The Ambassador Hotel's famed nightclub, where movie stars and big shots rubbed elbows with the rest of Los Angeles, I fell so hard for Franky Wyatt that I wouldn't have noticed if Charlie Chaplin tried to cut in. I'd meant to cement the details of the evening in my mind so I could share them with the girls back at The Rainbow. But I hadn't expected to be so distracted, so overwhelmed by my feelings for Franky ... or my guilt because of these feelings. Two tables down actress Miriam Hopkins was having supper with friends. Across the room Una Merkel dined with her husband. And a very young Joan Blondell danced beside us. I noted that I had two gin daisies and Franky had several gin highballs.

"Isn't it romantic ... " a tall, slender man crooned.

Now, one song blended into another, a slow song this time. Franky held me close, the movement of his feet and body attentive, direct, and easy to follow. Every inch of me felt alive and uncertain about how the evening would end. The pressure of his calloused hand on mine and the warmth of his breath on my neck sent intoxicating messages through me. I felt uncertain but more alive than I had in months.

Then, without warning, he disengaged. Taking hold of my hand, he led me off the dance floor, through the restaurant with its theatrical design of tropical plants. He abruptly shoved me hard against the wall of a dim alcove. Before I could question his motives, he lifted my chin and covered my mouth with his. The pressure of his lips, the sensation of his tongue probing mine silenced my protests and toppled my inhibitions as he pressed against me. His hard maleness dug into my dress, stirring me to new heights. I clung to him, inflamed by the taste of his hungry lips, the scent of his skin, the steel of his muscles, and the tang of whiskey on his breath. Until the hours between last week and this moment faded to seconds, like fragments of a dream. I wouldn't have protested if he'd lifted my dress, pushed aside my panties, and had me there against the wall. But a moment later, after I'd abandoned my will to resist, he was suddenly wrenched away.

I opened my eyes. And saw the alarm on his face. My heart lurched. *Nicky and Tito*, I thought. But no, hovering menacingly close was a large, silver-haired stranger in a white dinner jacket. Beneath his slim mustache, his lips were curled in anger and his dark eyes blazed with rage.

Before I could demand an explanation, Franky said, "Jeri Rose, meet my father–in–law, Caesar Cardona."

Cardona had the stance of an enraged bull. For several moments I stared up, too stupid to respond. Gathering my wits, I stuck out my hand. "How do you do?"

Caesar Cardona studied me and my outstretched hand as if he'd found a large gray rat flattened on his driveway under the wheels of his car. He turned to Franky and spoke in a heavy accent. "You never could make things easy for yourself, cowboy."

"You got somethin' to say, let's take it outside. But not in front of the lady."

Caesar gave me a contemptuous once–over. "Slow down, cowboy. I will be happy to instruct you in thee proper etiquette soon enough."

"Don't count on it. I'm pretty busy these days. Unless you're after a public scene to drum up publicity for Lupe's latest flop."

Caesar's olive-complected face became an inferno. At that instant, the restaurant captain and a waiter cornered us. "Is something wrong, Señor Cardona?" the captain asked.

Caesar Cardona ignored the question and moved nose–to–nose with Franky. "Watch yourself, cowboy. Or I promise, you will end up washing dishes in thee kitchen here. Good luck, *Miss* Rose." He stalked off.

Mrs. Rose, I thought. Why did everyone assume that every woman in Hollywood was an unwed aspiring actress. Maybe because it was often true. Or because no decent married woman would risk her reputation by kissing a married man in a dark corner of a crowded night club.

Back at our table, the festive mood had gone flat. "Sorry if I've complicated things for you," I said, reaching to touch Franky's hand.

Without looking at me, Franky gulped down the rest of his drink and stood. "Let's go."

Head down, hands stuffed in his pockets, he stormed through the club toward the exit. I trotted after him, anxious to catch up. Outside, an awkward silence settled over us. I tried to make conversation, to ask about the confrontation. But Franky seemed lost in an inner battle. Until I felt totally rejected and everything about me seemed wrong. From my height, to the size of my breasts, to my homemade dress. I saw myself as the world must. I was an unemployed married woman who lived at a brothel.

I absently watched the glamorous parade of men in top hats and dress suits and their magnificent counterparts in clinging satin gowns, fur capes, and opulent jewels, alighting from Cadillacs, Mercedes, Dusenbergs, Auburns, and Hudsons. Then Gary Cooper and Lupe Valez streamed by. And I realized that no one had stopped to greet Franky. To them, he was as invisible as I was.

At last Franky fished a cigarette out of his gold case and held the case open for me.

"No thanks," I said, watching him light up. "Is he always so angry with you?" I asked, determined to break through the uneasy silence.

Franky drew deeply on his cigarette then let the smoke curl out of his nose and mouth. "Angry? For him that was fatherly."

"Look, I know you're married. Remember, I saw you and Lupe together —"

"Not together. Just at the same table. Believe me, Caesar's not one bit concerned about his daughter's happiness. He's worried about the press. He doesn't want anyone getting wind of trouble in his daughter's marriage. Not before her latest picture opens. In case you haven't heard, she's supposed to be irresistible to all men."

In this era, bad press could hurt a picture. In the future, any press, good or bad, made money before a release and added to a star's popularity.

The Packard pulled up. The doorman helped me in. Without a word, Franky steered us down the boulevard. For miles we silently sped past filling stations, the occasional business, and acres of virgin land. I stared out the window, sorry things had been spoiled. Relieved, too, because I had nothing to be ashamed of.

"Does Lupe want you back?" I finally asked.

"She doesn't want me back. But she doesn't want a divorce either. Not when she has this new movie deal pending and her latest film is supposed to be another flop."

"If the picture isn't out yet, how can it be a flop?"

"The script. Her acting. The buzz around town."

"So a divorce is out of the question?"

"If I push for a divorce without Caesar's blessings, *he'll* make sure I never work in Hollywood again. And they'll both make sure I never see my daughter. Even if they have to hide her down in Mexico with the rest of the Cardona clan."

His daughter. How could I compete with such a sacred relationship? Even if I'd wanted to compete, which I didn't. A passionate affair with Franky was one thing. But I hadn't thought ahead about anything permanent. I wasn't ready to abandon Lex yet.

"I moved out of Lupe's house right after I met you," he said. "Most of Hollywood knows my marriage is finished. But the public doesn't. And Lupe doesn't like losing. She wants to be the one to call it quits."

"I suppose she sees other men," I said, remembering how shamefully Lupe acted toward Bobby Peacock back in Havana.

Franky glanced at me. "You're very direct."

"My mother used to think that was a good thing."

A smile crept over his face. "I'd like to meet your mother."

"Sorry. She passed away when I was thirteen." Decades into the future.

"My mom died when I was six. The same age as my little girl. It's a tough age to lose your mother."

"It's tough at any age. You haven't answered my question," I said.

"Lupe likes young boys fresh off the farm. The hungry ones looking for a movie career. To them, she's exotic. To her, they're gullible morons with corn for brains."

"Like you were once?"

"It's easy to get confused by French perfume and satin lingerie when you're used to sleeping in a bunkhouse with ten other guys, and the only females you know wear harnesses and saddles. But one day I realized I'd married a spoiled child. Unfortunately, I'd also married her father. A man I despise."

Franky changed gears at the corner of Beverly Glen, hit the gas hard, then charged up the hill toward Mulholland. The Packard sped over pitted dirt roads, past wild desert terrain, and small houses perched on precipices. Beyond the great hill was the San Fernando Valley and The Rainbow House.

But when the Packard reached the top of Mulholland Drive, Franky slowed to a stop and pulled over to the side. Without the engine grinding, the night became shockingly quiet with only a dog barking in the distance to remind me that civilization existed a few hills away. We listened to the dog and the cicadas. We studied the stars and filled our lungs with the cool night air. A fragrant air filled with the scents of dried grass and earth. Below, the San Fernando Valley glistened with lights, though the tiny communities such as Encino and North Hollywood were barren wastelands compared to what they'd become after World War II.

"Look, I'm sorry. I shouldn't have taken you there," he confessed.

"Why did you?"

"Should I hide you? Sneak you into a dark movie theater? Or act ashamed of what we're doing?"

"No, but The Coconut Grove is such a famous spot —"

"I didn't know Caesar would be there. Anyway, I'm working on this picture deal for Paramount in New York. With any luck, I'll be beyond his reach in a few weeks."

"Why's everyone so afraid of Caesar Cardona? His studio is on poverty row, and he only does low budget pictures."

"Caesar knows everyone in town. And he's vengeful. Never lets a slight go unanswered. And his movies make dough. I started my career at his studio." A long pause followed this outburst. Then, without warning, Franky reached for my hand. "Sorry about tonight, Jeri. I'll make it up to you. I promise."

Taking my hand, he gently kissed my palm. But he didn't stop there. He began to kiss my fingers, too. His touch was light, his breath was warm, and as his lips gently drew on each finger, pulling on them, kissing them, until goose bumps raced up my arms. The feel of his lips gently grazing my knuckles and palm made my insides tingle and grow ripe with a rising need. Franky had obviously gotten high marks in seduction, too.

Then, without a word, he let go of my hand, opened his door, and alighted from the car. He eased off his jacket, neatly folded it, then placed it over his seat. Standing at the edge of the mountain with his body outlined by the dim light, he stretched. He had powerful arms and shoulders, a small waist, and taut round buttocks beneath his trousers. He briefly gazed into the night. Then he slowly turned to face me. I had a fleeting thought that he was posing for me. That he understood his physical perfection and his power to seduce women with his remarkable looks. Lex was beautiful, too. But here stood a performer, a man who had once thrived on the admiration of millions.

"Step out here for a minute," he said.

"No thanks. I'm not wild about heights."

"I won't let you fall."

Chilled by nerves and the gusty winds which surged through the high hills, I clutched Lorena's fur wrap around me and climbed from the car to join Franky.

"Some view," he said, enfolding me in his arms from behind and warming me with his body.

"Nothing to what it will be one day."

"Better head back now," he said, dropping his arms, leaving me breathless and confused. Was this a game to him? Part of a plan to turn me on, then drop me like a lump of cold coal. Fine, I thought. Let him play his silly games. I wanted no part of his complicated life. I didn't need to cheat on Lex.

Back in the car, the engine roared to life. Soon, we were zooming down the hill, twisting and turning around tight corners as we sped through the dark with the engine grinding and the wind whipping through our hair. At the bottom of the hill, Franky abruptly swung the car off the main street onto a dark road, a mule path through the wild chaparral.

"Is something wrong with the car —" I began.

Franky cut the engine and reached for me. His mouth overwhelmed mine as his tongue penetrated my lips, driving deeply into my mouth, as his bruising eagerness smothered my complaints. I meant to pull away, to deny him. But the longing in my loins betrayed me.

Since last week, and even before then, I'd imagined making love to Franky. Tonight, on the dance floor, I'd filled my nostrils with the scent of his flesh, rejoiced in the iron of his strong arms and firm hands which gripped me. At the top of Mulholland , I accepted the truth, that it was only a matter of time before I succumbed. Now, as his mouth roamed over my throat and his hands slipped around me, reaching for my buttons and zipper, I stood back mentally and watched us. He was good. He undid my buttons in seconds before guiding my dress and chemise down to my waist. He was even faster with my brassiere, pulling it down and plundering my breasts as he tossed my bra into the car's backseat, leaving me exposed and chilled in the night air. He stared down at me, his expression unreadable in the dark. I shivered, feeling vulnerable as his mouth wandered over my breasts. Until his teeth sought out my nipples which grew harder than thimbles stirred by a sense of pain and desire.

I groaned.

Now, he put his weight against me and crushed me against the seat. I gasped as his other hand reached under my dress, rushed up my thigh to my garters, then searched between my legs.

Stop that, I thought, as his blunt, calloused fingers roamed beneath my silk panties. But I didn't shout or fight him. Instead, I seemed to stand apart from myself and observe the scene. I felt his lips glide across my stomach. And his gentle fingers stroke the area between my legs. From afar, I saw myself: breasts exposed, nipples hard, my new dress bunched up by my waist, legs splayed out, stockings down, panties open to his touch. The car quaked as he unbuckled his belt then fumbled with his pants. Which was the moment when reality spurred me into action.

No, I thought. *Not like this*. Not in a car. I wouldn't be treated like some dumb starlet. Like all Franky had to do was ply me with a few flattering words, a drink or two, and a garbled picture of the future before I betrayed my husband. With a rush of energy, I shoved him off me. "No. Stop. I can't do this."

Franky froze. His breathing sounded hard, irregular. "Jeri, please." He tried to tug me down, but I resisted.

"No, I can't do this," I barked, shoving him harder.

He withdrew. Leaning back against his seat, he let out his breath. Cold and ashamed, I fumbled with my things, feeling undignified as I dug for my bra and my chemise and struggled to dress. Using my compact, I managed a fast repair job on my hair and lipstick. Franky didn't look at me. Instead, he climbed out of the car and stood smoking.

When I finished, Franky held out his gold cigarette case to me. "Want one?"

"No thanks. I gave them up."

Exhaling smoke, he studied me. No doubt my hair looked like a haystack. My lipstick was on crooked, and my face was red having been rubbed raw by the stubble from his beard.

"Take a ride with me," he said softly, his hand gently reaching for mine.

"Thanks, but I'm tired. Maybe another time."

"Come on. It's not even ten. Come back to my place. Have supper with me. Meet my horses."

Horses? Was this a euphemism for etchings?

Instead of waiting for my answer, he dropped back into the drivers' seat, gunned the engine, and pulled onto the main road. Then we sped down the hill to the valley.

"Do you need directions to my place?" I shouted over the engine's roar.

Franky stared at me intently. The defiant glint in his blue eyes indicated he had other plans.

NINETEEN

Lupe Cardona's new driver Dennis swung the big Lincoln onto the dirt driveway and pulled into the Sunshine Bungalow Colony in Santa Monica. Lupe watched the back of his fat head under his black cap, hating him. She hated his haircut, the way his scalp showed through the stiff bristles, the way his ears stuck out. She hated his voice and the ruddy color of his skin. Even the shape of his fat piggy nose enraged her. Worse, Dennis, a nobody from Ohio or Omaha, was judgmental. The last three times he'd brought her here, he'd had a very annoying expression on his face. As if he, a lowly fat man, could judge her just because she happened to be meeting her lover at 9:30 at night, at a dirty bungalow colony by the beach.

She climbed out and purposely slammed the car door behind her – just before her white satin heels sank into the mud.

God this place was a dump. If only she and Boyd didn't have to sneak around. If only Boyd would propose so she could divorce Franky and marry him. She hadn't pushed Boyd hard yet because he seemed a tiny bit reluctant. Scared even. Like he was afraid of Franky and her father. So she'd made a special effort to look her best tonight. She'd worn her new white fox furs, a peach satin gown that hid nothing, and her highest heels. Too bad the shoes were like knives on her feet. Even after she'd told the stupid sales girl that she wore a size three, it felt like the girl hade given her a size one. Her large pearl earrings pinched, too. Well, she'd have to endure the pain because she was sure they made her look younger.

Tonight, everything must be perfect. She had to be glamorous enough to get Boyd to propose.

"Wait for me around thee corner," she growled to Dennis through the open window.

"Beg your pardon, madam."

"Are you deaf? I want you to wait for me around thee corner. Now get going."

"As you wish, madam."

What was that look he'd given her? A sneer? Well, he'd be sorry tomorrow. No matter what her papa said, Dennis had to go – with his Idaho accent – or was it Oklahoma?

Alone, she peered at the alley between a long line of white adobe bungalows. Now which bungalow had Boyd rented tonight? Number two. Yes, it was number two. Or was that last night? Damn it, these little hell holes all looked alike.

She hurried up to the window of the first, feeling her new satin shoes sinking into the dirt. But when she peered through the window, a frumpy house wife was making dinner in the tiny kitchen and a fat man in an undershirt, ragged shorts, socks, and garters sat on the sofa reading the newspaper. Meaning Boyd wasn't waiting for her in bungalow two.

Well, there were only twelve or eighteen bungalows in the whole place. It shouldn't be too hard to find him. But she could feel her make–up getting moist from the ocean air. If she arrived sweating, it would ruin the effect. Now where in the world was Boyd? She had no luck when she peered into the next three cottages. In fact, a lady drying herself off in a bathroom had seen her peering through the window and screamed her head off. Lupe had been forced to make a run for it. She'd finally hidden behind another bungalow and waited until the woman stopped shrieking. Lupe had been so upset, she'd needed to take a good long swig from the silver flask in her purse just to steady her nerves.

Desperate, she decided to stop in at the rental office. She'd never met Mr. Peters, the owner, but Boyd did a brilliant imitation of him. It was one reason she'd promised to find Boyd work in her next picture – providing Boyd behaved like a good boy.

Now, she hurried toward the neon sign above the first building that read *Office*. She was already an hour late for their rendevous, and Boyd might've spent too much time with a liquor bottle. And she was definitely in the mood for romance. She'd been dreaming about it all day. Even down at the studio while she was having her picture taken for a magazine, she'd thought of Boyd's kisses and that special way he touched her.

Hating to soil her new white gloves, she reached for the grimey office door handle. Entering the hot little room, she was annoyed to find another couple standing before the registration desk. The woman was big and wore one of those cheap two dollar dresses and a hideous old hat. An awful little man, who looked as if he hadn't shaved or bathed in days, waited beside her. Worse, they both had awful teeth. Lupe imagined they ate dirty vegetables and strained them through their teeth. She was so disgusted by them that she pulled out her perfumed handkerchief and held it over her nose.

It seemed that the woman had a bad leg and couldn't limp far and needed a bungalow up front. "Well, Pappy, what do you think? Should we take number six or number three?" the big woman asked the man.

"Anything you say, Mother. As long as it's got hot and cold running water and a working kitchen. I'm okay with either one of 'em. Now how much for three nights?"

"That'll be two dollars and twenty–five cents."

"Okay with you, Mother?" the man asked the big woman.

"Look, if you no mind," Lupe interrupted, holding the lace cloth to her nose. "I am in thee big hurry, and I must get thee information before it is time for my breakfast. So, you must forgive me."

The couple and Mr. Waters studied her as if seeing a ghost.

"I must find thee bungalow with Mr. Boyd Anderson," she said to Mr. Peters, a tall skinny man with big ears and a big nose. "You must know thee number, *si*?"

"My stars. Ain't you Lupe Cardona?" The fat wife exclaimed.

"Lupe is my sister," Lupe lied, making sure the handkerchief covered most of her face.

Mr. Peters eyed her skeptically, his lip riding up under his nose, exactly like Boyd's imitations. "Boyd Anderson, ya say?" Mr. Peters opened a book, ran his stained finger down a list, and frowned.

"Oh, no, no. I mean, Bill Anderson. Is his real name."

"Here it is. That'd be number eight. Around to the rear."

"Thank you *very* much."

It took Lupe another five minutes of sinking in mud holes and running into overhanging branches to find the ratty little building which turned out to be way in the back off a dark alley.

Lupe felt her nerves bottling up in her throat as she suppressed the urge to scream. Boyd was an idiot. How dare he drag her out to this rat hole when he could so easily propose, so they could be ensconced in her house. But no, Boyd was playing hard to get. Well, he better not play hard to get tonight.

At last she arrived at bungalow eight. She tried the door but found it locked. She knocked sharply but didn't get an answer. She knocked again but still got no answer. Furious, she began to bang and screech his name. Faces peered out of windows until she had to stop.

After all, she didn't need the press to hear about this.

In the end, she found the back window open. And there was Boyd snoring away on the bed, wearing just his shorts. A single light bulb glared down from the ceiling. And an empty whiskey bottle sat on the night stand,

"Boyd," Lupe growled, keeping her voice low. "Boyd?" She'd kill him when she got inside. But the doors were locked. Only the window was open. At least it didn't have a screen. But she hadn't considered the rose bushes, the wet soil, or her long dress and furs.

It took her ten minutes to get in. She ended up stripping off her stockings, after getting raked by thorns. Then she had to take off her shoes and tie her dress up around her hips, after she wrapped her furs around a tree limb. She arrived soaked in sweat. She could've murdered Boyd, who lay in a stupor across the bed, too pickled on booze to wake up. She was so angry, she slapped him hard across the face several times. And though he reacted by grunting and groaning, he refused to wake up.

She considered limping back to her fat driver Dennis and making him take her home. But she couldn't face the smug look on his face. So Lupe wrapped herself in Boyd's coat and fell asleep on the filthy sofa.

TWENTY

We reached Franky's house, *Casa Las Lunas* around
ten–thirty. The sprawling one story had been designed around a
courtyard where a tiled fountain spouted water and a hitching post
stood outside the front door. Beyond the house a thousand acres
stretched across the desert where ranch hands tended Franky's cattle,
horses, and citrus groves. Maybe it was the massive size of the house,
the splendid Spanish architecture, or the knowledge that Lupe
Cardona had probably designed every inch of its dark interior which
intimidated me. The decor, with its bulky furnishings, black iron
accents, stucco walls, and huge swimming pool out back, reminded
me of San Simeon, known as the Hearst Castle, the current residence
of newspaper mogul William Randolf Hearst and his mistress, actress
Marion Davies.

While Franky's cook made us a late supper, Franky showed
me around his house and his stables, where the familiar smell of
manure, hay, and leather reminded me of my childhood riding days.

"This is Josie," he said, rubbing a pinto's nose.

"How often do you ride her?" I asked.

"Every day, if I can." He moved down the line of stalls. "This
is her daughter, Eula." One by one, Franky introduced me to his
horses.

"Where's Fuerte?" I asked, referring to the horse he rode throughout his film career.

"Glue factory, I guess," he said, rubbing another horse's nose. "Fuerte belonged to the studio. But I rode him for years in pictures. His sister, too. The public couldn't tell the difference."

Franky was relaxed here, sharing the best of his world with me. I admired this other person in his faded jeans and worn flannel shirt. Clothes he'd changed into right after we arrived. Clearly, he felt more at ease here in his home.

"Anybody ever tell you, you oughta be in pictures?" he abruptly said.

"Sure, I can be the next Shirley Temple."

"Who?"

"I meant Constance Bennet." In 1933, the curly–haired child star Shirley Temple hadn't made her name yet.

"I'm serious, Jeri. You might very well be the most beautiful woman I've ever met."

It sounded like a line right out of a 1933 western, where the guy in the white hat pushes his faithful mount aside so he can lean in and plant one on the city girl's lips. Okay, I was flattered. But I wasn't batting my eyelashes and gazing up at him like some dumb pushover, even if I did enjoy his praise. I waited for Franky to make the anticipated move. Instead, he picked up the lantern and headed back down the aisle of stalls and outside to the main house. I followed, wondering what he had in mind. Because he'd changed tactics again.

No doubt he'd figured out that I needed a slower approach. Since a gallop had spooked me, he'd chosen an easy lope down a gentle trail with occasional stops along the way to show me the views. But I wasn't fooled. Franky meant to seduce me. And much as I hated to admit it, he'd probably succeed. Providing I didn't get thrown. Because I'd never felt lonelier. Because Lex hadn't written or given me a single word of encouragement in months. And because I'd discovered that I was a woman with strong desires, no matter how much I wanted to be a loyal wife. And because, other than Lex, I'd never been more attracted to anyone in my life.

TWENTY-ONE

Lex's hands flew across the ivory keys as he followed the notes on the battered sheet music. "I'm always chasing rainbows," he sang.

This song always brought back memories of his first day here last November when he and Jeri danced to the tune downstairs in the front parlor. Now it was April and still cold outside. He knew exactly how cold because the nurses made sure his windows were always open. After months of bed rest, he was allowed to bathe himself in a real tub, eat downstairs with the rest of the patients, read, listen to the radio, and play this old piano in the upstairs hall.

"Mr. Rose! Time to get back in bed. The doctor is here to make rounds," Nurse Bronson abruptly barked in a voice dissonant enough to kill a cardiac patient. She wore her usual disapproving scowl as she marched in and tried to drop the piano top on his fingers before she reached to feel his forehead. "You're warm. It's back to bed rest for you," she said, almost cheerfully.

"Did anybody ever tell you, you could charm birds from the trees?"

She frowned, making her face even uglier, if possible.

"Don't worry, they won't," he said, pushing out the piano stool and standing. He was sick of being a good boy. Sick to death of his room, including the view out his window. And the feeling that death sat right outside his door every night and enjoyed a good laugh at his expense. Because he hated the relentless regimen of cold air, pounds of bland food, unending glasses of rich milk, and husky nurses with facial hair who could wrestle a patient to the floor with one hand tied behind their backs. Nancy, the only pretty nurse, had moved to a bigger clinic.

Outside, during the hours of bed rest, he imagined how he would breakout. He pictured himself slipping out after the two a.m. bed check, carrying his shoes, and tiptoeing down the stairs and out the front door. Or he'd tie his sheets together and climb out his window. Then he'd hitch a ride to the station, board a train going south to New York, and disappear. Because he'd rather be dead than spend another year here where the isolation devoured all hope.

Back in his bed, Lex waited for Dr. Bergman. The young doctor, a new member of his medical team, had a mild case of TB, too, the reason he was up here in the mountains helping patients like Lex. For the last few days, during his second month of freedom, Lex had felt his fever coming back. He hadn't reported his night sweats because being out of his room with other patients felt too good to give up. Nowadays, he found the company of just about anybody as rewarding as good jazz music, French pastries, and a beautiful woman in an evening gown.

Dr. Bergman strode quietly into the room. His white lab coat hung loosely on his slight shoulders. "Afternoon, Mr. Rose."

"Lex, call me Lex."

Dr. Bergman smiled, his gentle green eyes sympathetic. "I always forget. Okay, Lex. Let's listen to your chest."

After the usual prodding and poking, Dr. Bergman pulled up the hard extra chair, sat, and scribbled across a page then clipped it to his board. "I'm afraid your fever is back. It's not bad for now, but you haven't gained any weight these last few weeks. So I'm going to put you on complete bed rest again."

At least Bergman, unlike the other doctors, didn't candy–coat the truth with questions like, "How're you feeling?" And, "Would you like to visit the clinic?"

As if he'd jump up and down and shout, "Goody, another trip to the clinic."

Unfortunately, the diagnosis meant he'd be shackled to his bed again, treated as if brushing his teeth was heavy exertion. He would eat, sleep, and bathe in his bed. At moments like this, he understood why grown men cried.

"I'm also recommending another series of *pneumothorax*. It shouldn't hurt and it will ease your discomfort."

"I don't feel any discomfort. I hardly even cough anymore."

"I know this is discouraging. But bed rest, good food, fresh air, and these procedures are the only weapons we have. One day soon …" Dr. Bergman's eyes conveyed sympathy. "I really would like to see you hiking through the hills tomorrow. But for now, I can't recommend it."

"What happens? I mean, what will you do to me?"

"The same as before. Gas in your lungs. It'll take about forty–five minutes. First we'll anesthetize the area and then put a thin needle in and you won't even feel it."

"You won't take out my ribs?"

"Not this time. That's a more permanent solution called a *thoracoplasty* where we permanently remove ribs to permanently collapse your lung. I know the other doctors have considered it, but I'm a bit more conservative."

"Guess I'm pretty far gone, huh?"

"No, you've improved these last few months. This is a minor set back. But we want you well."

The sentiment was nice but Lex doubted he'd be alive much longer. Either the Desanto brothers would find him, or he'd die from consumption. He'd rather be dead anyway than spend years in this place.

"Wouldn't you like to go home and be with your wife?" Dr. Bergman asked.

Lex studied Jeri's latest photograph on his night table. She'd sent him the picture a few months ago. In it she stood against a palm tree, smiling. But the picture didn't capture her beauty: her blue eyes, sensuous body, and glorious skin. And the word *home* had no meaning now either. His beautiful house on Riverside Drive had been sold to strangers.

Once he'd had the world by the tail. Now, he was stuck in bed on a Friday night. And when the lights went out at nine, he would wait, hoping not to hear a cup banging, a plea from some sick patient for help. He would pray that he and his fellow patients, his friends, made it through the night. That a hearse wasn't waiting downstairs out his window in the morning.

"Yes, I would like to go home someday," he finally said.

TWENTY-TWO

"Feel like a swim?" Franky asked, after dinner.

"The water's way too cold for me. You go in. I'll watch," I said.

We'd moved outside to his pool with a bottle of champagne. Sipping from an elegant glass, I tried not to spill any on my dress.

"I won't be long. Just a dip to cool off," he said, stepping out of his beach shoes and terrycloth robe before doing a perfect dive into the water, heedless of the frigid temperature.

Lying on the chaise longue, I surveyed the stars. Somehow, the nights seemed clearer in 1933 than in the future.

Franky swam laps. After about a dozen, he climbed out, wrapped a towel around his waist then stood dripping wet beside me. His body was even closer to physical perfection than I'd imagined from his broad shoulders and steel biceps, to his rock hard abdomen, and runner's legs. Even his well–formed chest was lushly covered in hair. Without asking, he dropped down beside me on my chaise and gazed at the sky. "Look at those stars. I love the valley. The wildness of it. Miles of open land and open skies."

We both silently stared into the darkness. Yet I couldn't ignore the closeness of his body. The sound of his breathing. And the pressure of his thigh against my own. My pulse raced. I waited, convinced he meant to make a move. Instead, he reached for his wine glass. When he finished the contents, he went back to star gazing. This languid approach unnerved me. I had no idea what to expect. Yes, I'd clearly rejected him earlier. Did that mean he'd decided to back off for the night, for good, or was he gearing up for a fresh assault?

"Getting cold out," I finally said to break the silence.

He faced me. His blue–eyed gaze caressed me all over me, stirring my insides. Without a word, he leaned toward me, took the champagne glass from my hand, and placed it on a glass side table. Then, without a word, he kissed me. The kiss was slow, gentle. His lips were cold from his swim but his tongue was fiery, warm enough to melt glass. He smelled of chlorine and water, of champagne and the fragrant night air. Changing positions, he moved closer until I reacted to his damp body pressed against mine and the underlying heat pouring off him. I felt his chest against my breasts. And his excitement beneath his swimsuit, that hard evidence that he wanted more than a walk through his stables. We lay there embraced, our lips searching, hungering, united. Running my hands over the smooth flesh on his back, I felt the network of hard muscles beneath his satiny skin.

"Jeri," he murmured, his hands on my shoulders, as his mouth drifted down my neck and he nibbled delicately on my throat.

His gentle kisses sent waves of desire through me. The mix of wine, cool night air, and a full stomach relaxed me, melting my resistance. Until the sensation of his hand roaming between my legs felt right. Until my own needs matched his own greedy ones, which swept through me, stirring a need for a release inside me. Without warning, he withdrew from me and stood. Then he tenderly guided me down on the lounge chair. I lay flat on my back, vulnerable and submissive. He began to remove my shoes.

"What're you doing?" I asked.

"Making you more comfortable."

Leaning on my elbows, I watched him as his warm mouth moved across my ankles, a mere sprinkling of light touches, as his lips climbed up my calf, arriving behind my knees. His efforts tickled but felt oddly good. He quickly undid my stockings, releasing my garters. It felt oddly freeing, pleasurable. Tired and giddy from the champagne, I shut my eyes and enjoyed his gentle ministrations. I waited, too, wondering how far up his lips would go. I wasn't afraid now. My resistance and reasons for saying no had gone up in champagne bubbles.

A moment later, he rose again. I watched him slide his wet trunks down his muscled legs till the suit dropped to the concrete revealing all of his remarkable body. And proving how much he wanted me.

I shut my eyes as he moved beside me then carefully climbed over me, his warm body covering mine. I felt joy in the bruising feel of his mouth on mine, the warm wetness of his tongue as it touched my own, and the feel of his hand kneading my breast. In the budding moments of Saturday morning, in the dark beside his pool, when my reservations had dropped to the ground beside his bathing trunks, my future and my past lost their relevance as my hunger for him engulfed me.

Under that brilliant California night sky, Franky Wyatt made love to me. I was vaguely aware when my panties floated to the concrete floor, when I felt his warm tongue, a magical instrument probe deeply, gently, yet provocatively between my thighs, igniting desires inside me. From a distance I wondered when I'd consented to this intimacy. An intimacy I'd only shared with Lex before tonight. Somehow, my body's pleasure overrode the critic in my head. A critic who usually weighed and examined my every move. I'd become an army of impulses and raw nerves, a sexual river driven by the tides of need and wild abandon. There was only the occasional glimpse of Franky's soft blond hair and my own throaty moans. Then, like an unbridled stream of pure energy, I arched my back as waves of a primal force, which felt like a mountain splitting in half, broke through me. I felt a rush, an urgent release, like liquid gold.

Franky pulled away, a half–smile on his tanned face. I was vaguely aware that my legs were apart. That I lay completely naked and exposed. I tried to sit. But an abrupt wave of nausea hit me. "Gosh, my head. I feel … "

Before I could finish, Franky pushed me down flat again. His face was a blur as he straddled me, thrusting himself inside me with a violent lurch. He rode me harshly, his face a mask of pleasure as I clutched his back. Until at last, he froze, shuddered, then rolled off me.

Without warning, the queasy feeling became overwhelming and unbearable.

"Want some more champagne?" he asked, his voice sounding far away, as swirls of cigarette smoke snaked their way from his nose and mouth.

"No, I … I feel sick. I'm going to …Is there a sink or a —"

He pointed. "Bathroom's straight ahead inside the *casita*."

I spied the doorway to a bungalow a few feet away. Snatching my dress, I held it to me as I managed to stand. Using the lounge chair to steady myself, I lurched toward the tiny bungalow. I shoved the *casita*'s door open and groped for the light switch. At last, I found the bathroom where I heaved into the commode. All thoughts of modesty and morality vanished. Minutes later, by leaning against the cold sink, I was able to stand. My pale face appeared before me in the mirror. And the sponge soaked in vinegar, meant to protect me, still waited in my purse, back inside Franky's living room. I tried to recall how I'd ended up here, drunk, and corrupted. Maybe it was the champagne. Then I hung my head over the toilet again and emptied out my stomach.

After, in the sink, I washed out my mouth and doused my face with cold water. I finally stumbled from the bathroom into the dark little room.

Franky slept on top of the blanket on the single bed. My new dress lay in a heap on a hard dark wood chair. My shoes and a lone stocking had been tossed on top of them. I suddenly longed for my room at the brothel. Taking Franky by the arm, I shook him several times. But he just growled to leave him alone. Cold and exhausted, with the threat of a painful headache, I crawled in beside him and passed out.

***

The bed shook. I stirred, feeling as if my throat and head were on fire. I was on my back, naked and cold. A tanned shoulder leaned into me. I glanced over at Franky. A lank of hair hung over his forehead. With a start, he made a noise and bolted awake. Rubbing his face, he observed me as if we'd never met before. He instantly rolled away, sat up, and reached for a cigarette.

"Want one?" He held out the pack to me.

My mouth felt like a desert. "No thanks. What time is it?"

"Around nine, I guess." With a sigh, he planted his feet on the floor, stood, and stretched. I couldn't help noticing the two perfect globes of his backside, the well–toned legs, and trim waist which rose up to his muscled back and broad shoulders.

"Got a lot to do today," he said glumly.

"That champagne really went to my head," I said, aware that whatever connection we'd had last night had faded.

"Me, too," he said flatly.

Not hostile, but not welcoming either. I covered myself with the sheet and stood. "I better get going."

He sighed. "Sorry, if I seem ... I've got a lot on my mind. I'll have Wolfie bring you some breakfast." He flashed me something less than his usual dazzling grin.

Somewhere a telephone rang. Swearing softly, Franky grabbed a towel off the bathroom rack and wrapped it around his waist. Without a word or a backward glance, he trudged barefoot outside. I retrieved my dress off the terra cotta floor and headed toward the bathroom. Then I heard Franky arguing with someone on the telephone. Dismissing a stab of guilt, I tiptoed to the open door and listened.

" ... and I told you I'd pay as soon as I got this picture deal, didn't I? Then don't make threats you can't – hey, you know I'm good for it. Do I need to remind you who I am? And who I'm connected to? Yeah, well, see that you do." He banged down the receiver. A second later, there was a loud splash and a shout.

Clutching my dress, I stuck my head out the door. Birds chirped and the sun was already bleaching the land. Peering through the limbs of a cactus plant, I caught a glimpse of Franky doing laps in his unheated pool, which had to be freezing this early in the day.

In the bungalow's bathroom, under a grim yellow bulb, I wrapped my hair in a towel and jumped into the shower. Afterward, I cleaned my teeth in the sink using my finger. Back in the bedroom, I slipped on my dress and faced myself in the mirror. For an instant, I imagined Margaret Maitland's horrified look if she saw me now. Never mind black lingerie. Here I was, wandering out of a married man's bungalow the morning after, wearing last night's dress without underwear, with my nipples visible through the material.

Outside, the air was fresh and cool. But in a few hours the heat would turn the dessert into a gigantic oven. Barefoot, I followed the stone path through the trees to the pool. My purse, garter belt, bra, and other stocking had been neatly placed on a lounge chair, no doubt by some discreet servant. In the pool, Franky powered through the water doing laps. A few yards away, the Mexican gardener clung to a ladder and pruned a tree. I settled onto last night's lounge chair and watched Franky swim. Based on his phone conversation, he had money problems, too.

An Asian man in a crisp white jacket appeared with a silver tray loaded with coffee, toast, butter, and jam. He placed it on the table under an umbrella. "Would you like eggs or cereal, Miss?" he asked.

"No, coffee's fine." I filled a cup, nibbled on a slice of toast, anxious to see how Franky treated a woman after he'd seduced her. A sick anxiety filled my stomach. I'd never cheated on Lex. And I wasn't prepared for rejection. Even in the future, I'd never slept around. A few moments later, Franky emerged naked from the water. He grabbed a fresh towel off the stack by the outside bar and stepped toward me.

"Come here, gorgeous," he said, pulling me to my feet as if I would instantly melt into his arms. Ignoring my cool reaction, he planted a wet kiss on my lips. He smelled of chlorine. "Feel like a swim?"

"No, I —"

"I probably have another bathing suit for you in the *casita*."

"No, I – I should get going. I have things to do."

Without warning, he grabbed me, lifted me up in his strong arms, and held me over the water.

"Let me go!" I shrieked, laughing, relieved to know he wasn't dying to see the back of me.

At last, he set me down. "Now be a good girl and have breakfast. I'll be right back." He sprinted toward the main house and disappeared inside.

At least I no longer felt like yesterday's oatmeal.

But during the half–hour drive back to The Rainbow House, as we sped over country roads, Franky stared straight ahead with his jaw tight and his expression tense. With the top down and hot dry wind whipping through my hair, I quickly fell asleep and woke to feel someone shaking me.

"Jeri? Jeri, wake up."

"Lex?" I gazed up confused to see Franky's face looming over me. Then I saw we were parked outside The Rainbow, and my whole life slid into place.

"Sorry, but I'm in kind of a hurry," he said, as I slowly climbed from his car and gently slammed the door.

Leaning over, he kissed me softly on the lips. "Thanks for a terrific time. I'm off to New York for a couple of weeks. Call you when I get back." Then he put his car in gear and sped off.

Standing in the car's dust under a blazing sun, I watched the Packard climb a small rise then disappear over the ridge. I wondered how Franky knew I lived at The Rainbow since I'd never told him. Or how long it would be before I stopped holding my breath every time the brothel's phone rang. Because a hollow feeling filled my stomach knowing my affair with Franky seemed to have ended as abruptly as it began.

Inside, the front parlor was already hot. Fanning themselves with magazines, Myra and Big Harriet played a card game called patience. Between the heat, the musty smell of old wood, booze, and perfume the house felt suffocating. The third floor would be hotter, staler. Out of habit, I glanced at the side table by the staircase in case, by some miracle, there was a letter from Lex. But the table was empty.

Diedre sat on the staircase painting her nails. She gave me her big southern grin. "Hi, honey. Did ya hear? Some of the gals are goin' skinny dippin' in a swimmin' hole. Wish I could go, too. But I got that rich young city boy comin' in at three. You should see this kid. All arms and legs with the biggest darn ears. But he promised me a bottle of real French perfume. I just hope he remembers," she said, blowing on her nails.

Today, I would gladly change places with Diedre, a pretty young girl who didn't mind sleeping with men for money.

"Is Lorena around?" I asked.

"Gee, honey, I ain't sure."

Racing up the three flights, I was drenched in perspiration by the time I staggered down the hall to my room. Inside, I slipped off my dress, dragged out a robe and slippers, then thumped on the wall for Jimmy. Unfortunately, he didn't return my signal. He was probably at the post office mailing a manuscript to his publisher or tending bar at a nearby saloon for extra money.

Back downstairs in the kitchen, Elvira, the housekeeper and cook, sat at the kitchen table shelling peas.

"Is Lorena around?" I asked.

"Miss Lorena went to get supplies. You stayin' for supper?"

"Guess so."

Elvira studied me. "Saturday night and you ain't seein' your young man?"

"No, not tonight." An awful headache began to throb behind my temple. And a combination of exhaustion and edginess left me too overwrought to sleep. "Is there any iced tea?"

"Help yourself. I fixed it with plenty of lemon and sugar."

I peered into the massive old refrigerator, a restaurant model Lorena had picked up for a song when the restaurant closed after the stock market crashed. I could've stood by that open door all day, it felt so refreshing.

"He be like all the others," Elvira abruptly said.

"What?"

"Your man friend." She gave me an understanding glance. "It'll be okay, honey. You'll see. Anyway, Lorena told me she'd be back at six. Meantime, tonight is a cold supper. We don't dare light up that stove in this heat. We might even shut down the water heater. Miss Lorena's afraid it might explode."

I wanted to bury my face in Elvira's massive bosom and cry like a baby. Instead, I said, "Thanks Elvira." I headed toward the back door. I meant to find a little shade outside to go with my cool drink.

"He ain't the only pebble on the beach," Elvira added, as I opened the screen door.

"No, but he's the one I have in my head now."

"A girl with your looks could have anybody."

Changing my mind, I slid onto the long wooden bench opposite Elvira. "If that's true, why can't I have him?"

"Maybe he's the wrong one. Maybe he ain't got a soul. Or he can't tell right from wrong."

I felt tears well up for a half–dozen reasons. For all the sick people at Mrs. Jankel's Cure Cottage. For all the poor people on the road. For the coyotes and bobcats killed by ranchers. For the downtrodden whores here at The Rainbow. I even felt sorry for Franky for not being a top star anymore. Mostly, I felt ashamed for being so disloyal to Lex and so typically female. A little sex with Franky and *wham* – I was besotted, lost in my memories from the night before. Desperate for approval from a man I hardly knew. I hated myself for being so predictable and pathetic.

"Now, it ain't all that bad," Elvira said, wiping her hands on her apron, before reaching for me, pulling me into her broad arms and holding me. "You cry it out, honey. You most likely tired, is all. No sleep. That's the problem with half the girls here. They don't get enough rest."

Sniffling, feeling better, I wiped my nose with a towel Elvira handed me. Then I stared into Elvira's kind face. "I bet you've done this plenty, working here. Consoling the girls, I mean."

"Lots of gals here need a hug and a shoulder to cry on. They find a man and believe he's gonna save 'em. He's gonna' be the one to take 'em away from all this. But we all gotta save ourselves. We gotta find our truth and be the best we can be. Especially when a girl be as different as you."

"Different? Why am I so different?"

"A girl as smart as you. Pretty as you. She gonna find the world hard. Too many choices. Too many men with one thing on their minds. You'll wise up one day."

"Think so?"

"Best you do before you leave this here earth. But first, you need some babies while you still young."

I hadn't thought about having a baby in a long time, since Lex went to prison. "I used to be all business and I never even bothered with men." *Back in the future.*

"You sure changed."

I laughed.

Elvira did, too. "See, you feelin' better already."

"Thanks Elvira." I picked up my drink and headed outside, wishing I had a swimming pool like Franky's, and a thick white terrycloth robe, too.

I fell asleep in the old hammock under an ancient oak tree and woke to the rumble of Lorena's old Ford truck chugging up the dirt drive.

TWENTY-THREE

"Sneaking around with a married man who keeps promising to divorce his wife? That sounds a lot like Roger and me. And I know how much faith you have in him," Lorena said later that afternoon, as we sat outside on the front porch and drank beer.

"What if Franky really does intend to divorce Lupe?"

"Then wait till he gets one. Look, I'll be thirty–four soon. And all I am is a nursemaid to a bunch of whores. But Roger Starling is no more gonna marry me than renounce being a Republican. I accept Roger's lies because he makes me feel like getting up in the morning and combing my hair. But a fact is a fact. Yours is called Franky Wyatt and mine is called Roger Starling."

If only I could hear Lex's voice. Maybe that would set me straight. But a night call to New York would cost fifteen dollars and fifty cents at night. During the day, it was twenty–seven dollars and seventy–five cents. A fortune. Plus, the last time I tried calling him, he'd been away at a special clinic for treatment.

I decided to focus on getting a job. For the next few days, I visited the May Company, Bullocks, Walker's, and The Broadway. But no one wanted me. I even tried Central Casting again, sure I'd run into one of the *wannabees*. But my old roommate Carol Ann had either skipped her daily visit, gotten a job, or seen the futility of her dreams, and headed back to her hometown.

As always, Central Casting turned me away with the usual, "Nothing today."

Still, I kept looking. I told myself that I just needed one lucky break. A motto I'd learned from the *wannabees* back at the Bayridge.

After another full day of job hunting, I took a bath and washed my hair. Up in my room with my hair in clips, I lay on my lumpy bed and read Myra's latest movie magazine. There wasn't any news about Franky. But I did find a brief listing of Lupe's latest picture, *Sonoran Princess*.

The phone rang downstairs. The good news was that Franky had sent me flowers the day after our date. The bad news was that he hadn't telephoned me in a month. I no longer expected someone to call out my name. But just then Lorena did.

"Jeri Devlin Rose! You got a letter."

The return address was from Saranac Lake. Finally a letter from Lex. "Guess I'll see if Elvira saved any lunch for me," I said, heading into the kitchen, anxious to be alone with my letter.

In the steamy kitchen, Elvira stood before the enormous old stove and stirred something in a large pot that smelled mouth–watering. "You paid up this week, Miss Jeri? Hope so. I made split pea soup with ham hocks and a nice tray of corn bread for supper."

"All paid up." *For now.*

Elvira worked for fifteen dollars a month plus food, board, and castoffs, when there were any. She had every Thursday and every other Sunday after breakfast off, when she took a long bus ride to Boyle Heights to see her sister's family.

"My own boy died two years ago in a knife fight," she'd once explained. "He wasn't a bad boy. Just fell in with the wrong company one night out in colored town where them darkies drink. He wasn't used to the scrap iron they call liquor and before you knows it, he goes mad over some little thing in a ruffled dress. 'Too much Brown Plaid,' the cops told me. 'Cause that stuff'll rot your gut and your head. I never did see my boy again. Not till he was stretched out in his blue suit."

Elvira's eyes had filled with tears. One of the girls had hugged her. Then Elvira said, "You gals are my children now. You gals, my sister Darlene, my niece Audry, and her brother Harmon."

But today, while Elvira made dinner, she hummed along to Bing Crosby on the radio.

Sitting on the kitchen bench, I tore open the envelope and instantly realized the handwriting had too many loops and curls to be Lex's.

Dear Mrs. Rose:

I'm writing to let you know that Mr. Rose is stable for the time being. Of course with time, rest and treatment, anything is possible. And we have high hopes that he will thrive for a good deal longer.

Mrs. Eva Jankel

The rest of her note listed Lex's current expenses.

I mentally ran through what was upstairs in my hat, Lorena's vault, and the few dollars I kept in my old cold cream jar. Not enough. I was no more capable of paying Lex's sanitarium bills than buying a home in Beverly Hills.

Rising, I headed out back where Lorena pulled clothes off the line.

"Darn, if I don't break my back doing this," Lorena griped, before noticing my expression. "What's up? You lose the picture game or something?"[3]

"How much could I earn at marathon dancing?" I asked.

Lorena put up her hand to block out the sun. "You must be

fried on that stuff Uncle Suds brews."

"I'm serious."

"Three of my gals tried that racket before coming here. First, you end up walkin' on your ankles cause your feet swell or turn bloody. You never sleep, you ruin your health, and then those sponsors don't pay you."

"More good news."

She sighed. "Help me carry this stuff in, and we can chat before I have to dress," Lorena said, grabbing one end of the basket while I took hold of the other.

Being Friday, the girls dressed earlier in case someone wanted a little fun in the late afternoon. Lorena would set up the bar – and charge a fortune for drinks – which came cheap because her suppliers exchanged beer for free visits to the brothel.

"Come on up. I want to show you something," Lorena said, leaving the clothes basket in the kitchen and heading up the old wood back stairs. We reached the attic, a small rough–hewn room with a peaked ceiling and a large round window which faced a gnarled old eucalyptus tree and the front yard. It was cooling off up here, but still warmer than the rest of the house. Oil paintings were stacked in corners. And the usual assortment of oils, turpentine, and paints sat in a box by a small table with a pallet and an easel where a half–done canvas waited to be finished.

Lorena painted when she had the chance, something even her beloved Roger didn't know about. Now, she plopped down on an ancient easy chair and directed me to a matching chair opposite her. "I had Diedre pose for this one." She pointed to a painting leaning against a post.

"Looks just like her," I said absently.

Lorena's paintings were full of vibrant colors and life. Modern, they defied any uniform idea of art, but were full of humor and faceless women in various nude poses.

"I got this,' I said, handing her the letter from the sanitarium. "I can't pay it."

Lorena read the note, while I gazed out the window at the chaparral that spread across the distant hills.

"What does Lex say?"

"Nothing. I haven't heard from him in six months. Whenever I call his cure cottage, they tell me he's asleep or away at a special clinic for treatment. I guess he stopped loving me somewhere along the way."

"But you still love him. It's somewhere so deep inside you've almost buried it. But it's still there."

"He's ... I never could stand to see him hurt. I'd sell myself like one of your girls before I'd see him sent to a state hospital. Sometimes at night in bed, I try to imagine him dealing with the disease. Knowing he won't get better. Staring at his own death. The indignities of being ordered around day after day for no purpose. How does someone with his passion for life deal with that?"

"Don't get all worked up. He's not dead, yet. And I can lend you whatever you need."

"You've done too much for me already."

"We're kin. What's more, I like you, which is more than I can say for the rest of my family."

"But you've worked so hard to be independent. I'd sooner take a room on the second floor and handle customers."

"Don't talk nonsense. I've never gotten paid for *that* myself."

"You mean, you've never had clients?"

"Hell no. I'm a business manager. Not a worker."

"But you always call yourself a whore."

"I say it before anyone else can. But I never took money to make love in my life. It's not that I'm ashamed of my girls for taking money. Being a *working girl* beats starving, or slaving in some beanery for nickels and dimes. But the other girls here aren't you. You were born to a better world – not men with dirt under their nails and jaws that haven't seen a razor since Wilson left office." Wiping her hands on an old rag, she casually said, "What about Franky? Can't he help you?"

"I guess he went to New York for a movie deal and hasn't come back yet."

Lorena reached into a battered old roll top desk, withdrew a movie magazine and turned to the section called "Hollywood Going's – On!" Under an old studio photo of Franky from his silent film days, a caption read, *"Cowboy heart throb of the silent era, Franky Wyatt, better known as Señor Lupe Cardona, celebrated his movie comeback at the Brown Derby last week."*

Last week? I felt sick. Franky had been home for at least a week without calling me.

> *... After career flops like **Dark Scavenger** and **Quarter horse Cowboy**, it seemed as if Franky would never climb back in the saddle. But with this new serial, **Ghost Rider**, he could see his star rise again. One thing's for sure, somebody in the Cardona clan needs a hit soon. In the meantime, tongues are wagging over the beautiful blonde Franky has been squiring around town. While Lupe and her pal with the initials BA have called it quits. So maybe Lupe and her cowboy will see eye–to–eye again.*

There were two more photos. One with Lupe and Franky at the party. And a close up of Franky and me at the Coconut Grove.

Lorena reached inside her old desk again and pulled out money. "Three hundred enough?"

"Put that away. I can't take your money. Not when the other gals here trek up those stairs every night with strangers who might give them syphilis or gonorrhea. Or some farm boy with too much moonshine in him who likes to get rough."

"Don't be an idiot. Take it."

"But I'll never be able to pay you back."

The phone rang, a distant sound from downstairs. Somehow I knew it would be for me. I even anticipated one of the girls calling my name.

And then Thelma yelled, "Jeri, it's for you!"

It was Franky. "It's been impossibly busy here. But I have to see you. Can you get away tonight? I could pick you up around nine."

Too bad I didn't have the backbone to tell him where to go. The best I managed was, "Not tonight. I already have plans." With a mystery novel and a radio program.

"Then how about tomorrow night?"

"Okay." Why did I agree? Because I felt as if I'd been holding my breath for a month and I could finally fill my lungs again.

Downstairs, Lorena rumbled past me with a basket of neatly folded laundry. "You're a real pushover, Jeri Rose. A prize sap." But after she said it, she winked.

That night I couldn't sleep. It was after three when I gave up trying and switched on my lamp. I figured Jimmy might be awake, too, since he hardly ever slept. Taking a chance, I knocked softly. A second later there was a faint reply. Relieved, I slipped into my robe, then tiptoed to my door. I reached the hallway at the same time as Jimmy. The stairs creaked as we headed down to the kitchen.

I sat at the table while Jimmy lit the huge old stove and put the kettle on for tea. We spoke softly since Elvira slept nearby.

"Franky Wyatt finally called."

"So the star of *Trusty Rusty and the Cattle Rustlers* is back,"

Jimmy whispered, as he put his hand in the huge old cookie jar and pulled out four cookies, setting two before each of us.

"He happens to be very appealing."

"And married from what I've read. Not to be mean about it, but so are you. So how does Trusty Rusty fit in?"

"I guess I've got what they call, squirrel fever." And another disease called loneliness.

The kettle whistled. "Stay put. I'll do it." He quickly fixed us tea.

I bit into a cookie. "Back in New York, I never thought of cheating on Lex. But now … the whole world seems upside down, including me."

"Plus Franky's rich, handsome, and healthy," Jimmy said.

"And dangerous."

"He didn't look too dangerous in *Trusty Rusty*."

"I'm afraid this whole thing is doomed," I admitted.

"No getting around that. Can Franky help pay your bills?"

"I'm not seeing him because of that." Although the thought had occurred to me even before Lorena had mentioned it.

"What's Lorena's new beau like?" he asked.

"High society. Out of reach."

Jimmy sighed. "Did Lorena ever tell you what happened to her back in Ohio?"

"Not a word."

Jimmy took a long sip of tea before he filled me in on Lorena's past. "She was about sixteen when she fell in love with some boy back home. One day, without warning, Clement packed up the family, including me, and moved us to Kansas. Claimed he got a deal on a farm there. Anyway, Lorena never even got to say goodbye to the boy. But as soon as we arrived in Kansas, she realized she was going to have a baby. So she told Violet."

I groaned.

"Who else could she turn to? She was young, scared, and stuck out on the farm with no friends."

"What about you?"

"We may be regarded as simple Oakies, but we don't marry our first cousins. Anyway, Violet told Clement, who went roaring after Lorena with a broom stick and beat her till we all thought she'd lose the baby. Not so. But when the baby was born, Clement took it away and sold it."

"I knew there was a reason I despised Clement. Did Lorena have any say in it? Did she know the new parents?"

Jimmy shook his head. "She spent the next year trying to find the baby but no one would tell her anything. At eighteen she ran away and came here to California. Then in 1930, when times got tough and the drought hit, Clement couldn't pay his loans and the farm went bust. So the family followed Lorena. By then Lorena had a taste for the worst kind of men. Users, losers, fellows who'd sleep with her one day and high–hat her the next. A year later, she opened this place." He gazed around the kitchen.

"Maybe that's why her opinion of men isn't very high," I said.

In many ways, Lorena and I were alike with one big difference: I believed my life would improve one day, when the Depression ended and times were better ... with or without Franky or Lex.

Lorena seemed to believe she'd come as far as she ever would. Of course I had hindsight on my side and she didn't.

TWENTY-FOUR

Lex woke confused. He was back in his room. He recalled the trip to the clinic and how they'd numbed an area on his chest then stuck in a long needle with gas. Now, there was a man in the room with him seated by the window. Lex recognized the pale craggy face, the long black coat, and those immense hands which toyed with a bowler hat on his lap. The pale face looked down at him. Something akin to a smile broke through the man's somber expression. Lex wondered if he was dreaming. Except there was his water glass by his bed. And the same relentless view out his window.

Then the apparition spoke. "Glad to see you're awake, sir. Feeling all right or should I call the nurse?"

"Harris?"

"Been a long time, sir. "

"How've you been?"

"Can't complain. Been fishing out on Long Island around Montauk. Staying with my half–sister. She and her husband have been most helpful. Good air out there, Mr. Rose. Good as it gets. Bracing and clean. Maybe, when you get out of here, you'll join me."

"Yes, I … let's hope. When I woke and saw you, I thought I was dreaming. Or dead."

"I know, sir. It was there on your face. But I'm really here. Been here for hours now. The doctor called me. Said I'd been mentioned as ... well, they wanted me here as a friendly face for when you woke up."

Lex reached for his water glass. Harris instantly rose to assist him. After a long swallow, Lex gave the class back to Harris, who replaced the glass on the night table.

"Wish I could go out to Montauk with you, Harris," Lex said. "But I won't be around long. It's written somewhere. Lex Rose dies young. I'll be thirty–four on my next birthday. Guess I was supposed to go down in Belgium."

"Slipped through the devil's fingers that time, you did."

"Not this time, Harris. I feel tired."

"That'll be the drugs in you. From the work on your lungs. Like a poison. But you'll improve in a day or two. And then we can play a hand of gin or whatever you like."

Lex had never been happier to see Harris. "Cards. I'd like that."

"You see, sir, I've rented a room just outside town. And I brought the old Dusenberg with me."

Lex grinned, thinking of the huge yellow vehicle, a reminder of grander times. "How is she?"

"Very well, sir. I look after her myself."

"We had some swell times with that machine, didn't we."

"The doc swears I can take you for a spin next week or the week after."

Lex's smile faded. "Harris, you know I can't ... I can't pay you."

Harris stared at the black hat in his large hands. "Been with you since you were eighteen. You saved my life a time or two back in Belgium and France. No need to worry about wages. I've come here as a friend."

***

"Hope you don't mind, but I've had my cook make us something at my place. I thought we could swim then have dinner and relax," Franky said, as he opened my door, and I climbed into his Packard the next night.

"Fine," I managed to say, feeling rejected and insulted. Because in honor of seeing me, Franky had donned an old flannel shirt, faded jeans, and dusty cowboy boots. In 1933, a gentleman didn't pick up cigarettes from a drugstore in less than a suit and tie. His attire, added to the fact that he'd been home for weeks before calling me, didn't help my mood. I'd spent most of the day dressing. I'd even worn a new gown, one Lex had ordered for me in Havana. A dress I'd never worn before.

"Look, if you're trying to hide me, maybe we should forget the whole thing," I said, through angry tears.

Franky's eyes widened. "Hide you? I'd be proud to be seen with you anywhere. I just prefer a quiet meal at home. I get sick of noisy supper clubs."

He reached for my hand. His fingers felt warm and calloused. His blue eyes oozed humble sincerity. He wouldn't be the first celebrity to eschew wild parties and glitzy nightclubs. But the truth might go deeper. I suspected he had money problems. Or he feared another confrontation with Caesar Cardona. Either way, it wasn't like me to be insulted so easily. What was wrong with having a casual dinner at a boyfriend's house? Especially since it meant I wouldn't run into the Caesar Cardona. Or the Desanto brothers.

By the time we pulled up to Casa Luna, twilight had descended over the mountains, and the smoldering valley had shifted from hot to frigid.

"Better get into the pool before it's too cold to swim," Franky warned. "Should be a few bathing suits your size in the *casita*."

Fifteen minutes later, after trying on a half–dozen suits hanging in the *casita's* tiny closet, I emerged in a nude toned bathing suit studded with rhinestones that enveloped my curves like a tight silk stocking. The bathing suit had been designed for a much smaller person; someone like Lupe Cardona with her penchant for flashy clothes. The average girl wouldn't be caught dead at a pool or public beach in something this revealing. In fact, it reminded me of a showgirl's costume from a Busby Berkeley musical. However, it was the only swimsuit in the closet long enough for my torso.

Barefoot and wrapped in a towel, I hurried to the pool. I intended to slip out of the robe and into the water before Franky saw me. I wasn't ashamed of my body. At five feet eight I might be considered tall. But I had the narrow waist, long lean legs and broad shoulders of Ginger Rogers. Too bad I had a chest like Mae West's.

Franky was too busy positioning himself on the diving board to notice me. Wearing black wool trunks, every inch of him looked chiseled and bronzed from his well–formed legs to his masculine chest. An instant later, he somersaulted into the water. Even his toes were pointed as he cut through the water's surface. Johnny Weismuller, the 1930's *Tarzan,* couldn't have done any better. I shoved my hair under a rubber bathing cap, mounted the diving board, then dove in after Franky. I surfaced to Franky's applause.

"Not bad," he said swimming toward me and taking me in his arms. "Now, I don't want to alarm you,' he said, in a low intimate voice. "But that suit you're wearing …"

I glanced down and cursed. The bathing suit had become completely transparent. Every inch of me from my nipples to my belly button showed through the wet fabric. I instantly shrank below the water line until all but my head and shoulders was submerged.

"Wait here." Franky quickly pulled himself out of the water, grabbed his terrycloth robe, and held it out for me.

"Turn your back," I insisted.

He laughed. "Not a chance."

"Then I'm staying right here."

"It's going to get very cold in that water soon."

Using my hands to cover my strategic points, I emerged from the pool shivering.

Franky gazed at my body, then slowly wrapped the robe over my shoulders. "I should make you wear that suit from now on," he said, his voice husky.

"What kind of material is this thing made of?" I asked, slipping my arms through the robe's sleeves, tying the robe sash, then ripping the tight rubber cap off my head.

"I doubt it's meant to get wet," he said, pulling me against him and giving me a warm kiss on the mouth.

"What *is* it meant for?"

"Posing around the pool. Or it might be one of Lupe's old show costumes from one of her movies."

One of Lupe's castoffs, exactly what I'd figured.

"Forget swimming. Let's have dinner. We can have it out here or inside," he said, releasing me from his embrace.

"Inside. And soon. I'm starving. It must be all this fresh air."

"You can change in the *casita*."

In bare wet feet, I followed Franky back to the tiny building. As before, the *casita* was damp and cold. The tiny building already held unpleasant memories for me from last time I'd been here. Now, in spite of the robe, I shivered.

Franky frowned. "Hey, we don't want you getting sick." He quickly withdrew a large beach towel from the small closet and, in a brotherly fashion, helped me out of the wet robe and into a large dry towel. He briskly rubbed my shoulders. "There, that should be better.

Why don't you take a hot shower, and I'll send my housekeeper Maria out to help you dress?"

He went back to the closet and began digging. "There should be some more towels here."

In the room's dim light, a vaporish yellow illumination created by the current light bulbs, I caught Franky's dashing profile and the beauty of his muscles. An involuntary rush of desire gripped me, a yearning to bury myself in his arms and press my body against his. Without a word, I dropped my towel then slowly pulled the shoulders of my bathing suit down around my waist, till my breasts were exposed. Barely breathing, I waited for him to turn.

"Found one," he finally said, holding out a towel and facing me. He froze. His eyes widened at the sight of my bare breasts.

For a moment, his gaze hungrily roamed over my body. From my taut nipples to the triangle between my legs, visible through the fabric. Then our eyes locked. An electrical charge surged through me. In a flash, he pulled me to him, crushing me. The sensation of his lips devouring mine, the aroma of his flesh, and the feel of his damp fragrant hair erased my reasoning and all my memories. There was only now. And him. Clutching the smooth burning flesh of his strong back, I molded myself against him just before we fell onto the narrow bed.

My mind stood back, judging me. Was this passion or love? A fling or an affair with a future? These doubts were flickers, spirited sparks, and just as fleeting. Weighed against the heat, the scalding fire that seared my cravings like a sizzling broiler, I forgot everything but the pleasure of his probing tongue and probing fingers. And the taste of his neck, throat, and lips. He silently guided my hand to his wet bathing trunks, and I found his excitement thrilling. Anxious to be closer, we battled the constraints of his bathing trunks which at last fell to the floor.

Unfortunately, my sodden suit seemed to have become a permanent part of me. The tight scratchy fabric still clinging to my hips burned my flesh as we tried to pull it down. After several frustrating tugs, we managed to yank the suit off. Until my body lay exposed, cold, and free.

Franky began to kiss me all over. My breasts, my hips, my navel, the whole length of my inner thighs. I was stirred by the warmth of his skin and his broad shoulders which towered above me like a warm shroud, a human shield against the room's damp chill. Until at last he positioned himself above me. With a gently thrust, he broke through my ambivalence and sent my reservations drifting over the edge of that bed like a goose feather falling from a pillow.

Afterward, Maria helped me get ready. Dressed, I followed her back to the main house to a large comfortable room off the living room, where a flames licked the insides of a large fireplace. And soft music played on a nearby phonograph. From behind a tall carved wood bar, Franky poured wine. Freshly showered, he'd changed back into a fresh pair of worn jeans and a clean flannel shirt .

"There's wine or I could make you something stronger," he said.

"What you're having looks good."

"Red wine," he said, fixing me a glass.

I dropped onto a large burgundy-colored sofa by the fire. But even with Lorena's fox wrap and the crackling fire a few feet away, I shivered. Like the *casita*, the large room with its tiled floors, oriental carpets, and high beamed ceilings felt damp, cold.

"Wolfie made us a roast. Should be ready soon," Franky said, handing me my glass then easing beside me until our thighs touched. Until I could smell soap on his skin. "Warm enough?"

"Better thanks."

In the fire's glow, Franky's skin looked like dark honey.

Firelight danced in his light blue eyes. I enjoyed watching him. But beyond his looks, cowboy charms, and a talent for pleasing me in bed, he was a stranger. It had been the same with Lex. I'd fallen in love with him too fast and learned too late that he had a bad reputation with women and didn't believe in marriage. In fact, Lex proposed *after* he believed he'd lost me.

"Are you okay?" Franky asked, breaking into my thoughts. "You looked so far away."

"Just day–dreaming. I read about your party in a magazine."

He frowned. "Sorry I couldn't invite you. An old friend insisted on throwing it for me."

"So you got your movie deal."

Franky stared into the fire. "Sort of. It's just a western series. One of those kiddy serials they show between the cartoons and the feature." He finished off his wine then rose to pour himself more.

"That sounds… exciting."

"Not exactly what I'd hoped for, but the public wants musicals this year. Or so I've been told. Down the road, if I'm lucky, there may be a feature film with some guy named John Wayne. At least the money's decent for the serial. In fact, I wondered, well, you and I never discussed money."

My heart stopped. Had I heard right? Did he think this was a business transaction? "I beg your pardon?"

"I know it can't be fun living at a place like The Rainbow. Since you aren't one of the regular gals. So I figured you might need a little help."

My pride told me to refuse. Then I realized my refusal would be idiotic. After all, Mrs. Jankel's latest letter had restated that she wasn't running a charity, and Lex's bill needed to be kept current. "Yes, I could use help."

Franky pulled an envelope from his back jean pocket and

handed it to me. He looked happy, expectant. I tore it open and stared at the contents. A hundred dollars. Relief surged through me. For the time being, Lex was safe.

Before I could thank Franky, he took my hand. Just his touch made my heart race. His hands were different from Lex's. Lex had always relied on weekly manicures. Franky's hands were rough and calloused.

Now, Franky studied my palm as if he intended to read my fortune. Then, like the flutter of butterfly wings, he began to run his lips over my palm and up the underside of my wrist, tickling me. My breathing picked up. My loins stirred. Soon my body quaked with an urgent yearning.

With barely a thought to my clean dress and freshly repaired face, I fell back on the sofa as Franky climbed on top of me. One hand massaged my breast as his lips traced a path down my throat and blue flames engulfed my insides. A thrill I recognized from as far back as Havana surged through me. Only the sound of the doorbell ringing and urgent pounding broke the spell. In a flash, Franky and I sprang apart. I pictured Caesar Cardona. Or the Desanto brothers armed to the teeth.

Instead a shrill voice rang out. A woman's voice with a strong accent. "How dare you tell Lupe Cardona what she can do! Thee whole house, thee *very* floor you stand on, belong to me. Now get out of my way, before I throw you into thee gutter."

"Please madam. Mr. Wyatt has company."

"I no care if he screwing his horse."

"Madam, I beg you to be patient and I'll …"

Franky bolted off the sofa. "Damn, Damn, Damn!"

Brisk footsteps echoed across the tiled floor. Wolfie rushed in. "Sir, your wife, that is, Mrs. Cardona, is here. I told her you had company, but she insists on seeing you."

Alarmed, Franky pointed to me. "Hide her."

TWENTY-FIVE

In a flash, Wolfie hustled me down a tiled hallway to a back bedroom. A heartbeat later, I heard Lupe storm into the living room. Due to the house's thick walls, I could only hear her in spurts. Determine to get better reception, I hurried into the attached bathroom and spied a water glass on the sink. With the glass pressed firmly against the carved wood door, Lupe and Franky came in as clearly as NBC's blue channel on the radio.

***

"Will you calm down?" Franky growled.

Lupe marched to the bar, helped herself to a full goblet of gin, and emptied it in a few swallows. Franky could tell this wasn't her first drink of the evening.

"Where is she?" Lupe growled. "Where is thee low–life *puta* you are hiding?"

"Inside my jeans," Franky said, dropping onto the sofa and managing a nonchalant pose, even though his heart was still bucking like a Brahma bull.

"I no messing around this time, Franky." Lupe banged her glass down on the bar then stumbled across the living room toward the opposite end of the house and called, "Come out, little *puta*, wherever you are? I going to tear your *estupida* face off." She sounded as if she was playing hide–and–go–seek.

"Fine, make a farce out of our lives," Franky muttered, trailing after her, as she staggered toward the dining room.

***

Their voices faded. Rushing back into the bedroom, I searched for a better hiding place. Based on the small bathroom and basic bedroom furniture, this wasn't the best side of the house. A framed picture of Wolfie and an older Asian man confirmed this. Franky had already told me that the main house had three bedrooms and three bathrooms plus a maids room with a bath off the kitchen. Then there was the *casita* and a bunkhouse for the cowhands.

In the distance doors slammed. But Lupe would be back soon, as soon as she didn't find me elsewhere. Hiding inside the armoire or under the bed seemed too obvious. Desperate, I unlocked the heavy lead–and–glass door and stepped out into the night.

Rocks encased a cactus garden. A low wall surrounded the garden. Ducking behind the rock wall, I tried to make out the shapes around me but couldn't. I just prayed there weren't any snakes, scorpions, or other critters in striking distance. A minute or two later, Lupe's voice grew louder, meaning she and Franky had arrived at Wolfie's room.

***

"Then who wore thee costume from my movie?" Lupe barked.

"Maria claimed there were spiders on it. She meant to clean it," Franky said.

"Is my favorite thing to hear you lie. You want Lupe to believe this is thee reason it was there on thee floor wet?"

"How should I know? Maybe Maria heard you arrive then peed on the thing from panic. God knows, *I* panic at the sight of you."

"My beauty has always made you nervous, no?"

***

Crouched behind the wall, I caught a glimpse of Lupe peering out the glass door into the dark.

"Tell me where you hide her? Or I will make you and thee *puta* very sorry," Lupe said.

A moment later, the voices receded. It seemed as if a year passed before I could stand, stretch my back, and sneak back inside the house to use my trusty water glass against the door.

***

Franky felt relieved. Somehow, Jeri had eluded Lupe. Now he settled back on the living room sofa and calmly lit a cigarette. "We're separated. I can see anyone I like."

Lupe's eyes narrowed as she crossed from behind the bar and stood over Franky. "You think I do not hear thee gossip? Thee way you have been fucking thee blonde woman with thee cow bosoms. Well, you better think again, because my father can make you very sorry. So you better listen to me good."

"I'm all ears," he said, wondering where Jeri could have escaped to.

"Send thee little *puta* home now and tell her she is finished."

"I have no idea who you're talking about."

"You must think I am thee idiot."

"Have I ever said that?"

"If she is not here, why do you have two wine glasses?"

Franky sent her his most condescending smile. "I used two glasses for two different wines."

"I am *sooo* impressed." Lupe rolled her eyes, then withdrew her gold cigarette case from her rhinestone bag and waited for him to light her cigarette. When he ignored her, she went back to the bar, poured herself a fresh drink, and studied him.

It wasn't fair, Lupe thought. She had to fret over every crease on her face. Franky didn't. He had aged, too. But it only made him more desirable. In fact, he was more handsome now than when they'd met twelve years ago. He still had a magnetism which drove women wild. His soft blond hair was still thick and shiny. Even his startling blue eyes didn't betray his passion for booze. And his physique made women stop and stare. Even in his cowboy clothes, clothes she'd often ridiculed, he exuded a breathtaking appeal. Deep down, she actually preferred him unshaven and rough. Still, she was glad she'd dressed for the evening in furs and a new satin gown that clung to her hips, belly, and thighs.

"Tell me thee truth. You no love this girl?" Lupe said, sure that the conniving starlet hiding in the closet or in one of the bathtubs couldn't please him in bed the way she could.

"What's your interest?" Franky asked.

"You are still Lupe's husband, no?"

"You might remember that when you're meeting Boyd Anderson in a public gin joint or one of those grubby bungalow colonies you're so fond of."

"As usual, you are not aware of thee latest news. But since your career is so pathetic, I tell you thee news myself. I no see Boyd no more. We are over with."

"What a pity. Did he slap you around like the last bum?"

She pretended to yawn. "That one, he drink too much. And I find out he is already married. He never bother to get thee divorce from his Ohio woman. I hear he is one of those hobo people now. A very sad story, really."

"Well, you still have your career. You're still a star."

Taking her drink and cigarette, Lupe moved back beside him on the sofa. Her voice became softer, more intimate. "This is very true. But little Lupe still gets lonely."

"Why? Is your father out of town?"

Lupe sighed loudly. "Why you make up such ugly stories? My

father is ... *mi padre, mi amigo*."

"Except when he's climbing into bed with you."

"I would prefer to discuss other things," she said, as her hand abruptly crept over his, and her red tipped nails began to gently stroke the back of his hand.

"How is your career? I understand Lupe Valez is doing quite well," he said, withdrawing his hand. "And Delores Del Rio, too."

Lupe exploded off the sofa, her dark eyes wild. "Lupe Valez? Delores Del Rio? I spit on them. They are nothing. Always they throw these fat whores up to me. But they are second–rate. I will drown them with my fame and beauty." Breathing hard from her outburst, Lupe reached for her purse and pulled out a lace handkerchief. After wiping her eyes and nose, she grabbed Franky's wine glass and chugged it.

"What about your new picture?" Franky asked.

Looking dejected, she dropped down beside him. "Thee newspapers hate Lupe. Already they say thee new picture stink. Even when thee fans who love me have not seen it."

"The press can be hard on anyone's career." He knew all about that, not that she'd ever shown him a whiff of sympathy.

"I want you to get rid of your other woman," she said.

"There is no other woman."

"Make her go away, and I will make you very happy." Taking his hand, she placed it on her small breast. "You are still very attractive to Lupe. And we are still married, no?"

"I told you, there's no one here."

"I no believe you," she murmured, stroking his chest, then kissing his face. First his chin, then his cheek, at last his lips. "I always like you better when you are rough with Lupe. It make me want you *very* much."

"Sorry to hear that."

Lupe crushed her mouth to his, while her hand roamed over his jeans until it rested over his crotch where she began to undo the buttons. "I make everything better for you. Your career will get bigger, harder, stronger until you are thee powerful star again, like before. We will be very happy." Her hand roamed inside his jeans, while her tongue probed his mouth. Lifting her dress up, she placed his hand between her legs. "Is ready for you, Mr. Wyatt. Is always ready for you."

As usual, her ministrations worked. Desire erupted between his legs. Every fiber of him screamed to throw her across the sofa and take her. But that was exactly what she wanted. And she'd rubbed Boyd Anderson and all the others in his face once too often. Shutting his eyes, he pushed her off him.

Still breathing hard, he said, "Let's try to retain some dignity, shall we?"

***

I heard the slap all the way down the hall behind the thick wood door in the bathroom without my water glass. My pulse felt as if it would fly through the roof beams.

Then I heard something smash and Lupe scream, "I kill you for this! You are finished. You are dirt. You will never see your daughter again. Never. And you will never work again in Hollywood. Not even when your dick shrivels up to thee size of Lupe's toe!"

I heard running and then a distant door slam. I hoped it meant Lupe Cardona had left.

A minute later, there was a gentle knock. I opened the bedroom door. Looking upset, Franky led me to the living room. A wine glass had been smashed across the floor. And Franky had a large red spot on his cheek, lipstick on his chin and mouth, and a look of sad resignation in his eyes.

"Are you okay?" I asked.

He nodded, rubbing where Lupe had slapped him. "Sorry. I guess …" His voice trailed off.

"Maybe it would be better if I went home now."

He nodded. His eyes were red. "This picture deal just has to go through. Then she'll never be able to touch me again."

Minutes later on the drive home, tired of the silence, I asked Franky about his marriage. "Weren't you ever happy?"

Franky squirmed. "Forget it. The story's boring."

"There must've been something you liked about her once."

Staring down the dark road as he drove, Franky started talking.

"We were both in this picture, *The Plains Drifter* back in 1923. The night it wrapped, there was a party. Lupe was twenty–one and very glamorous. Guess we both had a lot of tequila. We decided to take a drive. I'd taken actresses for drives before and never thought much about it. In this town, things happen fast. But when we woke the next morning in the back seat of her car, I was hung–over, sick. I couldn't remember a thing. So when Lupe swore she'd been a virgin, I was in no position to argue.

She told me she couldn't go home without a wedding band or her father would kill us. So we drove off to a Justice of the Peace and got married. When I got to know her – not to mention her father – I understood that she'd used me. Made up that virgin story because she was already pregnant."

"You mean your daughter Francesca isn't yours?"

"She is. Lupe lost the first baby. But there were so many other lies over the years. And we never could get her father out of our lives."

"There had to have been some good times."

"Not many. Even on our honeymoon in France, if we looked in a shop window and there happened to be a pretty young woman inside, Lupe threw a fit, claimed I didn't love her. That I was sorry I'd married her. In time her jealousy grew worse."

"So you stayed because of your daughter?"

"And because Caesar Cardona threatened to crush my career if I left."

"Why'd you finally move out?"

"My career hit a new low so what else could Caesar do to me? By then, Lupe had her sights on marrying Boyd Anderson so she agreed to a divorce. Unfortunately, it seems she and Boyd have had another spat and she's changed her mind about the divorce again."

"But you were in Havana together?"

"That was a public reconciliation to help with her last picture."

"*Sonoran Princess?*" I said.

"Another epic for the Guadalajara Spitfire. Full of gallant lads willing to lay down their lives for Little Lupe, just so they can worship her youth and beauty. Trouble is, she's gotten so she believes that nonsense."

It was almost two when we pulled up to The Rainbow. The place had closed early. Only a single light still burned upstairs. Tonight, Franky bounded out of the car to open my door.

"The studio school taught you some fine manners," I joked. When he didn't laugh or respond, I headed toward the house.

"Jeri, wait." He sprinted after me. There under a brilliant moon in front of The Rainbow, he pulled me into his arms. He held me so tight, his jean buttons pressed into my stomach. I reveled in the solid muscles of his back. Muscles formed as a ranch hand driving cattle, training horses, and later in the 1920s working in front of hand cranked cameras.

"Sorry about being such a bore. Guess I don't shake off these fights with Lupe so quickly anymore," he said.

I was touched by this admission and the feeling of intimacy it brought.

Then his warm lips covered mine and he slid one hand from my waist to my buttocks whiles his other hand pushed up the thin fabric of my dress, brushed across my thigh to the top of my stocking, to my panties.

I abruptly pushed his hands away. "Don't. Please."

"Jeri ... why?" he gasped, as he buried his mouth in my neck and his fingers worked between my legs.

"Stop it. Don't."

"What's wrong?" he asked, stepping back.

"Because tonight reminded me that we're both still married. Because I'm not the type to break up a family. I can't compete with Lupe, Caesar, and your daughter Francesca. And I can't forget about Lex either."

Franky sighed loudly. Then he tucked in his shirt, that soft flannel shirt which had seen dozens of washes and spoke of the cowboy who'd never been tamed. The boy who'd seen more action mending fences and sleeping in bunk houses than the interior of a department store or a bed made with satin sheets. The wrangler who still preferred his meat roasted on a spit, slapped on a plate full of beans, and washed down with beer. The young man who'd wandered onto a movie set one day and been asked to do extra work. Or so I'd read in a movie magazine.

At last, he slipped on his hat and said, "See ya," then headed to his car.

"Wait," I called softly. "Don't run off. Stay a minute."

"What's left to say? I'm married, you're married. My wife is determined to make my life miserable. I have no right to ask you for anything."

"I guess ... I guess I'm afraid of being hurt."

He leaned against his car and stared up at the old house. "Tell you something, Jeri. Lots of guys would stop in at a place like this, pick a gal, and pay to drive away their demons. Only trouble is, I've had you on my mind since Havana."

I searched his eyes for the truth in case he was acting. But bathed in gentle starlight his expression seemed genuine. I went to him. "Listen, I've only been in love once before. With my husband. I don't fall in love every day —"

"Love? You're in love? Who's the lucky guy? Anybody I know?"

I wacked him on the arm. "He's a skinny cowboy with bowlegs."

He glanced down at his own legs. "Can't be me."

Suddenly, a window screeched open and an angry voice shrieked, "Pipe down, will ya? Some of us is tryin' to sleep."

Big Harriet.

Franky and I exchanged looks. "Better get going," he whispered, kissing my cheek. "Call you tomorrow." A moment later, he drove off in his Packard. A cowboy driving a fancy roadster seemed like such a contradiction. But he wasn't just a cowboy. He was also a silent film star with a big house and an estranged, conniving wife.

Oddly enough, I felt giddy as I tiptoed up the front stairs to the house. I'd just confessed my feelings to Franky. And he seemed pleased about it. I considered waking Jimmy with my news.

But as I reached for the front door, I heard clothing rustle. I turned. In the ghostly grey dawn, I recognized Tito Desanto's dark cruel eyes, enlarged lower jaw, and Neanderthal brow just before he grabbed me and covered my mouth with his hand.

TWENTY-SIX

The hand over my mouth stank of piss. I sank my teeth in his palm and kicked as hard as I could. Tito withdrew with a yelp. For a moment, I screamed loudly enough to wake every dog and human in The San Fernando Valley.

Then he grabbed me again, clamping his hand over my mouth and wrenching me off my feet. Terror surged through me. Despite my struggling, he easily carried me down the porch steps and across the drive. My heart rate soared. I was sure he meant to deposit me in his car trunk and take me for a final ride. Instead, he dragged me to a nearby vacant field, away from the road and anyone who might see or hear me. Perhaps he intended to kill me as a warning to Lex.

Abruptly stopping, he tossed me to the ground. I fell hard on the roots of two tall eucalyptus trees. Tears and sweat streamed down my cheeks and my body shook with fear. Brushing myself off, I slowly climbed to my feet, terrified by the cruel smile on the big ape's face. He enjoyed beating up girls. Especially whores, from what people said. No doubt he'd have fun knocking me around, too.

I glanced toward The Rainbow. If I could run fast enough and get inside the house, maybe I could grab a weapon, get help. But if Tito caught me, he'd knock my brains out. Now, he studied me as if he'd read my thoughts.

And where was his brother Nicky? The brains of the two, providing Nicky's animal cunning could be considered intelligence. Nicky made the decisions. Tito was Nicky's attack dog. But Nicky wasn't around. Nor was the black sedan. Had the two brothers split up to search for me? Cell phones didn't exist in 1933. Plenty of families struck down by hard times didn't even have a telephone. So Nicky might not know Tito had found me. Or Nicky might be on his way here now. Meaning I had seconds to escape.

Grinning, Tito slowly took off his suit jacket and hung it over a bush. Then he rolled up his sleeves as if he intended to get sweaty. "Where's Lex?" he asked in his thick–tongued voice, while cracking his knuckles.

"How should I know? We're getting divorced."

"Don't play dumb," he said slowly.

"You're the expert at being dumb."

Tito caught me on the ear with an open hand sending me to the ground again.

"When I get done with you, nobody's gonna wanna fuck you," he sneered. "And if I'm so dumb, how come I found you? Nicky thinks you're still in Hollywood or by the beach. But I figured you'd wanna be close to your boyfriend. Yeah, I read about you and Franky Wyatt. So I came out here and waited in town for a few days. And there you were, comin' out of the drugstore."

"You're a regular Einstein," I said, stalling, wondering how to escape. We weren't far from The Rainbow, just in the next field over. I could still see The Rainbow's chimney.

Tito stepped closer and stood over me. "Stand."

"I can't."

He glared down at me. "Your old man got away with some heavy sugar. A million bucks. All ya gotta do, is tell me where he hid it. Then me and my brother won't bother you no more."

So that was what they wanted. Not revenge for their Uncle Carmine Ascencio's murder. Just money. A lot of it, too. Especially now with a quarter of the American population out of work. With two hundred thousand abandoned children wondering what had become of their parents. With thousands of men riding the rails in search of work, a meal, or an answer to how they'd lost their jobs, their homes, and their families. And the black dust storms which relentlessly devoured the plains, wiping out towns in Kansas, Colorado, Oklahoma, and Texas.

"I don't have your money. If I did, would I be living in a brothel?" I said.

From the ground, I watched him withdraw something long and slender from his double–breasted suit jacket before rehanging it on a bush. He slowly unsheathed a knife letting the smooth metal shine in the breaking sun. He ran his thumb over the tip, making sure I saw the blade.

Then he reached down, grabbed my arm, and lifted me to my feet. He yanked me close enough to smell his rotting teeth. Grinning, he pressed the flat part of the cold shiv against my cheek. "Start talkin' before I rearrange your face."

A shadow swept by. The merest flicker of a tree branch or a bird. Then I heard a clanging sound. Tito froze. The knife fell from my cheek as a strange expression filled his face. There was a second clang, as Big Harriet swung the iron frying pan again. Tito fell to his knees. Then I heard the crush of bone as the iron pan connected with Tito's skull a third time. Blood gushed from his scalp as he fell forward and his face hit the ground. His blood darkened the wild grass, pale dirt, and the roots of the trees. I hadn't heard Big Harriet coming. Not a footfall or the snap of a twig. I hadn't seen or heard Lorena or Elvira either. Now, the knife rested by Tito's still hand.

"Thank you," I gasped.

Breathing hard, Harriet glared down at Tito. "That fucker ain't never gonna mess with another girl again."

I felt dizzy. I swayed, only to be caught up in someone's arms.

"That's okay, baby," Elvira said, before I blacked out.

I woke, stretched out on the parlor sofa. Lorena, Elvira, and Big Harriet were clustered nearby talking softly. The room already felt suffocating and hot.

Harriet held Tito's knife. "I would've gelded that SOB, if he weren't already—"

"Never mind that now," Lorena said.

I sat up. I was on the sofa in the parlor. Fear clutched my throat. "But he'll wake up. He'll come after me. And he's got a crazy brother who's even meaner. A murdering lunatic named Nicky who —"

"Stay still," Lorena said, kneeling by my side, handing me an icy coke. "Drink this."

"You don't understand. We need to do something or he'll —"

"I promise you. This guy's never gonna hurt anyone again. Now drink up."

I reluctantly accepted the cold glass. The sweet drink helped, though my ominous feelings about the Desanto brothers lingered. And there was something Lorena wasn't telling me. "Lorena, I want the truth. Something's up. Tell me."

"He's dead," Big Harriet said.

Horror gripped me. "Dead?"

"Harriet didn't mean to do it," Lorena said.

"But sometimes, there ain't no stopping his type," Harriet said. "Not when the cops don't give a hoot who beats on a woman."

"You were asleep," Lorena added. "So Elvira, and Big Harriet helped me put him in the old cellar."

"My God."

"Believe me, he's long past caring," Big Harriet said.

"We buried him in the ground down there."

I pictured the three women tossing the lifeless body down the steep wood steps like a sack of potatoes. Big Harriet and Elvira digging the grave then tossing in Tito's suit–jacket and derby after him. "It sounds like something out of an Edgar Allen Poe story."

"No one's gonna find him," Lorena said. "I bolted the cellar door and put a padlock on it. And I'm the only one with a key."

"We'll need to move the body before it starts to stink," Elvira said.

"Not yet. Let's wait and see if the brother shows up," Lorena said. "We may have to move them both if Nicky's anything like his brother."

The facts were horrible. I'd seen dozens of violent films in the future. But this was real. Yet I'd brought these monsters into my friends' lives. And they'd saved me.

"Thanks," I finally said. Because even though I felt ill about the death, I was also relieved. Tito had meant to cut me up. He might've killed me, too, when I couldn't supply him with the information he wanted. And he and his brother wouldn't think twice about killing Lex. Now Nicky would have to operate alone.

"How about a nice cool bath?"Lorena asked.

"How can you be so calm after what happened?"

"I've had to knock sense into quite a few fellas. And not one of those stinkers ever threatened to cut up my cousin's face. He got what he deserved."

Upstairs, standing at the bathroom sink later, I applied medicine to my scratches and the welt on my upper thigh, which would turn into an ugly bruise soon. At least it would heal. But what about Nicky Desanto? He was bound to start sniffing around when his brother didn't return.

The Desantos' determination to find Lex didn't shock me. With their world collapsing, the brothers needed someone to finance their future. With their Uncle Ascencio gone and Samuel Seabury, who'd sent Lex to jail, prosecuting everyone who'd profited illegally during Mayor Jimmy Walker's administration, their world was ending. Seabury and his team were delving into payoffs, housing scams, and other dirty deals which had greased New York's politicians' palms and supported thugs like the Desantos during the 1920s. Even prohibition would be repealed this December when enough states ratified the Twenty–First Amendment, ending the bootleggers' reign.

By Monday, I was still fretting over Tito's murder and the possibility of Nicky Desanto showing up as I hunted for a job downtown. Every time I stepped off the bus or trolley I expected to see Nicky leaning against a car or hiding in the shadows. Maybe that's why nobody hired me, because I seemed spooked, afraid. They didn't hire me as a stock clerk, a soda jerk, or a bookkeeper.

Back at The Rainbow the following afternoon, I'd given up hunting for work and was sitting on The Rainbow's shady front porch trying to compose an upbeat letter to Lex. But other than Tito's death, there wasn't much to tell him. I couldn't mention Franky. And the rest of my life was nothing to brag about.

Also, a plump young woman, a possible candidate for an empty room on the second floor, sat on the top step scratching a bite on her thigh and jabbering to me.

"I been lookin' for work for ages. This friend of mine, Gladys, she told me about this place," the girl said. "I ain't never been in a place like this before, but what the heck, I figure it don't take much practice to do what comes natural. Know what I mean?"

I grunted.

"I heard this woman who runs the joint is pretty decent, too. I mean, compared to some I heard about. Cause I heard they can tie you to the bed and make you put out till you die. But I don't figure on bein' here long, cause I got prospects back home in Ohio. I'm from this little town you never heard of, but there's this boy there who's dyin' to marry me, and I may do it cause he has his own truck and some land we could farm. Grow taters and hogs and chickens."

More and more girls wandered down the dirt drive looking for Lorena. Hungry, tired, and desperate, they were willing to overlook the kind of work expected at The Rainbow.

"So your old man's sick, huh," the girl said.

I'd divulged this information to shut her up so I could finish my letter. But no matter how curt my answers or unfriendly my expressions, the girl wouldn't stop babbling.

"I been in one of them hospitals, too. Mine was a state run place, nothing fancy like the one your old man's in. Yep, I was a lunger once. That's what they call ya when you got consumption. I'll bet ya two–to–one he's up there *cousining* with some nurse right now. Probably got a swell set up. She probably climbs in bed whenever the lights go out. Or they sneak out and do it in the bushes during rest hours – which is most of the day in them places.

Had me an Italian fellow at the state home. He got me in a family way, and boy were them doctors sore. So I tells this doc, just wait till my old man comes along and I gotta explain how it happened. Well, them docs almost had strokes, so it was lucky I lost the baby —"

"Lorena can see ya now," Big Harriet barked, throwing open the screen door, startling the girl and me. Harriet stepped outside and glared down at the girl as if she were a rotting pile of rubbish. "Keep your big trap shut, too," Harriet warned her.

Rising, the girl shot Big Harriet a haughty glance, then

flounced through the door, an exaggerated sway in her hips.

"Never you mind what that piece of trash says," Big Harriet said. "You ain't got no proof your daddy's messin' around. The idea of that trashy girl spreadin' misery like that. I hope Lorena tosses her out on her keister."

Once again Big Harriet was offering me encouragement, coming to my aide. It seemed impossible. "Thanks. Would you like a chocolate?" I held out my box of chocolates, a gift from Franky, delivered an hour ago with a dozen red roses and a note saying he couldn't wait to see me.

Harriet studied the candy carefully. At last she chose one then settled down on the top step with a loud sigh, before daintily biting into the candy. She groaned with pleasure. "Been a long time since I tasted anything this fine."

"It is good," I said, overjoyed that Franky was making such a big effort to please me.

"So you ain't heard from your mister?"

"Not a word in ten months," I said.

"Well, livin' here, you get to see the way men really are. Like children every one of 'em. Lost and needy, lookin' for passion and tenderness one minute and bein' hard and selfish the next. They don't mean to disappoint us or hurt us. But they don't see beyond the moment. Like a kid with a nickel in his pocket that's torn between puttin' that coin in a charity box or blowin' it on candy." She gazed into the distance. "I know all about kids. I had a bunch of babies myself once."

I was speechless. I never thought Harriet would reveal her secrets to anyone, especially me.

"Then I got sick and seemed like I was about to die. Couldn't care for my babies no more. I was broke and alone, on account of my husband gettin' shot to death at a roadhouse over some girl the year before. I had me six children." Tears filled her eyes. Today she wore her everyday dress, a faded grey polka–dot dress with a white collar. She could've been a school teacher, a sales girl, or a housewife in that dress. Anything but a working girl waiting for business.

Just then the new girl stormed out letting the door slam behind her. She shot Harriet and me a merciless scowl and proceeded to march up the drive to the main road.

Big Harriet chuckled. "Lorena can spot the bad apples a mile off."

"Did you love your husband?"

"Love?" She snickered. "Honey, I was hitched at thirteen back in Tennessee. Had my first kid nine months later. Breast fed 'em till they was two – anything to keep 'em from starvin'. But they kept on comin'. And there was farm work and house cleanin'. My oldest girl worked alongside me till she turned twelve and run off with a boy from the next farm over.

"And then my man got shot, and I was alone with five young children. Then one day about a year later, I took sick, real sick. And some lawman showed up with a paper that said I was unfit. So they took my babies away. Seemed some rich lady wanted to raise 'em. She'd seen us at the dime store and decided she liked the looks of 'em." Harriet stared into space, remembering.

"At first, I held off them sheriffs with my shotgun. But I had this pneumonia. And I couldn't stand up for long. So one day, I just gave up.

It was early evening and I stood at the end of the drive and watched them sheriffs drive off with my babies. It was summer, like now, and the sky was still light. A Monday evening, I won't never forget it. Cause Monday was wash day. But I'd been too sick to do it. I'd just drop in the soap and boiling water and let everything stew. And when I found the energy, I'd try to finish. But not that day. I remember going back into that quiet house thinkin' I was about to die. I could hardly breathe to begin with. And I had this fever that wouldn't go away. I started to scream and tear out my own hair. I was in a bad way.

"But I still had hope. Only thing that kept me goin'. I'd stuck a piece of paper in their shoes. The paper said my name. It told my children what I looked like and how I loved each one special – like. My second daughter helped me write them notes just before the sheriff pulled in. One day soon, when I get enough dough, I'm goin' back and find 'em all."

"Have they ever written you or —"

"Nah. It wouldn't be right just now. They got to grow up and learn. So they won't make the same mistakes as me, see. So they'll live in a nice house. A clean place with sunny rooms and nice wallpaper. With gardens and swell food … what I couldn't give 'em."

"You loved them."

Tears filled her eyes. Swiping at them with a meaty hand, she said, "Maybe they'll be ashamed of me. Maybe they won't know me. Especially the little ones. But it's what keeps me goin'. So you don't pay no attention to that cheap little quiff. You go about your business and know that your husband's gonna get better. That what we done to that bad man needed to be done."

I swallowed, managing a nod. "Thanks."

"Know what I thought when I seen you coming down to breakfast with Lorena that first mornin'. I thought you was a movie star."

"I tried to be a movie star. It's not so easy."

"Ain't nothin' worthwhile that's easy." Big Harriet popped the rest of her chocolate in her mouth and rose to her feet. "Busy night comin'. Better go on up and take a bath."

TWENTY-SEVEN

Back inside later, I was on my way upstairs to wash my hair, when I spotted a letter addressed to me on the entry table. Lex. He'd finally written. But the handwriting on the envelope was wrong. So was the return address. This letter had come from Long Island, New York.

I quickly tore open the envelope and read.

... I've been living with my half–sister and her husband near Montauk. The only time I use my gun now is when I go hunting or shoot old bottles off a tree stump. Then I hear about Dillinger,[4] Pretty Boy Floyd or the Lindbergh Baby, and I'm tempted to grab my guns and head out on my own. But I don't, because I've found contentment. Some days I fish. Other days I head down to the old lodge where the hooch is bad and the conversation worse, but the fellows there accept me as one of them.

Have you been up to see Mr. Rose again? He may not say it, but I know he'd like to see you. I've been there twice. He looks fine, although he always did. I hope you are happy out there in California. Best regards. Harris

PS: Have the Desanto brothers given you any trouble?

I pictured Harris. The pale, hardened, scar–faced war hero. The silent, stoic bodyguard, who dressed in dark hats and dark coats and rarely spoke. Clearly, he was worried about Lex. Which was why I shut my eyes to the cost of a long distance call.[5]

With shaking hands, I sat at the tiny table in the telephone alcove behind the entry, under the stairs, and rang for the operator. "Operator, I'd like to make a long distance call to Saranac Lake, New York." I gave the operator Mrs. Jankel's telephone number.

"That number may take awhile," the operator said. "I'll have to get back to you."

Waiting for the call to come through, I killed time in the parlor. Someone had left a mystery novel behind and I read the first fifty pages. Two calls came through for other girls, tying up the line, making me grip the arms of the chair till their conversations ended. At four in the afternoon, the telephone finally rang for me.

This time the operator said, "Please hold the line for your long distance telephone call." Then I heard the operator speaking to a woman.

Then Mrs. Jankel shouted, "Hello, this is Mrs. Jankel!"

"This is Jeri Rose. Lex Rose's wife. May I speak to him?"

"Oh, my Mrs. Rose, of all times. He's not here at the moment."

"Not there? But it's after seven there. Where —"

"I'm afraid he needed another regimen of treatment, and he's gone to visit a clinic nearby. He'll stay there for a week or two."

"Treatment?" My heart thudded.

"They're collapsing his lung again. Putting it to rest. Takes several treatments over a week or two."

My lips trembled. "Will he … will he come back to the cure

cottage?"

"Yes, Mrs. Rose. I wrote you about this. Then again, maybe I didn't. You see his bill needs to be paid."

"I know. I sent you a hundred dollars. I'm trying to keep up but I need more time Mrs. Jankel."

"But the bill's only getting larger."

"Mrs. Jankel, please understand, I send you what I can. I'm not trying to be difficult, I just ... please, don't throw him out. I know I'm behind with his bill, but he deserves ... " Tears filled my eyes and my voice failed. At last I said, "I can't let him go to some awful state home."

"Many of them are very nice, Mrs. Rose. But to be honest, I've never thrown out a patient yet. One so sick, I mean."

One so sick. I swallowed, wiping my eyes and nose with my fingers. "Please tell him I called. And thank you ... thank you so much. I hope you'll keep me informed. Because Lex, that is Mr. Rose, he doesn't tell me much about his condition. I mean, in his letters."

"As you wish, Mrs. Rose."

I hung up. Tears raced down my cheeks. Lex was sick. Possibly dying.

Upstairs in my room, hidden in a box along with my garters, costume jewelry, and stockings, was the last of my money. Seventy–nine dollars and forty–eight cents. Not enough to support me for long and certainly not enough to pay Mrs. Jankel, too. Visiting Lex now was out of the question. Between the train fare, food, and a room in Saranac Lake, I'd go broke. Yet I craved the sound of his voice. The feel of his hand holding mine. If only I could see his handsome face again. A face no photograph could do justice to.

Days passed. I asked Lorena several times about Tito's body, but she always said the same thing. "Stop worrying so much. He's not going anywhere. We buried him real deep, honey."

During the same period that July, Franky and I saw each other constantly. We rode horses, swam, had dinner together, went to the movies, and made love. I also landed a job as a movie extra for ten days at almost eight dollars a day, after Franky told a director friend who needed girls for a saloon scene about me. I gave Lorena her seventeen for the next month's food and lodging, and sent fifty to Mrs. Jankel's for Lex's bill. And with the fifty dollars Franky had given me yesterday, I felt a lot easier.

I always meant to refuse Franky for anything more than dinner or the occasional small gift. But Mrs. Jankel's letters kept coming along with Lex's bills.

TWENTY-EIGHT

"Mother, you're wrong. *I'm* not paying my bills here. Jeri is," Lex said.

Ida gaped at her son. "I don't believe you. How could she afford this place?"

Lex didn't mention the account he'd left for Jeri at the United Savings and Trust. But then he'd heard the bank had failed. "I'm not sure. But she can't be having an easy time of it."

Ida stood. "Oh, dear, oh, dear. If only you'd told me. You should have said something." She saw herself tossing Lex's letters into the fire. Letters Jeri had never received. "I did something. Something hard to explain."

"Mother, what is it? Don't tell me you're marrying Sidney Shineman."

She faced him, her large eyes wide. "Absolutely not. That revolting little worm was already married. He deceived me."

"What happened? Did his wife call you?"

She stared down at her hands. "I went through his wallet one day when things didn't add up."

"You mean, he was suddenly pinching pennies."

"May I please finish my story or would you like to tell it?"

Pursing her lips, she brushed imaginary lint off her suit then said, "I got suspicious when we could never see each other Saturdays or Sundays. So one afternoon, after lunch, when he dropped by my place, I purposely spilled a drink on him. I made quite a fuss about cleaning his jacket. I told him to relax while I took care of it in the bathroom. When the door was locked, I went through his wallet. And found a family picture. One of those awful group portraits where everyone looks stunned. He was standing beside this big woman. Not very attractive. But clearly the wifely type."

"Unlike you."

"You act as if I've never been married."

"Only three times."

"I'd marry again, too, if I could find someone. But everyone's so poor now. I saw Darla Abernathy recently. In the glove department at Bergdorf's. I almost didn't recognize her. You know how la–de–dah she used to be with her big parties, four houses, and all those servants. Well, she looked poor as a church mouse. Dreadful really. I barely had the heart to greet her."

"But I'll bet you forced yourself."

"For old time's sake. She admitted that she and Thomas were barely eating. And there I was in a divine little fox jacket from Saks that Sidney had just bought me. So I offered her five dollars and she took it. Can you believe it?"

"Sorry to hear that."

She sighed. "Oh, dear, what were we talking about?"

"You regretted not telling me something."

She took a deep breath then sighed. "Yes, well, I seem to have forgotten what I meant to say." Why upset Lex now when he was slightly better after his last treatment? "You really should write Jeri more often. After all, she probably needs a little encouragement."

"Mother, you surprise me. I never thought you liked Jeri."

The following day, after his mother had taken the train back to the city, Nurse Bronson stuck her head in and saw Lex seal another envelope. Marching in, she instantly felt his forehead. "You should be out on the porch. It's a nice day."

"It's still cold. And it looks like a storm brewing."

She grunted. "I suppose it's warmer in California where your wife is."

"Probably."

"You gonna mail that letter or stuff it in the dresser like you did with the others?"

"Haven't decided yet."

"Since you wrote it, you might as well send it,

He was surprised to see concern in her eyes, green eyes hidden by spectacles. Joyless eyes which normally gave nothing away. Until now. Maybe she did have a heart. Maybe she even cared for him and her other patients, not that she ever showed an ounce of warmth to anyone.

To him, she behaved like an efficient machine. Pills, food, bedpans, thermometers, bathing, frigid air, and bed rest seemed to be the extent of her feelings. Except when someone like Mrs. Weiss died. He'd seen Nurse Bronson out his window by the hearse that night. The way her shoulders shook as she held a handkerchief to her nose.

She'd cried since then, too. Ten times now. It was always the same. Someone would call out and bang their metal cup in the night. He'd hear whispers, nervous voices outside his door before the hearse arrived. In a day or two, a new patient would arrive to fill the vacant bed. And later, Nurse Bronson would rattle off the rules, sounding like his army drill Sargent during the war.

Ten deaths in ten months.

"Here," he said, handing Nurse Bronson the envelope. "It

already has a stamp."

***

"Why can't I go to New York with you?" I asked Franky for the second time that night as we sped back to The Rainbow after another evening at his house with dinner in the dining room and sex out by his pool. "I'm not working now and ..."

Franky abruptly slowed down and yanked the wheel forcing the car off the road onto the soft shoulder where the engine conked out.

"What was that for?" I barked, startled by his reaction.

Franky took a deep breath. "Sorry. But I already told you about the tabloids and gossip columnists. Yes, they know you exist but they still don't know your name. Dancing, a few laughs, they can't prove anything. But if we traveled together and checked into the same hotel room, it would antagonize the press and Lupe's lawyer. If we aren't careful, you could be blamed for breaking up my marriage."

"And ruining your good guy cowboy image," I said, as acid rose in my throat. The subtle differences between our being seen together in New York or dancing together at a Hollywood nightclub escaped me. "You've always got some reason," I grumbled.

"Look, honey, I don't make the rules."

"But I'm not famous. No one cares about me."

"They'd turn up the heat on both of us. And with this new deal in the works, I need to keep my nose clean. Out here in Hollywood they're grumbling about the project, making excuses. They're fed up with westerns. All they want are gangster pictures and musicals. I need to convince the big money man back east that I'm the one he needs. He's a fan. He knows my pictures."

I shut my eyes, confused. "Look, I came here from New York. If I go back there, no one can be sure I'm following you. Why should all our plans be canceled just because Boyd Anderson refuses to marry Lupe?"

"Because Lupe and I are still married. And she's determined to keep me tied to her."

"So we can't even be seen together?"

"After I've signed the contracts and the studio can't back out of the deal, the newspapers can say what they like. We just have to be patient until I'm set. Then we can meet in New York like we planned. And once I'm on the payroll, I can do more for you financially. Get you settled in a decent place. Lupe might get so fed up with the bad publicity, she'll hop on a train to Reno and divorce me."

Putting my head back against the seat, I shut my eyes. Why was I pushing so hard? I wasn't even sure I'd want Franky if both of us were free to get married. Because in spite of Lex's ten month silence, I still loved him. Maybe I just wanted to go east because September had finally arrived. Here in the valley the heat was punishing. But in New York, Central Park would soon be full of fall colors and the fragrance of burning leaves. Store windows would fill up with the latest fashions. And street vendors would be selling chestnuts. I imagined the brisk air on my face and the sense of renewal.

"When are you leaving?" I asked.

"Friday."

In five days. I envied him. Back in 1930, I'd briefly shared a Brooklyn flat with a girl named Mary Alice, the sister of a coworker at Saks. At night we'd listen to the radio. On Sundays we'd see a movie. It seemed comforting now, even cozy, providing I overlooked a few things. Like the police hounding me to catch Lex in an illegal act. Or the fact that Lex couldn't turn a corner without some woman trying to seduce him. And the painful memory of Lex's initial reluctance to marry me.

"You can reach me at the Waldorf. I should be there for a

week or two," Franky said.

"How long till things get settled?"

"Three months tops. I should be filming in New Jersey and Long Island by early spring."

"Are you sure you want me with you?" I expected to hear a hesitation in his voice, a lack of conviction.

Instead, his expression was deadly earnest and entirely believable when he said, "Of course. More than anything else."

"In the meantime, Lupe might meet someone new," I said, thinking how improbable this seemed. Lupe would be back like a hound on the scent of quail as soon as she heard Franky was working again.

Franky reached for my hand. As always, his hard–earned calluses surprised me, because he never sounded like an illiterate cowboy. Those studio voice coaches certainly knew their business.

"I suppose this all sounds pretty complicated. I didn't mean to upset you," he said.

Before I could respond, he pulled me to him and smothered my doubts with a kiss. I clung to him, relieved. In seconds, my body responded to his attentions. To his warm cheek pressed against my own, the feel of his lips as they traced the flesh over my throat. And the desire that overwhelmed me like an addiction.

He quickly slid the shoulders of my new satin dress down. A dress worn without a bra. Under the stars, he brought his mouth to my breast until his lips gripped my nipple making me cry out. Without a word, he roughly lifted my dress to open a path for his lips and burning hands.

"Jeri," he gasped, pressing me to him, as he buried his face between my legs and guided me further down on the seat, as his fingers tore at my silk panties.

I hardly noticed the car's door handle digging into my back or the fire engines roaring by in the distance. Or the sweet scent of orange blossoms, chaparral, and smoke, as he roughly separated my thighs and his fingers rose tantalizingly between my legs.

Breathing hard, he fumbled with his pants. With a soft groan, he slowly entered me. Tonight, he took his time. Eyes shut, he rose powerfully above me. His handsome face and well–formed shoulders loomed against the night sky, lit by a golden moon and fiery stars. For those few seconds, his desire for me gave me power. Only the blissful movement of our bodies counted as we both rode a passionate wave to a climax. Franky abruptly gasped and shuddered.

A heart beat later, he collapsed on top of me then rolled away. At least I'd worn the sea sponge soaked in vinegar this time. The one Lorena had given me.

Then a sudden breeze washed over me, making me shiver.

"It's cold," I said, sitting up.

Franky didn't answer. He was too busy fastening his pants, tucking in his shirt, and combing his hair. For me, dressing in the car was nearly impossible. I gave up trying to pull up my girdle and stockings and finally stuffed them in my purse. I did manage to slip my dress over my head but couldn't reach the buttons in back. After struggling for several seconds, I hoped Franky might offer to help. But he hadn't looked at me since he'd climbed off me.

"Gimme a hand here," I finally said, turning my back so he could help me. Dressed, I sat back in my seat and pulled my skirt down over my knees until no one could tell what we'd just done.

"Getting late," he said, easing the car back onto the rural road and heading toward The Rainbow. His beige cowboy hat sat on the seat between us and his hair blew in the wind. His shoulders, under his sports jacket, were relaxed as he focused on the road. As usual, I worried that his post–coital silence meant something. I'd just formulated what I'd say to him when the Packard crested the hill and

I tried to comprehend why thick smoke hovered over The Rainbow and foul fumes cloaked the clear night air. Seconds later, as the car descended toward the house, I spied flames.

TWENTY-NINE

Fire and scorching heat enveloped The Rainbow house. Flying embers and demonic flames gorged themselves, licking at the wood and paint, threatening anyone foolish enough to get close. Without a word, I abandoned Franky and raced down the dirt hill on foot to the group of girls in robes and bed sheets. Like a flock of birds, they clustered together and silently watched the wood structure as it crackled and burned like old newspapers. Fire fighters, with their primitive hoses, had given up trying to save the old structure and now fought to keep the flames from spreading to the dry grasses nearby.

Without warning, Lorena appeared by my side in her robe. Her eyes were red and swollen, and she held a crumpled handkerchief in her hand. "Where've you been?" she cried.

"Lorena, what happened?"

She stared at the old house. "It's all gone."

"What about Jimmy? Where's Jimmy?"

Lorena shook her head and blew her nose.

"He got out, didn't he?" I asked, grabbing her shoulders.

"I don't know. He never came out of his room. He must've gotten drunk and fallen asleep with his door locked. We tried to rouse him. I banged and banged on his door. I screamed for him, but he wouldn't come out. I couldn't find my keys and there wasn't time to look for them. The fire... it happened so quickly. My artwork, the furniture, even my damn cat's gone," she sobbed.

Horror ripped through me. "I don't understand. How could this happen?"

"One minute we were closing down for the night and the next … there was smoke and heat. I tried to save everyone. But Pumpkin ran under my bed …"

In a flash, Elvira appeared. She grabbed Lorena in a bear hug. Lorena clung to Elvira.

"Ain't nothin' in the world to do but pray the mornin' comes," Elvira soothed. "And thank the Lord we all still here."

The flames seemed to spit and jump as they hungrily lapped at the edges of the brick chimney trying to consume it, too, having already devoured everything else.

I stared at what was left of the house, the place where my room had been. I only hoped Jimmy was okay. Maybe he'd gotten out. Maybe it was all a misunderstanding. Of all the people I'd met in California, Jimmy and Lorena meant the most to me. I trusted them. I'd even considered telling them about my being a time traveler. Now, I'd missed my chance with Jimmy.

Suddenly, I remembered the body. Tito's body. It was buried under the rubble, too.

"Someone was smoking," Lorena said, shaking her head. "That's what the fire chief thinks. Or it could've been an electrical fire. He's not sure yet. When I think of how many times I warned those gals about smoking in their rooms."

Jimmy had always laughed at that rule. He constantly smoked, absently lighting up, dropping matches on the floor as he banged away on his old Royal, counting words, worrying if anyone would like his stories.

All at once, trucks filled with people from nearby farms arrived. Dazed people wearing old clothes swarmed across the land, their expressions filled with awe and fear. Exhilaration too, because of the wrath before them. Many offered to grab a bucket or a shovel to help. But the head fireman said there was nothing left to do. So the onlookers joined the whores and watched The Rainbow burn.

I thought of Lorena's new washing machine, the sewing machine, the refrigerator. Pumpkin the cat, Jimmy, and Tito Desanto down in the basement.

"Had me five hundred bucks saved. Stuck in my old Bible," Big Harriet said, rubbing her eyes and squinting at the burning house. "I was countin' the days till I could bring my two youngest babies out. Don't know if I'll ever find 'em now."

"My dough was under my bed, stuffed in a sock," Thelma whined. "I was gonna open up the nicest little dress shop you ever seen back home in Ohio."

"Guess we all shoulda kept our dough in the bank," Myra concluded.

"I was afraid to trust a bank with so many of 'em goin' bust. And Pretty Boy Floyd and Bonnie and Clyde on the loose," Thelma added.

"Bonnie and Clyde? Ain't they back in Missouri and Louisiana?" Big Harriet said.

Around four in the morning, when the bones of the house stood black and pitted, the girls tried to peer into the debris to see if anything had survived. Some things had. A metal spoon. A china bowl. But there were no signs of Jimmy or the cat. Kneeling, Lorena retrieved an old coffee creamer and gazed at it.

"The tin box?" I asked, suddenly remembering a metal candy box where Lorena stored her cash.

Lorena stuck her hand under her robe and pulled out the box.

"First thing I grabbed."

The clopping noise of a horse and wagon broke through our stupor. A farmer, curious about the fire, sat on an old horse–drawn wagon and gazed at the charred remains. "Sorry to see her go," the farmer said, shaking his head at the blackened mess. "Sure gonna miss you ladies. Be happy to drive anyone who needs a ride into town later. Just drop by my place."

"Jeri?" a voice called.

I turned. *Franky*. I'd forgotten all about him.

"A few of the girls can stay at my place, " he said softly. "No one will bother them on my ranch."

"Thanks. That's … very generous of you. I'll tell Lorena."

Every time I thought I knew Franky, he surprised me. One moment he was selfish. The next moment he was thoughtful and generous. When I felt neglected, he sensed it and sent flowers. But this morning I suspected the invitation was a polite gesture, the right thing to say at the right time.

Lorena and I exchanged looks. She, too, recognized the sentiment behind Franky's offer. "Thanks for being so kind, but these are my girls, and I need to get them situated for the long haul."

Franky tipped his hat. "I'll be in my car," he said to me.

"All right, listen up," Lorena said, her voice surprisingly solid.

The girls stopped digging through the rubble with sticks and stared hopefully at Lorena.

"Old man Quinn from next door is willing to drive you girls to town on the back of his truck," Lorena said. "Just walk over to his place. There's a rooming house called Mrs. McCawber's. They say it's clean with food that won't put you in the morgue. Though I doubt it'll be up to Elvira's standards. Or there's Bunny Blaine's. Anybody here ever worked for Bunny?"

The girls glanced at each other and shrugged.

"She's got a house off Sunset in town. Pretty spiffy. I got her telephone number. You can call her when you get to the city." Lorena handed Big Harriet a scrap of paper. "Maybe she needs girls." Lorena shot me a look.

I understood. Bunny Blaine liked them young and pretty, the small town beauties with big aspirations. Girls who arrived in Hollywood hoping to grab the brass ring and break into pictures but ended up broke, doing another kind of acting.

Elvira stood apart, clutching the few things she'd rescued from the fire. Her dark eyes looked weary, dejected. I imagined how she felt. An aging black woman with references from a brothel would have a hard time finding work when there were hundreds of white girls willing to clean houses in 1933. At least Elvira had managed to grab her son's picture, her wrist watch, and her bed quilt before escaping, the one benefit of sleeping in the servants' room off the kitchen on the first floor.

"There's a room over the stables at my folk's place," Lorena told Elvira. "My family might try to work you to death. But as soon as I set up housekeeping, I'll bring you along."

Elvira nodded solemnly. "I'll be ready."

After endless hugs, promises to write, and quite a few tears, the girls of The Rainbow began to walk up the hill to the neighbor's farm.

Lorena stood beside me. "Even if I rebuild the place, it'll never be the same. That perfect blend we had. You can't plan something like that. It just happens."

Tears filled my eyes. A whole world had gone up in smoke. A place where I'd never been lonely. Knock on a wall and there was Jimmy, Lorena, Elvira, or one of the working girls. But at least now, no one would ever find that body in the cellar.

As we trudged up the road to the neighbor's house, an old car screeched to halt, and the passenger's door sprang open. Lorena and I stared as Jimmy jumped out. He froze as if hit by an alien's beam and gaped at the charred remains of The Rainbow. Maybe he was thinking about his typewriter. Or a story he'd almost finished. A second later, he spied Lorena and stumbled toward her.

Lorena's eyes widened. "Damn you!" she sobbed. "I thought you were dead." She rushed at him, grabbed him by his thin old jacket and sobbed into his chest.

Jimmy's voice was hoarse. "I was tending bar in Hollywood. For God's sake, Lorena. What happened?"

"I thought … Thank God, you're here. But Pumpkin disappeared."

"It'll be okay. I'll find her," Jimmy said, rubbing her back.

But Pumpkin couldn't be found. Maybe she'd escaped into the hills when the fire started or she'd gotten trapped in the house. No one knew.

For a little while that morning, Lorena, Billy, Elvira, and I dug through the blackened remains. By ten, we were ready to face the dreaded move back to the Coopers' farm. Lorena had the idea of fixing up the old bunkhouse for The Rainbow girls. Franky drove me over. Lorena followed in her truck with Elvira. Jimmy moved into a place in downtown Van Nuys.

By the time Franky parked out front, the sun had turned the desert into a kiln. Uncle Clement, dressed in the filthiest longjohns imaginable, shuffled across the yard feeding the pigs and chickens in between spitting tobacco juice.

"So you're back again," Clement sneered, sending an especially large glob of brown juice at Lorena's feet as she led Elvira across the yard toward the shabby farmhouse.

Franky and I stood by his Packard. He stared down at the powdery dirt and kicked a pebble in between gaping at the squalid farm or squinting into the glaring sun.

"I better get going," he said. "I'll call in a few days. We can have dinner before I leave." Taking me by the shoulders, he planted a kiss on my cheek. He looked tired.

I was half dead myself. Plus a dozen questions raced through my mind, but I was too tired to talk. My puny savings and all my things were lost. And I had this awful feeling that while my uncle scratched his ass and the pigs nosed through the table scraps strewn across the yard, Franky was making a final exit from my life. And I had no idea how to stop him. Or whether I even wanted to.

"Sure, see you sometime," I breathed, turning my back to him and crossing the dusty yard to the house. It took a heroic effort not to look back. Or beg. Instead, I dragged open the creaking screen door and let it slam shut. Tears spilled down my cheeks. Then I heard the Packard's engine and the crunchy sound the tires made as they rode over dirt and gravel as the car pulled away.

Inside, pots banged in the tiny kitchen. Then I heard Aunt Violet say, "This is God's wrath upon a sinner, Lorena. You get down on your knees and thank the good Lord that he saw fit to spare you. You and them other sinners."

To which Lorena replied, "Guess that's why you're livin' so high yourself."

My heart sank. Being here was a mistake. Mrs. McCawber's boarding house would have been better. And if her boarding house was full, I'd move back to The Bayridge. Anything but this rundown farm and with its so–called good people with their pious damnation of everything.

Upstairs in Lorena's room, I began to plan my future. Tomorrow, I'd put on one of my good dresses, now stored at Mr. Chin's Laundry. I'd haunt every studio in town until I found a job, even if I had to hitchhike across the county. I'd make a pest of myself until somebody hired me as an actress, a waitress, or a typist. What's more, I'd pay that sanitarium bill and take care of Lex myself. Maybe Franky Wyatt wouldn't take me back to New York, but I could damn well get there on my own

That evening, after a dismal dinner of tough fried meat, turnip greens, and butter beans, served alongside an awkward silence, deep sighs, and scathing looks from Uncle Clement, Lorena and I shivered through cold baths in the upstairs metal tub, then escaped to her room. By 8:30, we were dressed for bed. Lorena's folks had turned in by seven. Elvira had settled in the barn with Rufus.

"Stay still or I'll smear your nails," Lorena growled, balancing a bottle of red polish on her knee while painting my nails and getting tipsy from the bootleg brandy in her flask.

"Don't tell me you lost everything that wasn't in that little tin box?" I said.

"Not everything. The First National has a few bucks of mine."

"Trust you to have a backup plan."

"Yeah, I'm a genius when it comes to money. I just don't have any sense about men." She let go of my hand and twisted the polish cap back on the bottle and slipped it back in her night stand.

My hands sparkled with fresh red polish. "Thanks, they look great."

"You're welcome." Lorena took another swig of brandy. "Want some? It'll help you sleep." She held out the silver flask.

"No thanks. Guess you're pretty devastated."

A soft utterance told me she was. "It's not just the house fire. I'm tired. Really tired. And on days like this, I'd like someone strong to lean on."

"What about Roger?"

"He took a powder. Not a word from him in ten days."

"Maybe he's out of town or —"

"Maybe. If I get enough horse liniment in me, I might even give him a call and find out."

"Lorena, don't. Not tonight after the fire and everything. Wait till you feel better."

"I happen to think this is the perfect time. Roger's either a good guy or a stinker."

"But what if he's just … busy? You're upset right now. He's bound to hear your desperation. And you know how scared fellas get when you need them too much."

Lorena's expression grew icy. "What makes you such an expert?"

"Nothing, I —"

"You're just so sure he doesn't love me, aren't you? You can't imagine a swell guy like Roger Starling loving a no–account whore like me."

"But you told me yourself, there was no real future with him."

"Did I? I forget. Anyway, I don't intend to let him slink away without consequences. And he's no worse than that has–been western star you're stuck on. A guy with a wife and kid." Eyes blazing, she rose off the bed, shot me an angry glance, then strode from the room, shutting the door with a sharp click. A heart beat later, I heard her slippers flapping on the steep stairs.

My mouth felt dry. Everything Lorena had said about Franky was true. But Roger was no better. He'd never been serious about Lorena. To him, she was a diversion like fishing or golf. Because guys like Roger understood their social position from birth, since the day they tried on their first pair of knickers. Roger was expected to share his life with someone from the right family, with the right money. In 1933, people from Pasadena society didn't marry farm girls from Kansas, let alone a brothel madam. Still, I would've sliced off my thumb rather than hurt Lorena. She was my best friend. Even so, it was time to find my own place.

I woke at dawn before the Coopers' rooster crowed. I quietly rose off the parlor sofa where I'd slept, preferring to keep out of Lorena's way. I put my few things in an old laundry bag and scribbled a note to Lorena. The note thanked her for everything, apologized for saying the wrong thing, and promised to be in touch as soon as I had an address. I stuffed the note in Lorena's beaded bag and left it on the kitchen table.

At 5:30, around the same time my uncle was pulling up his suspenders and stepping into his boots to milk the cows and feed the chickens, I slipped out of the house. A lot had happened to me since I'd first arrived here in the valley. But like so many other people living during these hard times, I never managed to stay in one place long.

Outside, a burst of light over the hills to the east meant the sun would soon be up and the earth would begin to broil. In the waning coolness, I hurried down the long drive to the road. Minutes later, at the edge of the property by the wheelbarrow, where yesterday's vegetables had begun to stink like garbage, I sat down on a worn tree stump to wait. I had a quarter for anyone driving by willing to take me to town. From downtown Van Nuys, I'd catch a trolley into the city.

It seemed as if a few seconds had passed when I woke to someone shaking me. Lorena stood over me, a basket of fresh eggs under her arm. "Jeri, what in blazes are you doing here?"

"Morning," I said. "Pretty early for you to be up."

Lorena glanced at my purse and laundry bag. Her eyes were red and puffy. "Where exactly are you headed?"

"Town, if I can hitch a ride."

Lorena placed her eggs on the ground and slid beside me on the tree stump. "It's cause of me, isn't it? Cause of what I said last night."

"Forget it."

"I can take losing the girls, even my house, but not you. Who will I talk to?"

Relief warmed my insides. "Elvira's still here. And I'll visit when I can."

Hope flooded Lorena's face. She stood. "Stay where you are. I'll take you to town myself."

I felt as if I could breathe again.

Minutes later in Lorena's truck, as she concentrated on the road, she confided in me. "You were right about Roger. The stinker said he'd enjoyed knowing me, but he was on his way to Saratoga to meet his fiancé. *Men.* You'd think I'd know better. Guess I'm just thickheaded about love."

"It's not your fault for wanting someone exciting and wonderful."

"At least I still have a little cabbage. I checked with my bank yesterday and my account has over twenty grand. Before the fire, I was gonna retire in five years. Take a long cruise around the world, then pick out a swell house on the beach. I was gonna put all this behind me.."

"Lorena, you're rich. That's a fortune. If I were you, I'd buy a place at the beach right away. Then I'd take the rest of my dough and buy stock in GE and GM and hold onto it for about fifteen years."

"What're you, a fortune teller?"

"Yeah, that's me, the fortune teller with fifty bucks to her name. And that's only because Franky shoved the money in my hand yesterday before he took off. "

The bar Lorena drove us to was packed. Drunken laughter, loud dance music, and pounding feet made my head hurt. "What're all these people doing here so early in the morning?" I asked.

"Night workers. Girls having a fun day off."

"Let's try Mrs. McCawber's telephone again. I need to lie down," I said, massaging my temples.

"Just a little longer," Lorena pleaded. "I can't face that farm unless I'm smashed."

"Why not get a place together? A little house or an apartment. Just until we get back on our feet," I said.

"What about you and Franky?"

I gazed at her from under heavy lids. "With or without Franky Wyatt, I'm going back to New York. If he doesn't want me, I'll take up where I left off before I married Lex. Maybe I'll even get my old job back."

"What job?"

"Salesgirl at Saks or Hirsh's, a shop for ladies. I miss seeing the leaves change colors and Halloween decorations everywhere. I miss having coffee and pie at The Automat."

"Say the word, and I'll put you on a train."

"Sure. One day soon."

"Why not leave today?"

I shrugged.

"Because of Franky?"

I nodded. "He's on his way to New York himself. He's still trying to get that cowboy series made. He should be back in a week or two. And when he gets back, I'll decide what to do."

"You're scared about seeing Lex again, aren't you?"

I sighed. "What if he's thin and hollow–eyed? He used to be so handsome. And I'd like to remember him that way. Besides, I'm not anxious to break his heart. If only I could get a job. I swear I'd drive a truck loaded with dynamite if I could just earn a few bucks."

Unfortunately, Mrs. McCawber's boarding house was full, thanks to The Rainbow girls. The Bayridge had no room either. So with no place to go, I took the long journey back to the farm with Lorena, promising myself it was temporary.

THIRTY

"Jeri Devlin's waiting to see you, Mr. Bianco," the secretary announced over an intercom, a bored expression on her aging, powdered face.

A moment later, the door labeled *Casper Bianco, Publicity*, opened and Mr. Bianco emerged. Under five feet, in spite of his shoe lifts, he had a thick nose, a bushy mustache, and a hairstyle meant to cover an expanding bald spot. Lorena's description of the former Rainbow client was accurate down to his expensive dark flannel suit and bay rum aftershave.

"Come in, come in," Bianco said, sweeping me inside with his hand, and shutting the door tight. Biting on his cigar, Bianco settled on the edge of his large brown desk and stripped me bare with his small eyes, starting with my broad hat and narrow dress to my slender ankles. "How about a good look," he said, gesturing with his cigar for me to turn around.

I gave him the full treatment, moving slowly, so his puffy dark eyes could feast on every curve.

"Have a seat," he said, pointing to a low chair beneath him. Dropping down, I let my skirt ride up just enough to keep his interest.

"So, tell me about yourself. How'd you meet Lorena?" His gaze settled on the front of my navy dress with its white collar and modest neckline, which only hinted at my cleavage.

"She's my cousin."

"Really. You in the same line?"

"I'm an actress."

"Done anything to prove it? I mean, besides the eighth grade play back home."

Here came some real acting. "I was an extra on Broadway. I had a walk on in *King Kong*. But I'm currently between jobs." I used my most educated voice, which didn't impress him. To be fair, there were millions of college graduates who regularly ate out of garbage cans.

His hand moved to my knee. "How anxious are you to break into pictures?"

It occurred to me that he might simply pull down his pants or open his fly. This had never happened to me – so far. Mostly, the sleazy producers I'd met just suggested what they wanted. But I'd heard stories. Even waiting tables would beat having Casper Bianco's dick in my mouth. "I'm anxious to get work but I'm not starving," I said, removing his stumpy fingers.

"Too bad. Sometimes a hungry girl has an open mind." His sweaty hand returned to my knee. "I can help you, honey. Make sure your name gets around with producers, directors. I'll see you get a small speaking part in our next picture. Would ya like that?"

His hand had inched up my thigh. "Sounds wonderful," I said, smiling, wondering how he'd react if I hit him with my purse.

Rising, he stuck his head out the door and said. "No calls, Doris." After shutting his door, he dropped onto an old leather sofa and patted the space beside him. "Come sit by me, sweetheart."

"It's Mrs. Rose. And this chair's just fine."

He raised a curious brow as if this was just the first round and he had bigger ammunition to come. "First, I'll need some consideration from you, Mrs. Rose. Understand?"

I didn't need an Oscar to fall on me. I grimly thought of the expense of getting here. New stockings, fresh heels on my shoes, and trolley fare. Not to mention those sanitarium bills waiting to be paid. I pictured myself emerging empty handed into the glaring sunlight. And Nicky Desanto waiting for me.

"So how about drinks tonight?" he asked, leaning forward and putting his hand up my skirt all the way to my panties. I was an inch from walloping him in the jaw, when a woman's shrill voice from the outer office broke the spell.

"When I get my hands on that ugly midget, he going to be sorry he was born!"

Lupe Cardona. I'd recognize her voice in my sleep

Bianco cursed softly, shot to his feet, straightened his tie, and quickly said, "Look, Mrs. Rose, it's no good right now. But I know a swell little place. Great drinks. Good steaks. We could meet there tonight. Have a bite. Discuss your career potential. Pickup where we left off."

The shrill voice outside the door reached a crescendo. "I going to murder him!"

"I can't. My husband and kid expect me for dinner."

Bianco's expression turned to ice. "Look, honey, I'm a busy man —"

"With a wife named Annabel, three children, and a big house in Beverly Hills."

Bianco's eyes widened. "You ... know?"

"Please Mr. Bianco. I can answer phones, type, anything. Anything that we won't have to be ashamed of."

"But I already have a secretary and —"

"Think Mr. Bianco. A secretary, an usher in the theater, a script girl."

"This isn't Central Casting. And there are hungrier girls. Girls willing to —"

"A job Mr. Bianco. A prop girl, a receptionist, a stand in …"

Without warning, the door exploded open, slamming me in the back. I gasped and fell forward out of the way.

Lupe Cardona charged in. "You disgusting little worm!" she shrieked. "You fat little nobody. Three times I call. Three times thee puta out front tell me you no can come to thee telephone. And all thee time you are in here fucking thee starlet. I have you fired for this. I have your pathetic little penis stuffed and hung on thee Christmas tree."

"Lupe, darling, please hear me out. I just got back this very minute and —"

"You think I am stupid? You think you can lie to Lupe and she no understand?"

"Please, Lupe. Tell me what I can do. Anything …"

Lupe loomed over Mr. Bianco, all four feet eight inches of her. Dressed in a brown silk dress, her hair scraped back into a bun, six pounds of make-up, and a dozen dead foxes hanging around her shoulders, she clutched her snake–skin pocketbook as if she meant to strike Bianco with it. "My maid, that whore–faced puta, is fucking thee chauffeur. So tell me, Mr. Pig, who is going to drive me to thee gala tonight? You?"

"Well, *I* would but my wife —"

"You better come up with thee answer now, you ugly little fat man. Because I angry enough to have your little thing stapled to thee door."

Bianco's eyes widened. "But Lupe, honey …"

Thumping her purse against his chest, she moved nose–to–nose with the little man. "My father owns this studio, you disgusting boil. Do you forget? And now, today, *I*, Lupe Cardona, thee Guadalajara Spitfire, have been forced to drive here alone."

"My God, Lupe, I had no idea —"

"I am fed up with this *sheet.*"

Bianco plastered a sickening simper on his sweaty face and spoke calmly, softly. "Now, Lupe, you know I'll find you someone."

"Don't *Lupe* me. I want a man. And I want him *now.*"

"Haven't you got a friend? What about your husband? Or that nice boyfriend Boyd —"

"How dare you mention this disgusting name to me. My father is going to hear about this. Now, get me a *man!*"

Sweating profusely, Bianco's hand shook as he picked up his phone and mumbled into the receiver. "Lupe, darling, please have a seat and I promise —"

"No more of your stupid promises. I want action."

Bianco's gaze abruptly settled on me. Trapped in a corner, I'd been watching Lupe's tirade hoping I'd escape her notice. But seeing me, Bianco hung up the receiver. "Lupe, I've got the perfect answer. This young woman here is exactly the person you need. She's educated, willing, and very reliable." His eyes begged me to concur.

Disgust filled Lupe's expression, as if she'd just found me on my hands and knees under Bianco's desk. "I am not interested. I want thee man, not another dirty slut. And *she* cannot drive me to thee gala tonight, or did you forget? Am I supposed to walk there tonight? Or maybe you like for me to crawl? Is that what you want, you fat, pathetic little —"

"Now Lupe —"

"Listen good, *mi amigo*. I don't care who you get, but he better be handsome and he better be on time. I will be ready at 5:45. And he better fit thee uniform. *Understand?*"

Bianco bobbed his head. "I'll call the agency immediately. Or find you a handsome young actor."

"Don't just stand there," Lupe suddenly barked at me. "Carry thee packages and hold her hand." She pushed a little girl, who'd been hiding behind her, at me. Wearing a baby doll dress with a smock, a hat, gloves, and black Mary Janes, the child looked terrified.

So *this* was Franky's daughter Francesca.

Bianco pushed me toward the door. "Go on. Take Mrs. Cardona home. And drive carefully," Bianco ordered.

Horrified and dumfounded, I gaped at Mr. Bianco who dismissed me by fluttering the back of his hands. Discouraged by this unseemly, I grabbed the child's hand and packages and trotted after the tiny Guadalajara Spitfire who marched out briskly, in spite of her extremely high heels and tight skirt.

An enormous cream colored Lincoln Sedan Convertible blocked the front path to the building. After tossing her keys at my feet, Lupe marched around to the passenger door and waited for me to sprint around the car and open it for her. Like a good chauffeur, I stood at attention as Lupe tossed her furs over her shoulder, pushed Francesca ahead, then slid into the back seat. "Hurry up. I no like thee sun," Lupe barked.

I refrained from asking Lupe why, if she hated the sun, did she have the car's top down. But I clammed up. I was more terrified of the gear shift than anything else. The car might have an H shift like I had back in 1997 in my antique Carmen Ghia, or it might be something entirely new.

"Don't sit there like thee dog." Lupe snarled. "Drive."

I managed to put the car in gear and start it. The car hummed to life, and we were soon sailing out the studio gates. Lupe stared into space, seemingly engrossed in an inner movie of her own. We emerged onto a busy street without the benefit of a light or stop sign.

Glancing at Lupe in my rearview mirror, I thought it strange that neither Boyd Anderson nor Barry Arlen, the young actor spotted with Lupe swimming in the nude at Rosarito Beach, Mexico, had offered to squire her to the gala tonight. Mostly, I struggled to comprehend the extraordinary circumstances which had thrown Lupe and me together.

Then Lupe said, "We have met before, no?"

I glanced at the rearview mirror and lied. "No, madam." Could Lupe, who'd been drunk and otherwise occupied that night at the Rio Rosa Club in Havana, remember me?

"How old are you?" she abruptly asked in an almost friendly manner.

"Thirty," I said, aging myself by two years so Lupe might regard me as less threatening.

"I will be twenty–three next month."

Francesca was eight, meaning Lupe would've given birth at fourteen. Besides, Franky had already told me that Lupe was thirty–three and had been twenty–one twelve years ago when they got married.

"You don't look bad for thirty," Lupe went on. "Still, I no can believe we will get along. I no like pretty girls in my house. But today I keep you. I will have Mr. Bianco find someone better tomorrow."

"In that case, I need fifteen dollars for today," I said.

Lupe's mouth opened. Her eyes flashed fury. "You are not to speak to Lupe this way. I am thee *patróna*."

"Good, I've always wanted to meet a *patróna*." Pulling the great cream colored boat over to the curb in the middle of a busy intersection, I opened my door and climbed out. "See ya."

"What you do?" Lupe screeched. "No, wait!"

Without a glance back, I headed down the street hoping to find a streetcar stop.

Lupe jumped from the car. "Stop, you *estupida* fool. I tell you to stop!"

According to Franky, Lupe never walked unless positively desperate. In her four inch heels, walking would be like crossing the street on *pointe.* My shoes weren't much better. Knowing this, I'd crammed a comfortable old pair in my purse for just this kind of emergency.

"No, no. Don't go – please," Lupe whined, as she stumbled after me, waving her arms. "I pay you twenty dollars. Anything you want. But please, you must take Lupe home."

I paused, turning. "I don't like your attitude." Working for Lupe was out of the question. First, she was a bitch. Second, I didn't like the idea of sleeping with my boss's husband.

But when Lupe caught up, she grabbed my arm and held on as if she meant to drag me back. "I am sorry. I no fire you tomorrow. And I pay you very well. I make you thee promise. Okay?" Lupe's dark eyes blazed with appeal. She obviously hadn't expected a confrontation with a human being with a backbone.

"It won't work. I don't like temperamental actresses."

"No, I treat you very good. You will not be sorry. You will meet many important men. Maybe you will even get thee movie contract. Maybe you play my mother in thee next picture."

I studied Lupe's earnest expression and started to cackle. Lupe's mother of all things with my blonde hair and blue eyes and her black hair and dark eyes. Not to mention the fact that Lupe was at least five years older.

Suddenly, Lupe began to laugh, too. She laughed so hard tears filled her eyes. "Please. I not thee bad monster you think," she said, gasping for breath. "I just work for monsters. Now you must come with me to *mi casa.*"

By the time, we arrived at Lupe's vast estate above Sunset, I'd mastered the car's steering and gear shift, though driving it was like maneuvering a sixteen wheeler without power steering.

THIRTY-ONE

The estate dwarfed anything I'd ever seen before in Hollywood, both in the present and the future. Driving through the front gates up the hill, we passed acres of cultivated grass and manicured bushes. There were gardens with ponds, a tennis court, and a mountainous staircase which wound down from the grand Spanish Colonial estate to a swimming pool complete with fountains, gazebos, and topiary in the shape of serpents.

Once inside, a tiny housekeeper in a grey and white uniform with a crown–shaped white headpiece greeted us. Without any acknowledgment, Lupe swept past the tiny woman, dropping her hat, gloves, and furs into the maid's arms. After kicking off her shoes, she marched up a grand staircase. Tension filled my stomach as I scooped up Lupe's things from the maid and trotted up the stairs after the star.

Halfway up, Lupe froze in her tracks and cast a horrified glance over her shoulder at me. "Why you follow me? You must take thee back stairs."

"I don't take the back stairs for anyone," I said calmly, not that I was in a position to argue anymore. After all, Lupe was now home and could easily find someone else to drive her car. But it would be better to establish a few ground rules first. Even penniless and desperate, I refused to be a third rate human being for my lover's wife.

Lupe's frozen stare thawed and she continued up the stairs and down the hall to an immense room where a bed the size of a small yacht sat in a corner by a pair of iron and glass doors leading to a tiny iron terrace. Lupe instantly flopped face down on her bed before rolling on her side. "Send for Mr. Pepe. And rub my feet. They killing poor Lupe."

Taking a seat at the foot of the bed, I began to rub Lupe's feet.

Lupe groaned with pleasure. "Very nice. Did you call Mr. Pepe yet?"

"How could I?"

She sighed. "Must Lupe do everything herself?"

Scowling down at her, I stood. I was already exhausted and the day stretched ahead to infinity. "What's the phone number?" I asked, not hiding my annoyance, as I reached for the elegant gold–plated phone.

"Is in thee little gold book," Lupe said meekly.

I located the number in a small leather book engraved with Lupe's name. In the middle of my conversation with Mr. Pepe, about rushing over to do Lupe's bidding, Lupe abruptly muttered that it was time to fix her bath.

In the bathroom, tiled in green marble, I dumped in an array of bath salts and perfume, set out the thick white terrycloth robe and pink silk mules, then switched on a heater built into the wall. When the tub had filled with bubbles, I returned to the bedroom and gently shook Lupe awake.

She stared up at me as if we'd never met before. "What you want from Lupe?"

"Your bath, madam. You'll need one before your hairdresser and manicurist arrive."

"Sí. Undress Lupe. And hurry up. I very busy."

Lupe's immodesty shocked me. She seemed to regard me as either blind or akin to a nurse. Once she'd settled in her sunken tub, she sighed contentedly. "Now, you must wash Lupe."

Using an enormous natural sponge, wondering what Franky would think if he saw this, I obliged *Madam Lupe* and began to scrub her back and shoulders.

Nude, Lupe had small breasts, narrow-hips, and a tiny waist. However, her legs were extremely short, a flaw she overcame by wearing extremely high heels.

Relaxed and in a better mood, she talked about anything and everything. She quickly explained how she kept in shape with massages and a careful diet. She actually had decent skin tone, a miracle considering she never exercised and never left her house without a girdle. Exercise to her was a fast foxtrot or sex.

"... For many months I like Boyd thee best. He is very passionate with Lupe. He make Lupe crazy with his kisses, until I no can think straight. But he drink too much. And he very unreliable. He always late or he forget to come. But he very handsome with a very big ..." Lupe held her hands apart making us both laugh.

"What about your husband?" I asked, feeling as if I were posing as a priest in order to hear a confession.

"He no love me no more. Lupe no love him either."

I noticed that Lupe hadn't put much emotion into the word *love*.

"And he always want thee money. And he refuse to give Lupe thee divorce until he take thee money, thee ranch, everything."

Was Lupe's assessment of Franky's greed true? Or was Lupe manufacturing unpleasant stories out of bitterness? After all, I'd overheard that scene at Franky's ranch when he'd turned her down for sex.

Lupe rested her head back against the tub, shut her eyes, and said, "Play thee music for me. Thee record player is by thee closet."

Back in the bedroom, I sifted through a pile of 78s, found a soft love song, and wound up the RCA portable. Soft music filled the room.

When I returned to the bathroom, Lupe had fallen asleep in the tub. Taking a seat on the chair by her vanity table, I listened to the music and watched the star to make sure she didn't slip under the water and drown. Even though her death would solve quite a few problems.

A few seconds later, there was a knock on the bedroom door.

Lupe's eyes fluttered open. "Tell them to go away. Say to them I no feel well."

The tiny uniformed Mexican maid from earlier waited outside Lupe's door in the hall. "Please, you must tell thee Señora that Francesca wishes to speak to her. Francesca is upset. She say her mother no let her see her papa tonight. She cry all thee time."

"Her father?" *Jesus, was Franky here, too?*

"Sí."

Back in the bathroom I gently shook Lupe. "Señora?"

Lupe's eyes flickered open.

"Madam, your daughter wants a word." I tried to recall what Franky had said about Francesca but couldn't remember a thing.

"Must thee child always ruin my sleep? Tell her she must stay in her room tonight and have her supper alone. I fed up with her. Why must she always cry to be with that stupid cowboy? He is no good for her. He say to everyone, I am a bad mother. Today, she cannot see him. Is finished."

I quickly relayed the message to the maid then asked, "Is her father here now?"

"No. He call on thee telephone. He ask when Francesca will be ready." The maid shrugged. "I tell him, no."

So Franky was back in town. He'd been gone for three weeks. Three weeks during which I'd lived at the Cooper's farm and hunted for a job. Now, Franky had no idea how to reach me. Providing he wanted to.

On my fourth day as Lupe's gopher, an unattractive new driver named Harlan took us to Lupe's hairdresser on Sunset. As soon as he stepped from Lupe's car to help us in, I knew Harlan would be fired soon. Lupe seemed to expect Douglas Fairbanks, Jr., or Ronald Coleman to schlep her around. She also seemed to find pleasure in firing the help.

While Mr. Pepe and his entourage administered a mud pack, a massage, a permanent wave, a manicure, and a pedicure, I slipped out to call Lorena.

At the corner drugstore a few doors down, I found a telephone booth. After depositing a nickel, I patiently waited while the operator took a good five minutes to connect to the correct exchange and reach the family farm. By some miracle, Lorena answered right away.

"I can't talk long. I got a job working for Lupe Cardona," I explained.

"Have you been drinking?"

"I wish. Look, I can't stay on the phone. She likes me bowing and scraping every second. Can you meet me Sunday at 1:00? I'll fill you in then."

"Where?"

"That Mexican joint you like in Hollywood."

"Sure, no problem. I'll leave right after the folks head for church," she said.

"Has Franky called yet?"

"Not yet. Maybe he's still in New York."

A pang of misery barreled through me. "No, he's back. I better go. Lupe's bound to need her cigarette lit or her purse opened."

"Sounds peachy."

"See you Sunday." I hung up.

The next day, a Friday, after morning fittings at the studio, Lupe relaxed out by her pool. Meaning I relaxed by the pool with her. Lupe had fallen asleep on a lounge chair with her face in the sun. As if the rays could permeate the six layers of foundation, powder, three inches of lipstick, the false lashes, and heavy white robe.

Dressed in my heavy navy work dress, with my hair pulled into a spinster's bun, clod in heavy brown oxfords, I hid beneath an umbrella and read Lupe's latest copy of *Vogue*.

It seemed The Casino in Central Park, a favorite spot of Lex's and mine, had been refurbished and was still regarded as the best night spot in New York City. Now, the nightclub featured torch song singer Georges Metaxa as well as pianist Eddie Duchen and the Casino orchestra. Fashions included a stunning tailored jacket over a full length black skirt for evening by Milgrim, my favorite designer back in the days when I could afford a famous designer. Lupe had already circled an apricot satin gown trimmed with Russian Sable from Henri Bendel's. And Helena Rubenstein advertised a new lipstick called Flaming Red Poppy.

"Bring me ice coffee," Lupe abruptly barked, sitting up and ripping off her eye guards. "And thee little sweet cakes I like."

"Your diet, madam."

"I no ask for your opinion."

Slapping down the magazine, I marched back to the house. In the kitchen, Vicente the chef cursed at me in Spanish. It took him a good fifteen minutes to make a fresh pot of coffee and create an elegant plate full of pastries. I emerged from the house twenty minutes later lugging a bone crushing tray laden with cookies, cakes, and coffee. Praying not to trip, I slowly descended the stone steps leading to the pool. I was a few yards away when I realized two men had joined Lupe. One of the men had dark hair and wore an elegant suit. The other one ... was Franky.

THIRTY–TWO

My heart raced. How could I face Franky? What would he think when he saw me here working for Lupe? I glanced back toward the house. Maybe Lupe hadn't noticed me. Maybe I could turn around and pretend I'd forgotten something in the kitchen. Once inside, I could send Maria or Pilar out with the tray.

Unfortunately, at that moment Lupe yelled, "Hurry up. We no have all day."

Lugging the heavy tray down the staircase with my back hunched to support the enormous silver service, I crossed the patio and approached the table. Seeing me, both men rose, an oddly polite gesture, considering I was a servant.

Across from Franky, peering at me curiously, sat Harry Ambrose a movie executive I'd met weeks ago during my hunt for work. I cringed, thinking of my bland, unpainted face and my horrendous attire: A dowdy gray dress, thick stockings, and heavy work shoes. At Lupe's insistence, my hair had been scraped back, too. And thanks to my indoor duties, endless work hours, and lack of sleep, I was pale enough to be embalmed.

Averting my eyes, I carefully unloaded the tray onto the long glass table where the three sat, shaded by an umbrella. Franky tactfully stared at the pool.

"I do not understand why you are always so slow," Lupe grumbled as I placed the costly china dishes before them. "You are like thee lazy burro."

Taking a deep breath, I steeled myself against Lupe's incessant griping and fought to keep my composure. Unfortunately, a spoon from my tray plunked down on the glass table with a loud bang.

"*¿Qué hace usted, estúpida?*" Lupe bellowed. "So clumsy. Leave now before you break thee whole table. And bring more cakes for thee guests. And do not dawdle this time or I take thee belt to you."

I openly glared at Lupe, daring her to strike me. She averted her gaze, and I controlled my rage. *Think of Lex*, I told myself. *Lex needs care.* Like a mantra, I repeated these sentences in my head whenever Lupe became abusive, a daily event. Then I'd picture Lex at the cure cottage or one of The Rainbow girls trudging up the stairs with a sour smelling farmer. Not that I wouldn't have loved to toss a drink in Lupe's mean painted face. But I'd gotten used to the money, used to having a job. And thanks to Franky's help, I was almost caught up with my payments to Mrs. Jankel.

Now, trying not to grunt, I carefully lifted the heavy tray, slowly crossed the patio, then climbed back up the stairs. But not fast enough to avoid hearing Lupe say, "I think she have thee crush on thee cook or something. That one is always in thee kitchen throwing herself at thee serving boys. And she is so slow, so stupid. Also, she never take thee bath. Many times I must tell her to take thee bath. Or she will stink like very old shoes."

I prayed Franky saw through Lupe's ugly stories. Mostly, I wondered why he was here and why he hadn't called me at Lorena's.

In the kitchen, Chef Vicente glared at me as I place the silver tray on the counter and reached for more china plates.

"Don't take the whole china cabinet," he roared. "Just take what you need. And that mess by the pool better be cleaned up before supper, after Madam finishes with her guests." Shoving another plate of cookies in my hand, he growled, "Hurry."

This time, Lupe eyes filled with venom at the sight of me. "Idiot. I tell you to bring thee tea sandwiches, too."

"Don't bother on my account," Harry Ambrose said, standing. "I've gotta run."

Clutching a huge gold cross around her neck, Lupe stood, anxiety covering her face. She forced a smile and said, "No, no, Harry. Why are you always in thee big hurry? You must stay. We still have many things to say, no?"

"Perhaps another time. Nice to see you again, Franky. Mrs. Rose."

I glanced up, startled. He'd remembered my name. I searched Lupe's face to gage her reaction. The star might not like her guest greeting a servant. But Lupe was anxiously fluttering around Harry, asking if he needed anything and when he might call again.

Head down, unwilling to look at Franky, I quickly loaded up the silver tray again with dirty dishes and crumpled napkins. I kept my eyes averted until I was inside the house. I never even saw Franky leave. But minutes later, hunched over the kitchen sink with my hands in hot soapy water and a pile of dirty dishes waiting to be washed, I resented the painful tears which fought to come out. Franky didn't deserve my tears.

By four that afternoon, Lupe had withdrawn to her room for a nap. Needing to be alone, I hid in the butler's pantry under the guise of filling out invitations for Lupe's next bridge luncheon. In the privacy of the room, tears finally broke through my self–control and streamed down my cheeks. Unfortunately, Clark, the butler, a tall handsome young man, chose that moment to bolt through the kitchen door wielding silver candelabra. Seeing my tears, he tactfully averted his gaze and knelt by a cabinet. Using a crumpled hankie, I quickly dried my eyes and nose.

"Now, where did I put that silver polish?" Clark said aloud, whistling, digging through the lower cupboard. "There you are." He pulled out a jar and chose the seat down the table from me and began rubbing the polish on. "You're new here, aren't you?" he asked, keeping his eyes on his job.

I cleared my throat. "Yes I ... I'm Jeri Rose."

He extended a large hand. "Clarence Berns. Clark to my friends. Nice to meet you."

We shook hands then both returned to our chores.

"She gave you a hard time, huh?" he abruptly said.

"You heard?"

"Everyone did, honey. Look, she acts mean because she's not very bright. She probably has no idea how she sounds. Or what she's saying."

"I don't usually cry, but ... " There was too much to explain. My whole life felt like a disaster.

"Honey, we've all been at the receiving end of that Guadalajara tongue. She put the curl in my hair and a permanent frown line between my brows." After grabbing another rag off the pile of freshly laundered rags, he continued rubbing the silver.

"How'd you get started here?" I asked, glad to find a friend in the house.

"You could say my theatrical career got sidetracked by The Crash. Not that I was a head– liner yet. But back in New York, I did vaudeville, burlesque, night clubs. Then *kaboom*. The stock market took a dive and the work dried up so I headed here. Have you met Papa Bear, yet?"

"Who?"

"Caesar Cardona. The big man himself."

"Haven't had the pleasure," I lied, recalling that night at the Coconut Grove with Franky.

"You're lucky. At first I thought, Holy Mother, he's guessed I'm no football player. I even waited for the axe to fall. But nothing happened until he dropped by one day and said in a deep, accented voice, "Young man, I do not like thee way your butterballs are coming out."

I laughed out loud over Clark's imitation.

"I mean, there are fifteen servants slaving here and that doesn't include the fruit pickers that come to harvest the grapefruit, yet he's always wandering into the pantry to complain about the cocktail nuts or flower arrangements. Anyway, he makes Lupe seem like a saint. So beware."

"Thanks for the warning. And for cheering me up."

"Another afternoon of tea," he said, frowning at the pile of stationery, lists, and stamps before me.

"Monday. And a bridge luncheon the following Thursday. I just hope I get Sunday off. "

"Don't count on it. She manages to create a catastrophe just about every weekend which holds everyone up."

"But I have plans."

"Ever heard of the Depression? She can do whatever she wants."

"But I'm supposed to meet my friend. When will I have a chance to call her?"

He glanced out the door. "Once Lupe goes out, things are pretty quiet around here."

"Sneak a telephone call?"

"An emergency is an emergency. And the next time she starts yelling, think of something pleasant, like the rotten state of her career," he said. "And that handsome cowboy who's about to divorce her."

I opened my mouth to dig deeper into the household gossip when Juanita rushed in and handed me a letter. "This is for you. And thee Señora, she wants you upstairs."

"... and make sure you put thee stockings together before you get thee drops for me at thee pharmacy," Lupe said five minutes later. "I no feel like Lupe today. My head, she is very bad – like she going to break in half. And thee new frock, she is to be ready for tonight at thee dressmaker. So you must pick that up, also. I have not told you before, but my new friend, he is very rich and very handsome. He no like blondes – so you are not his type – because he like small woman with small feet and brown eyes like Lupe have."

As usual, Lupe sat in her bed and sipped her coffee as she directed me from chore to chore, bragging, trying to irritate me. Aside from her jealousy, she clearly admired me. It was obvious whenever I advised her about clothes or a new young man she had a yen for – usually an inappropriate young actor who wanted to attach his name to hers for selfish purposes. But today she'd been extremely cruel, and I couldn't help wishing she'd get a taste of her own medicine.

"And you must wait up for Lupe tonight," she rambled on. "I going to be very late, but I cannot undress alone. I must be perfect tonight. Everyone will be looking at me. Tonight, Lupe is thee queen, no?"

I curtsied. "Yes, your highness."

Lupe nodded. "I like this. From now on, you will curtsy for Lupe all thee time. Now, fill thee tub for Lupe's bath. And put in lots of French perfume."

That evening, Lupe stood before her tall freestanding mirror and scrutinized herself in a new black silk dress with puffy white organza sleeves. "Now you will put on Lupe's diamond tiara. But do not mess up Lupe's hair."

I gently placed the tiara on her head. We both studied the results of our work in her tall wall mirror. Four hours of ministrations from head to toe and even I had to admit she looked stunning. Her hair, thanks to Mr. Pepe, was perfect. Her make-up was dramatic, including false eyelashes, kohl, and every other artifice known to flatter. Max Factor himself couldn't have achieved more enhancing results.

"Lupe is a knockout, *si?* Did I tell you that after thee picture premiere tonight my date will take Lupe to a very big party for all thee important people? You are jealous, no?"

"I'll probably slit my wrists as soon as you leave," I said.

"Good."

"I still can't find your other stockings," I griped, wondering why Lupe had seven mismatched stockings, as I shoved the rest of her delicate lingerie back in her bureau.

"So what? I can always buy more. Now you must wipe down thee tub and pick up all of Lupe's things," she added, dropping onto her dressing table chair and wincing. "My head … she is still bad. Like she wan' to break in half. But I must go tonight anyway. Is my movie, no? Besides, champagne always make me feel better. I have not told you before, but my new boyfriend is crazy for me. Maybe I even marry him one day, when I get thee *divorce*."

In reality, Lupe and her "new boyfriend" had spoken exactly once. The boyfriend was actually a paid studio escort hired to accompany Lupe to her premiere. But I ignored her needling because I knew she was terrified that *Love Flies to Montevideo* would be another flop.

Lupe covered herself with a silk hand towel, took a sip from the rum–and–coke she'd ordered earlier, then made a face. "Thee drink is not strong enough. Why you always make them so weak?

And another thing. I no like thee new driver. He very dull. And he no look good in thee uniform. Tomorrow you will call thee studio and order another man. I want someone young and handsome. Dark or blond is okay. But he cannot be ugly. Understand?"

"I'll make it my life's work."

Lupe's last driver had been dismissed after Lupe had found him holding a crap came in the garage with her gardeners. Since my arrival two weeks ago, three drivers had come and gone.

"I very nervous. Thee picture tonight is stupid. But thee public want thee musicals. I just hope they like Lupe." She held out her glass and I poured in more rum. "Soon thee new script be ready. Maybe I like, maybe not. But at least they want Lupe. Is good, no?"

"You'll probably save the studio from the Great Depression single–handedly."

Lupe sighed. "*Sí*, Lupe is very lucky. Beautiful, talented, and young."

"With a brilliant command of English," I added, handing Lupe a lace hankie doused in Shalimar.

Lupe stuck the hankie in her beaded bag, stood, tossed her white fox stole over her haughty shoulders, and ambled out the bedroom door. I followed her downstairs and out to her car where an aging uniformed driver, doomed to be fired tomorrow, waited to drive her and her studio escort to Graumann's Chinese Theater for the premiere.

Seconds later, as the car sped away, I filled my lungs with the cool California night air. As always, my thoughts turned to Franky. Where was he tonight? Home alone? Drinking with his buddies? Reading a script? Or out with another woman? I faced the huge house dreading the lonely night ahead. Being young, I wanted to enjoy life, too. A part of me *was* jealous of Lupe. She went to glamorous parties, lived in a mansion, and shopped till she needed a phalanx of servants to lug her packages up to her room. On the other hand, I had the honor of rubbing her feet, mending her hems, and washing out her bathtub. Worse, Lupe was married to Franky and didn't even want him.

Heading inside, I thought back to New York, to Riverside Drive and Keely. Had Keely envied me when I dressed for dinner and decided on which fur coat to wear?

I returned to Lupe's room and waited until her car had been gone a good ten minutes before I picked up the telephone. My hands shook as I lifted the receiver. What if Lupe decided she wanted different gloves ? Or her other diamond bracelet? Or her silver flask? No, she wouldn't be back for that. I'd put it in her evening bag myself, after I filled it with brandy.

I stared at the telephone. Franky might be home. But no, I refused to crawl to him, especially after this afternoon. If he was interested in seeing me, he could damn well find a way. I thought of calling the farm to warn Lorena about being late Sunday, too. But what if another servant was watching me? Although Clark was the only one who actually lived in the big house. The other servants quarters were across the courtyard in barracks. Right now, the rest of the staff were either resting, reading, writing letters, playing cards, listening to the radio, or sleeping.

Still, if I were caught using the telephone, I'd be fired. And even though I resented my job, it paid well, and kept me out of Nicky Desanto's reach.

I began to straighten up Lupe's room. Six matched pairs and three orphaned stockings later, after organizing Lupe's upper bureau drawer, her closet, and her cosmetics, I was almost asleep on the settee when I remembered the letter.

My first letter from Lex in over ten months.

October 1, 1933

Dear Jeri:

I may be one of the sicker chaps here, but it sure feels good to be with people again, I mean besides Nurse Bronson and my doctors. I'm eating with the others downstairs now. We have quite a few New Yorkers here. One I actually met before in the city. We laughed like school kids at the rules – although some patients apply them without question and believe everything they're told. Me, I'm still trying to believe. Love Lex.

After a good cry, I fell asleep on the sofa. At two when Lupe still hadn't returned home from the premiere, I wandered downstairs and across the yard to the servants' quarters where I fell into my own bed and drifted off instantly.

THIRTY-THREE

" ... *Unfortunately, the audience's love for Lupe Cardona also flew to Montevideo last night when Lupe Cardona tried to sing and dance in LOVE FLIES TO MONTEVIDEO, a fluffy piece that begs for a story and a talented leading actress ... "*

By six the next morning, every servant at the Cardona compound had read this crushing newspaper review of Lupe's new picture. The actress and her film had been shredded by columnists from New York to Los Angeles.

At seven I left the servants' quarters and crossed the dusty yard to the main house. Today, the kitchen smelled like a KFC franchise. And there was no fresh coffee in sight. Instead, Juanita, Vicente's second in command, hovered over two enormous frying pans brimming with grease and chicken. While Juanita flipped chicken thighs, breasts and wings, her assistant Pilar, rolled chicken parts in egg and flour.

Clark had warned me about Lupe's fried chicken episodes. "It happens when she's depressed. She eats till she practically explodes."

"Pull my other leg," I said, laughing, sure he was trying to be funny.

"You won't find it so hilarious when she's knee deep in necks and gizzards," he added, folding his feather duster under his arm, and replacing an imported Chinese figurine in a cabinet, a job he alone was permitted to tackle as opposed to the maids whom Lupe referred to as "clumsy putas."

"You mean she gets drunk?" I said, thinking *necks and gizzards* could be yet another euphemism for getting drunk.

"I mean, she eats fried chicken. You'll see. After Franky moved out, I thought she'd grow feathers and start pecking for ticks in the yard."

Now, steeling myself for the worst, I crossed the butler's pantry, took the hallway to the dining room, passed the living room, and headed up the main staircase. Besides the smell of chicken, I could hear the sad strains of the La Traviata– an Italian opera about a courtesan dying of consumption – playing on the Victrola. Which instantly made me think of Lex and the letter I intended to write him.

At the top of the stairs, after knocking twice, I opened Lupe's door. "Good morning, madam," I said cheerily, crossing the threshold into total darkness.

"Why you so late?" Lupe groused.

It took a moment for my eyes to adjust. With the help of a few slender threads of light slipping under the heavy red velvet drapes, now drawn tightly against the day, I eventually managed to make out shapes in the room. Sitting up in bed, Lupe's small form was hunched over a tray. Her tiny hands clutched a wing as she gnawed like a furtive rat, before dropping the bones on her plate and licking her fingers. The odor made me dizzy. I hadn't had time for sip of coffee and now the smell of garlic fried chicken made my stomach churn.

Picking up a leg, Lupe added, "I been very upset. And you were not here to help, when thee whole world saying Lupe is finished. Lupe's career *es muerte*. And I been so, so —"

"Hungry?" I offered, unable to stop myself.

A hideous pause followed this outburst. I hated myself. My one moment of triumph at Lupe's expense could get me fired. And where would I find another job? But as Clark had reminded me earlier this week, Lupe liked me.

"Considering she hates all women, even the servants, Lupe seems positively smitten with you," he'd remarked. "Maybe she likes big–chested blondes."

But even if Lupe did like me, she could fire me with a flick of one eyelid.

A sudden sob interrupted my thoughts. "Lupe? I mean, madam?" I said, rushing to her side.

"Sit down and no speak to Lupe. I no talk now. But I no want to be alone either." Picking up another chicken part, Lupe used it to point to the bench by the end of her bed.

"Are Mexicans fond of fried chicken?" I'd asked Clark that day.

Clark explained that Lupe had been raised by a black maid named Georgia. "Big woman, great cook, wonderful second mother type. So Lupe – with her buck teeth, tadpole figure, and tiny brain – called her Googi. Apparently, Googi could whip up fried chicken and mashed potatoes better than any slave on the old Mexican plantation where Lupe grew up. And when Lupe got a bad grade in school for miscounting her toes or messing herself in the sandbox, she'd run to Googi who would comfort her with fried chicken. Until our dear Mistress looked like a fat little pigeon."

"What happened to Googi?"

He shrugged. "Maybe she was sold to another plantation when she got too old to cook. After all, she was here when *Our Lady of Cardona* was a child – about forty years ago."

I laughed. "Lupe claims to be twenty-two."

"Which would make her about fourteen when she had her daughter, meaning she was thirteen when she married Franky. Which isn't possible since Lupe's daddy was probably still sleeping with her himself back then."

"That's an awful thing to say."

"Okay, it's gossip. But the man stays with her in that room for hours. Not that I've personally seen anything. But there's been a parade of maids dismissed over the years for walking in on them. That is until Franky Wyatt rode into town with his manly muscles and insufferable good looks. I guess Lupe spotted him one night at a barbecue, pointed a chicken leg at him, and grunted. So Daddy came through and got Franky a studio contract and a wedding ring."

I cringed at the ugly gossip about Franky. This story was nothing like Franky's version of his first meeting with Lupe on a movie set. "You mean they bought him?"

"I'm just guessing, pet, so don't look so distraught. But consider this. Dear Franky started out as a western rider back before talkies. A nobody. Then, he met Lupe and bingo, he's suddenly a major cowboy star. And we all know who Lupe's daddy is. My guess is that Franky's rise to stardom was no coincidence. I also think little Lupe wants Franky back. That's why there's been no divorce. I mean, he *is* irresistible. Have you ever seen the yummy pictures of him Lupe has stashed in her old hat box in the guestroom closet?"

"No, I —"

"Take a quick peek when you have time."

Now, the morning after the big premiere, after the critics had shredded Lupe and her latest film with a few savage paragraphs, I sat in the dark at Lupe's feet and listened to her chew.

"Rub my feet," she abruptly barked, kicking off her silk coverlet and sticking a manicured foot out.

After bringing in lotion from the bathroom and leaving the

door ajar for light, I rubbed her little feet till my shoulders ached. Which was when Lupe pushed her tray aside and snapped, "More chicken."

"Madam, are you sure you should eat —"

"Now. Or I fire you."

Five minutes later, I returned with a full tray and silently placed it on Lupe's lap. Lupe instantly picked up a greasy breast and sank her teeth in.

Scattered on the floor by her bed, lay the very newspapers which had attacked her talent, her charisma, and her movies, while suggesting that Lupe was *past* playing young *femme fatales.*

Initially, I'd felt like gloating. Lupe had been so insensitive to me yesterday, so mean to the servants and Francesca, who seemed to be nothing more than a pawn in her war with Franky. But watching her eat, I saw her differently. Lupe was a vulnerable woman. A woman in a man's world. She could buy clothes and do her best to look young. She could try to act before a movie camera or put on a happy face at dinner dances. She could even give birth. But she could never escape the truth: She was beholden to the studios, the press, to her rich and mighty father, and the men who ruled the system.

And *if* those men decided she was too old, that the public no longer liked her, she'd be out of a job like the rest of us. Lupe might rule her house, but on the streets of 1933 Hollywood, she was a ninety–eight pound victim. And she would soon be a two hundred pound *has been* if she didn't stop eating.

A door downstairs slammed, startling us. Caesar Cardona's booming voice rose from below. "Where the hell is she?"

Lupe and I heard thunderous footsteps coming up the stairs. I pictured Caesar Cardona. His tall, powerful frame, the dark double–breasted suit, thick silver hair, and imposing strut. The degrading way he'd looked at me that night at The Coconut Grove.

This was a man who never asked for anything. He demanded it.

Lupe and I panicked. "Thee closet," she hissed.

I dove inside her dress closet. It reeked of old Shalimar perfume, a scent I now found nauseating. As the closet door snapped shut, Caesar Cardona burst into the room. Peeking through the door slats, I saw him approach Lupe's disheveled bed.

"What nonsense is this?" he bellowed.

Lupe's eyes widened. Fear covered her sallow face. At this time of morning, her smoldering Latin appeal had yet to be painted on.

"What do you think you are doing?" Caesar barked.

Biting her lip, Lupe stared up, her dark eyes blinking.

Glancing at the tray, at her, with her hair in disarray and the overall state of the room, Caesar Cardona's face reflected disgust.

"After all I have had to sacrifice to make you a star, this is how you thank me? By stuffing yourself like a pig?" he growled.

Tears rolled down Lupe's cheeks.

Grasping a rolled newspaper off the floor, he slapped her with it across the chest and head several times making her shriek. Grabbing a handful of her nightgown, he pulled her face to his, until their noses almost touched. "You are pathetic. We do not have time for this."

She began to whimper.

"Stop crying, or I will use my belt on you, party or no party tonight. Or did you forget?"

"No, please. Not tonight."

"You *will* go."

She began to sob. "But thee things they say about me —"

"Shut up," he barked, sliding off his jacket. Next, he unbuttoned his shirt, then ripped off his tie before neatly folding his things on the chaise lounge near the closets and me. Down to his shorts, he moved to the bed and flopped down beside Lupe. "Why must it always be like this? You and your mother, thee same thing. When I brought you up here from Mexico to live like a queen, to be a woman of the world, I had dreams. But all you want to do is to lie here like a dog in your own filth. To eat until you turn into a fat, old woman."

Lupe's head bounced with each sob.

In the shadowed light, I recognized triumph on Caesar Cardona's face. He abruptly stood and pulled aside a drape to peer out the window. Then he turned back toward Lupe and moved to the bed where he lifted the tray and placed it on the floor. His voice softened as he moved to her, and gently turned her face to stare up into his.

"Now, now. Don't make me hit you again. You make Papa happy, no?" he said.

Sniffling, wiping her nose with her hand, she nodded.

My heart raced as Clark's ugly stories flashed through my mind.

Caesar began to kiss Lupe. First her forehead, then her cheek, then her mouth. I heard Lupe give one convulsive sob, then she seemed to collapse, as if her energy or her will had turned into a vapor and drifted into space.

"You aren't going to fall apart over a few bad reviews," Caesar murmured, as his mouth closed over hers and he gently slid her from a sitting position till she was down on her back.

Don't watch, I told myself. But it was like passing an ambulance on the road after a major accident. You just couldn't look away.

Caesar lifted Lupe's silk chemise. How nimble his fingers were as they undid those tiny silk–covered buttons before his mouth sought her breasts, his lips pulling hard on her nipples, until she cried out in pain. He advanced down her body, yanking at her gown before he undid his pants before jamming his fingers between her legs, making whimper. Then he fell on top of her, entered her quickly, and began to move. Lupe stared at the closet where I hid, her dark eyes blank, dead.

In seconds, it was over. In one swift move, Caesar pulled up his pants, patted back his mane of lustrous white hear, tucked in his shirt, and headed into the bathroom. I heard the sound of water running. Minutes later, he marched back into the room, pulled on his shirt, tie, and jacket. Then he strode directly toward the closet, toward me.

THIRTY–FOUR

I held my breath sure he'd heard me breathing and had come to expose me. Instead, he paused before the tall mirror to button his shirt and knot his tie. He gave himself a slow approving glance, then turned back to his daughter who lay nude on her back, her breasts flattened, her body vacant, lifeless.

"You have ten minutes to shower and clean up. Have thee girl clean up this food. It stinks in here."

Lupe slowly sat up, her small firm breasts exposed and forgotten as she faced the closet. Her eyes grew wide and I saw that she'd just realized what I'd witnessed.

"Papa, an hour, *por favor*," Lupe begged.

Sighing, he nodded. "Very well, wear thee green satin."

She hung her head. "*Sí*."

"Be quick. I do not like to see you like this." Holding up his arrogant head, he opened her door and marched out.

I stayed put. Then I heard her feet padding across the floor to the closet. The door opened. I moved past her. Without a word, I picked up the dinner tray and headed toward the door.

Lupe stared down at her manicured hands, her expression vacant. "Go home today," she said softly. "I give you thee holiday.

Come back tomorrow."

"But my paycheck, madam."

"Ask thee butler. He will give you thee money."

"As you say." I left, shutting the door behind me, feeling sick. Nothing I'd seen or heard at The Rainbow had prepared me for this.

Two days later, a few days before Halloween, Lupe had a breakdown. Her studio announced to the papers that she had a serious case of bronchitis. But the truth went deeper. The actress couldn't cope with her life. Neither sleep, a new lover, nor heavy drinking could wipe away her pain over her bad reviews, her fears, and her bullying, destructive father. Production on her newest picture, *The Vaquero's Daughter*, ceased temporarily while Lupe recuperated at a sanitarium in Tucson.

After I answered Lupe's fan mail, I left, too. With money Lorena lent me, I bought tickets to go east to see Lex. But first, I met Franky to say goodbye.

***

"But why leave now, when we can see each other every day? When Lupe's stuck in Arizona and there's nothing for you to do?" Franky complained, leaning on his elbow and staring down at me, after we'd made love again in the *Casita*.

"It's time I saw Lex. I need to find out how he is," I said, rising naked from the bed and heading into the bathroom for a shower. This once I managed to ignore Franky's bronzed good looks, knowing he meant to convince me to stay.

"I swear Lupe's haunting me," he complained, following me into the tiny bathroom and studying his face in the mirror above the sink.

Standing in the shower with blissfully warm water cascading off me, I listened.

"Between her father, her lawyers, and her phone calls, it's

nice to have her away," he griped.

An icy hand gripped my intestines. "She still calls you?"

"We still have Francesca to consider. Although Lupe's trip to Tucson's been a nice break."

"Of course," I said, managing to sound congenial, as I shut the water off, reached for a towel, and exited the shower stall. Not that Franky or Lupe seemed to really care about Francesca. From what I'd seen, Francesca spent most of her time in school or with a loyal servant down at the far end of the house in her room. Out of everyone's way.

"Promise me you won't stay in New York, too long," Franky purred, ripping off my towel and pulling me against him, letting me know he was ready to make love again.

Too bad I didn't have time. "Honey, we need to get to the station before three. And I need to dress. I don't want to miss my train."

He sighed. "Don't worry. I'll get you there on time."

***

It took over four days to reach Saranac Lake. Days of dusty trains which raced along for hours then sputtered to a halt and remained immobile for hours without any explanation. Five days without a shower and only foul–smelling sink water to brush my teeth in. Days without exercise, unless I counted walking through crowded, smoky cars as exercise. And sleeping in a hard seat, freezing in the coach car.

After a brief stop at Grand Central where I changed trains, I arrived at the tiny station at Saranac Lake where the temperature had dipped to the low forties. I rented a room in town not far from Mrs. Jankel's. A room with linoleum floors, a cracked sink, and a sagging mattress that rested on noisy springs. I bathed in a bathroom down the hall, in a tub I cleaned myself. With shaking hands I fixed my face in a broken mirror above the sink under a dim yellow bulb. I wore a dark grey dress trimmed in plush fox, a remnant from better days. A dress which had been stored at the dry cleaners and therefore escaped The Rainbow fire. I set out early that morning to find a hairdresser. At a place called Peggy's, the owner, a stout Irish woman, shampooed and pinned my hair, then stuck me under a hair dryer. Two hours later, just after noon, I emerged ready to face Lex.

I negotiated a cheap fare with a local driver to take me to Mrs. Jankel's, that grim little cure cottage which had filled my nightmares for almost a year now. Today, however, surrounded by brilliant fall foliage and wild flowers which crept across gentle hills, the huge Victorian cottage looked cozy, even inviting. Clutching my purse, I clumped up the well–swept stairs and entered, causing a bell to ring. Inside, the same odors from last time assaulted my senses. The smell of food, urine, and disinfectant.

In seconds, a nurse in a crisp white uniform emerged from a back room and saw me. "Please have a seat in the parlor. Someone will be right with you."

A half–hour later, I still sat alone in the parlor. Finally, another young nurse hurrying down the stairs noticed me. After a harsh once–over, she said, "May I help you?"

"I'm here to see Lex Rose. I'm Mrs. Rose, and I've been waiting here for almost an hour."

Was it my imagination or had the young nurse's expression become more inquisitive or down right judgmental?

"You'll have to wait. Mr. Rose is having an afternoon snack. Please be patient."

With no choice, I dropped back into the large comfortable chair. I'd just pulled out my compact to check my hair and lipstick when a voice startled me. "Jeri?"

My heart lurched. I bolted to my feet and turned. "Lex?"

As if in a dream, I saw him standing a few feet away, tall and dark haired, if thinner than before. Even his bulky sweater and baggy grey slacks couldn't hide his weight loss. And he was paler than baby powder. But he still had a look nobody else ever would. My eyes filled up, and I groped through my purse for a hankie.

"Darling, how are you?" I asked, suddenly self–conscious. I longed to grab him and hang on but wasn't sure I should. Was he still contagious? Or had that passed? Would he want me to hug him?

Now I noticed a nurse standing in the background smiling, hanging onto a coat.

"Good to see you," he said, as his beautiful blue eyes swept over me, approval in them. Then I was in his arms as we clutched each other.

He abruptly pulled away and sent me a wicked smile. "Better stop this right now. I may be ill, but I'm not dead. Besides, they're very snippy about affection here. How about a nice walk?"

The nurse stepped forward and helped him into his coat. Then he reached for my gloved hand.

His hands felt warm and alive and he smelled of a tangy cologne he always wore. Side by side, we headed out into the chilly afternoon. Without a word we followed a narrow path through the fragrant pines toward the lake. The air was pristine and the autumn temperatures hovered in the high forties. Above the pines, the sun was strong with a sprinkling of glossy clouds.

"Is this okay for you?" I asked, as we hiked up a gentle hill.

Instead of an answer, he grinned at me, and his fingers squeezed mine. He felt both familiar and strange. I heard birds and the crunch of our feet over the moist earth and pine needles as we ascended a small hill and ended up on the same tiny bluff where Harris and I had ventured that first day here, months ago, when we'd brought Lex to Mrs. Jankel's Cure Cottage.

"So, how do I look?" he asked, tossing a stone into the lake.

"Fine. You look fine."

"You don't look too bad yourself," he said, grabbing me by the arms and pushing me up against a tree before burying his lips in my neck. "God you're still the sexiest woman alive. I thought I was dreaming when I came downstairs and saw you."

"Is this okay? I mean, are you well enough to have visitors?"

"I won't kiss you on the lips again, I promise."

I froze. "Darling, are you still contagious?"

He pulled back and gazed into her face. "Not for now. But I can't stay out too long anyway." In his eyes, understanding blended with sadness. "It'll be rest time soon. Wanna take a rest with me?" he joked, winking.

I laughed, relieved. Linking arms, we strode back to the cottage. "You haven't changed a bit." I teased.

"Have you met someone else out there?"

My foot faltered and I briefly stumbled. I felt my face flush. "No, I ... I didn't mean to surprise you like this. But I needed to see you."

He briefly gazed into my face. And though I averted my eyes, I knew he'd seen the answer in the blush of my skin. Lex was bright, intuitive. And now, thanks to my bumbling evasions, he knew the truth. He knew I'd met someone else.

"Sorry, for not writing more," he said. "Guess I've never been good about writing letters. It's not like I don't think about you. I think about you every time I breathe. At night in bed, I even plan what I'll say to you when I write. How I'll word everything. But in the morning, I can't write. Half of me wants to tell you to get lost, to find someone else. And the other half of me ... wants to beg you to wait forever."

Heaven, help me, I'd betrayed him. And yet, he'd pushed me

away with his silence. Or were these my justifications for being with Franky?

He abruptly paused to gaze into the distance toward a small meadow. "Look, there's no use in mincing words. I'm not going to make it. It's not a death wish or anything. I even follow most of their idiotic rules. But I'm not gaining weight. I still have fevers. And every time they give me a few lousy privileges, I end up sick again, back on complete bed rest. I don't want to write you about the food, the deaths, or the bloody coughs. But I hold my breath every day hoping for a letter. I want to hear everything about your life."

Tears flowed down my cheeks. "Thank you. Thank you for saying that. I wish … I wish you'd written me these things." *And maybe I wouldn't have been so lonely. Or fallen for Franky Wyatt.*

"You shouldn't love me," he finally said. His face was calm when he said it.

"You don't mean that."

"Better head back now. It's almost nap time." Shoving his hands in his pockets, he set off down the path toward the cottage. Clouds had drifted across the sky, shutting out the sun, turning the afternoon gray.

"Are you tired?" I asked, as we approached the house.

He paused and waited for me to catch up. "Don't linger here, darling. Turn around and go back to California. Go back tonight or take the first train out in the morning. I won't be around much longer. At night, I cough. They're going to collapse my lung again, but the doctors aren't optimistic."

"Oh, Lex," I said, wishing I didn't feel so emotional. Wiping my eyes with a handkerchief, I blew my nose and managed to calm down.

"Be realistic, Jeri. You have to go on without me. Make the best of it. I just hope that whoever you fall for deserves you. That he loves you as much as I do."

I understood what he faced. The current cures. Rich foods, bizarre procedures to collapse his lungs, constant bed rest in the cold. I also knew that he probably wouldn't survive. Some night, he would call out. He would bang his cup. Foamy blood would bubble up in his throat and they would take him away.

"Tell me about California," he abruptly said, as we climbed the outside staircase to the front door. He sounded as if we'd dropped by some chic bar in the city and were chatting over Manhattans.

My guard went up. The details of my life seemed too sordid. *I was living at a brothel, while dating a married man, but now I'm a domestic for my lover's wife.* "It's okay, I guess."

"I meant, how are you making out with money?"

I didn't want to talk about money. I didn't want to whine about my problems. Or worry him. I wanted to talk about us. In a minute or two, he would slip inside and disappear. "I'm okay. I have a job working for an actress as her assistant. She's in a sanitarium in Arizona right now for emotional reasons."

"Which actress?"

"Lupe Cardona."

His eyes widened. "The Mexican Fireplug?" he said, screwing up his face.

I laughed. "The Guadalajara Spitfire for your information."

"If ever an actress had a knack for overacting and ruining a picture, it's Lupe Cardona. You should've written me about that. At least it's an interesting detail, unlike my health, or those endless sad stories about people dying in the gutters from starvation or typhus. Now come inside and tell me every nasty detail you can remember about little Lupe and her father, Caesar Cardona, king of the low budget picture."

Inside, a plump blue–eyed blonde nurse in bright lipstick,

flashed Lex a shy smile and said, "See you later for your bath."

Janice, a beautiful, dark–haired patient, wearing a flannel robe, waylaid us in the hallway and said, "We on for a game later, honey?"

"Sure," Lex said, before introducing us.

"We think your husband's swell," Janice said. "Best gin player I ever met. See ya later, handsome," she purred, as if she had more in mind than counting cards.

I'd heard the rumors about sanitariums. Sex filled a void. It gave patients a sense of life. To the nurses and lonely female patients, Lex would seem as dashing and handsome as Clark Gable or Douglas Fairbanks, Jr. And thanks to my relationship with Franky, I had no right to complain. But I still had to take several deep breaths to avoid making a shrewish comment about his friendships here at Mrs. Jankel's.

When we reached his room, I asked if I could sit with him while he napped. "I brought a good book to read, and I won't make any noise. I promise."

"It's against the rules."

"Well, then I could use a nap myself," I said.

"I wish that were possible. But that's against rules, too." He stood in front of his room, barring my way. "Actually, there's not much to do or see here, Jeri."

He was urging me to leave. A physical pain surged through me for all the things still unsaid. "You look good, darling," I said.

"You too." He gazed into my face as if he wanted to memorize every bone. Bending down, he kissed me softly on the cheek. He still looked like the old Lex, that handsome Lothario who'd changed me forever. Now, as the clouds outside Lex's window darkened, he took my hand and squeezed it. "Have a safe trip back, darling," he said slipping a folded piece of paper into my hand.

I wanted to say I still loved him. That I would always love him. Instead I said, "Promise me one thing. Promise me you'll fight hard to get well."

***

Outside, wrapped in blankets, with rain threatening, Lex stared into the dark clouds and thought of Jeri. His heart ached and he was sure he'd start coughing soon. Oh, to be young and healthy again. To see the future as if it was an enormous buffet and all he had to do was reach for what he wanted, and go where he wanted. To feel the excitement of tomorrow and the promise that just around the curve something wonderful waited. But now the end seemed near. And Jeri had found someone else. He'd seen it in her face.

"Lex?" A woman whispered.

He glanced up. Janice again.

"A little game of gin later? How's about it?" she said.

"Sure." Why not, he thought. Anything to kill time.

***

In the taxi ride down the hill to my hotel, I read the folded paper.

> ... *Nicky Desanto's back in New York. They say his brother Tito is missing and might even be dead. So be careful and don't linger in the city.*

> *Lex*

THIRTY-FIVE

"Don't go back there. Call Lupe and tell her you're sick or going back to New York," Franky urged, as we sped down Sunset Boulevard.

Franky had picked me up at the train station. And he'd been after me to quit my job with Lupe ever since I'd climbed in beside him. We were practically at her house now.

"I don't understand your attitude. I need to work," I said.

"No you don't. Not anymore. I have money now. And a real future with this western serial. Besides, it's awkward having you in her house."

"I promised Lupe I'd come back."

"And you think that means something to her? She can replace you in an hour."

"Maybe she can replace a maid or a driver but I mean more to her than that."

"What if she hears about us?" he asked.

"She won't hear anything unless you tell her."

"Fine. Just call me when you can." He pulled over to the side of the road and stopped. We both stared up the hill, at the long drive which led up to Lupe's grand house. "That's quite a hill. And your bag's a back–breaker," he said.

"I'll manage."

Even though I'd only spent a few hours with Lex at Saranac Lake, my view of Franky had changed. He seemed shorter. And I'd begun to question his stories. "Tell me again, how you met Lupe," I suddenly said.

Franky chuckled. "Not now my love. Better get you back in harness before you're missed and the empress gets upset."

"Sure. See you," I said, climbing out and managing to pull my suitcase off the rear of his car. A moment later, Franky pulled away. The dust from his wheels settled on me. Then, under an intense sun, I slowly headed up the hill. It turned out that Lupe had returned early from her stay in Tucson. Apparently, she'd grown restless. Or her father had grown impatient to be with her.

A short while later, with butterflies in my stomach, I waited outside Lupe's room. It seemed as if months had passed since I'd stood here, though it had been less than two weeks. Repressing the nervous buzz in my stomach, I knocked twice and entered. Lupe sat at her dressing table.

Seeing me, she smiled. "Is good to see you."

I studied her eyes to detect any insincerity. But there was none. Her delight filled me with guilt. This frail human being depended on me. And one day soon, no matter how hard Franky and I tried to keep our relationship hidden, she would discover the truth and feel betrayed.

Today, she was made up to the hilt and wearing a cool summer frock and high heels to deal with the eighty–degree weather brought on by Santa Ana conditions. But under her eyes the telltale purple stains spoke of sleepless nights and fear.

"I'm glad to be back," I said, picking up her things off the floor and disposing of them while she chatted to me.

"Tomorrow, we will be working very early again. I no like,

but my father … I mean, thee director, say it is best to work in thee morning."

"I'll make sure you're up and on time. Would you like breakfast in your room first?"

"Just coffee and toast, not thee butter or jam."

"Very good, madam." I avoided her eyes. Eyes that recalled what I'd witnessed through the slats in her closet door. "What are your plans for today?"

"I must study my lines. There are many. You will help me."

The following week, while waiting for Lupe to return from a date, I fell asleep on Lupe's armchair. In the early hours of the morning, a rough hand shook me awake. Groggy and startled, I stared up into Caesar Cardona's suspicious dark eyes.

"Who are you? And what are you doing in Lupe's bedroom?" Caesar Cardona demanded.

In a flash, I saw it was after sunrise, though there was no sun, just the steady sound of rain hitting the gutters. Then I recalled that Lupe had gone on a date last night and insisted I wait up for her. Eventually, I'd passed out on her chair as I often did.

Keeping my face averted, I sat up slowly. At least my lipstick had worn off and my old tweed suit, low chunky shoes, and heavy cotton stockings might temporarily conceal my identity. I looked as if I should be ringing a school bell not seducing a Hollywood leading man. On the other hand, Caesar still wore evening attire, as if he'd just come from a formal dinner dance at the Coconut Grove. Tall and imposing with his thick silver white hair and mustache, he stood several feet away and scrutinized me as if deciding if I were worth ordering off a menu. As if he might say, *"Give me that blonde for dinner but leave off the garlic."*

"You work for my Lupe?" Caesar's accented voice boomed.

I nodded and stared at the carpet, wishing I'd had time to

shove on my glasses and pull back my hair. For eight weeks I'd managed to avoid *Don Cardona,* until now.

He stepped closer, wagging his finger. "We have met before?"

Keeping my gaze on the green carpet, noting how often wall–to–wall carpets buckled these days, I slowly stood and moved away from the morning light and Caesar Cardona. "I've been working here for quite a while, sir. No doubt we've met before."

"I do not think so. I would have noticed someone so pretty. My Lupe did not mention you were so striking."

"Maybe she doesn't think I am."

"Maybe. But I am sure we have met before. Somewhere …" He sat down on the chaise lounge, lit up a long cigar, and oogled me from my ankles to my breasts. "I never forget a face."

Too bad he was staring at my breasts and his expression said he wanted to see me without the spinster get up. Like he'd prefer me stretched out on Lupe's bed in ostrich features. Or floating in Lupe's sunken tub in little more than soap and water. I just hoped that among my duties of dressing Lupe, rubbing her feet, and taking her abuse, I wasn't expected to sleep with her vain, lecherous father. I'd heard about Caesar Cardona and the parade of secretaries and starlets he'd bedded long before I'd ambled up the drive of Casa Cardona to be Lupe's lady–in–waiting.

Turning my back to Caesar, I began to organize Lupe's lingerie drawer, aware that his gaze now rested on my haunches. He meant to remember where he'd seen me before. I prayed he wouldn't. That he'd never connect the glamorous doll he'd met months ago at a nightclub with the plain frump organizing his daughter's girdles.

I heard him stand. I glanced over my shoulder to see him pointing, looking confused. He'd obviously found part of the puzzle, but it didn't fit in with what he remembered.

"Couldn't be," he said, chewing on the idea. "And yet … do

you know Franky Wyatt? Lupe's husband."

"Beg your pardon?"

"What is your name?"

Which name had I used that night at the Coconut Grove? Jeri Devlin? Or Mrs. Lex Rose. "Jeri Devlin."

He wagged his finger. "No, is not right. Your hair, your clothes, even your name are different. But is still you. I am no fool. I dress and undress actresses every day. And when I see a beautiful young blonde out with my daughter's husband, I no forget thee face."

"Your daughter's husband?" I repeated, feigning shock.

We both heard the car drive up. Caesar's expression said: *Now we'll get to the bottom of this.* Trapped, my mouth tasted dry and my stomach threatened to heave across that annoying carpet. No explanations could excuse the fact that I was in love with Franky.

The front door slammed. We listened to the unsteady clip of heels on the tiled floor, footsteps on the stairway, and along the hall. It seemed like forever till Lupe staggered into the room, dragging her fox fur. Her hair was awry, her lipstick was gone, and her eyes were half–shut. Holding onto the back of the chaise lounge to steady herself, she tossed her purse and fur on the cushioned seat, then kicked off her shoes, unaware she had company. When she finally spotted us, she squinted as if she could hardly make out who we were.

"Papa? What are you doing here so early?"

He smirked at her. "What do you think I am doing here, you stupid cow? Are you so blind, so drunk, you don't even know that you have been sheltering thee very woman who is stealing your husband?"

She frowned and rubbed her head. "Papa … I do not understand."

"*Idiota.* This woman has split up your marriage." He pointed a damning finger at me. "She has been spying on you for months."

Backing up, I eyed the door. And steeled myself to sprint to it. Too bad Lupe and her father were blocking my path.

"I no believe you," Lupe cried. "She is nothing. A servant. A stupid girl who need thee job. I pick her up to drive my car, to clean for me."

"From where? Central Casting?"

She squinted at me. "You and Franky? But I treat you like my *very* own sister. How come you do this to Lupe?"

I shut my eyes, unable to explain.

"Get out," Caesar growled, moving toward me, rage on his mustached face. "You are finished in this town. Crawl back to Kansas or Detroit. Whatever hole you crawled out of."

"And Franky no marry you," Lupe sobbed. "I never give him thee divorce. I make you both sorry."

It was time to get out. Caesar could easily reach for the fire poker or grab me by the throat. I'd be easy to erase. In Hollywood, I was just another blonde actress, a nobody. And Lupe and her father had no idea just how invisible I was, having been born in 1972, decades from now. I needed a decent bluff to make sure they didn't try anything.

"Just one thing," I said, my voice quaking. "If you ever try to hurt Franky or me, I left papers with a friend who'll tell everyone about the filthy things you do to your daughter."

Hollywood could forgive some things. A good press agent could work miracles. But incest wouldn't wash well. The stain would kill their careers.

Caesar's eyes widened then narrowed to dark, murderous slits. His hands tightened into fists. His mouth compressed with anger, as he stared at me in silence. I began to inch back slowly toward Lupe's door. Then I ran. I crossed the hallway and flew down the back staircase.

As my foot reached the last stair, Caesar leaned over the iron railing and thundered, "Get her out of here!"

Tearing across the living room, I headed toward the rear entrance. I meant to cross the back yard to the servants' quarters, grab my things, and call a cab. But before I could reach the dining room, strong hands grabbed me from behind, lifted me off my feet, and propelled me across the dining room, the butler's pantry and through the kitchen, where my feet barely grazed the terra cotta floor. A sheepish blur of familiar faces – wide eyed and stunned – gaped at me and my assailant. With a final shove, he rammed me against the screen door and shoved me out into the yard. I fell, hitting the hard-packed earth now wet from the rain.

My purse, coat, and hat were tossed out after me, ending up on the ground. I looked up at my attacker. At Clark, my former friend. Peering down at me, regret covered his face.

"My things," I shrieked.

"Leave now. *Please*," he urged, glancing over his shoulder in fear before slamming the door shut.

Gasping, sobbing, I managed to stand. Retrieving my things off the wet ground, I fought my rage and humiliation, and slipped into my new polo coat, a ten–dollar bargain from a Sears Catalogue. Then I sped down that driveway as if pursued by demons. Hanging onto my navy beret, which was worthless against the rain, I couldn't help glancing back to make sure no one had followed me. Like a tough young employee Caesar might send after me to silence me forever.

In spite of the rain and my heavy work shoes, I made good time. Moments later, I spied Sunset Boulevard. I thought about my things, about the money I'd sewn into the lining of my suitcase, which was back there in the servants' quarters in a room I'd shared with Luisa, a young Mexican girl brought up from the interior to work in the kitchen.

On Sunset Boulevard with my feet aching and my mind churning, I spied the Rexall Drugs three blocks down. Pushing myself on, I made it there quickly. I finally dragged open the door causing a bell to ring. Inside, I smelled ham and eggs on the grill and realized I hadn't eaten since yesterday afternoon. I'd been too busy getting Lupe ready for her date last night to have supper. And this morning's fight had taken care of breakfast. Now, the big clock above the Ex-Lax advertisement said it was after seven in the morning.

I had thirty cents in my purse. Calling Lorena would cost a nickel. If she couldn't come, it would be another nickel to reach Franky. If I couldn't reach either of them, I'd need another nickel for a streetcar. For now, I couldn't even afford a five cent candy bar.

Seeing the telephone sign, I hurried toward the back of the store. Tears filled my eyes as I slid inside the phone booth and shut the door. Cold and soaked to the bone, I'd never felt more wretched. Everything on me from my coat to my dowdy tweed jacket was wet right down to my panties. But at least this tiny space was private. I briefly caved into self–pity. Tears flowed down my cheeks. I thought of The Rainbow, Jimmy, Lorena. Elvira, Big Harriet and the rest of the girls. I'd been surrounded by friends there. Whores, yes, but friends. Now I was all alone and broke. Today would've been payday, too. In a few hours, I would've gotten my wages, the spare change Lupe tossed at me every Friday. But those few dollars helped me pay for Lex. Now what would I do? I couldn't expect Franky to pay for me *and* Lex's sanitarium.

Why had I stuck around for the Great Depression? Why hadn't I been smart and traveled forward in time with my brother Paul when I'd had the chance? At the moment, I missed every blessed thing about the future. From my credit cards to my cell phone. From my career prospects to my indifference to men.

I pulled out my compact to fix my face and hair. My sodden

beret and soaked hair hung in soaked clumps. I found a wad of toilet paper from my purse and wiped my face dry. Then, with a shaking hand, I applied lipstick. Too bad the effect was clownish on my tired, dispirited face.

"Help you?" a strong masculine voice rang out, startling me.

Heart pounding erratically, I stared into the bespeckled eyes of the sour looking druggist. "I just need to use your phone, thanks," I croaked.

Frowning, he marched back behind the counter and eyed me suspiciously.

With a shaking hand, I carefully took a nickel from my change purse, dropped it in the slot, and dialed Lorena's telephone number. As the phone rang, I kept my eye on the drugstore. What if Caesar Cardona charged in with the police to have me arrested on some trumped up charge? Or Nicky Desanto wandered in and found me? But no, Lex's note had said Nicky was back in New York.

When no one picked up at the Cooper farm, I hung up, waited for my nickel to be returned, then called Franky's house. On the second ring, Wolfie answered. Then it felt like years before Franky said hello.

"It's me. Something's happened," I sobbed.

"Jeri?"

"I ... Caesar Cardona showed up and recognized me."

"Where are you?"

"The drugstore on Sunset."

"Look, it's raining pitchforks here and the roads are pretty much washed out. But I'll get there as soon as I can."

"How long?"

"At least an hour. Maybe more."

I bought a two–cent newspaper then took a stool at the lunch counter. I ordered coffee and a donut to kill time and stay dry. Fifteen minutes later, I'd finished the paper, gone through a dozen magazines off the newsstand, perused the store's collection of lipsticks, powders, creams, and hair treatments, and found the druggist eyeing me as if he suspected I might run off with a movie magazine or a candy bar.

On a better day, I might've chatted with the old man, explained that I was waiting for someone. But today, broke, jobless, and homeless, I felt ashamed. In the same way a hobo riding the rails might feel ashamed. Somehow, in spite all I'd read and seen about the Great Depression; from the bank closures, homelessness, and desperation for work; I blamed myself for my hard luck just as every other hungry, unemployed victim of the era blamed himself.

A moment later, I reluctantly exited into the morning rain. The clock outside the drugstore said it was almost eight. The rain had begun to spiral and shift, twisting palm trees and electric light poles. Three doors down, a small awning in front of a bakery offered shelter. Running through the rain, I eventually ducked underneath it to wait, as shivering pedestrians hurried by, intent on keeping their hat brims low against the blinding downpour. Hoping to spot the Packard, I combed the traffic for Franky's car, knowing it was way too early for him to arrive. Cold and miserable, I envied the people rushing from the warm, well-lighted bakery with their boxes of cookies, cakes, and bread. I just hoped the bakery owner didn't come out to shoo me away.

Over and over I imagined Lupe shrieking, "… Franky no marry you. I never give him thee divorce."

What would Franky say when I told him? What if he got angry? He'd been counting on a comeback and a divorce. What would happen if Caesar Cardona put out the word against him, had Franky blacklisted?

Then a huge Lincoln sent a wave of water toward the curb, and I barely stepped back in time to avoid another soaking. Instead of speeding on, the grand car stopped. My heart lurched. I expected Nicky Desanto or Caesar Cardona to step out of the car. Instead, the uniformed driver jumped out and opened the back door.

A friendly voice from inside called out, "Jeri?"

THIRTY-SEVEN

I stepped forward. For one tantalizing instant, I imagined Lex inside. Lex as he used to be: rich, handsome, and healthy. As if Lex could've managed to get well, travel all the way to Hollywood, hire a car, and find me here at the exact moment I needed him.

Of course the man inside wasn't Lex. It was Harry Ambrose, the studio executive I'd met while job hunting and later out by Lupe's pool.

"Remember me?" he asked, sliding to the edge of his seat and peering at me from the car's dry interior. "You look like you could use a lift somewhere."

"I'm waiting for someone."

"Any chance you could use a cup of coffee?"

It was still way too early for Franky to arrive. And I was cold and lonely.

He opened the door wider. "Come on, let's get a cup of coffee and a sandwich. How about it?"

"I can't stay long," I said, sliding in beside him. The car smelled of cigars, leather, brandy, and my wet clothes.

"Harry Ambrose, in case you forgot." He held out his hand. "We met in somebody's office."

"And at Lupe Cardona's." I managed a weak smile and shook

his hand. "Jeri Rose." Then I spied the ring on his finger. "You're married?" I blurted out, without thinking.

"Fifteen years." He sat back.

His voice said New York but not Park Avenue. His tone said he found me attractive and vulnerable but that he wasn't desperate to seduce me. Which I liked. And didn't. I wasn't used to it. It made me feel unattractive, old. Ever since I'd turned fourteen back in 1987, back in my own generation, men and boys had found me attractive, even beautiful. Being blonde, long legged and full breasted, men had paid me attention, too much in many cases. But here I was on my way for coffee with one of the most infamous men in Los Angeles after one of the most awful mornings of my life, and he didn't seem one bit attracted to me.

Harry Ambrose was known to be a man who got things fixed. He wasn't a mobster like Tito or Nicky Desanto. But he probably knew who to contact if he wanted to get rid of someone. Harry was the man you called when you got into trouble. Or you wanted to get rid of trouble.

In an objective way, I found him very attractive. He looked to be in his late thirties. He was around five ten, muscular, and beginning to go gray, though his barber cut his glorious thick hair to perfection. His fine wool suit looked custom made, making him appear even more powerful, more handsome.

"Musso's," he told the driver.

"Oh, no, not there," I said. "I mean, the way I look and … well, your wife might not like it."

He gave me a long once over, which under the circumstances made me squirm. Then he said, "Honey, I'm a big boy. I do business in this town which means I often see other women for breakfast, lunch, and dinner."

Self–confidence emanated from his eyes to his pores. Next to him, I felt like a gawky, ignorant school girl with braces on my teeth. Yet, no one had ever considered me a dumb blonde before. And I couldn't be called a kid since I was twenty–eight. So maybe Harry Ambrose had a good heart and really meant to rescue me. Then I recalled a story about his being linked with a young actress, a gorgeous brunette, who wasn't his wife. However, the brunette's name eluded me as the big car pulled up to Musso & Frank's, and I spied several men closing umbrellas and hurrying inside.

"Fix your face before we go in," Harry said.

My heart sank at his abrupt tone. Of course I did look like something that had crawled out of a drain. Opening my purse, I withdrew my compact, two lipsticks, and a brush. Taking my time, I painted on a first coat, blended a lighter shade on top, and topped it off with a layer of Vaseline. Next, I powdered and rouged my face. Using a comb, I tried to make sense of my wet hair, but it was a hopeless mess, and so was my hat.

"Maybe I can help," Harry said. After reaching into a small leather box on the floor, he withdrew a small chic little red hat and handed it to me.

I gaped at the costly item. "Are you a haberdasher or just psychic? I mean, how did you know I'd be joining you for breakfast today?"

"I do business with a lot of gals who get caught in the rain." I'd just bet he did.

Once Harry approved of my appearance, the driver opened our door and we dashed under the restaurant's awning.

"Hold on a second," Harry said, as his driver extended a black jacket with a luxurious fur collar toward me.

My guard went up. "Look, I may be wet and hungry but —"

"You're only borrowing it. Relax, it's part of my wardrobe department. You never know when a girl will need to dress up," he said calmly, dropping the jacket over my shoulders and opening the restaurant door for me. Inside, it felt twenty degrees cooler, and I was relieved to have the jacket to cover my wet dress.

Seeing Harry, the restaurant captain immediately led us to a choice center booth.

"Order me steak and eggs and have whatever you like," Harry said, when the waiter handed us menus. Then Harry grunted an apology and sped toward two gray–haired men, joining them in their booth.

It was a relief to be alone. I ordered steak and eggs then searched the crowd for famous faces but found none. Perhaps it was too early for anyone really famous to be out having breakfast.

A few minutes later, Harry returned. "Sorry, but mingling is part of my job. Have you ordered yet?"

"Steak and eggs," I said. Harry made me nervous. His teeth were too white, his smile too dazzling, his sincerity too practiced. And he was too worldly, too jaded. Of course his best feature was his power. He could do things for me. But the cost of his help might be expensive.

"I saw your picture in the papers or in a movie magazine," I finally said.

"Possibly both. So how did I look?"

"What do you mean?"

"I'd like to think I'm better looking in person."

I actually laughed.

Our food came. But I was too tense to eat. My battle with Lupe and her father was still too fresh. And Harry Ambrose intimidated me too much.

"So, what're you doing out here in California?" he asked, cutting into his steak, chewing, and studying me.

"I came here to work. To pay my bills," I said, pushing my

food around my plate.

"Where ya from?"

"New York."

"By way of The Rainbow House."

His remark shocked me. I studied him, wondering what he wanted.

"It's my business to know what goes on in this town," he explained. "Eat up."

I took a bite of toast which went down like a chunk of sawdust. "I met Franky in Havana. I was there with my husband. Until this morning, I worked for Lupe Cardona. Then her father had me thrown out."

"Consider this a lucky day."

"Sure, let's order champagne," I said flatly.

"Why not go home and stick it out with your husband?"

"Is that what you tell all the actresses you meet?"

His dark eyes became earnest. "Trust me, it's wise advice based on years of experience. This is a miserable business."

"So I've seen."

"So what's keeping you here?"

"There's a depression on. The weather's good here. The California economy beats the rest of the country hands down, and my husband has medical bills."

Harry nodded. "Is he very sick?"

I nodded, hating the painful tears which filled my eyes. Harry reached inside his pocket, pulled out a clean handkerchief, and handed it to me.

"Thanks," I said, wiping my eyes and nose.

"Look, I know about you and Franky Wyatt. And I'm sorry to say, he probably can't help you, if that's your angle. He's washed up in this town."

"I'm not interested in Franky for what he can do for me," I snapped, though it had crossed my mind at first. Just not lately. It seemed that traveling back in time had wiped out my business instincts. In 1997, I'd been all business. In 1933 all I seemed to care about were love and passion.

"Good, because he's dog meat these days," Harry said. "First, his father–in–law put out the word. Plus, he's a relic from the silent days. Not much interest in western stars right now."

"Is that so? What about John Wayne and Gary Cooper?"

"John Wayne's got a chance. And Cooper's got a name. Franky's yesterday's news."

"For your information, Franky has an offer and ..." I stopped. Franky had forbidden me to discuss his plans with anyone.

"The western series?" Harry said, cutting off a huge piece of meat and cramming it in his mouth. "That deal won't fly. Too hard to film in New Jersey or Long Island now. Hollywood's where it's all happening."

Of course he knew all about Franky's big deal, about Franky's dream of doing a western series away from Hollywood. Worse, Harry already knew the outcome. My heart sank. Franky and I needed that deal to get away from Lupe and her father. I watched Harry wash down his steak and eggs with coffee. He showed more passion for food than another man's life.

"I don't understand. Franky's still young and handsome," I said.

"Handsome? Every Tom, Dick, and Harry who gets off a bus in this town has a leading man's profile and broad shoulders. But you gotta be smart. And lucky. Otherwise, you'll end up mopping floors at the Ambassador."

"But if Franky made it big in pictures before, surely he can make it again," I said.

"Baby, his style went out with racoon cats and the Charleston. So don't hang your hopes on him."

"So all of you power brokers have decided he's through. Well, you'll be through one day, too. In 1997 you won't even be a faint memory. Your name won't even show up in an old movie magazine. You'll be another dead press agent who clawed his way up the ladder, screwed a bunch of starlets, and acquired a car with pigskin seats. Everything else of yours will end up in a scrap heap or stuffed inside a stuffy consignment shop for strangers to poke at."

Standing, I took off his fur jacket and hat and tossed them down in the booth. "And that, Mr. Ambrose, is a fact. If you live long enough, you can take it to the bank. On the other hand, Franky's films will end up at the UCLA film school or in the Academy's film archives."

In spite of my wet hair and sodden dress, I marched to the door with my head up. Even if telling Harry off had been my last bridge in Hollywood, I didn't care. I hated him, Caesar Cardona, and all the big shots who thought of people as surplus meat.

THIRTY-EIGHT

Back on the street, my eyes burned with tears. Everything I'd touched had turned sour. And who was I to condemn Harry Ambrose when I'd betrayed Lex for months by sleeping with Franky?

As I hurried toward the drugstore to wait for Franky, a wave of loneliness washed over me. I missed Lex. If only he hadn't gotten sick. If only he could wrap me in his arms and tell me he loved me. But he wasn't here. And he wasn't getting better. Besides, things with him had never been simple. Not from the first night to the last.

Fifteen minutes later, I reached the familiar bakery and its protective awning.

Now, as the time slowly ticked by and I combed the traffic for Franky, I knew he'd abandoned me, too, that he was never coming. Desperate, I dug out my last nickel and went back inside the drug store to call Lorena again. Once again no one answered. Which was when I went back outside and spied Franky's Packard up the street, caught in traffic.

Thanks to the downpour, the Packard's top was up.

Standing by the curb, I waved madly. After navigating through the tight traffic, the Packard pulled over to the sidewalk and the door opened. Franky's outstretched hand felt like warm sunshine.

"Hurry up, before you get hit by a wave."

I slid in smelling the pigskin seats. Franky stared ahead not speaking. I glanced at him, hoping for a kind word, but his gaze stayed on the traffic and the road, as he headed down the boulevard. Out my window the scenery drifted by, as rivers of water trickled down the window.

"How're things on the ranch?" I finally asked, aching over Franky's blank expression, the uncomfortable silence, and the slick sound the tires made on the wet dirt road. "Any trouble with the rain? I mean, are the livestock okay?"

Franky changed gears and kept his eyes on the car ahead of us. "Horses got to high ground in time. I got some men taking care of things till I get back."

"That's good," I responded too quickly, ignoring the flat tone in his voice.

I suddenly felt ashamed in front of Franky. As if I'd done something to be ashamed. But he'd known about my working for Lupe before this. Sometimes, I'd even shared information about Lupe and Caesar with him. Information about new pictures Caesar and Lupe talked about producing.

Using a handkerchief, Franky wiped the window which kept fogging up. At last, he pulled alongside a shabby little sandwich shop that looked as if it had been chipped off another building and placed in a parking lot. Large pits filled with water surrounded the tiny place.

Franky shut off the engine."Let's go in," he said, as the rain abruptly let up.

Inside, two forlorn souls, heads bent forward over coffee and the blue plate special ate silently as Franky and I entered. The radio played a dismal love song. The counterman quit wiping off the counter, placed coffee cups in front of us, and held the coffee pot expectantly.

"Two joes, black," Franky told the counterman, climbing onto a stool.

I slid onto the one beside him.

"Anything else?" The counterman asked, pouring coffee for us.

"I'm not hungry," I said.

"Have something," Franky said.

"Okay, a hamburger and fries. And a chocolate milkshake with lots of ice cream." I suddenly felt famished.

"Make that two," Franky said.

I pulled out my compact and checked my face. Without Harry Ambrose's red hat and fur coat, I looked ready for a breadline. My dress and coat were damp, and my hair had turned frizzy from my permanent wave. Still, I wanted Franky to tease me or take me in his arms and swear everything would work out for the best – even if I did look like a chunk of lead.

"Take off your coat," he abruptly said, standing. After helping me out of my coat, he took off his trenchcoat and hung them both on a rack by the door.

"Better?" he asked, sliding back onto the stool.

I nodded. Somehow his kindness made me sadder, lonelier. But I wouldn't cry yet. Not until I was in bed tonight – wherever that would be.

"I have no place to stay tonight. Unless I can reach my cousin," I confessed. Maybe if I moved back in with Lorena and her folks, I could help Lorena rebuild The Rainbow. There had to be something I could do now besides wait tables and sleep with strangers.

"We'll find you a room," Franky said, stirring his coffee and staring into space. So far he hadn't offered me a room at his place. Not even his bungalow by the pool

I studied Franky, the faded cowboy star, and tried to see him the way Harry Ambrose did. But I couldn't. To me, he was still painfully handsome and desirable. Today, it seemed impossible that I'd once had an MBA from UCLA and a condo in Malibu. Or that I'd lived in a big house on Riverside Drive with servants. I even doubted my abilities. Now, as rain splattered the roof above us and we silently ate, it seemed as if nothing would ever work out again.

Twenty minutes later, Franky tossed a dollar down then helped me into my coat.

"Wait while I get the car," he said, not looking at me. Then he dashed outside as the skies opened up with a downpour of a biblical magnitude. Something bad was about to happen. I felt it. Something worse than all the bad things which had happened in the past few months.

So that later, at the Coopers' farm, I wasn't surprised by Franky's little speech.

"Maybe we should take a short break from each other. See if Lupe and her father calm down," he said as we sat outside in his car.

"Suit yourself," I snapped, climbing out and slamming the car door before picking my way through the muddy yard to that grim faded farm house. I dreaded my reception. I hadn't been able to reach Lorena by phone, which had probably been disconnected. I prayed she was home.

Franky abruptly bolted from his car. "Jeri, wait. Look, I didn't mean what I said. It's just... I got a lot on my mind between the ranch and all. I'll find you a room in town later, as soon as the rain lets up. I'll call you tonight," he said, as rain pelted his hat and coat.

I faced him too beaten to react. "You can't call. The phone's been disconnected. When I get the chance, I'll call you. We can finish this conversation then. Thanks for lunch and the ride."

Without a backward glance, I ran to the mottled front door and hammered until my uncle answered. When my Uncle saw me, his grim, weather–beaten expression said it all: Here was another mouth to feed. And tonight was Thanksgiving.

THIRTY–EIGHT

"You got a letter from Lex," Lorena said, that night, after a grim dinner with the family, who'd eyed me with the same disgust as they did Lorena.

"Gosh Mom, you're a genius when it comes to peas, onions, and potatoes," Lorena had chirped, swallowing a fork filled with the current dinner offerings.

Violet glared at Lorena then daintily helped herself to a tiny fork full of peas. "You be grateful for those peas. In Kansas, we didn't have nothin' before we left."

"Let's have a little music and lighten up the atmosphere," Lorena said.

Clement scowled. "Electricity ain't been paid or did you forget?"

Lorena sent me a look. "Guess you need my help after all, Daddy. I'll take care of that in the morning. Gosh, I'm beat." She turned to me. "You must be tired, too."

My head bobbed rapidly. Then we escaped upstairs to her tiny room.

"Hope you don't mind sharing a bed," Lorena said, lighting an oil lantern then pulling down a pile of worn quilts. "It's clean. And I won't bite."

I burst into tears, then spilled out my heart to Lorena.

" … you've had a bad day, that's all. And being a man, Franky couldn't think of anything to say. He's no better or worse than any of them," Lorena said, trying to calm me down.

"But all our plans."

"Maybe it's time you read that letter from Lex. And there's another one from his landlady, Mrs. Jankel."

"When did they arrive?"

"Few days ago at the post office." She opened the top drawer from her bureau and handed me both envelopes. "Hope they aren't more bum news."

Dear Jeri:

Last night I coughed up blood again. The doctors and nurses say it's because I don't willingly submit to the regime, that my attitude stinks. Swell, I think. But how does an attitude make your insides bleed? And why won't they admit that sick guys like me get out of here feet first or not at all. I hear the cries in the night and see the empty rooms the next morning. I hear the whispers, too. Twenty–five percent don't make it. One quarter won't ever sing and dance again while holding a golden girl in their arms. I've been here thirteen months, but it feels longer than the Great War,

and that lasted an eternity. I may go mad. Maybe
a mental hospital would be more fun anyway.
Write me. Your letters help. And please send me
a new photograph. Love Lex.

If I'd rented a room up in Saranac Lake to be near Lex, would he be better now?

The current theory behind keeping a patient at rest was sound in its way. The doctors felt that a patient at rest would form a capsule around the tubercular region. Like a gossamer fabric, a silky thread like spider webbing, this membrane built up over time. If the lung rested and the patient gained weight, if the capsule formed, then maybe the patient would get better. But the truth was, a real cure was years away.

I read Mrs. Jankel's letter next.

"... and it has been weeks since I received a payment from you. I can't keep Mr. Rose here and pay for his hospital procedures, too. You currently owe $212.00."

I hardly slept that night. I worried about Franky. I worried about Lex. Words and phrases raced through my head. Things I meant to say to Franky. Ways in which I could tell Lex about Franky.

Around three, I abruptly sat up in bed, glad Lorena slept soundly beside me. Why should I tell Lex about Franky? Or bother to mention a divorce? Franky had never proposed to me or suggested marriage. All he ever said was that when the contracts for the cowboy serial were signed, we could get a nice place and not worry about being seen together in public. Hardly a diamond ring or the graceful chimes of church bells ringing in the background.

***

The early February sun slanted across the crumpled white sheets. Franky yawned, picked up the alarm clock, and glanced at the dial. "Damn, it's after eleven already."

In two seconds he would bound out of bed, yank on his pants, and rush off as if he had a dozen pressing things to do. Where he went after he left me here in this grim little room with its ancient bed, scratched chests of drawers, and chipped sink was a mystery. Maybe he saw his barber for the works then rushed home to his ranch to mend fences. Maybe he had another girl on the side. At least he'd rescued me from the Cooper's farm and found me this place, pathetic as it was.

"Guess we should dress," I said before he made some excuse to dash off. I tried to sound upbeat, though my cheerfulness rang false.

"Take it easy," he said, placing a pillow behind his head, then taking my hand. "I'm in no hurry."

Grateful to share even a few extra minutes with him, I leaned back against the iron headboard and studied him, finding myself as entranced as always by his muscled flesh and brilliant eyes. "So it's all set for New York, right?" I said, hating myself for harping on the subject.

He dropped my hand and sighed. "Like I told you before. I'll meet you at The Waldorf on the twenty–fourth."

"But what if Lupe complains or threatens you? What if —"

"Darling, how many times do I have to say it? You're my

gal now. Okay?" He leaned over and pecked my cheek. "Lupe means nothing to me."

For the moment my anxieties abated. Too bad they'd return tonight with a vengeance. Alone in this airless room, in this old house in Boyle Heights, accommodations Franky paid seven dollars a week for, my head would fill with images of him dancing close to another woman, kissing her, whispering promises in her ear. I'd pace the floor questioning my right to happiness. I'd blame myself for betraying everyone from Lupe to Lex.

"Promise me if you change your mind about us, you'll tell me. Okay? I'd rather know the truth," I said.

With a loud sigh, Franky kicked off the sheet, dropped his feet over the side of the bed, and ran his hands through his thick blond hair. "Damn, but you got a one track mind." In a flash, he rose off the bed, pulled on his shirt and pants, before studying himself in the mirror above the bureau. Rubbing his hand over his jaw, he frowned at the beard stubble. "Has Lex written you something upsetting? Is that why you're so jumpy?"

"No, it's not that." A lie. Mrs. Jankel's most recent note said the doctors wanted to remove Lex's ribs to permanently collapse his lung. And his bill had escalated to over four hundred and fifty dollars. Mrs. Jankel had also included a list of cheaper cure cottages, since I hadn't paid her in two months for the weekly rate or Lex's additional surgical treatments. She'd also given me a final due date.

... I need your final payment of four hundred fifty dollars before February 15, or I will have to give

> *Mr. Rose's room away. I think you should*
> *consider moving Mr. Rose to one of the newer*
> *public sanitariums which deliver good care, but*
> *don't charge anything.*

Today was January 29, 1934, and I barely had local bus fare. Yet I couldn't let Lex end up in a public institution, some ward where the beds stretched as endlessly as the Great Wall of China. And I didn't dare ask Franky for another dime. Not when he was already paying for everything from my rent and to the aspirins I needed for the headaches I'd been having lately.

"Is he getting any better?" Franky asked, pulling on his boots.

"Sure. But I guess it takes a long time to get well."

His sudden interest in Lex's health alarmed me. Would this be his excuse to back out of our relationship? "He's not the reason I'm so nervous," I said. "Guess I'm still upset over Lupe and her father."

Plus the endless hours which inched by while I waited to leave Wednesday, three days from now. I'd never been so aimless. In the 1990s, I'd attended college, graduate school, then worked in advertising. Back in 1929 and 1930, I'd sold lingerie. Then I worked at Saks as both a model and a sales girl before ending up at Hirsh's, a small women's store where I met Zaza Pavlova, a dear friend who helped me through some tough times before I married Lex. Here in California I'd done extra work in the movies. But until Lupe, my hardest job had been hunting for work.

Now, the four walls of my little room felt like a rat cage in a house with three other cages filled with strangers: A salesman down on his luck, a small family barely scraping by, and a single girl desperate for a job or a man. At night, my only company was the radio.

Dressed, Franky fastened his wrist watch. "What about your cousin? Isn't she around?"

Was that derision in his voice? Not that his opinion differed from everyone else's. Once a girl ran a whore house, she was forever labeled unfit for decent society. But people were wrong about Lorena. My cousin, the whorehouse madam, was the kindest and most generous person I'd ever known. And she'd never made love for money in her life. Which was more than I could say, considering how financially dependent I was on Franky.

"She's trying to rebuild her house. Since the fire, she's been very busy," I said.

"Here's your train ticket and something for clothes," Franky suddenly said, digging through his pants pocket, then tossing a train ticket envelope and a thick wad of cash on the bed. "Get something at Hattie Carnegie's or Saks when you get to New York. A tailored dress with a jacket and furs. Something sophisticated but conservative."

He sounded as if I usually looked like I hustled sailors in Times Square.

Dressed, he opened the door to leave. Then, as if remembering something, he turned, pecked me on the lips, and rushed out. I listened to his boots clumping down the stairs then

I raced to my window to see him climb into his car and drive off.

Once again, that empty feeling filled my stomach as I dropped down on my bed to count the money. Two hundred dollars in cash and a one–way ticket on The Twentieth Century for a small, private stateroom. The ticket alone had to be worth over a hundred bucks. Maybe even a hundred twenty. And with the fifty I'd dug out from behind the lining in my suitcase, after Clark had mailed me my things, I was sitting pretty. Unless I blew everything at Saks when I got to New York. Or Franky was unexpectedly detained here in California.

Don't think like that. Stay positive.

After a fast bath in the tub down the hall, I donned an old dress, then dashed down the street to mail money to Mrs. Jankel. I sent her seventy–five dollars, over two weeks rent. Later, I'd trade in my expensive train ticket for something cheaper, even if it meant sitting all the way to New York. The extra money might postpone Lex's eviction. Unless Mrs. Jankel was determined to find another tenant for his room, a better paying tenant.

Alone that night, I wondered where Franky was and what he was up to. And why he never saw me at night anymore. To kill time I read and listened to the radio. Someone in the house had left behind Agatha Christie's *Lord Edgeware Dies.* I tried to get absorbed in the story but the hours passed slowly.

The next morning, still damp from my bath, with my hair clipped and pinned into appropriate waves, as I hung stockings on the clothes–line out my window, a knock on my door startled me.

"Who is it?" I yelled, tying the belt of my robe tight and wondering why my landlady, who always sat on the front stoop, had allowed anyone past her.

"Telegram."

With my door open an inch, I stared down at a Western Union boy. After scribbling my name on the receipt and tipping the boy a nickel, I locked my door, then dropped down on my bed. The pale yellow envelope terrified me. *Don't let it be about Lex*, I prayed. With a swift rip, I tore open the envelope and read.

> *Please come to Casa Cardona tomorrow afternoon at three. I must talk to you. My car will arrive for you at two.*
>
> *Señora Lupe Cardona.*

THIRTY-NINE

Lupe's new driver Rupert had sparkling dark eyes, white teeth, a body–builder's physique, and enough raw sexual energy to make my hair curl from the Lincoln's back seat. At last someone had cast the right actor for the role of Lupe's chauffeur. No doubt Lupe now spent her free evenings down at the Casa Cardona garage drilling Rupert on left hand turn signals and which sexual positions worked best in a rumble seat.

The sun was still high when I mounted those familiar grand stairs to Casa Cardona. I regretted wearing my reliable old brown dress from two seasons ago.

Clark answered the door. After bowing slightly, he glanced around furtively, then whispered, "Sorry about being so rough that day. The big cheese made me do it."

Clark immediately resumed his bland butler's expression as he led me to the grand living room. But just before he opened the double doors to announce me, he paused. "I forgot. Some nasty hood came looking for you. I told him you'd left."

Nicky Desanto. Thank heavens he was back east now, providing Lex's information had been correct. "Thanks."

With a nod, Clark knocked twice, opened the living room

doors, said my name, then silently backed out, shutting the doors behind him.

In the center of the room on the white sofa with a leopard skin rug draped behind her, Lupe reclined in pink silk lounging pajamas. Her feet, in pink ballet slippers, were tucked beneath her, and a white cashmere blanket rested on her lap. A fire burned brightly. Rita, her maid, busily set out an elaborate tea service on the coffee table. I suddenly wondered if Lupe expected company and was daft enough to believe I'd help serve.

Instead, Lupe rose slowly and extended her hand. "It was very good of you to come. Please have thee seat."

Apparently, the elaborate tea service with sandwiches, scones, and pastries *was* meant for me. Too bad I couldn't see the point in dragging out the scene. "Look Lupe, there's nothing you can say or do about Franky that will —"

"Tea?" Lupe interrupted, as she tipped the silver pot toward a small china cup and saucer.

"Sure, fine, whatever," I said, resigned to the charade, though I knew Lupe was about to drop a bomb on my head, some deadly item meant to rip Franky and me apart.

I reluctantly settled onto a tall, elegant chair opposite her. Trying to remain calm, I mentally ran down my list of unfinished chores which needed attention before my train left Wednesday. Like getting a final permanent wave. And forwarding my mail to the Grand Biarritz in New York.

"Please help yourself to thee food," Lupe said, gesturing toward the feast I would've enjoyed under different circumstances. I grudgingly accepted a crust–less sandwich wedge and tea before Lupe got to the point.

"Look, Jeri, I no intend to fight you," she said. "And I no beg you or Franky to come back to me. I only wish to explain my side of thee story. You must believe, I no want you to hate me. You been like thee big sister to me. So for me it is only right to warn you about thee mistake you make with Franky. He is not thee man you believe he is. And this I must assure you —"

"Wait just a second —"

"Please." Lupe held up her tiny hand to silence me. "I no take long for this. Maybe you will listen and understand that I tell thee truth. Yes, you can make up many ugly stories about me and my father for thee newspapers. But you cannot forget that I take you in. That I pay for you. That I trust you with my life."

I stood. "You worked me like a slave. And what has any of this to do with —"

"Please, I must ask you to listen to me now."

I sat.

"Maybe I not easy to love. And I know you have seen many things. Things which are not very easy to understand."

I swallowed. Lupe was alluding to her father's incestuous demands. I stared at the oriental rug unable to face her, amazed she'd brought it up.

"But I like you. When you were here – thee house, it was better. Not so lonely. When I no can sleep or I have thee bad headache, you try to help me very much.

But you must understand my husband. He was all thee time with thee young girls from thee first day to thee last. So I warning you, he will disappoint you, too. Not because he love me, but because he is afraid. He is afraid to make my father angry. And he is also afraid for his career. Because he know that Hollywood is finished for him. But he also know that my father can help him. So he cannot marry you. Because he still want with all his heart to be famous," Lupe said.

No, I thought. She's just trying hold onto Franky, to

manipulate me. She wants to upset me, fill me with doubt, drive me off.

On my feet again, I realized I was shaking. "I really don't have time for this *Lupe*," I said, using her first name for once. "I'm amazed you can live with so many crazy illusions and lies. Have you been such a saint? What about your little trysts down by the beach?"

Without warning, Lupe's eyes filled with tears, meaning she was either very upset or a much better actress than anyone believed. Curious, I dropped back onto my chair.

"Yes, I lie," Lupe whispered. "I must lie. Or I would be dead. I work in thee business where I have to say yes when I want to say no. I make thee pictures they say for me to make. Every day I must ask: Will thee people like me? Will they like thee way I look? Thee way I dress. All I can do is work hard. I must always pray that they will think Lupe is still young, still beautiful. That I am still thee Guadalajara Spitfire." Sniffling, Lupe pulled out a lace hankie and gently wiped her nose.

I studied Lupe reluctant to feel sorry for her. But I did.

"I no want thee divorce," Lupe added. "What woman wants this thing? But you must believe Lupe. Franky has done this many times before. He meet thee *chica* he like, so he make up many stories. He tell thee *chicas* that he grew up with nothing to eat or to drink. He say to them that he was thee poor cowboy on thee ranch in Arizona. But he was not living with thee horses and cows when I meet him. His father owned thee food store in San Diego. And I no make him marry me either. He want to marry me for what my father can do for him. For many years, he make thee movie pictures because my father want him to be popular. But always, Franky is drinking and sleeping with thee young chicas from Idaho and Kansas who believe that he will make them famous. But he will never divorce me. No, that he will never do. He love himself too much. And he know that you cannot help him with his career, but my father can."

"I have to go." I grabbed my purse and stood.

"Please, Jeri, I no hate you. I tell you thee truth. Franky will not make you happy. Me either. But I am his wife and we have thee daughter. And I am used to him."

Rupert drove me home. In spite of my quaking nerves, I finished the items on my list. With or without Franky, I planned to go east.

The next morning, as Rose Tencil clamped the electric rods in my hair and the putrid odor of permanent wave solution and singed hair filled the salon, I replayed the scene at Lupe's house. *She had liked me.* In a strange way, I'd liked her, too. Maybe because Lupe had needed me so much. Or because I saw through her games and found her sympathetic underneath. But I refused to scurry back to New York like a whipped school girl because of what she'd said. Or for that matter, anything that Harry Ambrose had said that day in the rain.

The next morning, the phone downstairs rang early.

"Mrs. Rose, telephone," my landlady called upstairs.

It was Franky. "I heard about your tea party yesterday," he said, sounding defensive. "And as much as I'd love to drive you to the station, I've got a sick calf and a lame horse to deal with. Is there anyone else who can take you to the station?"

How easily he broke his promises lately. How I longed to tell him to drop dead. Instead I mumbled, "I'll try my cousin. Or call a cab."

"Good, fine. I'd come myself, but we're short of help right now, and I need to get things squared away before I meet you in New York."

"No problem." *Asshole.*

"See you at The Waldorf. And don't forget, I love you," he

said.

I had to believe him. What choice did I have? Because in a moment of clarity, I realized that I was hooked into Franky from A to Z. Not only did I desperately want the SOB, I needed him, too. For money.

"That's some get–up," Lorena said the following afternoon, as we drove to La Grande Station at Second Street and Santa Fe Avenue, the current railroad station. Union Station wouldn't be completed until 1937. "You look ready to do a screen test."

"Thanks," I said, as my stomach somersaulted from nerves. "You look pretty decent yourself."

Today, Lorena wore a tailored brown dress which fit her as if Hattie Carnegie herself had sewed it on. Her dark shoes were conservative yet elegant. And her freshly permed honey–blonde hair was styled just right. She didn't look like anybody's idea of a whorehouse madame, but then she never had.

"How about a little *Gordon Water*? My flask's in the glove compartment," she said.

"I'm okay, really."

"Here's a little something you might need." Lorena held out a fifty–dollar bill.

"Keep it."

"Don't be an idiot, take it."

"You're pretty quick about passing around the heavy sugar," I said, shoving the money in my purse, knowing it would put me one step closer to securing Lex's place at Mrs. Jankel's. "Franky gave me a bundle, too. And how come you're still living on the farm if things are so swell? I've been worried about you. I thought your bank might've gone under."

Lorena grinned. "Nah, things are peachy. I'm just biding my time so I can build a really great house. A mansion with all the trimmings."

I imagined the new Rainbow would look like Tara in the epic film, *Gone With The Wind* which wouldn't be released until 1939.

"Did I ever mention that the fire insurance clerk was a steady Rainbow customer, and we had a fire insurance policy after all?" Lorena added.

"I'll just bet you did. Wish I had more of your iron running through my veins. Once upon a time I did. Now all I do is worry about Franky. Will he come? Does he love me?"

"You'll know soon enough," Lorena said softly. "Either way, you'll survive."

"I guess so. What's the latest news about Roger?"

Lorena never took her eyes off the road. "He's back from Saratoga with his fiancé."

"You've spoken."

"Twice. In fact, he's gonna help me rebuild The Rainbow."

"He actually offered to help?"

"Not exactly. When I called him last week, I casually mentioned that I might like to write our state senator."

"So?"

"Our state senator happens to be Roger's daddy. I thought I'd let the senator know that his son has a habit of promising hookers he'll marry them when he's already engaged. Naughty boy."

"That's —"

"Gentle persuasion. Roger thought he was having fun slumming around with a dumb floozy."

"He found out about you and The Rainbow?'

She sighed. "It seems he knew from the start. I'm not surprised. I'm well known around town. Anyway, it turns out he's gonna be a big help. With a few thousand dollars from him – a drop in the bucket for his fancy Pasadena family – we'll be able to keep twenty women off the dole. And with his dough, what I've got in the bank, and the fire insurance money, The Rainbow's gonna rise from the ashes better than ever. I may even trade in this hayburner for something that raises your blood pressure when you put her in gear. Something sporty and fast like a Packard."

I laughed. "I'd like to see that."

"You'd better. I expect to see you back here one day. Now what did Queen Lupe have to say?"

Out my window, the buildings which now made up downtown Los Angeles would be eyesores by the time I grew up in the late Twentieth Century. But today they were a tribute to the town's optimism and growth. "I felt sorry for her."

"You're soft in the head."

"Why? Because she's a rich movie star? Face it. She's closer to forty–four than twenty–four. The whole industry's waiting to see her go down for the count. And one day soon, life's gonna hand her a steep bill."

"What did she say about Franky?"

"That he'll never leave her. That he's a liar and a Casanova. Which may have been true once. But I have to believe he loves me. That he'll follow me to New York. And one day, when the time's right, we'll get married." I waited for Lorena to contradict me.

"Not to be a wet smack, but just how's he gonna get this new movie deal if he's on the outs with the studio boss's daughter?"

"Different studio."

"I thought there was like a club, an unwritten agreement that the studios circle their wagons when the natives attack."

"I don't think anyone's gonna worry about a low–budget western serial."

"And Lex?"

His name made my heart jump. "Once Franky arrives, I'll go

to Saranac Lake and explain everything in person. It'll be better that way." *Sure.* I might as well stick a knife in Lex's ribs and collapse his lungs myself. Because this time I'd have to confess that I'd fallen in love with another man. Okay, Lex had pushed me to do this. But I knew Lex's true wishes. He dreamed of me pining for him. He imagined me hurling myself across his coffin, crying and screaming. The rest of his lofty pleadings for me to survive well without him had sounded good at the time. But it would be painfully different for him to hear me say I loved another man.

"By the way, Lex sent you this." She handed me an envelope from Saranac Lake. "I just picked it up at the post office this morning."

I studied the envelope and recognized Lex's handwriting. I tried to imagine Lex's reaction to my confessions about Franky. Would he be sarcastic and make clever quips? Or would he hide his pain and wish me luck … even if it killed him?

"If you need me, I'll be at the folk's homestead," Lorena said, cutting through my reverie as she pulled over to the curb by a tall Moorish building.

My heart lurched. We'd arrived. Thanks to the Long Beach earthquake the previous March, the station's domed roof had been removed and scaffolding supported part of the building.

"Did I tell you Jimmy moved to San Francisco? He wrote. Says he loves it up there. He's working in some fancy new saloon and writing on the side."

I wasn't listening. My stomach rolled, my heart raced, and my mouth felt like the Dust Bowl. I forced myself to breathe as I stared out the window at the people hurrying into the train station. Lorena climbed out of the truck and began to pull my two suitcases and hatbox off the back. She found me a porter and sent him off with my things. Until there was nothing left to do but say goodbye.

"Guess it's time," she said. "You better get a move on."

But I couldn't move. Without a word, I grabbed her and hugged her tight. She smelled of My Sin and hair lacquer. When we pulled apart, her eyes were red with tears.

"Thank you, Lorena. Thank you for too many things to mention. I can never repay you."

"Listen… if stuff doesn't come out like you planned, like he chews with his mouth open, picks his toenails, or ends up being stingy, write me, and I'll wire you whatever you need. We're kin. And always will be."

I fought the urge to cry as I stood by the station doors and watched her drive away. I wanted to believe that I would see her again. But it was a big country. And I doubted I'd make many trips west once I settled in the east. Maybe one day, when World War II ended and air travel improved, I'd see California again. For now, I'd had enough of Hollywood. Clutching my purse, I entered the busy station, relieved that the ticket line wasn't too long. I intended to trade in my ticket for a cheaper one even though it meant I'd have to sit all the way to New York.

"How much to New York in coach?" I asked the ticket counter clerk.

"Eighty–nine dollars."

"Can I trade this one in?"

"Yes, ma'am."

An hour later, as the train pulled out of the station, I shut my eyes, wishing I could sleep all the way to Chicago. I'd spent the previous night sitting in the dark on the window ledge fretting over Lex and Franky and staring out at a neon sign that read Nick's Steak House.

Back in the future, I'd been a career woman. Now, my life revolved around men. No one in 1933 would be shocked by this admission. A girl who didn't pine for a home and marriage was a freak. Even Lorena didn't blame me for being stuck on a guy. But I knew there was a saner way to live. And if I'd been braver, I would've told Lorena about my being a time traveler. I would've described the future when women could be doctors, lawyers, accountants, bankers, and engineers. Lorena might've even believed me.

A half–hour later, sitting beside a grim faced older woman, I stared out the window, as the train chugged out of the station and the view out the window spoke of a burgeoning city. And the vast, wild lands that still remained virginal for now. In seconds I grew drowsy. Just before I slipped into an unconscious state, I thought the sound of the train seemed to repeat: *He's not coming, he's not coming.* Then I drifted off.

TWENTY–SIX

I felt Lex's presence as soon as my foot hit the pavement outside New York's Pennsylvania Station and a freezing February wind whirled around me. This had been his city once, his empire. I imagined him rushing through the crowd, a head taller than the other pedestrians, his stylish hat tipped over one brow, and his blue eyes focused straight ahead. But he wouldn't be here today or tomorrow. Nor would Harris who'd retired out on Long Island. Still, New York felt magical as I gripped my overnight bag and waved down a passing cab before a porter loaded my suitcases into the back.

Today, warmed by my old sable coat and my favorite black velvet hat, luxury items which had been stored for almost two years at Mr. Chin's laundry, I felt ready to face the world. As always, traffic crawled along Fifth Avenue. But the skyline had changed with the tops of the new Chrysler Building and Empire State Building reaching for the forbidding gray sky. Much had been added, too, from the new Radio City Music Hall to the new Waldorf–Astoria, the world's largest hotel in 1933.

Unfortunately, the Grand Biarritz had slid downhill. The lobby still smelled of furniture polish but today the palm trees looked tired. And a joyless hush blanketed the hotel, as if this was four in the morning, not noon on Saturday.

A longing for my first day here in 1929 surfaced, when a parade of haughty women in expensive furs, a thread of French perfume dangling in their wake, had crossed this same marble floor. When the phones at the busy front desk rang constantly. And the lobby had percolated like Grand Central Station at rush hour thanks to the stock market's grave stumble and the growing fear which had filled the guests. And yet, there had been an energy that morning, too, as the last aura of prosperity radiated through the lobby.

But that was over four years ago. And the crowds had moved onto The Pierre, The Plaza, The St. Regis, and The Waldorf.

Now, a tired looking businessman stood before the registration desk, a scarred leather grip at his feet. Another man sat in a broad chair in the front lobby by the window facing out toward Central Park South, a newspaper on his lap, his mouth open as he snored. By the elevators, a bored looking uniformed black man stood waiting, as if he'd been waiting years for somebody to ring for him. When my turn came at the front desk, a short, officious young man, a stranger, briskly greeted me with an automatic smile. "May I help you, madam?"

"A room please."

"Do you have a reservation, madam?"

"Yes, Mrs. Lester Rose."

"Please sign here." The young clerk turned the guest book to face me. I quickly scribbled my name.

"I believe there's a telegram for you, Mrs. Rose," he added, opening a drawer then handing me a Western Union envelope.

Praying for good news, I instantly tore it open and read.

Missing you. See you at the Waldorf. Love Franky.

My whole body relaxed. Franky was coming after all. He'd be here tomorrow. I felt as if I'd dropped fifty pounds, as if I could float across the lobby.

"Here's your key, madam. Is there anything else I can get you? A newspaper or dinner reservation?"

"Wait," I said, staring at the key to an unfamiliar room. "Is number 552 available?"

"But I gave you a much nicer room, madam. With a view of the park. It's been completely redone, and I'm still charging you the three–dollar rate."

"I'd prefer 552. I've stayed here before. And I have sentimental reasons for requesting the room."

Leaning forward, the desk clerk glanced around the lobby, then spoke in a low tone. "But 552 hasn't been refurbished."

"I don't care."

"And guests say … it's haunted."

"Haunted?" I laughed. "Surely you don't believe such nonsense."

His expression turned blank. "As you wish, madam." After giving me a hard second glance, he checked the warren of pigeon holes behind the desk, then handed me another key. I studied the key. Judging by the metal medallion on the key chain, it might be the same one I'd used in 1929.

Up on the fifth floor, I followed the tired carpet past walls in need of fresh paint and new wallpaper. The ghost of an old cigar hung in the air, and the din of men talking, perhaps playing cards in one of the rooms, added to the hotel's faded grandeur. The hotel would be ready for a wrecking ball in the late 1990s. Now, it was like a beautiful lady past her prime, with eyes that have witnessed too many disappointments.

The bellman appeared from the service elevator and hurried to unlock the door. Inside, while the bellman placed my luggage on the stand then turned on the lights in the bathroom, I dropped onto one of the twin beds and surveyed the room. A room which had been my refuge several times.

As before, the old Crosley radio rested on the night table

where the Magic Fingers Massage Machine had been. But I still had no idea what prompted it to appear. Did the machine only materialize on certain dates? Or did you have to be true in your heart, like Dorothy in her quest to go home to Auntie Em?

"Would you like ice or a room service menu?" the bellman asked, jarring me from my thoughts.

"No thanks." I handed him a quarter then shut the door behind him.

I quickly unpacked then luxuriated in a hot bath. But even the soothing hot water couldn't relax me. I expected to look up and catch a glimpse of Paul leaning against the wall, a flask of bootleg whiskey in his hand, a drunken smile on his handsome face. Or I'd catch his spoiled wife Sylvia smirking at me, a judgmental hatred in her dark eyes.

Or I'd imagine I heard an air conditioner or a TV, indications that the room was moving forward in time. Why not? It had happened at least three times before. First when Paul had been sent back in time in July of 1997, and later when I'd followed in his wake that October. And again that fateful summer night in 1930 when Lex lay in bed in the next room with a gunshot wound in his shoulder; when both Paul and Sylvia had slipped into another era, and I'd stayed behind with Lex.

After my bath, I dressed in my robe and sat down at the small round table to write letters. I sent another eighty–five dollars to Mrs. Jankel, which included Lorena's money and what I'd received for exchanging my train ticket. I included a note saying she could reach me here at the Grand Biarritz Hotel.

Then I dug out Lex's letter from my purse, the one which had arrived five days ago, right before my train. I'd read it so many times, the ink had faded and the paper had deep creases.

His words, "… it would be impossible to blame anyone for

finding you beautiful or falling in love with you," indicated he sensed I'd met someone like Franky. Worse, he told me he still loved me. Twice.

In the morning, Pierre, my former hairdresser, who'd managed to stay in business, washed and set my hair. Then I took a nostalgic walk up Fifth Avenue and found myself staring into Hirsh's store window, thrilled it had survived these hard years of the depression. As always, the bell rang when I crossed the threshold.

My old friend Zaza Pavlova stopped dusting the glove counter and graciously swept toward me. "Good afternoon, madam," she began a second before her expression lit up. "Well, well, if it isn't Jeri Devlin Rose."

"Zaza," I breathed, before we hugged.

"Enough of that," Zaza said, wiping her eyes with a lace handkerchief. "Now stand back and let me look at you." Squinting, Zaza gave me a ruthless once-over. "I see you've kept your figure. Including that impossible bust of yours."

I laughed. "Good to see you, Zaza."

"It certainly took you long enough to drop in and visit your old pal."

"I've been in California for fourteen months. But I'm back now. For good."

"Glad to hear it. Now have a seat and tell me everything."

For two hours, I filled her in. About Lex being sick and my decision to come back east. But I never mentioned Franky. Franky, who was the key to my life. Even with his telegram tucked inside my purse, it seemed unlucky to broadcast our plans. Mostly, because we were both married to other people.

"So you'll work for me," Zaza concluded. "Mr. Rose can hardly resent that, considering how hard things have been."

"Sure, that is ... I'll have to see what he says. In the

meantime, I need a tailored day dress." I'd almost decided not to get a new outfit. I had Lex's bill to consider. But since Franky was definitely coming and would be flush with money from his new series, I felt safe in purchasing a few things.

"So it's to be that kind of visit," Zaza said. "Nothing like a good challenge, I always say." Tapping a long finger against her cheek, Zaza began to pace before the store's various clothing racks. Occasionally, she pulled out a garment, then instantly shoved it back on the rack. At last she snapped her fingers. "I've got it. Right off the truck and so stylish Coco Chanel could've sewed it herself. With matching shoes and a gem of a hat."

"I'll need furs, too."

"Furs, shoes, a suit? You must've hit it big."

"If I'd really *hit it big*, would I be shopping here?"

Zaza laughed. "I've certainly missed you, Jeri Devlin Rose."

Then Zaza was in motion. I found myself in a whirlwind of suits, shoes, stockings, and hats. Zaza also sold me everything at the wholesale price. "It's the least I can do for a former employee," she said.

At last in the finished ensemble, I studied my reflection in that familiar free–standing oval mirror. Zaza had made me look expensive. Even the Russian fox collar for nineteen–ninety-five could've come from a renowned furrier.

"You've done it again," I said. "You're a genius."

Zaza raised a brow and nodded. "I never argue with facts. Now, how about the truth? You've been acting like you're standing on a bed of hot coals since eleven this morning."

Zaza dropped down onto the familiar red velvet sofa and patted the spot beside her. I quickly joined her. In an instant, the truth tumbled out. Facts about Lorena, Lupe, and of course Franky. Zaza silently listened. Being a quiet Tuesday, we were interrupted exactly once by a woman hunting for a purse.

Finally, after I'd revealed all, Zaza shook her head and said, "Why didn't you write me?"

"Ashamed I guess."

"No matter. Here's how I see it. That cowboy is married. So much as it hurts me to say it, I wouldn't put much faith in him." She held up her hand to show there was no arguing. "I know what he said. I know he *thinks* he'll be here with bells on. But don't forget, your friend Zaza has seen it all. And don't forget, you're married, too. For better or worse. Maybe times are tough and Lex hasn't been a saint, but I doubt you'll find happiness with this actor. Actors..." she grimaced, "conceited fools. I knew a few of them myself in my day. Most of 'em don't know there's another soul on earth. It's all about them. Their careers, their heartaches, their money problems."

I laughed. As in the good old days, Zaza's remarks were harsh but perceptive.

"So don't be too broken hearted if Mr. Franky Wyatt doesn't come through," Zaza added. "And if you need a job, you can work here. You were the best sales girl I ever had. That's what I used to tell Mr. Leon Hirsh, whenever he crawled out of his office." Zaza made a face and cocked her head toward the back, toward owner Leon Hirsh's door, as she'd done a hundred times in 1930.

"Won't he resent my coming back after all this time?" I asked.

Zaza's expression grew smug. "Well, it seems the news never reached the West Coast. I suppose Walter Winchell was too absorbed with other things to mention it on the radio. But I married that miserly Leon Hirsh six months ago."

"Zaza, you didn't."

Zaza shrugged and made a face. "It was about time the old skin flint asked me."

TWENTY–SIX

Franky looked nervous. *Good*, Lupe thought, as she made her grand and *very late* entrance into the Ambassador Hotel's dining room.

Today, she'd donned her dark navy suit. The one he liked. Draped in furs that rose up high behind her, she knew she'd never looked more attractive. Strutting behind the restaurant captain, she crossed slowly, head high, gaze intent on the carpeted route to Franky's table by the window. Even here in Hollywood, at this famous hotel where stars congregated nightly, heads spun to glimpse the Guadalajara Spitfire. She heard the buzz of voices and felt a flood of satisfaction. She hadn't faded from the public eye yet. Maybe one day soon, but not today. She could see the women jealously admiring her slimness, her clothes, her perfectly made–up face.

Seeing her, Franky bolted to his feet and reached for her chair.

His cheeks were flushed, and she could tell he'd already had a few drinks.

"Thank you very much for coming to see me," she said smiling, placing her lizard bag on the chair between them. They ordered cocktails. Then more cocktails. It felt good to drink legally again. For this, she thanked President Roosevelt.

At last the sun, which had been high when Lupe arrived, began to sink, casting a magical burnt orange glow over the room.

Lupe was glad her hands looked pretty with her polished nails and gleaming bracelets. She was glad Franky was half–plastered. It would make things easier.

Still, he eyed her warily. "All right, let's settle all this and stop being polite," he slurred.

She wouldn't answer him right away. She would create a sense of drama.

She withdrew a cigarette and ebony holder, then waited for him to light it. He managed but only after she helped steady his hand. She exhaled slowly, letting the smoke curl sensuously out of her nose and mouth. "I been thinking about us. You are still very angry with Lupe?"

He sighed. "I wouldn't call it angry. I'd —"

"You had thee good time with Francesca Saturday?"

"Sure, she's … she's gotten so big. We went riding," he said.

Lupe had no desire to discuss Francesca. "I want to tell you that my father has thee new picture idea. Is very good for you. Perfect."

Franky froze and stared. "What?"

"He want to offer you thee leading role in thee new picture of his."

Franky's heart pounded. He studied her hard, wondering if she was toying with him. "What kind of picture?"

"With thee horses, thee pretty girl from thee saloon. He ask me to tell you."

"What's the part?"

"You would be thee star. Thee sheriff."

He picked up the olive from his drink and ate it. "Why me? Why now?"

"He want you and me to be together. For us to be happy."

He stared down at his butter plate, his silverware. Lupe and her father had a plan. They wanted him back. New York was still haggling over the details of his contract for the western serial. A serial that would be shown along with the live comics, a cartoon, and two feature films. In other words, he'd be back in the cheap end of the theater. Unless … "When does he need me? I've already got a six–month commitment."

Lupe smiled. She placed her soft hand over his. "We have many things to do first. For now, we no fight anymore. Also, I no want you to leave California. We must be together, a family. For Francesca."

He studied her, annoyed by the sensations the touch of her hand brought.

"Is all I want. My father want this very much, too," she murmured, gazing directly into his eyes.

Franky withdrew his hand. He squeezed the arms of his chair. That trapped feeling overwhelmed him, like an anvil resting on his chest. He'd been feeling this way a lot lately. First because of Jeri. And now Lupe. He wanted his career back. Period.

"You are still very handsome," Lupe cooed, tickling his hand. "Did you know I am staying here at this hotel. I have thee big room upstairs. Is very nice. Would you like to see it?"

Maybe he could do the series *and* the movie. Two pictures back–to–back. Just like in the old days. He'd be on top again. Caesar might give him his whole career back. Or the new studio might get wind of his picture deal with Caesar and offer him a better contract. He could easily cash in his train ticket to New York.

He took a cool sip of his drink and sent Lupe the look that always melted her right through her panties. "Which floor are you on?"

"Come, I show you."

***

It was after three when my taxi pulled up to the glamorous new Waldorf–Astoria's Park Avenue entrance. The February sunlight and clear blue skies struck me as a wonderful omen. Still, my hands shook as I paused outside the hotel entrance to steal a last look in my compact to confirm that my rouge hadn't faded, my lipstick hadn't caked, and my mascara wasn't smudged. At last I adjusted my fur, stuck a small mint in my mouth, and hurried inside up the escalator to the lobby.

Proud in my new clothes, I strode through the grand room beneath its enormous crystal chandelier and across the huge circular mosaic by Louis Rigal on my way to the registration lobby. Both the men and women eyed me as if Marlene Dietrich herself had crossed their paths.

Moments later, I paused by the long front desk to get my bearings while searching the crowd for Franky. The huge room hummed with couples chatting, bellhops pushing luggage carts, guests waiting to be checked in, and business travelers with bulging briefcases. The few children with their parents, danced about, excited to be in such grand circumstances. In the background, musicians played.

The mixture of cigar smoke, furniture wax, French perfume, and odors from the bar and restaurant were ambrosia to me, adding to my excitement.

But Franky wasn't standing in the lobby, slouching on one of the chairs, or standing by the famed nine foot tall clock. Not that there was any need to panic. Not after his telegram had confirmed his intentions. His train was probably late. Trains were often late. Especially trains arriving from places as far away as Los Angeles. His train might've come through Chicago, Kansas City, or Detroit. It could easily have been delayed by the weather or engine problems.

So I began a casual search of the hotel which felt like a great adventure. After all, this new hotel was regarded as the biggest and most dazzling hotel in the world. It even had its own railway platform downstairs.

Since Franky wasn't in the main lobby, I quickly searched the smaller reception rooms which ran from Park to Lexington Avenue. I peered inside restaurants, bars, even telephone booths. I completed my circuit twice then stopped at the front desk to see if Franky had registered yet.

"No madam," a friendly desk clerk said. "Not yet, but we do expect him shortly."

I found a comfortable armchair in a prominent location in the vast lobby where I sat down to wait. A half hour later, I bought a *Herald Tribune* newspaper.

February 15, 1934. Clear skies. Temperature 36°. John Dillinger had been captured and sentenced to twenty years in Indiana.[3] In Germany, the police raided homes of dissident clergy. Germany had signed a non–aggression pact with Poland. And the Nazis had the Psalms rewritten with modified references to the Jews. President Roosevelt declared "… the New Deal is here to stay." Books like *Miss Lonelyhearts* by Nathaniel West, *Tender is the Night* by F. Scott Fitzgerald, Henry Miller's *Tropic of Cancer*, and William Saroyan's *The Daring Young Man on the Flying Trapeze* topped the charts .

In music Cole Porter's "Anything Goes," "Blue Moon," and "All Through the Night," filled the radio airwaves. At the movies, Claudette Colbert starred with Clark Gable in Frank Capra's *It Happened One Night*. Marlene Dietrich played in *The Scarlet Empress* and Greta Garbo appeared in *The Painted Veil*. Fred Astaire and Ginger Rogers danced their way through Cole Porter's *The Gay Divorcee*. And actors William Powell and Myrna Loy starred as Nick and Nora Charles in the film version of Dashiell Hammett's *The Thin*

Man.

Tired of reading, I put down my paper and stretched my neck as I perused the busy lobby again. As the minutes ticked by, a serenity enveloped me. I pictured Franky on the train peering out the window, frustrated.

At 5:30, a tall gentleman crossed toward me. He was hard to miss with his athletic build, thick dark hair, tanned face, and magnificent suit. But as he drew closer, my heart sank. *Harry Ambrose.* Next to Caesar Cardona or Nicky Desanto, he was the last person I wanted to see. Holding up the newspaper to block my face, I prayed he'd pass me by. Our last meeting, on the day I'd escaped from Casa Cardona in the rain, had been awful. I could still hear him denigrating Franky over steak and eggs at Musso and Frank's in Hollywood.

Now, I sensed someone standing over me.

Harry Ambrose peered over the top of my *Herald Tribune.* "Hello, Mrs. Rose. Good to see you again."

He had a nice speaking voice, I'd give him that. He'd probably gone to Hollywood with the same tired aspirations as everyone else. He probably thought he'd end up a movie star but found out he had a natural talent for being a shark.

I lowered my paper and gazed impatiently up at him. "I'm waiting for someone. Don't let me keep you from wherever you're headed."

"You're waiting for Franky. That's why I'm here. Lupe Cardona sent me," he said.

My heart lurched, and my stomach turned queasy. "Lupe? But what does she have to do with me?"

"How about a drink?" he asked.

"No thanks."

"I think you may need one."

Fear gripped my stomach. I reluctantly stood. My head felt light, as if I might faint. Being excited about seeing Franky, I'd skipped breakfast and lunch.

"Take it easy," Harry said, taking my arm to steady me.

"Where is he? Just tell me," I said.

Concern covered his face. "Let's get you settled first." He helped me across the room. Each step felt like an effort. People glanced our way thinking I was drunk or seriously ill. We settled at a tiny table in a glamorous lounge on the edge of the lobby.

The Waldorf could've been a luxurious ship in the midst of a turbulent sea. Inside, it was hard to imagine that outside there were bread lines and an ocean of ragged human beings sleeping in doorways and using newspapers as blankets against the cold. Or that a famous shanty town for the poor, a Hooverville, had erupted where the old city reservoir had once been.

Only the highly varnished paneled walls, and lavish Art Deco decor seemed real. In fact, it was hard to imagine anyone in this hotel experiencing anything more awful than indigestion or a hangover. I doubted anyone here had ever suffered from a broken heart... until now.

I gazed into Harry's deep brown eyes and fleetingly wondered if his affair with that actress was still fiery. Or if his wife had heard about it or even cared. "Are you still married?" I suddenly asked.

"Of course, why shouldn't I be?" he stated, sounding neutral on the subject.

"I just wondered."

"Want one?" he asked, pulling out a gold case and offering me a cigarette.

"No thanks. Look, I promise not to fall on the floor and start beating my breast, so please tell me what happened."

Harry glanced at me then motioned for the waiter and ordered us coffee.

"I'm hungry," I said.

"Change that to coffee and club sandwiches," Harry told the waiter. Harry faced me again. "Sure you don't need something stronger?"

I braced myself for the worst. "No."

"Remember our dinner together?" he said.

"Breakfast. We had breakfast, although I never stayed long enough to eat. Please stop changing the subject."

"I wasn't very nice about Franky, was I?"

"Why the hell do you keep dragging this out?" I snarled.

Instead of answering, he reached for his copy of *The New York Times* and opened it to the rotogravure supplement that included pictures of famous people and events. And there it was, a photo of Lupe Cardona and Franklyn Wyatt. The caption read:

> ... *The beautiful couple are expecting a new bundle by spring. Both are delighted and will be celebrating their good news in Mexico City with Lupe's family this month.*
> *"We are more in love than ever," Lupe explained, a glow on her face, a tiny gloved hand on her flat tummy.*
> *Both Lupe and Franky will be starring together in a new western picture, **The Fiery Breed**.*

My mouth felt like cotton. My heart actually hurt. Because Franky wasn't coming. Not today or tomorrow. We would never speak again. Never see each other again. Never make love again.

Harry took my hand. "Listen, Jeri. You can't blame yourself. Franky's like most stars who find their moment in the limelight has passed. They feel lost. Most would do anything to climb back on top. Franky used to be a star. He did dozens of pictures. Then one day his telephone stopped ringing. The parade had moved on. He's been desperate for a break ever since. But if it helps at all, he meant to be here today. He even had his train ticket. Lupe and her father talked him out of it. They can be very persuasive, and you can guess how a starring role opposite Lupe would sound to him. Especially after the serial here in New York was canceled."

"Canceled? When?"

"Two days ago. Maybe even yesterday. I'm not sure."

"Did he know about it before I left Los Angeles?"

"I doubt it."

Franky had traded me in for a better deal. Meaning Lupe had been right about him. She'd known all along what motivated him and how to get him back.

Rage coursed through me. Then sadness. I wanted to scream. Instead, I rose slowly and gripped the back of my chair for support. "Look, you've been very … considerate, but I need to go back to my hotel room and lie down."

The waiter appeared with a tray laden with food: Thick sandwiches, french fries, and cole slaw. I couldn't imagine eating any of it.

"Let me take you back," Harry said.

"No, I'll be okay. Anyway, I refuse to cry in front of you."

"Look, we got off to a bad start that day back in Hollywood. But I've got nice broad shoulders to cry on. And I can be very sympathetic."

"Please go away."

"Why, because I've seen you at your worst?"

Was that it? Yes, he'd seen me that day in the rain, lost and alone. And even back then he'd known that Franky had no spine. And here Harry was again, elegant, handsome, and invulnerable. "Why did they send you to tell me?"

"I'm the fixer, Jeri. I handle what the big shots can't."

"I'll bet you've never been hurt in your whole life. I bet you could lose your family in one afternoon and never shed a tear."

His deep brown eyes probed mine and I could see he was mulling over my statement and its intended meanness. "I only wish I were that invulnerable. But like most people, I handle other people's problems better than my own." Without asking, he pulled me into his arms.

I meant to push him away, to hurt him. Instead I buried my face in his soft expensive coat where it was dark and safe, a refuge from the cold winter I faced alone. "Why does it have to hurt so much?" I cried.

"Because you cared." At last we pulled apart and he handed me a fresh handkerchief. "Better?"

"I just need to think. To make plans."

"Maybe I can help with those plans."

"You've helped enough."

"Jeri, don't go to pieces. You'll find someone else. What about your husband?"

Tears filled my eyes again. "He's sick. He needs ... I need to pay his sanitarium bill."

"And Franky could've helped with that, couldn't he?"

"It wasn't like that. I loved him."

When I calmed down, Harry sent me back to the Grand Biarritz in a cab. He made me promise to meet him later back at the Waldorf for dinner, though I planned to cancel.

"And buy a new dress," he said, handing me two fifty–dollar bills.

I stared at the money then felt my fingers close over the bills before I shoved them in my purse. Forget pride. Franky wasn't coming, and Mrs. Jankel wanted payment in full by next week.

As my taxi rumbled back to the Grand Biarritz, I felt like one of The Rainbow girls. One year I was with Lex, the next Franky. And now Harry Ambrose. Even with Harry's money and what I'd brought with me, I had a little over a hundred dollars left, after sending Mrs. Jankel her money and purchasing a complete ensemble at Hirsh's. Maybe if I told Zaza my story, she'd take the outfit back. And if I moved to a cheaper hotel and went to work right away, maybe … tears filled my eyes as I tallied up what Franky's rejection meant.

Without Franky's help, Lex would be evicted.

If only I could talk to Lorena. But an expensive long distance call was out of the question. I'd have to write her instead.

Back in my room, I slept for several hours. When I woke, I put on a green silk dress with a low back I'd worn a few times since Havana. Dinner with Harry suddenly seemed better than eating alone.

***

"Your dress is stained," Harry said, his voice husky, his dark eyes cloudy with desire, as he dropped down beside me on the hotel bed in his room and stared at a wine stain over my breast.

I hadn't intended to end up in Harry's room. But after dinner in the Waldorf's famous Empire Room, I'd consented to a slow dance. There I was in the middle of the dancers with my chin on Harry's shoulder, when I spied Nicky Desanto and his men bulldozing their way past the other patrons waiting to enter.

Desanto and his men wore their usual hit–men suits. Although Nicky still looked as if he needed a booster seat and a nose job. Too bad the disappearance of his brother Tito hadn't erased his cocky smirk. At least I was sure Tito wouldn't show up tonight.

"Meet me by the elevators," I suddenly whispered to Harry, wondering if he already knew about Nicky Desanto the way he knew about everything else. I quickly blended in with several women heading to the powder room. Which was how I dodged Nicky Desanto but ended up on the twelfth floor on Harry's bed, sharing a bottle of imported champagne with him.

"Did I tell you that I almost left my husband for Franky?" I slurred, trying to sit up while Harry reached toward me and gently, like a tickle, traced the wine stain over my left breast. His fingertip felt warm through the material. I held my breath, disturbed by his touch which focused on the area over my nipple. His eyes seemed drugged by the sight of me in his room, on his bed.

"Take it off, " he said, in a breathy whisper. "Take off your dress, and I'll send for the maid."

Leave, I told myself. But I'd had a lot to drink. More than I'd ever consumed at one time in my entire life. Even back in college. And I'd never felt so lonely. Lonely down to my veins. Afraid, too. Afraid of the future, of Nicky Desanto, of being hungry and broke.

Of course, Harry was another bad choice. Another handsome married man. A fixer who bought off the police and kept the stories of illegal abortions, actors on heroin, and stars caught in hotel rooms with the wrong lover out of the newspapers. Harry was everything I should be running away from.

As if reading my mind, sensing my resistence, he reached inside his coat jacket and pulled out his wallet. With a flick of his fingers, he withdrew three fifties and held them out to me. My fingers itched for those bills. Harry clearly understood my desperation. Hadn't I confessed my troubles to him at dinner? Hadn't he surmised that Franky was my lover but also the means for paying my bills?

The money was inches from my face. If I took it, I was no better than the girls at The Rainbow. On the other hand, that money would keep Lex safe. And Harry was handsome and clean. Not one of those dirty farmers Big Harriet dragged into her bed. And in the morning, I'd still be myself. I wouldn't really change. And in time, this memory would fade. So I'd take his money, shut my eyes, and get through it.

"Have you got a bathroom?" I asked, wobbling to my feet.

Harry placed the bills on the night table. "Don't keep me waiting. I hate to be kept waiting."

"Be right back." Inside, the bathroom I avoided looking in the mirror. Moving slowly, I carefully took off my dress and under things. I folded them and left them on the toilet seat. Then I wrapped myself in a large towel and padded barefoot back into the room.

Harry's back was to me and he was cursing into the telephone. I quickly slipped between the cool starched sheets, feeling strange from the drinks and the odd events which kept unfolding. As if I were watching life from a distance. But at least I wasn't alone tonight. I couldn't be alone right now. And the bed felt heavenly. So I tried to keep my mind blank and not notice that a man I hardly knew was about to climb in bed with me and touch me in my most intimate places … for cash. A ruthless man. A man I'd hated up until a few hours ago. Not that liking someone had much to do with sex, according to Lorena. After all, I'd more than liked Franky and where did that get me?

If only I could talk to Lorena now. She'd put me straight.

"Wives and girlfriends trade sex for money all the time," she'd say.

But I kept seeing my old neighbor seducing the milkman to feed her baby. And the dirty farmers trekking up The Rainbow stairs. So I told myself that Harry was attractive, and I could do this for Lex.

Harry hung up the receiver. The lust in his eyes had been replaced by weariness. "Look, there's a mess I need to clean up for the studio, so I gotta head back to California right away. You weren't hot to do this anyway, were you?"

I stayed quiet.

"You're a decent gal, Jeri. You just fell in with the wrong people. Stay here as long as you like. Have a grand meal on me and keep the dough. Just leave me your telephone number. Maybe you'll change your mind about me. Decide I'm not the big bad wolf."

I wasn't sure how I felt about him. But watching him pack, put on a clean shirt, knot his tie, and slip into a jacket made me feel lonely. But even drunk and filled with despair, I knew I'd gotten lucky. This was one mistake I wouldn't have to live with later on.

I heard the gentle click as the hotel door shut behind him.

I was alone again. But not out on the street, and not a girl for hire either. And I'd just put away a hundred and fifty dollars more. A fortune.

I slept until three, until I felt sure Nicky Desanto had left the hotel to go home. Then I caught a cab back to the Grand Biarritz. In the lobby, I debated about stopping at the front desk for messages. I still hoped Franky had sent a telegram or a letter explaining how much he missed me, how he planned to be here soon, how the news about Lupe and him had been a publicity stunt. But deep down, I knew better.

I slept till noon then went out for a long walk. I ended up at the movies and saw the Marx Brothers in *Duck Soup*. Today, their antics left me cold. My heart felt too heavy.

Back at the Grand Biarritz, I crossed the marble floor so tired I doubted I could stay awake for the elevator ride up or the long trek down the hall to my room. But as I approached the front desk to get my messages, I froze. The hair on my arms stood up. From behind, a man standing before the front clerk looked exactly like Lex.

His height, the tilt of his head, even the way he held his hat, reminded me of Lex. Of course this man's hair was longer with more gray in it. But the superb cut of his navy suit was exactly like Lex's navy suit. And yet, I knew Lex was still up at Saranac Lake fighting for his life.

Only yesterday Mrs. Jankel had repeated her usual reason for Lex not coming to the telephone. "Sorry, Mrs. Rose, he's resting."

Then we'd gone on to discuss his bill.

"… But you gave me until February 15, Mrs. Jankel," I'd

argued.

"I never dreamt that you would come up with the money."

"But I just sent you another a hundred sixty dollars."

"But before this, you didn't pay me for months. And I'm afraid I found another patient who —"

"You can't move Lex now. You promised. You said you never evicted anyone so sick before, and you can't do it now," I'd argued.

"Very well. You have less than one week to come up with the remaining funds."

And now this man with his broad shoulders and narrow waist made my heart spin. He brought back feelings for Lex I'd almost forgotten about. In that moment, the newspaper picture of Franky and Lupe could've been an old photograph of two silent film stars I'd barely heard of.

I moved behind the stranger and waited for him to turn. I caught a whiff of cologne, a scent Lex had never worn. Still, I longed to stretch out my fingers and tap the man's shoulder.

Instead, I waited for Ed, the chatty older desk clerk, to finish yakking about how tough times were even though President Roosevelt had made things better.

"... take my brother Thomas. He was part of the Bonus Army. All he and them other veterans wanted was what the government promised. Compensation for what they done for America in the war. Men who lived in them awful trenches in France. Lost their arms and legs. And died. Those fellas needed to feed their families. And what did that stinker Hoover do? Gave 'em the bum's rush. Ran 'em all out at gun point. Used American soldiers against starving American veterans."

Again, the familiar angle of the stranger's head and the shape of his long fingers made my heart catch. If only this stranger would turn and end my imaginings. I knew what I'd see. His chin wouldn't be as chiseled or his smile as dazzling. His eyes wouldn't be the same thrilling blue. After all, I'd been through this same fantasy a dozen times over the past fourteen months.

Then he turned.

TWENTY–SEVEN

I blinked several times trying to accept the truth. That the man standing before me was Lex. My husband.

Gazing intently into my eyes, Lex repeated the very words he'd used on me so long ago that night at the Plaza Hotel when I intended to crash a party to find my brother Paul. "Would you mind teaching me how to dance? I never did learn."

Throwing my arms around him, I sobbed into his lapel. At last, I let go.

Lex gazed down at me, his expression filled with awe. As if my enthusiasm had surprised him. "Are you all right?" he asked, his slight English accent surprising me, the way it always had.

"What're you doing here? Mrs. Jankel never said a word about your coming down," I said, noting a network of tiny lines around his eyes. Lines which spoke of pain and worry and the dark places he'd visited. Eyes which were still clear blue pools, lustrous and appealing. He'd filled out again, too, gained back most of the weight he'd lost so that he looked like his old self. "Are you better? You look better."

"Sure, much better."

For months, alone in bed at night, I'd imagined what I'd say if he ever got well. Now I could barely conjugate a sentence. Instead I linked arms with him and led him away from the front desk to a large sofa where we sat. "Why didn't you call or write that you were coming?"

"I wanted to surprise you. When Mrs. Jankel told me you were here, I had to come see you."

"Are you really cured?"

"Better. Not cured, but well– enough to be released."

"But Mrs. Jankel, she acted like you'd be staying with her for a long time. I just sent her more money."

"Don't worry about that. We'll get the money straightened out. She just didn't want to tip you off about my surprise."

Relief filled me. "It's great to see you."

He grinned. "Guess I look a little different." He stared down, unable to meet my gaze. Then hope filed his face. "Not too bad though, huh?"

In 1929, he'd been invincible. Now he seemed vulnerable, afraid. He was struggling to sit up straight and one side of him seemed concave.

"There's still nobody like you," I said, squeezing his hand, as my eyes filled up again.

"How about dinner? They feed you like crazy when you're a lunger, and I've been dreaming of a steak. A big juicy one."

I laughed. "Sure, just give me five minutes to freshen up."

I heard my heels clicking across the shiny marble floor before I stepped into the elevator. I felt his gaze on me the whole time. Upstairs in my room, while I brushed my teeth, combed my hair, applied lipstick, and changed into my new suit, I managed to drive out my demons, those memories of Franky, Lupe, and Harry Ambrose. Only Lex mattered now. Except, I felt a niggling concern about the discrepancies in what Mrs. Jankel had told me about Lex's health and Lex's assessment of things. Because Mrs. Jankel had pushed for her money like an angry loan shark. Unless, she really had wanted Lex to surprise me.

My phone rang. It was Lex. "What're you doing up there,

making beds?"

"I'll be right down."

Outside, we headed up Central Park South to Broadway. Lex moved awkwardly as if compensating. When he noticed me watching him, he hailed a cab.

A moment later, as our taxi rumbled down Broadway, he took my hand and stared at the intricate lines that filled my palm. "It's my chest," he abruptly said. "The doctors took out a few ribs to permanently collapse my lung. It makes my left side stand out. It's called a *thoracoplasty*. It's what saved me."

"It doesn't matter. You look fine," I said.

But when we got out, I saw he was having some difficulty. He held onto the taxi door a beat longer than normal, and he was suddenly sweating. "I could use a drink."

"Is that okay? With your doctors, I mean."

"They're up in Saranac Lake and I'm here. Not much they can do."

"So, you're really better," I said, as we took our seats in the restaurant and studied our menus.

"A capsule has formed around the lesion. For now, as long as I live like an invalid, I may be okay. I intend to live while I can. And be grateful for the time."

Which was how I decided we had to return to the future no matter how many tries it took to get there.

***

"Look, it's silly for us to stay in different rooms," I said, on our way back inside the hotel after dinner. "After all, we're married. And this way, I can be near you in case you need something."

"Okay." But on the way up in the elevator, Lex leaned back against the wood paneling and stared down at his shoes. He seemed shy, awkward.

"What is it?" I asked.

"At Mrs. Jankel's, the other lungers expected a fault or two, a scar here and there. I fit in there. No one worried about catching the disease. We all had it. But you … I don't want to scare you."

"I'm not that fragile."

"No, but I am," he said softly.

I took his hand. If only I could undo my life from the past year. My visits to the pool house with Franky. And my plans to leave Lex. If only he would get well, I'd never leave his side again.

At last, I unlocked the door to my room. "There are still two beds. And we won't push ourselves tonight. I'm too tired to be romantic anyway."

"Sure. We'll get a good night's sleep. Rest, that's the ticket. At least that's what they always told us." He stared into space as if he was still there, recalling the rules, the routines, the rigid order of life at Saranac Lake.

"You once showed up here at this very room with flowers after we had a fight," I said. "I remember you wore this incredible tuxedo, and I could hardly resist you."

He chuckled. "But as I recall, you did." He dropped onto the bed by the window. "I sent for my things."

"Good. Did they give you any medicine to take or —"

"Honey, you don't have to worry. I swear I won't be a grumpy old burden. I can do everything I used to." He winked seductively, making me laugh.

"I'll bet you can. Just let me take a nice long bath," I said.

In the bathroom, I turned on the tub faucet then poured in bath salts and perfume. Items I'd brought to smell good for Franky. For some reason Franky and my affair with him seemed to have happened years ago. As if time was being kind to me, altering the intensity of my feelings about yesterday. Maybe it was because Lex was still miraculously handsome and sophisticated. Or because he could still make me laugh in a way Franky never could.

"Can you reach my bag?" I called, as I settled in the tub and felt a tiny headache coming on.

"Be right there." A moment later, Lex entered the bathroom.

Buried by bubbles, I grinned up at him. "Keep me company."

He showed me my purse. "What do you need? Maybe I can find it for you."

"Aspirin." I studied him, surprised to find him extremely desirable again. As if time had stood still and California had been a dream. As if our marriage had never been interrupted.

Frowning, Lex dug through my purse. "Fascinating what you ladies hide in these things."

"Just the tricks of any good magician. Darling, back in Havana were you really... I mean what about that street girl?"

His head jerked up. Looking pained, he sighed. "You must hate me."

"No, I don't. But that evening's haunted me for a long time. I always meant to ask you about that night. But up until today, I wasn't sure I could deal with your answer."

He crossed his heart. "Nothing happened with her. I let her use the bathroom then I paid her off. But I wouldn't touch her. Still, I apologize for her. And for those awful dinners with those stuffy people. I needed to keep you angry, to avoid contact with you. Even then, I guessed I had something more than a cold. Especially the first time I coughed up blood. I just couldn't face life in a sanitarium. Guess I never knew anyone who came back alive from one. So I flirted with other girls so you'd stay away, so I'd never infect you. And other than that lapse in the car that night after dinner with your favorite couple, the Maitlands, when I couldn't keep my hands off you, I managed to behave like a good little gent. Which was no cakewalk. Anyway, you never did get sick. It's what gave me hope up there at Saranac Lake when I felt so blue I wanted to end it all."

I stared into the water. If only I'd been as brave. "I'm glad you're here."

He went back to digging through my purse. "Aspirin, huh? You're sure you have aspirin in here?" He suddenly pulled out a scrap of paper and studied it. "You should see this. It's got this hotel's address but it says *The Roosevelt Grand Hotel*."

I froze, heart pounding. Could it be? Could Lex have found that elusive scrap of hotel stationary? A scrap I'd been chasing since my brother Paul and his wife Sylvia vanished from this very room.

I rose, soapy and wet. I reached out for the paper. "It should say the Grand Biarritz," I shouted, grabbing a bath towel, as the room seemed to grow murky and dark.

"Jeri?" Lex said, as I pushed past him and his voice seemed to echo from far away.

Cold and wet from my bath, I charged into the bedroom. And there it was on the night stand: The Magic Fingers Massage Machine, my time travel vehicle. I'd tried to conjure it up dozens of times over the last four years and failed. Now, here it was. I pointed, unable to move or speak.

"Jeri? What is it" Lex called, moving toward the machine in a kind of slow motion, until his finger moved toward the lever.

"Lex!" I shrieked, as the room went dark and I seemed to fall in a hazy whirling motion onto my bed.

TWENTY–EIGHT

With a hard jolt, I woke. Heart racing, I bolted up to a sitting position. Sunlight flooded the hotel room, a very different hotel room. The current decor didn't match the interior of the Grand Biarritz or the Roosevelt Grand. And yet, as details from the last few days filled my head, I realized it had to be one or the other.

Across the room, Lex lay on his back, snoring.

Today, the hotel room had brilliant blue drapes and matching bedspreads. On my night table a turquoise princess telephone and a dial–faced clock radio had replaced the old Crosley radio and Magic Fingers massage machine. The dark–brown high boy and round table with chairs had evolved into modern blond–colored furniture, including a small desk and a long low bureau. What's more, a large TV sat on a stand opposite Lex's bed.

Covering myself in last night's discarded bath towel, I tiptoed to the double windows. By leaning to my right, I bypassed the tall hotel wing directly across from me and managed to see a portion of the sidewalk and street below. These same windows had given me my initial glimpse of the world back in 1929.

What year had we landed in now?

Today, long flat rectangular cars inched their way down the busy street below. Women in low heels, short A–line coats, berets, and colorful knitted caps hurried by. I quickly combed the room for a travel guide or a magazine, something which would give me today's date. But there was only a match book resting in a green glass ashtray with the logo: The Roosevelt Grand Hotel, proving we'd arrived sometime after World War II. Judging by the old television and room decor this wasn't the late1990s. I tried not to feel too disappointed. At least this time, I hadn't arrived in some distant era alone.

Lex sighed in his sleep. I told myself it didn't matter what year it was as long as there was a modern cure for tuberculosis. Still, my fingers itched to reach for the TV knob or the dial on the blue princess phone so I could learn the truth. But I didn't dare wake Lex. He needed rest. Yesterday's trip down from Saranac Lake had exhausted him.

I quietly unearthed my robe and slippers from the closet, dressed quickly, then slipped out the door to find a hotel maid. According to my watch, it was only seven, and I soon learned, too early for the cleaning crews to start their rounds.

Down the hall by the elevators, I found what I needed. A hotel guest had left a newspaper on top of a dirty room service tray. Heart pounding, I snatched up the paper and read: February 1967. The truth dried out my mouth.

Back in our room, Lex had kicked off his covers. With the bedclothes bunched up down by his feet, I could see his bare torso down to his shorts. In spite of the bright pink scar below his chest, he still looked extremely desirable from his muscled shoulders, arms, and chest, to his narrow waist. The few grey strands in his beautiful thick dark hair actually added to his appeal. Even last night, the tough–talking cigarette girl at the supper club had stammered and blushed when Lex teased her. Last night, back in 1934.

As if sensing my scrutiny, Lex opened his eyes.

"Morning," I said.

He smiled. "Nice to wake up to someone who isn't about to empty a ripe bedpan."

I laughed. "Sleep well?"

"Strange dreams actually. What happened last night?"he asked, moving to sit on the edge of the bed and stretching. Then he glanced around the room, frowned and pointed to the television. "What's that?"

"It's a TV, a television. Here, I'll show you." Kneeling, I twisted the *on* knob. Several seconds later, after the old–fashioned tubes heated up, a black & white picture showed a woman happily mopping her floor. Music from a commercial filled the room. *"It's so easy when you use Lestoil,"* a female sang.

Lex stared into the screen, fascinated. "I've heard of TV. But …" he slowly surveyed the room. "Am I crazy or has everything in here changed? The colors —"

"Darling, I think I should explain what happened."

"Judging by your expression, a stiff drink would be in order."

"Maybe this will help." I handed him the newspaper and waited for his reaction.

His eyes roamed over the paper. After several seconds he put down the paper and glanced toward the TV where a rerun of the 1950's *Father Knows Best* aired. Facing me again, he said, "Nineteen sixty-seven? How?"

"I'm not exactly sure."

"The newspaper said there's a war on."

"Vietnam. It's in Southeast Asia."

He chewed on this idea for several seconds. "I really could use a cigarette and a drink."

I crossed to him, sat down beside him, and took his hand. "Prohibition's over. We can order anything you like."

He squeezed my hand. "Guess I owe you an apology. It's a relief to know you weren't raving mad, making all that stuff up about coming from the future."

"Actually, I never thought you listened. I always figured you were hoping I'd shut up."

He chuckled. "Only whenever you brought it up." He was staring at the TV again.

Being Lex, he refused to let me see his fears. But I knew how he felt: disoriented, confused, afraid.

For a few minutes, we stared at the old TV, and I wondered if we'd enjoy living through the 1960s, one of the most turbulent decades in history. A span that included the Vietnam War, feminism, the birth control pill, and the future assassinations of Bobby Kennedy and Martin Luther King. At least Lex and I would experience these changes together. And he could be cured now.

"Are you okay? You've been through quite a lot between yesterday and today," I said.

"I'll be fine. Really. As long as I have you." Then he reached for me.

He pulled to him, encircling me in his arms. After studying my face, he gently pressed his lips to mine. Until I felt a pressure rise inside me as his tongue probed my mouth, and my hands sought the muscles on his back.

Under the circumstances, I was surprised to find myself responsive. Ever since he'd appeared in the lobby yesterday, I'd been afraid I'd find his touch repugnant. Instead, I found him as intoxicating as a new lover from his masculine jaw and seductive smile, to his prize-fighter's body and glistening blue eyes.

I began to devour his neck, his broad shoulders, his throat, and his lips. My attraction to him burned as powerfully as it had the first time he kissed me back in 1929. He groaned, his need for me evident and ready, as his hands roamed over my body and his mouth moved down across my chest, his tongue reaching out to probe my nipple as his hands weighed my breasts. Then he was over me, above me, powerful and dominating. Lust blurred his expression as our bodies connected. As the TV blared in the background, we found that place we'd lost long ago. And I thanked Mrs. Jankel for keeping my husband alive to be here with me again.

Side–by–side afterward, glistening with sweat, we laughed and made plans.

"Thank God we don't have to worry about money," Lex said, kissing my shoulder. "A short trip to Havana and we'll be sitting pretty again."

I studied him. "What?"

"You remember, the money I deposited in Havana."

I was suddenly sure the TB had spread to his brain, a medical possibility. "Take it easy, sweetheart. You've been through a lot."

"Don't you believe me?"

"Darling, where did you get such an idea?"

"Remember Havana? I didn't just plan a vacation down there to avoid the sanitarium. That's where I deposited our dough to hide it from the Desantos. Now all we have to do is go down there and get it."

His news stunned me. I thought of my struggles to pay his bills, the months of chasing every kind of job imaginable. How I'd allowed Lupe to degrade me. And what I'd almost done with Harry Ambrose. "You should've told me. Tito Desanto almost killed me over that money."

Lex frowned. "I did tell you. I wrote you all about it in a letter."

"No, you didn't. What're you talking about?"

He was silent. I could see him trying to work things out in his head. At last he said, "My mother was supposed to mail you my letters. I had her do it from the city so no one could trace me up at Saranac Lake. I wrote you that if something happened to me, or either of our banks got into trouble, you were to go down to Havana and collect the money. I left the account information with a New York attorney."

I leaned back in bed, hardly able to absorb this news. "I never got your letters. Not a single one until my last month in Los Angeles."

He appeared stunned. Then he chuckled bitterly. "Ida always was ruthless. I should never have trusted her." He reached out for my hand. "Sorry. I never knew. Since you always wrote me, I assumed you got my letters."

I sighed. How many things had happened because we hadn't communicated. If only we'd had cell phones, the internet …

"How you must have resented me," he said.

I avoided looking at him. I hadn't been an angel myself. "So you deposited this money down in Havana in the fall of 1932?"

"Exactly. And with interest and inflation, it should be worth millions now."

I was tempted to explain about the Cuban Revolution, the Cold War. About our money being confiscated by Fidel Castro. How we'd never see a dime of it again. But for the moment, Lex had been through enough. I refused to wipe away the happy look on his face.

I'd tell him later, after we went to a hospital to find out about the new cures for tuberculosis. After I searched for my brother Paul.

At the moment, the only things I wanted were room service and the feel of my husband's warm arms around me. I wanted to float here for awhile, to feel safe and content.

The challenges of living in 1967 could wait.

An hour later, after we'd showered and dressed, we headed down to the lobby to go out.

"First, we'll go to Mount Sinai and find you a good doctor," I said.

"Darling, I've seen enough doctors for now. Today, let's pretend we never heard of TB. Let's go shopping instead. I feel distinctly frumpy."

"But they have a cure now. And —"

"I see myself in a swell new suit and a cashmere coat."

He looked so happy, I agreed. "Okay, but tomorrow we're going to find a good doctor."

So we went shopping. We would've gone to Hirsh's, but the phone number had been disconnected, probably long ago. That was the hardest part of being a time traveler. You had no advance warning, no time to say goodbye to friends. I imagined Zaza wondering why I never returned to see her. And poor Lorena waiting for a letter which would never come.

As our cab crawled through the congested streets, Lex held my hand and gazed contentedly out the window at the 1967 skyscrapers which competed with the old Chrysler Building and the Empire State Building. Studying Lex's handsome face, I wondered how he and I would cope with this new world.

Oddly enough, my affair with Franky felt as if it had happened thirty years ago. Overnight, my agony had evaporated. Yet, we'd only left the 1930s hours ago, with its radio shows, dirt roads, two dollar dresses, permanent waves, and Busby Berkley extravaganzas. Instead, Lex and I had emerged into the Swingin' Sixties. The world of The Jet Set, Mod clothing, The British Invasion, and Twiggy.

On the driver's radio, The Young Rascals sang, "Groovin." Out our window a billboard advertised the Broadway musical, *Cabaret*.

At Orbach's, a store famous for selling high end items at bargain prices, the five dollar dresses from 1933 now cost eighteen or more. In the women's department, shoppers mobbed bins over–flowing with discounted items. Most were so intent on their quest, they didn't notice Lex in his double-breasted pin-striped suit or me with my hem around my ankles and my hair in ridges and curls. We could've come from a costume party, we looked so out of place.

In 1967, dresses were worn mid–thigh. Hair was either long and straight or styled in the ubiquitous flip or a helmet–like bouffant hairdo called a bubble. Headbands, bows, and scarves were popular. Dresses had dropped waists, empire lines, or were unfitted shifts. Lips were pale. Eyes were dramatic with heavy eyeliner and fake lashes.

While I dug through a dress bin for buried treasure, Lex located a chair and read the newspaper. With my tiny stash leftover from Harry and Franky, I bought a navy and red geometric wool dress, shoes, and large dangling earrings. Then, while paying for a new black coat for Lex, I spied a familiar looking salesgirl briskly crossing the floor. The tiny, dark–haired woman was the image of my sister–in–law Sylvia.

"Honey, I'll be right back," I called to Lex, who absently waved back at me, as I charged after the young woman. Unlikely as it seemed, this girl could be Sylvia. After all, she and my brother Paul had vanished in 1930 from our hotel room. And since Lex and I had landed here and now, why couldn't Paul and Sylvia?

In spite of her high heels, Sylvia's lookalike moved at a brisk clip. Seeing her, salesgirls from hosiery to cosmetics grew intensely busy. After she passed, the employees' hateful frowns convinced me that this unpopular young woman might very well be my sister-in-law. Not that I'd gotten a direct look at her face. And her appearance had changed dramatically due to the current fashions. This girl's hair was in a perfect flip, stiff from hair spray and teasing. She wore thick black false eyelashes, pale lipstick, and a short green dress.

Moving fast, I fought to keep up. But the tiny woman's rapid pace made me wonder if she knew I was tracking her and meant to give me the slip. I expected her to suddenly jump onto a service elevator or disappear through a locked door. At last, she paused by an older saleswoman, giving me time to catch up.

"Why aren't these sweaters neatly folded and organized by

color? They look like rags thrown in that bin," Sylvia's lookalike snarled.

"But I was told this morning that these were supposed to look tossed around because —"

"Listen. I'm the buyer here, and what I say goes. If you can't follow a simple order, then you'd better start looking for another job. Is that clear?"

The older woman's face turned red. Tears glistened in her eyes. "As you say, Mrs. Devlin."

My pulse rate soared. *Mrs. Devlin.* It *was* Sylvia. And she still had the charm of a poisonous spider.

"I'll be back later." Turning on her heel, Sylvia marched through a curtain and yanked it shut behind her.

Ignoring the *Employees Only* sign above the doorway, I pushed through the curtains to find myself in a typical store hallway with boxes, untagged garments, bins, and clothing racks lining the hall. Winding my way down the corridor, I ended up peering through the door of a small back room crowded with old desks, piles of hangars, boxes, fabric scraps, clothing, calendars tacked to the walls, and the stench of cigarettes.

"Hello," I said softly.

Sylvia's head jerked up. Her eyes widened. "Damn it, lady. You practically gave me a heart attack. This happens to be a restricted area and ..." Sylvia paused. Her eyes widened. "Jeri?"

"You aren't dreaming, Sylvia. I'm really here."

Sylvia regarded me and my 1933 dress as if I'd appeared at her door in a loin cloth, dragging a dead carcass behind me. "What're you doing here?"

"Lex and I just arrived. Sorry, I scared you but —"

"I hope you aren't looking for that brother of yours. We're divorced in case you haven't heard."

Thank God Paul had come to his senses. Though still pretty, Sylvia now had tiny lines around her eyes and her mouth seemed frozen in misery. "We just arrived this morning from 1934. I had no idea what happened to you or Paul."

"Not so loud," she grumbled, reaching for a crushed pack of cigarettes and holding them out to me.

"No thanks."

Sylvia lit up, took a heavy drag, and gazed into space. "So you just got here, huh?"

"A few hours ago."

"Seems like I've been here forever. Maybe if Paul and I'd stayed back then ..." she shrugged. "Things got pretty rocky once we landed here. And that was over three years ago."

"When did you get divorced?"

"Six months later. Guess I didn't dazzle Paul anymore. He suddenly preferred girls who went to college. Brainy types with blonde hair and money."

"Is he around here? I mean, have you seen him?"

She blew smoke at me. "Well, it's not as if we take Sunday drives together."

"I just meant —"

"I haven't seen him since our divorce. Right before he started running around with some debutante from Smith or Vassar. Far as I know, he's down on Wall Street. He sends me money regularly, I'll say that for him. Otherwise, I'd starve on the peanuts they pay me here. And I'm the head buyer."

"Good for you."

She glared at me. "Don't tell me you're looking for work."

"Not today, but I will be."

"Well look someplace else. You and I never hit it off."

I was struck by Sylvia's toughness, her anger. Back in 1929, she'd been conceited and spoiled until the Stock Market Crash rocked her world. But she'd still been softer. Now, she looked as if she might crack her gum and start cleaning her nails with a switchblade.

"Trust me, I won't ask for your help, Sylvia."

Sylvia laughed bitterly. "Nothing personal, really. I wouldn't wish this place on my worst enemy. If I were you, I'd go some place snazzy. Some place where they pay a commission and the customers are civilized."

"Then why are you here?"

"I got sacked at a few of the city's finer emporiums. I'm a drunk, for your information."

Sylvia had been drinking heavily back in 1930, but her honesty about her problem still shocked me. I thought of suggesting an AA meeting but decided to bow out quickly. "Well, thanks for the information. And no hard feelings."

"By the way, did Lex survive? He was pretty messed–up the last time I saw him."

"He has TB, but he's alive."

"I'd really love to shoot the breeze with you, but I'm not a lady of leisure anymore. I assume you can find your own way out," she said, picking up a black phone receiver and dialing a number.

"Just tell me how to find Paul." .

She frowned. "He's just off Wall Street. Here, I'll write it down for you."

A few minutes later, I found an empty phone booth by the restrooms. My hands shook as I deposited a dime then dialed the brokerage firm's number. The receptionist connected me to a secretary who informed me that Paul was in a meeting and would soon be gone for the day. She politely asked if I would like to leave a message. I considered leaving my name, but Paul might be too shocked by the news. He might even think it was a hoax. After three years of being sure I'd never see him again, I wanted to greet my brother in person.

Before Lex had time to pull on his new coat, I was pushing him out the store's door.

But everything seemed against us from the rain to the stagnant Friday afternoon traffic. With each passing minute, I grew more frantic. I wanted to kick myself for not leaving Paul a message. I stared out the window. A poster showed the cover of *Sargent Pepper's Lonely Heart's Club Band* by the Beatles. A movie theater marquee advertised showtimes for *Bonnie and Clyde.* It seemed as if a month passed before we pulled up to an impressive front door of the brokerage firm Winston & Barlock. We crossed through the stately front doors and followed the directions to Paul's office. My pulse throbbed.

"I'm sorry, but you just missed him," Paul's secretary, an older woman, with a heavy New York accent said when we finally reached Paul's office. "And he's just left for a two week vacation,".

I stared at her, shaken, deflated. I cursed the rain. I cursed my stupidity. Paul would've waited if he'd known I was coming.

"You can always leave him a message. He may check in before his flight. And he'll probably call here in a day or two."

"Would it be possible to get his flight number? Could you at least tell me where he's going?"

"Sorry, but I can't give out such personal information."

"But I'm his sister. I've come all the way from California." *And thirty-three years from the past, too.*

"I wish I could tell you. But you see, this is his honeymoon. It's the first chance he and his bride have had to get away. But I'll see that he gets your message as soon as he checks in."

So Paul had gotten married again. I hoped this girl was nicer than Sylvia. "Well, thank you," I said, accepting the pad and pen she offered, wishing there were cell phones and computers. I'd just begun scribbling a note when I looked up.

A young man in a wet wool coat charged toward us. "Miss Levine, I forgot my umbrella and it's raining like mad…" He paused.

I smiled "Paul."

"Jeri." Then we were hugging and I knew everything would work out.

EPILOGUE

By the autumn of 1968, Lex was well. After a long regimen of drugs, he turned a corner and was pronounced cured. He instantly reopened Rose Construction, and we soon moved from a garden apartment in Queens built in the 1930s to a large home in Great Neck's swanky King's Point. We had a baby girl and named her Jessica. She instantly became the apple of her Uncle Paul's eye. But while many doors opened, others closed.

I found out that Leon Hirsh had died from a sudden heart attack in 1935, and Hirsh's went out of business. Zaza now lives in a rest home in Yonkers and no longer recognizes me. Harris passed away last spring while fishing. Lex cried as if he'd lost his own father and can't speak of it to this day.

One afternoon, alone in the city after a dental appointment, with time to kill before meeting Lex for dinner, I visited the big Fifth Avenue public library hoping to uncover the fate of people I'd known in the past. Without the Internet, my quest proved challenging. But in many cases my diligence paid off. By sifting through old newspapers from the 1930s and 1940s, I was able to uncover quite a lot.

For instance, *The Vaquero's Daughter*, Lupe's last picture, made her previous movie flop *Love Flies to Montevideo* look like a whopping success. Worse, Caesar Cardona had a stroke within weeks of Lupe and Franky's reunion. And without Caesar's iron fist and his ability to push through movie projects, it appeared that Lupe and Franky never worked again. News of Harry Ambrose stopped right after Pearl Harbor. And even though he'd wanted to corrupt me, I hated to think what that meant.

Of course there wasn't a line about anyone from The Rainbow House. Those women simply vanished. Who could say if Big Harriet ever found her children? Whether Thelma ever opened her dress shop back in Ohio? Or Lorena ever found true love? I dug through newspapers and telephone books searching for news of them. But I never found a word.

Then, I accidentally stumbled across Lorena's obituary. There was the date: July 13, 1944. I must have read the words a hundred times wishing I could erase their finality, make things come out differently. In 1944, on her way home from The Hollywood Canteen, where she volunteered, a drunk ran a stop sign and hit her car killing her instantly.

A memory surfaced of my mother and grandmother exchanging looks when someone mentioned Lorena. As a child my curiosity had been aroused by their odd behavior, the way they shook their heads, made faces, and the inevitable hush that followed. But my mother and grandmother never knew Lorena. They never needed her as I had and found her heart brimming with generosity and kindness.

And now, Lorena would never meet Jessica or Lex. We'd never gossip over coffee or get sloppy again over gin fizzes as I'd dreamt of doing a thousand times. We'd never talk honestly about growing old and how we felt about life. And yet sometimes when I'm drifting off to sleep, I imagine I hear her laughing. I still believe she exists out there in the past, in the vast vapors of time. Lex, my brother, and I are proof that parallel worlds do exist.

I believe all of the people I knew back then live on a parallel plane. And if I wanted to, I could check back into the Roosevelt Grand on the right day at the right time and travel back there.

Lupe would still be misusing pronouns and bragging about her beauty and talent. Lorena would still be offering advice about life and men. And Franky would be atop his favorite stallion on a ridge gazing down at the wild expanse of the San Fernando Valley.

For me, it's a fading memory.

And yet, whenever I take the train into the city and meet Paul for lunch, which I do fairly often, I make a point of walking by the Roosevelt Grand, the former Grand Biarritz. I stare up at the aging hotel and try to imagine how I am forever linked to it.

The End

Endnotes:

1.Lillian Gish was a famous silent screen actress.

2. Judge Joseph F. Crater, like Jimmy Hoffa, became one of the most famous missing men in America when he vanished on August 6th, 1930, after telling friends he would be attending the Broadway play, "Dancing Partner" that evening. He was never seen or heard from again. Nobody has been able to explain why Judge Crater disappeared, although there is no shortage of theories.

3.The picture game was from *The Los Angeles Times*. Readers were encouraged to dream up advertising copy to go with a weekly published picture to win money.

4. Dillinger will escape. He will leave a trail of dead in Minnesota but be gunned down outside a Chicago movie theater on July 22, 1934.

5. Current data is only available till 2008. In 2008, $27.00, the cost of a long distance phone call from California to New York in 1933 is worth:

$448.55	the Consumer Price Index
$372.42	the GDP deflator
$1,297.67	the unskilled wage
$2,816.72	nominal GDP per capita
$6,828.80	using the relative share of GD